UNFINISHED BUSINESS

Wendy Hewlett

Unfinished Business
Wendy Hewlett
Copyright © 2014 Wendy Hewlett
All rights reserved.
ISBN: 099216673X
ISBN-13: 978-0-9921667-3-1
ISBN: 978-0-9221667-1-7(eBook)

To My Sister, Nanci — I don't know a more beautiful soul. I owe you the world for always being there for me, for catching me when I fall. I am truly Blessed to count you as my sister and my friend.

Chapter 1

Taylor Sinclair looked out of the small window over the city of Toronto from her seat in first class. God, it felt good to be home after thirty-two days, six hours and – she glanced at the time on her iPhone – thirty-six minutes. When she thought about how excited she'd been at the start of the tour to promote her book, *Leila's Locket*, she couldn't believe how naive she'd been. She should have known the media would hound her all over North America. It didn't seem to matter how many times they announced she would not talk about Sarah Johnson or her reign of terror over Taylor. In every city they travelled to, the media was out in full force, incessantly calling out the same horrific questions.

She took a leave of absence from her job as a Police Constable with the Toronto Police, so she wanted to get the promotional tour done and over with as quickly as possible. It made for a gruelling schedule, but that wasn't what caused her so much stress. She could handle the sixteen to eighteen hour days filled with interviews, book signings, and constant travel. She could even handle the flashbacks triggered by the media's constant harassment. After all, she lived through those moments over and over again. In most cases, people had no idea she was having a flashback, unless it was a particularly brutal one.

It was the nightmares that she couldn't handle – the strange melding of past and present which had her flailing about and screaming primal, guttural screams. It used to be Taylor could wake herself up at the onset of a dark nightmare, but over the last month she lost that ability. One of the worst nightmares gripped her in a hotel room in Calgary, Alberta on the first week of the tour. Emma Brinkman, her publicist, was in the room next door and ended up forcing the night manager to open Taylor's door so she could get into the room. Taylor awoke to find Emma shaking her, screaming her name and the night manager gawking at her with wide eyes and his mouth agape. Thank God the guy had the sense not to blab what he'd seen to the damn media. Since Calgary, Emma insisted on staying in the same room as Taylor or at the very least, having a key card to Taylor's room. Taylor's only defence against nightmares now was to stay awake.

She leaned her head back in the seat, closed her eyes, and brought a picture of the tall, dark, and ridiculously gorgeous Caillen Worthington into her mind. She'd never been attracted to a man until she met Cail. She hadn't known she could be attracted to a man before him. It was those deep blue eyes, framed in thick, jet black lashes that first sent a thrill through her. Then he smiled his brilliant smile and those adorable dimples formed on his cheeks. Add to that the hard, chiselled body and was it any wonder all those glorious sensations surged through her? Just thinking about him sent a thrill straight to her core.

Okay. She sat up, gave her head a little shake. Time to put that out of her mind before she got herself all worked up. She watched out the window as the black asphalt of the tarmac got closer and closer, until she felt the wheels touch down on the runway.

"You made it." Emma Brinkman covered Taylor's hand with her own and gave a little squeeze. "Welcome home."

Emma had been with Taylor through every step of the tour. She'd been travelling with authors on promotional tours for nearly fifteen years and she never experienced anything like the media attention Taylor drew. Everywhere they went, they had to fight through crowds of reporters. They'd been mobbed, pushed and shoved all over the continent. But, the worst of it had been the nerve of the reporters to ask the questions they did. Even a seasoned veteran like Emma was shocked at the abhorrent questions they shouted at Taylor.

Taylor offered Emma a weak smile. "You too." The tour may be over, Taylor thought, but the media frenzy was about to get worse with Sarah Johnson's trial due to begin in five days.

They were whisked off the plane while the other passengers were still seated and escorted to an electric cart. "If you could have your passports ready," the young man in an airport uniform began. "I'll take you through immigration and into a private lounge where you can wait for your luggage to be collected."

"Thanks," Taylor and Emma said in unison.

"Are there a lot of reporters out front?" Taylor asked.

"Oh, yeah," he answered. "And a lot of fans, too."

Great, Taylor thought. She could be rude and try to ignore the reporters, but she couldn't do that to the people buying her book. She'd have to take some time and sign a few autographs.

They were taken to the front of the line and passed through immigration then Taylor was dropped off at a private lounge while Emma went to claim their luggage. Taylor set her bag on one of the chairs, picked up a magazine and settled in for the wait. She had no idea how many planes she'd been on in the last month, but she was thrilled the last flight was finally behind her and she was home. She set the magazine down again, unable to concentrate on it, and leaned her head back against the wall.

That's how she was sitting when Cail looked in through the glass door. God, did she have any idea how beautiful she was? No, Cail thought with a smile, of course she didn't. He watched her for a minute, sitting there in an oversized sweater that slid over her shoulder, leaving it bare and undeniably sexy. He wasn't sure if it was the way she was sitting or if her trapezoids and shoulders were more defined than they had been. Black leggings clung to long, lean legs, and black leather ankle boots with a short heel adorned her feet. Her dark hair was tied back in its usual pony tail. Cail quietly pushed the door open. "Hey, gorgeous."

Taylor sensed him standing there watching her before he spoke. She hadn't been expecting him to meet her here. Her vivid, emerald eyes took him in, standing there in faded blue jeans, a tight t-shirt that showed off rippling muscles of his lean, hard body, and a battered black leather jacket. A slow grin spread across her face as she took in his beautiful smile, those dimples and his sexy eyes. "Hey."

"Are you going to come over here or am I coming over there?"

"Why don't we meet somewhere in the middle?"

He missed that voice, an exotic mixture of smoke and honey. Cail waited until Taylor stood then they slowly walked to each other.

Her arms wrapped around his neck as she pressed her body to his. A long sigh of relief escaped from deep within her as Cail's strong arms wrapped tightly around her, his heart beat against her chest in complete unison with hers. This was what she needed. This was where she needed to be. "I've never felt as safe as I do when I'm in your arms," she whispered.

It ripped at his heart. How many times in her life had she felt safe? Not nearly enough. So he held her tight with his cheek resting against the side of her head and he gave her the comfort she needed. She'd always been thin with a runner's body on a six foot frame, but now she appeared to be more muscular. He ran his hand up and down her back, feeling every ridge and valley of her muscles.

Taylor stayed in his arms, feeling his heart beat against hers, listening to the rhythm of his breathing. Leaning back, she took his face in her hands, studying him. "Your hair's grown." Gone was the Police Academy regulated brush cut, replaced by soft ebony curls. "I like it," she said as she ran her fingers through his hair. "Kinda sexy."

"Mmm, how about you take that band out and I'll run my fingers through your hair?"

"I'll make you a deal. Take me home and I'll take it out."

"Oh, that's tempting, but we're not going home. We're going straight up to Gray's."

Taylor's grin vanished. "I haven't seen them since the wedding and I'm dying to, but I thought we could spend a day or two alone first."

"There have been reporters surrounding our building for the last two days waiting for you to come home. I think you need a few days away from all that."

He was right, but she figured she needed him more than the break. Besides, they could go up to Gray's in a couple of days and take the break then. She brushed her lips over his. "Just a day ... or two."

Cail's hand slid up her back to the nape of her neck and he kissed her hard and deep. A month apart had been excruciating. He requested a leave of absence to accompany her on the tour and was denied. Never again. If she ever had to go out on a tour like this again, he'd quit the damn force before going a month without her. "God, I missed you."

"Missed you, too," she grinned. "So we'll go home first?"

* * *

Emma finally made it back to the lounge with Tony Crawford, the owner and CEO of Crawford Publishing, in tow. When Emma pushed through the door, Cail was leaning back against the wall with Taylor in front of him, her back to his chest. His arms wrapped around Taylor, their hands entwined at her belly. Tony went straight to Taylor and she took a step forward, accepting his quick hug.

"I'm sorry for all of the media hassles," Tony told her.

"Not your fault."

"Still, I apologize for it. You did an awesome job, Taylor. Both you and Emma did great. The book is still holding at the top of the best-seller list."

It still blew her away that she was a best-selling author. She figured one of the reasons the book was doing so well was people thought she'd spill some of the details of the terror and abuse she lived through. She hadn't included any of that in the story of her life on the streets. She wanted to inspire young people who found themselves in a similar situation, not scare them half to death. "Thanks, Tony."

"Your luggage is in the car. We're ready to head out."

Taylor took a deep breath and nodded. "Okay," she turned to Emma. "Let's get it over with."

Two body guards and two police officers escorted them out to the main terminal. Barriers had been erected to keep the fans and the media controlled. As Taylor neared the sliding doors, the murmuring of thousands of voices grew louder and louder. She wrapped her arm around Cail's waist and stuck her thumb in the waist band of his jeans. "Stay with me," she pleaded. She took a moment to take a few deep breaths to shake off the nerves. As they stepped through the doors, the roar of the crowd engulfed them.

They made their way along the barricade as Taylor talked to fans and signed copies of her book. She'd become adept at blocking out the reporters yelling out their hideous questions. At one point the fans must have tired of the questions because they began chanting Taylor's name at the top of their lungs, effectively drowning out the media. They were rewarded for their efforts with a blinding grin from Taylor before she moved on to talk to a girl who looked no more than fifteen. Taylor lifted the baby from her arms. "What's his name?" she asked, smiling at the baby as she tucked him in the crook of her arm and swayed back and forth.

"Justin," the girl answered shyly.

"And yours?"

"Amanda. Mandy. My friends call me Mandy."

"Are you on the streets, Mandy?"

"No. I was, but I get help now that I have the baby."

Thank God, Taylor thought. "Are you in school?"

"I missed a lot of time last year, so I'm doing grade ten over again."

"Good. Keep at it," she smiled at Mandy, brushed her lips over the soft peach fuzz on the baby's head, and reluctantly handed Justin back to his mom. "Have you got a copy of Leila's Locket?"

"No, not yet." Mandy couldn't afford to buy it, but didn't want to tell that to Taylor Sinclair.

Taylor turned to Emma, who handed her a copy of the book which she signed and handed to Mandy. "For you," she said when Mandy looked like she was about to refuse it. "I want you to have it. There's a card inside with my cell number on it. If you ever need someone to talk to, give me a call."

"Thanks," Mandy whispered. "Thank you." She hugged the book to her the same way she was hugging her baby.

Taylor was almost to the door when she spotted Cheryl Starr from the National News Network. She tightened her grip on Cail. Starr had been calling Emma every day for the past month requesting an interview. It got to the point where Taylor told Emma not to bother mentioning her calls, just tell her no.

"Taylor," Starr called from behind the barrier.

She spent an hour with Starr before the tour, promoting her book. Taylor didn't forget Starr hadn't drilled her about the abuse, but it didn't mean she was going to talk to her about it now. "The answer's still no."

"Taylor, NNN is airing a two hour special based on interviews with Sarah and Darryl. Don't you want to have your say?"

It was the first Taylor heard of this special and she wasn't impressed. It hit her like a fist to the gut. Why the hell would anyone air a program based on what those two had to say? Even worse, why would anyone watch it? "The answer's still no. I won't be changing my mind, so you can stop wasting your time." Ignoring the last few fans standing at the barricades, Taylor sailed out the door. The limo driver opened the door and she turned to wave to the fans then disappeared inside with Cail right behind her.

* * *

Two hundred kilometers to the north east, Gray Rowan sat in her great room watching the live broadcast on the National News Network. She was an incredibly striking woman with extremely short, spiky blonde hair and platinum highlights. Her new husband, O.P.P. Sergeant Patrick Callaghan, sat next to her on the bronze leather sofa with one arm around her shoulders and the other resting on her baby bump. At twenty-two weeks, she was more than half way there and just beginning to deal with back pain and discomfort. Her belly had fascinated her as her ripped abs gave way to a growing round mass.

Detective Sergeant Chris Cain sat in one of the deep, comfortable leather chairs which stood on either side of Gray's large, square coffee table of unfinished oak. Beside her was her girlfriend, and Cail's sister, Kate Worthington. They all stared up at the large screen TV mounted on the stone façade above the fireplace.

Cheryl Starr appeared on the screen with a sea of reporters and people filling the airport terminal behind her.

"NNN has confirmed Taylor Sinclair's flight has landed safely here at Lester B. Pearson International Airport and the aircraft is making its way to the gate. Sources here at the airport tell us Ms. Sinclair will be the first off the plane. She'll be escorted through customs and immigration before coming out the double, frosted glass doors you see behind me. We expect that to be in approximately thirty minutes time. Back to you, Dan."

Callaghan picked up the remote and pressed mute. He glanced at his watch. "So she'll be coming out about twelve fifteen. Why don't we have some lunch while we're waiting?" He gave Gray's belly a gently pat.

"Don't worry, Patrick. I'm not going to starve to death," she laughed. "Besides, Maggie's whipping up something."

"Can you feel the baby moving yet?" Chris asked, eyeing Callaghan's hand gently circling Gray's belly.

"Just little flutters every now and then."

Callaghan laughed. "She's not sure if it's gas or the baby." He laughed again when Gray slapped his arm.

"It's the baby," Kate announced confidently.

"How would you know?" Chris grinned, poking Kate's belly.

"Lots of my friends have had babies. They all describe it as a flutter when they start to feel the baby moving." She snuck in a poke to Chris's ribs.

"See," Gray said to Callaghan. "It is the baby."

"Oh." Callaghan nearly screamed. "Did you feel that? I felt the baby. Did you feel the baby move?"

Gray laughed now. "That was probably just gas." But she felt it and knew it was the baby. "God, I don't know if there is anything better than that feeling," she grinned, bumping Callaghan's hand out of the way for hers.

"I can think of one." Chris smirked then grabbed Kate's hand before she could poke her in the ribs again.

They dined on Maggie's soup and sandwiches in front of the TV as they waited for Taylor to come through the doors into the main airport terminal. When Cheryl Starr appeared back on the screen, Callaghan turned the sound back on.

"We're just a few minutes away from seeing Taylor Sinclair come through the sliding doors behind me. We're hearing reports Taylor has been reunited with her boyfriend and fellow Toronto Police Constable, Caillen Worthington, in a private lounge inside the terminal."

As Cheryl talked, the doors behind her slid open revealing an airport representative. Emma Brinkman and Tony Crawford followed him out then Cheryl turned back towards the doors. "As you can see, the doors have just opened and Taylor's publisher, Tony Crawford, and her publicist, Emma Brinkman, have just come out." Several seconds went by with Tony and Emma looking back inside the doors before Taylor walked out, with her arm around Cail's waist while his circled her shoulders.

"And here she is," Cheryl announced while the noise level in the terminal rose to deafening with the crowd cheering and the reporters calling out their questions. "Don't they make a gorgeous couple?"

"She hates this," Chris announced. "She hates all the attention."

"She doesn't understand why people are so interested in her," Gray stated.

"Everyone loves to look at beautiful people. Is it like that for you when you go out on book tours, Gray?" Chris asked.

"I don't go out on them anymore, but no, not to the extent Taylor experiences. I think a lot of it has to do with what she's been through and the person she's become despite it. She's still an innocent."

The camera closed in on Taylor and Cail as Taylor moved to the barrier and began talking to fans and signing books. "She looks very pale," Cheryl continued. "Obviously, the busy schedule of her book tour has taken a toll on Taylor Sinclair. Forty-two cities in thirty-two days was quite an ambitious goal, but they managed to attend all of their scheduled interviews and book signings with a few extras added in along the way. Sinclair's book, *Leila's Locket*, continues to rank at number one on the New York Times Best-seller List."

"It's not the schedule that knocked her for a loop, you dumb bitch," Chris said to the TV. "It's all of you fucking reporters."

"Chris," Gray admonished quietly.

"Well, it's true. You've seen enough of the coverage on her to know that."

She had. And she knew Chris was right. Watching the way they treated Taylor had made her heart sick. Although she'd only known Taylor personally for about seven months, she considered her family and they were very close. She knew Taylor well enough to know the questions she was constantly being asked would trigger horrible flashbacks.

Cheryl Starr's commentary ended, giving way to live reports from a helicopter, which picked up the coverage outside the terminal. They watched as Taylor waved to the crowd and preceded Cail into the limo. Behind them, Emma and Tony got into Tony's car and sped off before the limo pulled away from the curb and began to slowly drive away from the airport. As they headed for the highway, the limo disappeared into a tunnel and the helicopter picked them up again coming out the other side, following it towards Toronto's downtown.

"I thought they were coming straight here," Chris commented.

"Taylor probably wants to stop at home first," Gray thought out loud. "You can't blame her after being away for a month."

"She didn't know Cail was meeting her at the airport," Kate announced. "He wanted to surprise her. Knowing my brother, he'll probably want some alone time with her."

"They can have their alone time in the limo," Chris grinned.

Kate's poke made it past Chris's defences this time. "You've got a one track mind."

The cameras followed the limo along the 401, heading eastbound. Callaghan leaned forward to pick up the remote, ready to turn the TV off, when the limo suddenly came under rapid fire.

"Oh, my God," Kate and Gray cried out in unison. Gray's hand flew up to cover her mouth as the tears began to flow.

Chris and Callaghan sat in stunned silence, watching the nightmare playing out live.

"We're not sure where the shots are coming from," announced the reporter in the helicopter, a hint of panic in his voice. "At this rate, the survival of anyone inside the vehicle is doubtful." Bullets continued to blast the limo and then a massive ball of orange and yellow flames ballooned around the car and shot skyward followed by thick black smoke. The helicopter lost coverage for a moment and then the screen filled with the flaming remains of the limo.

Callaghan wrapped his arms around his hysterical wife. There were no words he could think of to comfort her or settle her, so he just hung on and rocked her back and forth, his jaw clenched in anger.

Kate had come to love Taylor, just as much as Gray and Chris. But Cail was her brother, her little brother. She let out a wail that didn't sound human before Chris wrapped Kate in her arms.

Maggie ran into the great room to see what the commotion was about and saw the flaming limo on the screen. "Don't tell me that's Taylor and Cail. Oh, dear God." She ran to retrieve the remote and turned the TV off before dropping to the sofa, sobbing.

Chapter 2

Well over an hour passed before Callaghan was able to settle Gray down. They sat in the great room, watching the updates on the TV with the sound muted.

Maggie brought in an herbal tea and set it in front of Gray. "Try this," she pleaded. "It should help you to relax."

She needed a sedative, Callaghan thought, but that just wasn't possible with the baby on board. "Maybe we should call the doc. There must be something you can take to help calm you."

"I'm not taking anything, Patrick. It'll be fine. I just can't believe–" she broke into tears again.

"We're all in shock," Chris said as she stared blindly up at the ceiling. There has to be a mistake. This just couldn't be happening. She went over what they watched play out on the news over and over again in her head, desperately trying to find an explanation that didn't end in Taylor and Cail being killed. She placed a call to Toronto Police Inspector Cal Worthington, Kate and Cail's father, but was still waiting for a call back praying he would tell them that it had all been a horrible mistake, that Cail and Taylor hadn't been in that limo.

"Gray, why don't I take you up and you can lie down for a while?" Callaghan suggested.

"I couldn't sleep right now, sweetheart." She placed a hand on his cheek. "We'll be okay. We're okay." Gray planted a kiss on his lips then sat back, wiping her tears away with a tissue. "Should we be calling anyone?"

"I think everyone knows," Chris responded. "Besides, everyone she loves is in this room."

"What about Cail?" Gray looked at Kate, her face so pale framed by all of those thick black curls. She looked so much like her brother with the bright blue eyes and strong features.

"My dad's taking care of that. I should probably go to my mom's. She's a wreck. I need to get to my mom."

"I'll drive. Just let me grab our stuff." Chris started up the stairs to retrieve their bags from one of the guest rooms. Half way up she heard Maggie's scream coming from the kitchen. She turned to see Maggie running into the great room.

"There's a car ... there's a limo at the gate." Maggie huffed out. "The driver said Taylor and Cail are in the back."

Gray was up out of her seat and on her way to the door with Kate right on her heels when Chris shouted, "Stop. Don't go out there until we know for sure who's in that car." She bounded down the stairs, drawing her gun and ran into Gray's office. Pulling back the drapes a fraction, she watched the limo pull up in front of the house. "Callaghan," Chris eyed him on her way out of the office. "With me."

Chris opened the front door and darted behind a pillar on the porch. Callaghan took the opposite pillar while Gray stayed in her office, peeking out the window with Kate and Maggie. Raising her gun, Chris called out, "Step out of the car, keeping your hands where I can see them."

The door flew open and hands appeared above it. "For Christ's sake Cain, what the hell are you doing? Put the damn gun down."

Chris lowered her gun with a huge sigh of relief. "Please tell me Taylor is in there with you."

"We're stepping out. For God's sake, don't shoot," Cail yelled. He stepped out of the car and offered his hand to Taylor.

Taylor stepped out behind him and watched Gray and Kate come barrelling out of the front door sobbing. "What the hell is going on?" Kate ran down the porch steps, quickly followed by Gray who all but threw herself into Taylor's arms. "Hey," Taylor soothed, rubbing Gray's back. "What's wrong?"

Chris, Callaghan and Maggie watched, in stunned relief, from the porch.

"Does someone want to tell us what the hell is going on?" Cail asked, while comforting Kate.

"We watched you die," Callaghan replied. "On live TV, we watched you both die."

"What?" Taylor asked, confused now.

"The limo. Shots were fired at your limo until it blew up."

"That's crazy. No one fired on our car." Taylor stared at him before it began to sink in.

Cail explained, "Tony didn't want the media to know Taylor would be up here, so he arranged for another limo to wait in a tunnel before the on ramp to the highway. We waited there for a few minutes while the other limo headed out of the tunnel and towards downtown."

They stood in the driveway until everyone's nerves had a chance to settle then everyone grabbed a suitcase to bring inside. Callaghan reached for a four by six foot package wrapped in white paper with thin silver lines in the shape of wedding bells. "Ah, ah, ah," Taylor warned him off. "I'll take that one."

It was all he could do to surrender it. He figured Taylor had done some drawings for them and had them framed as a late wedding present and he was itching to see them. He picked up one of the remaining suitcases, but stuck close to Taylor, following the package inside.

* * *

Taylor sat staring up at the TV screen in shock. A banner at the bottom of the screen read:

Taylor Sinclair Murdered

She watched the replay of the limo coming out of the tunnel, driving along the highway for several minutes and then the shots hitting it before it exploded. "It's my fault that driver's dead."

"You don't know they were targeting you," Chris stated. "They may have been after Cail."

"How do you figure that?"

"Cail was involved in an arrest last week netting over a million dollars in crystal meth. It's looking like the meth belonged to Vincenzo DeCosta, who's linked to the Romano crime family."

Taylor turned to look at Cail as he took over from Chris, "Turns out the kid we arrested, Carlos Spanner, was DeCosta's nephew, his sister's son. We think the kid may have stolen the crystal meth from Uncle Vinnie seeing as he turned up dead in his cell two mornings ago. Someone stabbed him in his side and he bled out. The odd part was that the kid was locked in his cell alone all night. The only person we can think of who'd have that kind of reach is DeCosta."

"So the mob is out to kill you because you confiscated their drugs?" Taylor tried to process it, but her mind was a muddle after what she watched on the screen. This all sounded like something out of a mystery novel.

"It's possible. It's also possible that you were the target."

When Chris pulled her phone off her belt and answered a call, all eyes were on her. She wandered to the other side of the room, her back turned to them. When she ended the call, all eyes stayed on her and complete silence filled the room as they waited for her to give them an update. "Here's the plan," she announced as she crossed the room back to her chair. "We're going to let the media believe Taylor and Cail were in that limo. Hopefully, it will keep you both safe until this mess gets sorted out. Kate and I will stay here with you as protection. Looks like we're on lockdown for a few days."

"At least you'll have a few days break from the media harassing you," Cail said to Taylor.

Taylor was still trying to process everything. If it wasn't Cail they were after, the only person she could think of who wanted to do her harm was sitting in a jail cell. "Would Sarah Johnson have been able to hire someone to take me out? She tried to get Darryl to do it."

Chris sighed. She hadn't wanted to upset Taylor with news of Sarah Johnson. With the trial so close, she was sure Taylor was under enough stress. The prosecutor needed Taylor's testimony to put Sarah Johnson away and Chris wasn't sure Taylor would be able to handle sitting in the court room talking about the atrocities Johnson had done to her. "It's possible, but not likely."

"Who's the lead in the investigation?" Taylor asked. She thought Chris would be spared from investigating this one. She was a Detective Sergeant in the Sex Crimes Unit and this case would surely go to Homicide.

"This is either related to the Carlos Spanner case or to the Sarah Johnson case. I'm leaning towards Spanner based on the fire power that hit the limo. We're talking about assault rifles, possibly AK-47s. I can't imagine Johnson would have access to anyone with that kind of fire power. Right now they've got Detective Warren Boone from Homicide leading the investigation, but Detective Ian Pierson from Vice and I are being kept in the loop. If evidence points to Sarah Johnson being involved, I'll become more involved, but Boone will remain the lead investigator."

"You said AK-47s," Taylor said. "So, there was more than one shooter?"

Chris nodded in acknowledgement.

"It's gotta be DeCosta," Cail offered and felt Taylor's grip on his hand tighten.

"That's my gut feeling," Chris replied then turned to Taylor. "You've got the best instincts of anyone I know. What's your gut telling you?"

"That it was a hit on Cail. I was just collateral damage." Taylor found herself relieved that the media wasn't being advised she and Cail hadn't been in that limo. If DeCosta could get to a kid locked up in jail, he could get to Cail. She only hoped Boone cleared the case in the next couple of days. The media would find out they were alive by the time Sarah Johnson's trial began on Wednesday. If the case wasn't cleared by then, Cail was in serious danger.

"Hey," Cail said to Taylor, raising his hand to cup her face when he sensed her fear. Her hand covered his. "He's not going to get to me. We'll take him down before he gets another chance."

"You could use your –" Chris began and was quickly cut off by Taylor.

"No, I can't." If she used her ESP to try to see what was going to happen, she was scared to death she'd see Cail die.

The room fell silent as everyone pictured what Taylor was so scared of. Callaghan decided it was time to change the depressing atmosphere, mainly because he was itching to get his hands on the package Taylor brought in. "Is that a T. Grace Sinclair original over there?" he asked, drawing everyone out of the deep pool of depressing thoughts.

"Maybe," Taylor smiled weakly. It was probably a good time to give it to them. It would pick up the somber mood. "But, I can only give it to you if you want to know the sex of your baby." She turned to face Gray. "I had a vision when I first figured out you were pregnant. Instead of telling you about it, I thought it would be cool to draw it. I tried a few times, but it just didn't look right in black and white. So I painted it."

"It's a painting?" Callaghan looked like a kid at Christmas, his grin spread from ear to ear.

"It was supposed to be part of your wedding present, but I didn't have it ready on time."

Gray waited until Callaghan's big brown eyes met her deep blues. "Do you want to know?"

"How can we not? I'm dying to see it."

With a laugh, Gray said, "Okay." Her hand spread across her belly. "Let's see what we've got."

Cail picked up the wrapped canvas and laid it on the coffee table in front of Gray. Callaghan sat down beside her and when she started to meticulously peel the tape back, he grabbed onto the paper and ripped it wide open. "Patrick," Gray scolded. But she could see the painting now and her eyes filled with tears. Callaghan lifted the canvas so they could view it straight on.

Taylor had painted their baby girl at about two years of age, wearing a pretty white sundress and running barefoot on the grass in the back yard. Her blonde hair and blue eyes matched Gray's, although her hair was a mass of soft curls like her father's. Her fine, delicate features were as impeccable as her mother's. Callaghan was behind her, grinning as he chased his giggling daughter with Lake Balton in the background. Gray watched from the deck with laughter in her eyes and her belly swollen with baby number two.

"Oh, she's gorgeous," Gray exclaimed through her tears.

"She looks just like Mommy." Callaghan leaned in and kissed Gray's temple. "She's as stunning as her mother."

"Oh my God. I look like a beached whale." Gray laughed when she saw herself in the painting.

"No, you don't. You look amazing." Taylor had a tear in her eye as she watched their reactions. "You look as beautiful as you do right now."

Chris, Kate and Cail moved around to the back of the sofa so they could see the painting. "It's amazing, Taylor," Kate said. She put her arm around Chris's waist and leaned into her as they studied the canvas.

"I taped the drawings of her on the back of the canvas," Taylor explained. "I thought you might want to have them, too."

"I think we have to hang this in the baby's room," Callaghan beamed. He peeled the sketches from the back and went through the five drawings. "We should frame these, too," he suggested. "We could put them in our room."

Taylor offered up her room when Gray and Callaghan announced their pregnancy. It was the closest to the master bedroom and made the most sense. "How's the baby's room coming?" Taylor asked.

"It's nearly done. I'm just waiting on Gray to pick out the furniture," Callaghan announced proudly with his eyes still glued to the drawings.

"We've still got lots of time, honey." Gray patted his hand. "I'm only five months."

When she said five months, Taylor got a sick, twisting feeling in her stomach at the tail end of a nasty flashback. She closed her eyes for a second to push the memories out of her head. When she opened them again, she found Gray staring at her.

"You okay? You've gone a bit pale."

"Fine," Taylor answered. "My stomach's just a little upset."

"When was the last time you ate?"

"I had some breakfast on the plane."

"Patrick, could you get Mags to put something together for Taylor and Cail?"

Callaghan rested the painting against the wall, stood back looking at it for a minute then turned to Taylor. "This is so much more than a gift you've given us, Taylor. I don't know what to say. You've got amazing talent and I absolutely love the painting and the drawings. Thank you." He walked to her, grabbed her face in his hands and planted a big kiss right on her lips.

Taylor's entire body stiffened at his display of affection. "You're welcome." She blushed then pinched her ear lobe in an attempt to calm herself. It was a technique taught to her by Dr. Lane McIntyre, the Toronto Police psychologist who Taylor saw regularly, and helped her to deal with her haphephobia or fear of being touched.

Gray got up to thank her and Taylor placed a hand on her baby bump. "You've gotten a lot bigger since I saw you last." She winced when Gray slapped her arm. "Ow, maybe I didn't say that right." Taylor closed her eyes and concentrated on the baby. "You've been singing to her. She likes it. She loves the sound of your voice."

"Okay, I take back the slap." Gray placed her hand over Taylor's. "What else do you see?"

"You can feel her moving now." Taylor let out a quick laugh. "Mostly in the middle of the night. That's when she's the most active."

"Yeah. That's when she delights in dancing on my bladder."

Taylor laughed again then removed her hand to give Gray a hug. "God, she's beautiful, Gray. Callaghan is right. She's as beautiful as her Mommy."

"How'd you do that?" Kate asked. She'd been watching Taylor closely, intrigued by both the painting and what she was doing with Gray.

"She's got an incredible gift of sight," Gray answered. "When she chooses to tune in to it." She placed her hands on Taylor's cheeks and looked deep into those bright green eyes. "Thank you for that. And for the painting and the drawings." She kissed Taylor's cheek and then hugged her again. She'd been devastated when she thought Taylor and Cail had been killed, but she thanked God for not taking them. Twice now, in the last few months, she thought she'd lost Taylor. She prayed that she'd never feel a loss like that again.

* * *

Taylor stood at the great room window watching Callaghan and Cail attempting to clean up the millions of leaves covering the lawn like a carpet. Behind them, Lake Balton looked cold and forbidding. The trees were nearly bare, giving them a cold, skeletal appearance. When Cail got his hands on the blower, he showered Callaghan in leaves. Callaghan retaliated by scooping up a huge pile of leaves and dumping them on Cail's head. "They're like little boys."

"That looks like fun," Kate said with a laugh. "I haven't played in the leaves since I was a little kid."

Taylor frowned, thinking of what it must have been like to play in the leaves as a kid. She'd never done it. She was too busy trying to stay alive on the streets, too busy trying to hide from the monsters who terrorized and molested her for years.

"Do you want to talk about it?" Gray asked Taylor. She'd watched Taylor's shoulders slump and knew she was thinking of her past.

Taylor turned to face Gray on the sofa. "Talk about what?"

"About the media hounding you on the book tour. About what has stressed you out so much. You're not sleeping, are you?"

Taylor turned back to the window as she wrapped her arms tightly around herself. "I just need to get back into my routine and I'll be fine."

"You really think they're going to leave you alone because you're getting back into your routine?" Chris asked.

"No. I think it's going to get worse with the trial starting on Wednesday." Unless she could put a stop to the trial, she thought. She'd been thinking about it the entire time she was away and she came up with a plan she prayed was going to work.

Chris dropped her head to the back of the chair. She couldn't help but blame herself for the media hounding Taylor. She kept second guessing herself. Maybe she shouldn't have pushed Sarah Johnson. Maybe she shouldn't have made Taylor tell her what they'd done to her. She'd worked in sex crimes for over eight years and she never heard anything as horrifying as what Sarah and Darryl Johnson had done to Taylor.

"It's not your fault," Taylor said, still staring out the window.

"What, are you still tuned in to the ESP shit?" Chris shot back.

"I can feel the tension in you all the way over here."

"It doesn't do any good to argue about blame," Kate said. "Taylor needs to deal with what she went through on the tour so she can make it through this damn trial."

"There's nothing to deal with. It's done." Taylor turned from the window and went to sit next to Gray on the sofa.

"Are you going to sit there and tell me you're not having flashbacks and nightmares?" Gray reached out and took Taylor's hand in hers. "We sat here and watched the way the media treated you, watched you slowly deteriorating. I let you get away with telling me you were fine over the phone, but it stops now, Taylor. We're not going to sit around and watch you slowly die."

Taylor's head fell back and she stared up at the ceiling. "I don't know what you expect me to do. I don't know what I'm supposed to do."

"I've invited Dr. McIntyre up here for the weekend. If anyone can help you, Taylor, it's Lane."

Taylor turned her head to glare at Gray. "That was a little presumptuous of you."

"We watched you and Cail get blown up this afternoon." Gray choked back her tears. "I can't go through that again. I can't go through losing you again."

Taylor scooted over and embraced Gray. "I'm sorry," she whispered. "I'm sorry."

Chapter 3

When Dr. McIntyre arrived, Taylor carried her bag up and showed her into one of the remaining guest rooms. She leaned back in one of the chairs and stretched her long legs out while Lane unpacked. It was the first time Taylor had seen Lane in anything other than what Taylor considered her 'professional gear'. She wore a pair of jeans and a sweatshirt. Her heart shaped face was framed by dark curls, highlighting her doe like brown eyes. Gray was right. If anyone could help her it was Lane. But what Taylor had in mind wasn't what Gray meant.

"So, I guess you've seen some of the news coverage from when I was away."

"Yes, it's one of the reasons I'm here, Taylor."

"One of them?"

Lane smiled. "Who wouldn't want to spend a weekend at Gray Rowan's lakeside home?"

"I hope we're not taking you away from your family."

"My kids are grown and my husband passed away a couple of years ago."

"Oh, I'm sorry." Taylor winced. What was she supposed to say to that? Should she have known that? "It must get lonely," she heard herself saying and winced again.

"Sometimes. Were you lonely being away from Cail for a month?"

"Yeah, but not just in the physical sense. For some reason I feel safer when he's around. He can be pretty goofy sometimes, like when he was playing in the leaves with Callaghan this afternoon. I like those sorts of things about him."

"You wished you were out playing in the leaves, too."

Taylor let out a quick laugh, wondering how Lane picked up on these things. "It's kind of crazy, isn't it? I mean I'm an adult for crying out loud."

"An adult who never got the chance to be a kid. You should do those kinds of things when you have the opportunity. It's good to feel like a kid every now and then." She stopped putting her things away and took a seat beside Taylor. No time like the present to delve into one of the other reasons she was here. "I don't know if you've heard or not, but NNN is airing a special based on interviews with Sarah and Darryl."

Taylor twisted the bottom of her sweater in her fingers. "I heard it from Cheryl Starr this morning."

"How do you feel about it?"

"I don't want them to air something like that, but apparently there's nothing I can do about it." She'd grilled Cail in the limo and got the song and dance about freedom of speech.

"Any particular worries?"

With a long sigh, Taylor stood and began pacing. "You want a list?" she asked with a slight laugh. She paced a bit more before continuing. "I'm worried they're going to say things I've never told anyone; things I don't want anyone to know; things that I couldn't talk about, can't talk about." Taylor sat back in the chair, resting her forearms on her thighs and stared at the floor. "You know there are things the police and the media haven't discovered. Some of those things I should have told Cail at the beginning of our relationship, but I just haven't been able to make myself do it. What if those things are aired on this special and I haven't told him?"

Lane glanced at her watch. "You've still got a few hours if you want to talk to him."

"What? It's on tonight?" Suddenly, the room felt like it was starting to spin and Taylor leaned over so her head was between her knees and placed her hands on her head. "Oh God, I don't think I can watch it."

"Well, that's another reason I'm here," Lane said, her voice soft and calming. She laid her hand gently on Taylor's shoulder. "Breathe, Taylor."

She hadn't realized she was holding her breath. She tried to take a few calming breaths, but she still felt light headed. The sick, twisting feeling in her stomach made it even worse. "I just don't understand how they can go on TV and talk about the crap they did."

"In Sarah's case, she craves the attention. She wants to be the star of the show."

"Won't it just make matters worse for her with the trial coming up?" Darryl at least had the sense to plead guilty. He had nothing to lose at this point, but Sarah was still hoping to win her case.

"All along she's insisted she knew all of the details because you told them to her."

"Do you believe that?"

"No, of course not." Lane ran her hand up and down Taylor's back, surprised at the muscle definition she could feel through the thick sweater. "You've been working out a lot. I'm surprised you found the time."

Taylor figured Lane was going to find out sooner or later anyway, she might as well get it over with. "I've been working out at night. I haven't been sleeping." Drawing or reading made her drowsy, so she'd taken to hitting the fitness centres in whatever hotel there were in to keep herself awake.

"Nightmares?" Lane asked.

Taylor only nodded in response.

"I'd like you to come in for a full physical before you go back to work."

"Geez, you're full of good news," Taylor frowned.

"Yeah, well I've got more. There's a houseful of people here that really care about you. They've been very worried. I thought it might be a good idea to talk about what you went through on the tour with everyone present."

Taylor's cheeks puffed out before she blew out a long breath. "I guess I owe them at least that."

"Okay."

Taylor took her time getting to her feet to ensure she wasn't going to pass out, and then walked to the door before turning back. She had one more thing to talk to Lane about and she was too nervous to ask. "I appreciate you coming all the way up here."

"It's my pleasure. They're not the only ones who care about you, Taylor." Lane smiled again, in a way that Taylor found comforting.

Taylor started to turn again and stopped herself. She wasn't sure why she was afraid to ask, except that Lane was the only one who could put the brakes on what she wanted to do. She leaned against the door, looked Lane in the eye and just spat it out, "I want to talk to them. Both of them. Before the trial."

Lane sat studying Taylor for a minute, her brows drawn in tight. "Taylor, I'm not sure you're ready for that."

"I need to do it."

Maybe it wasn't such a bad idea. If she wasn't ready to face them one on one, she sure as hell wouldn't be ready to take Sarah on in court. "Alright. I'll ask Chris to arrange it, but I'm going to be there in case you need me."

"I appreciate that, too." She walked down the hall, turned into her own room and closed the door behind her. Leaning back on the door, she took a deep breath, relieved to have gotten the wheels in motion to face her demons. God, she was tired. Thinking a nice hot shower would help revive her, she walked into the bathroom and found Cail pulling his shirt off. "You taking a shower?" she asked. Her eyes were drawn to that deep V cut in his lower ab muscles, disappearing below the waistband of his jeans.

"Want to join me?" He grinned. "I know that look in your eyes, Bean."

"What?" She couldn't stifle her smile or the slight blush. She stepped towards him and splayed her hands over his abdomen, ran them slowly up over his chest, cupped his strong shoulders then brushed down his strong arms. Her eyes locked onto his as his arms circled around her.

"Did you know your eyes glow when you're turned on?" Cail asked.

"Who says I'm turned on?"

"Your eyes," he said and laughed. "Remember that first night you touched me? You let me touch you the same way? It was the first time I really saw your eyes light up like that. You looked absolutely radiant. That was the single most intimate and memorable experience of my life."

"You can't be serious. Not with all the women you've been with." And that was a really stupid thing to say, she thought. It wasn't a secret Cail had been with a lot of women. He'd been very open about his past with Taylor, which only made her feel worse that she hadn't told him things he deserved to know about her.

"I've never been with a woman like you, Tay. I don't want to be with anyone else but you for the rest of my life."

It scared her when he talked about being with her forever and she knew part of it was because of what she hadn't told him. It was time to face this demon, too, she thought. "You might not say that after I tell you what I need to tell you. We need to talk."

His first thought was that she met someone else while she was travelling around North America. He wasn't sure he wanted to hear what she needed to tell him. Cail's arms tightened around her as he whispered in her ear, "Why don't we have that shower first? We'll work off some of this tension in you."

Taylor reached over her head and pulled the band holding her ponytail out. Cail knew having her hair down was one of her triggers. She'd taken it out for him on occasion, but it didn't stay down for long. As soon as she released her thick, silky hair, his fingers were running through it. It spilled out of his hands, hanging below her shoulder blades before he was sinking his fingers into it again. Brushing his lips over hers, he whispered, "God, I missed you, Tay." The kiss started off so tender and slow, gradually deepening in sync with their breathing until they were desperate to quench their thirst for each other.

She gasped as he devoured her neck. "I think I might be addicted to you. I've been going through withdrawal for the past thirty-two days, ten hours, and … crap." Her phone was in her pocket and even if she could get it out, she wasn't sure she could read it, wasn't sure she could focus. "About thirty minutes, I think."

Cail straightened and looked into her eyes, astonished as he worked out the hours and minutes in his head. "You counted from the last time we made love."

Her cheeks reddened with embarrassment. "A little over the top?" The glowing smile that slowly spread across his face made her even more embarrassed.

"No. No, it's … you." He ran the tip of his finger over her perfectly shaped eyebrow then slowly traced it down the hollow between her high cheek bone and strong jaw to her lips. "You have a hard time saying the words sometimes, but you do little things like that and I know you love me as much as I love you."

"I don't say it enough," she whispered, more to herself than him. It hurt that he would think she had a hard time saying those words.

"You don't have to say it, Tay. You show it all the time."

"I do love you, Cail. I love you." She leaned her brow against his, wondering how the hell to say what she needed to say. "It's just … I can't give you the future you deserve."

Cail let out a nervous chuckle. "What are you talking about? You are my future." Was she breaking up with him?

"I can't be everything you need me to be."

"Tay, I don't need you to be anything but who you are. I love *you*. You."

Deep down she knew that wasn't quite true. She'd seen that his vision of the future included a family similar to the one he'd been raised in. "Cail, I can't … God, this is hard. I should have told you this at the beginning of our relationship and I couldn't."

Cail leaned back and took her face in his hands, staring into her eyes. "Hey, you don't have to tell me right now. There's nothing you could say that would stop me from loving you. You've got enough pressure on you right now."

"I don't want you to hear it from Sarah or Darryl."

Ah, now he understood. "You're worried they're going to say something on this program tonight that you want me to hear from you." He watched as her eyes filled with tears, watched as they quietly spilled out and he gently wiped them away with his thumbs. "Just say it then. Just let it out and know that I love you no matter what."

He was right. She just had to say it and be done with it. Whether he chose to stay or go, she would deal with it. She'd have to deal with it. Leaning into him, she rested her head on his shoulder and closed her eyes. "I can't give you children."

"What do you mean? You can't have kids? How could you know that?"

"That didn't come out right." Taylor shook out her hands to relieve some of the tension she felt. "It's not so much that I can't. I won't have children."

Cail didn't understand. He'd seen the way she was with the baby at the airport. He'd seen the way she was with Gray's unborn child and thought she'd make a great mother. "Why? What the hell did they do to you to make you swear off having kids?"

Taylor let out a shaky breath. "I was only thirteen when I was pregnant."

He pulled Taylor into his arms, kept his grip tightened around her as he tried to reign in his anger. He was sure whatever happened to the baby, Sarah Johnson was responsible. "There are other ways to have a baby if and when we decide we want kids, Tay."

She pulled back sharply to meet his eyes. She wasn't sure what she expected, but his reaction shocked her.

"Did you think I wouldn't want you anymore because you don't want to have children?" he asked.

"I don't know what I thought, but you deserved to know what you were getting before we got involved. I didn't understand how you could want me when you knew what they said about me on the news;

about what happened to me at that foster home and living on the streets. Then I thought you wouldn't want me when you heard me tell Chris about Sarah and Darryl. Even now I don't get how you can look at me and not be grossed out knowing what was done to me."

"Jesus, Bean. I love you. I could never look at you and see the violence that was done to you. You know that, but if you need me to keep saying it, I will. I saw how you were with that baby today at the airport. You've got so much love in your heart. You're going to make an awesome mom one day, if that's what you want."

Leaning back into him, she buried her face in his shoulder and whispered, "I love you." It amazed her that he didn't shower her with questions, wanting to know the details of what happened. How could this beautiful, wonderful man know many of the dark things about her and still love her for who she is? It was a miracle to her.

"Are you okay?"

"Yeah."

"Good, because I'm about to restart your clock. What were we at? Thirty two days, ten hours and thirty something minutes?"

"It's probably forty something minutes by now."

"Well, we better get started before it gets any higher." He swept her off her feet and carried her to the bed.

"What about the shower?" she asked with a giggle. Oh my God, she thought, surprised at herself. Taylor Sinclair did not giggle. Ever. At least she'd never giggled until that moment.

"We'll get to it ... eventually."

* * *

Taylor walked out of the bathroom wrapped in a towel and eyed the five suitcases sitting on the floor. She left for the tour with two suitcases, but she couldn't keep wearing the same outfits for all of the TV appearances, so she bought a lot of clothes along the way. Right now she just wanted to put on something comfortable, like sweat pants and a sweat shirt. Somewhere, in one of those cases, she had a few things that would do the trick, but she was pretty sure they needed laundered. With a sigh, she kneeled in front of one of the cases and began the tedious job of rifling through them, leaving one aside, unopened. As she went through the other four cases, she pulled out two or three sketch pads from each and piled them off to the side.

Cail came in from the bathroom and grabbed clean clothes from his duffle bag as he watched Taylor. "How many sketch pads did you take with you?"

26

"Two," she answered.

He figured she wasn't sleeping, but the number of sketch pads she brought back and the fact that she put on all of that muscle pretty much confirmed it for him. "Are they the kind of drawings I can look at?"

Taylor looked at the pile and then up at Cail. "You really want to see some of them?"

"Yeah." She was a talented artist, but he knew there were drawings she didn't want anyone to see – drawings of the darker experiences of her life. But she also drew her good memories now and those were the ones she usually let Cail see.

"Look at this first," she said, and handed him a small white box with a gold crown design on it.

Taking the box from her, his eyes widened. "Rolex?"

Taylor shrugged, smiling up at him.

He wasn't sure why he felt so uncomfortable all of a sudden. "Tay, you really shouldn't do this."

She understood the look on his face. She knew how she felt when Gray kept giving her things, so she stood and put her arms around him. "You said I have a hard time saying the words. Maybe it's just that I'm not used to saying those words. I'm not used to caring about anyone. But, I care about you. I love you, Cail and if you ever doubt it, you can look at that watch and know that I do."

"Do you have any idea how much these things cost?" he asked as he brushed his lips over her temple.

"That doesn't matter. What matters is that it's a token of my love for you."

Cail sighed. With one arm wrapped around her waist, he flipped the box open with his free hand. He was expecting some fancy, flashy gold watch with diamonds all around the face or something crazy like that, something totally not him. But the watch she'd picked out was very masculine with a dark blue face, glow in the dark hands and digits, a window box displaying the date, and a dark blue outer ring with the gold numbers of the twenty-four hour clock. The links of the band were brushed silver with a gold strip down the middle. It was the kind of thing he could wear to work or even to the gym and it suited him perfectly. "Tay." His eyes moved from the watch to her eyes. "It's awesome. I love it." He kissed her gently. "Thank you."

"You're welcome." She gave him another quick kiss and went back to routing through her suitcases. "I've got nothing to wear."

Cail laughed. As he removed the watch from the box and secured it to his wrist, he said, "You've got five suitcases. How can you not have anything to wear?" He held his arm out and admired the watch with a smile.

"I want something comfortable and everything I've got needs washed."

"Gray should have something that fits you."

Cail was still admiring his watch when there was a quick knock at the door before it flew open.

Chris's eyes just about popped out of her head before she let out what sounded like a short scream and slammed the door closed again. She'd gotten an eye full of Cail wearing nothing but his new Rolex. "Put some damn clothes on for Christ's sake," she yelled through the door.

After seeing the look on Chris's face, Taylor was nearly bursting at the seams trying not to laugh. She glanced up at Cail and saw he was doing the same thing. The two of them burst out laughing as Cail put the Rolex box in his duffle bag and threw on his boxers and jeans. He went to the door and opened it to find a red faced Chris still standing there wearing her trade mark cargo pants with a Toronto Police sweatshirt, her honey blonde hair as short as Gray's.

Taylor roared with laughter at seeing Chris blushing. She'd never seen her so embarrassed. It was usually Taylor who was red faced.

"What the hell's so funny?" Chris asked, walking in and leaning against the dresser as Cail closed the door.

"God, that was hilarious. You should have seen your face." Taylor continued to laugh. "I've never seen you get so flustered before."

Chris's brow furrowed, still a bit embarrassed. As she watched Taylor, she realized she'd never seen her laugh like that before, never seen her doubled over in the throes of a full on belly laugh. She couldn't help but smile. "I didn't mean to interrupt. I just came up to talk to Taylor."

Taking the hint, Cail put on his shirt and leaned over to give Taylor another kiss on the temple. "I'll see if Gray has something you can borrow."

As he was going out the door, Taylor quietly said, "Cail? You didn't read the back." He continued out the door, closing it behind him as Taylor got up off the floor, ensuring her towel was secured around her.

"I was talking to Lane," Chris began. "Taylor, I don't think it's a good idea for you to go see Darryl and Sarah."

"It's something that I need–" Taylor was cut off when Cail came flying back into the room with the watch in his hand, picked her up, whirled her around and then planted a deep, passionate kiss on her. Taylor's surprise gave way to sensation and she sunk into the kiss. When he pulled back, he was grinning at her. "I love you, too." He put her down, gave her another quick kiss and was out the door again.

"Okay," Taylor said with a grin once she'd caught her breath. "What was I saying?"

Chris couldn't quite remember after watching one hell of a hot kiss. "What was that about?"

"Nothing." Taylor brushed it off with a wave of her hand.

"You're glowing for Christ's sake." Chris stared at Taylor, but she was smiling too.

"I feel good," Taylor said then sighed. "Better than I've felt in …" she tried to think when she'd ever felt better. "God, I don't know. It just feels really good to be home."

"I bet," Chris said with raised eyebrows.

Taylor felt the little flush in her cheeks that she was well used to by now with Chris's teasing. Before it got any worse, she tried to remember what they'd been talking about. "Sarah and Darryl," she said, as if to remind them both. "I need to see them, Chris."

"Why? Why put yourself through that?"

"It's time I stop letting them terrorize my thoughts and dreams. I need to find a way to put all this crap to rest and get on with my life."

"Why don't you wait until after the trial?"

"I don't expect you to understand why I need to do this, why I need to do it now, before the trial. But, I'm asking you, as a friend, to arrange it."

"You're looking for closure, right? You're not going to get that before the end of the trial. I don't think you're thinking this through."

"I've been thinking it through for over a month now," Taylor yelled. "I know what I'm doing. I know what I need to do."

They stood staring at each other. Chris was a little taken aback when Taylor raised her voice. It just wasn't like her. She's determined, Chris thought. And who was she to stop someone from facing their attackers head on. She had to admire Taylor for it because it was something she'd never been able to do herself. "Okay," she said softly.

"Okay?"

"I'll set it up." She suddenly realized why Taylor looked so different. Her hair wasn't up in its usual ponytail. She wondered whether to mention she looked great with her hair down, but she was worried it would set Taylor off.

A little calmer now, Taylor consciously relaxed her shoulders. "Thanks," she said as there was another knock at the door. She walked over and opened it, then stood back to let Gray in.

"I've got sweat pants, a tank top, and a sweatshirt. Is there anything else you need?" she asked, setting the clothes on the bed.

"No, that's great. Thanks, Gray." Taylor picked up the clothes and went into the bathroom to change.

"Everything okay?" Gray asked Chris.

"She seems to be doing great," Chris answered. "She's in for one hell of a nose dive in a couple of hours though," she added in reference to the special airing on NNN.

"Chris," Gray said quietly, but Taylor heard Chris's comment from the bathroom. She appeared in the doorway in panties and a tank top with the sweat pants dangling from her hand at her side.

"You don't think I should watch it."

Chris turned to see her standing there and thought, shit. "No, I don't. I don't see the point of putting yourself through that."

"Gray?" Taylor nodded toward Gray, looking for her opinion.

"I'm not a fan of you watching it, but when I put myself in your shoes, I'd want to know what the hell they're saying. I would watch it."

Taylor turned back to Chris. She knew Chris had been raped and she assumed it had been her ex-partner who pled guilty to attempted rape. She felt there was a lot more to Chris's story than that, but Chris never talked about her past. "If it was whoever raped you, talking about what he did to you, would you watch it?"

It pissed Chris off. She'd admitted to Gray and Taylor, after Taylor and Cail had a fight about Taylor scrubbing herself raw in the shower, that she too had the urge to scrub herself clean on occasion. In a roundabout way, it was her admission that she'd also been raped. Other than Dr. McIntyre, Chris had talked to no one about her past and even what she told McIntyre was limited. She wouldn't be seen as a victim, refused to be a victim. Her immediate reaction to Taylor's question was defensive. She crossed her arms and said, "This isn't about me."

Taylor tapped her head against the door frame a couple of times in frustration. "I'm just asking for your opinion. If you were me, would you watch it?"

"Your situation is completely different from mine. I didn't spend the last month having my past thrown in my face everywhere I turned to the point I couldn't sleep. I don't know how you're fucking standing there as if everything's okay. Watching what that she-devil has to say could be what sends you over the fucking edge."

"How the hell would I know what your situation is?" Taylor yelled back. "You don't reveal anything about your past. I have no idea if you have family somewhere or if you grew up in Toronto or somewhere else. I don't know anything about you. You never let anyone get past that tough cop exterior – Detective Sergeant Chris Cain who doesn't take any crap from anyone. I don't know who the hell you are, so I don't know why your opinion even means anything to me."

Chris stood there taking it, staring at the floor as anger burned through her veins. When Taylor finished, she pushed herself off the dresser and stormed out the door, slamming it behind her.

"Crap." Taylor took a deep breath and looked at Gray.

"She's very sensitive about revealing anything about her past," Gray said quietly.

"Ya think? The only person who really knows her is Lane."

"Well, at least she's got her."

"You're saying I should have been a better friend and kept my mouth shut."

"No, I'm not. She got angry and you responded to her anger. Don't start feeling guilty." Gray sat on the bed while Taylor finished getting dressed. "So, what are you going to do about this program then?"

"I don't want to watch it." Taylor sat on the bed next to Gray.

"Taylor, I know there's a lot you haven't told anyone. Aren't you worried about what they'll say?" she asked, taking Taylor's hand in hers.

Taylor let herself fall back onto the bed with a long sigh. "I don't understand how anyone could go on TV and talk about the horrors they've committed. It doesn't make any sense to me that they would publicly talk about what they've done, especially in Sarah's case, because her trial hasn't even started."

"I think it's going to be more them pointing fingers at each other as opposed to admitting what they've done."

Sitting back up again, Taylor repeated, "I don't want to watch it. I don't want them to air it." She sucked in a shuddering breath. "God, I've gone from happy to angry and now I'm fighting back tears. I'm so damn tired. I don't want to deal with this crap anymore. I'm so sick of it."

Gray put her arm around Taylor's shoulder and pulled her in. "You just have to get through this and the trial. After that, I really think it will all die down." At least she hoped and prayed that would be the end of it.

Chapter 4

After dinner, everyone gathered in the great room. Taylor felt everyone's eyes on her during dinner, but she'd eaten a good serving of Maggie's Caesar salad and spaghetti with meat sauce. She didn't think she could eat another bite until Maggie brought in Taylor's favourite dessert – apple crisp. Now she was stuffed and struggling to stay awake. She settled onto the sofa with her head resting on Cail's shoulder and closed her eyes.

"I know you've all been very worried about Taylor over the past month," McIntyre began. "So she's agreed to talk about what she went through on the book tour with everyone present."

Oh crap, Taylor thought. She kept her eyes closed and said, "There's nothing to talk about. It's done. Let's just move on to the next thing."

"You've been experiencing more flashbacks than normal," McIntyre stated.

"Not since I've been home."

"What about the nightmares?" This was going to be a lot more difficult than Lane expected with Taylor not cooperating.

Taylor lethargically lifted her head and opened her eyes to find everyone staring at her again. Chris was sitting right in front of her. They'd hardly spoken since they yelled at each other in Taylor's room. Taylor focused her eyes on the fireplace which was only making her sleepier. "I only have nightmares if I fall asleep."

"So you've been forcing yourself to stay awake?" Chris asked. She didn't wait for an answer. "Jesus, Taylor."

Kate's hand covered Chris's on the arm of the chair and she gave Chris the calm down look.

"Do you ever get nightmares, Chris?" Taylor asked.

"This isn't about me."

"Would you want to go to sleep if you had horrific nightmares every time you dozed off? I used to be able to wake myself up at the onset of a nightmare. That's why I only sleep two or three hours a night." They all knew she only slept a few hours and then spent the rest of the night drawing, but, except for Dr. McIntyre, they hadn't known why. She told them about the nightmare in Calgary and Emma getting the manager to let her into the room. "Would you want to fall asleep if you were doing that every night, Chris?" When Chris started to say something, Taylor cut her off. "I swear to God, if you say it's not about you one more time, I'll hit you."

Chris closed her mouth and stared across the coffee table at McIntyre.

"We've been trying to treat Taylor's nightmares in therapy," McIntyre explained. "I think it's time that you tried Prazosin, Taylor."

"I'm not taking drugs."

"You can't keep going without sleep."

"Maybe I'll be okay now that I'm home."

McIntyre let out a sigh of frustration and rubbed the spot between her eyes. "If you try to get some sleep tonight and don't have a nightmare, I'll let it go for now. Otherwise, I can't clear you to return to work unless you're taking Prazosin."

Taylor's anger flared, but she didn't say anything. She continued to stare at the fire, her body tense. She wanted to run up to her room or go downstairs to the gym and run on the treadmill. Cail leaned over and brushed his lips over her temple, which usually had a calming effect on her. She closed her eyes again and tried to concentrate on Cail, but she was getting more and more agitated at the thought of not being able to go back to work unless she was taking a drug that she didn't want. "I guess I won't be going back to work then," she spat out.

"Tay, give it a day or two and see how you sleep," Cail said softly, still trying to comfort her.

"You're angry," McIntyre stated the obvious.

"You know how I feel about taking that stuff. Making it a condition of me going back to work makes me angry."

"Taylor, you can't function properly if you don't get regular sleep. I can't justify putting you behind the wheel of a vehicle when you haven't slept for a month."

"Fine, I won't go back to work."

Chris turned to glare at her. She'd been waiting six months for

Taylor to come to work for her. After twelve weeks at the Academy, six weeks with a training officer and her leave of absence, Taylor was finally going to be assigned to her. That Taylor would give up on going back to work so easily made her angry.

"It's not about you," Taylor snapped at her.

Kate gripped onto Chris's wrist and gave it a little tug. Chris turned her head to look across the table again and said nothing.

"You're angry with Chris." Again, McIntyre stated the obvious.

"Chris is angry with me."

McIntyre sighed in frustration again. "Taylor, Cail is right. Let's just give it a day or two and see how you're sleeping."

"Fine, are we done?"

"We're all sitting here because we're worried sick about you, Taylor," Gray offered in a calm voice.

"I can't do anything about what happened on the tour. I don't know what you expect me to do. It's done. It's over. If anything, I'm stronger physically and emotionally than I was before the tour. They can spout their questions all day long and it doesn't get to me like it used to. I'm sick of it, but it doesn't affect me. I don't let it get to me. So let's just move on to the next thing."

"The next thing is the NNN special which starts in about five minutes," McIntyre said.

"Shall I make the popcorn?" Taylor asked.

"Damn it, Taylor Grace." Gray leaned forward to look past Cail at Taylor.

"It's a coping mechanism, Gray," Chris said. "Don't let her upset you."

Taylor felt like punching Chris, but she was also feeling guilty. "I'm sorry, Gray. I didn't mean to upset you. I just feel like everyone's pissed at me for stuff I can't control. I don't know what you want me to do."

"We're not pissed at you, we're concerned."

"I don't want you to be." She wanted to say she was fine, but she knew that would just upset Gray even more.

"All anyone is asking you to do is talk about what you went through on the book tour," McIntyre stated. "That's all we expect. Getting it out can go a long way to getting over it."

"I'm over it."

"No, you're not," Chris said under her breath.

"What the hell's wrong with you?" Taylor yelled at Chris as she got up, stormed out of the room and through the laundry room into the washroom, slamming the door behind her.

Everyone sat in silence. After a few minutes, Callaghan said, "That went well."

"Maybe she wasn't quite ready for a group session," McIntyre suggested, still frustrated. "She feels like we're all ganging up on her."

"Why are you getting on her case, Chris?" Cail asked. "Why are you pushing her buttons?"

"Gray, is there somewhere I could speak to Chris privately for a few minutes?" McIntyre asked, rubbing the spot between her eyes again.

"You can use my office. Chris knows where it is."

"Great," Chris said under her breath again as she stood and headed towards Gray's office opposite the laundry room. It was like being called into the principal's office for Christ's sake.

McIntyre followed Chris in and closed the door, admiring the impressive collection of books lining the walls. Gray's antique desk sat in front of the window, facing two wing backed chairs separated by a table and tiffany lamp.

"What are you doing?" McIntyre asked gently as Chris dropped herself into one of the chairs.

"I'm not doing anything. She's the one who keeps putting me in her situation."

McIntyre took the seat next to Chris. "And your situation is so different from hers?"

"I wasn't hunted down on the streets."

"No, you were hunted down in your own home." She watched Chris roll her eyes. "You consider her to be your best friend and she counts you as hers."

"Gray's her best friend."

"She sees Gray as more of a sister, even motherly at times. She considers you to be her best friend. Neither one of you has allowed yourself the luxury of a best friend before."

Chris was surprised Taylor thought of her as her best friend. It touched her in a way she wasn't prepared to admit. "She's better at it than I am."

"Are you worried she'll abandon you, so you're trying to sabotage the relationship before that happens?"

"It's not a relationship, it's a friendship." Her abandonment issues were what caused her to sabotage all of her relationships or end them when they started to get too serious. Better to leave before you were left.

"Which you've never had before."

"So you think I'll sabotage our friendship? I want to work with her for Christ's sake. I'm not looking to ruin our friendship." Chris leaned forward and rubbed her hands over her face. "I'm scared. I'm scared shitless she won't make it through the stress of this trial after what she's just been through."

"Have you told her that?"

Chris sighed. "No." She raked her fingers through her hair then looked over at McIntyre who was just sitting there watching her. "You think I should tell her. Shit."

"It wouldn't hurt you to be more open with her. She's someone you could talk to and trust."

"I know. She's proven I can trust her over and over again. I don't want to talk about some shit to anyone."

"You don't want to talk about anything to anyone."

Chris huffed. "I see what I put her through and I don't know how the hell she stands it. I couldn't –" Chris covered her eyes with the heels of her hands when she felt the burn of tears. "Shit."

"You feel guilty for making her do what you can't."

"I feel like a damn hypocrite."

"Everyone is different, Chris. Everyone heals at different rates, deals with trauma in different ways. The Johnson case has taken as much of a toll on you as it has on Taylor. It's made you compare how you've dealt with your trauma to how Taylor is dealing with hers. It's not something you can compare. She's asking you to put yourself in her shoes when she asks for your opinion or advice and it's not somewhere you're willing to go. What you need to consider is that she doesn't understand how painful putting yourself in her shoes is for you. She's only asking for your opinion because she respects it."

"I gave her my opinion." Chris already talked to McIntyre about the yelling match in Taylor's room.

"You gave her what you think she should do, not what you would do in her position."

"Okay, so I'll apologize to her or whatever."

"I know how painful that will be for you." McIntyre smiled.

"Ha, ha."

"Why don't I go and get her." McIntyre walked to the door then turned back with her hand on the door knob. "She's a lot stronger than you think, Chris."

"Meaning she's stronger than me."

"No, meaning she'll make it through the trial come hell or high water. She won't let Sarah take her down." McIntyre studied Chris for a minute. "You're just as strong, working in Sex Crimes for the past eight or nine years, facing your demons every day."

Chris watched McIntyre walk out and got up to pace. "Facing everyone else's demons but my own is more like it," she said to herself.

When the door opened again she turned and saw Taylor lean against the door frame. "Isn't Lane coming back?"

Taylor leaned back and craned her neck to look out towards the great room. "Guess not."

"Could you close the door then?"

Taylor stepped into the office, closed the door then leaned back on it. "I didn't mean to be such a bitch," Taylor began. "I guess I'm more stressed out than I thought … or tired and grumpy, I don't know."

Chris looked up at Taylor then continued pacing. "Lane asked you to come in here so I could apologize. Don't steal my thunder."

"Oh," Taylor said and watched Chris pace.

"Your hair's down."

At that Taylor started gathering her hair up and tied it back in its usual ponytail with the band she'd stuck in her pocket.

"Shit, I just screwed that up too, didn't I? You were probably on some kind of record for having your hair down." She paced back and forth a few more times. "I'm scared, Taylor. I'm scared half to death you don't have enough left in you to get through this trial." There, she'd said it. Now she just had to swallow this damn lump in her throat. There was no way in hell she was going to cry.

"I lived through the reality, I'm sure I'll live through the trial." She didn't know what else to say as she watched Chris pace. It was starting to make her sleepy so she leaned her head back and stared at the ceiling.

"Look, I've never done this whole friendship deal before. I'm worried sick and I don't know how to deal with that."

Taylor dropped her head down again to look at Chris. She knew how she felt, not knowing how to deal with caring about people again after so long on her own. "Why haven't you done the friendship deal?" When Chris didn't answer, Taylor said, "I'm sorry. I wouldn't want to pry into your past."

"Damn it, Taylor, I'm trying here. I'm trying."

"Trying to what?"

Chris stopped pacing and looked Taylor in the eye. "Trying to explain why I've been such an idiot, trying to apologize for it."

"Okay, we're both sorry. Are we good now?"

"Christ, you're frustrating me."

"Ditto." Taylor smiled. "Are we in the whole friendship deal again?"

"I'm about to kick your ass."

"I'll take that as a yes." She walked to Chris and circled her arms around her. "I'm sorry."

"Me too," Chris said with a sigh, hugging her back. "There's something else I want to say."

"Yeah?" Taylor asked as she took a step back.

Chris shoved her hands in her pockets and rocked back and forth on her feet. "I don't talk about my past."

"I got that."

"Ha." She felt herself shaking and hoped Taylor didn't notice. "You said you didn't know me."

"I was angry, I'm sorry."

Shaking her head, Chris said, "No, you were right. Let me get this out." She inhaled deeply and blew it out slowly as she closed her eyes. "I was born in Toronto. My family … my parents and my two older brothers … disowned me when I was fourteen."

"What? Why? Why would anyone disown their only daughter?" Taylor was shocked.

"They disowned me when I came out. They did me a favour, really. I was better off staying in youth hostels until I graduated from high school and went to the Academy."

"I'm sorry, Chris."

"No, don't. Would you want my pity?"

"No. I wish I had met you when we were both out there on our own." Chris was only two years older than Taylor, so she would have been in the youth hostels when Taylor was twelve. They had so much more in common than Taylor could have known. It helped, she thought, to know a little bit about Chris's past. She felt she understood Chris just a little better now. "Thanks, for telling me that."

"Yeah, well, besides Lane you're the only one I've ever told."

Taylor stepped back into Chris and hugged her again. "You can trust me not to repeat it, Chris."

"If I didn't know that, I wouldn't have told you. God, how much have you been working out?"

Taylor stepped back again. "I needed something to do to keep me awake at night."

"Shit, Taylor. How long do you think you can go before your body shuts down? You need sleep."

"Lane thinks so. She's making me go in for a physical."

"Oh, shit. That sucks."

"Why? What's she going to do to me?"

Oh God, Chris thought. She didn't want to be the one to break it to her. "She'll, you know, poke and prod. Then send you for a blood and urine sample at the lab."

"Poke and prod where?"

Waving a hand around with a disgusted look on her face, Chris answered, "Everywhere." When Taylor's face lost its colour, she started to laugh.

"Not funny," Taylor said with a furrowed brow.

"Neither was when I opened your bedroom door."

Taylor started laughing. "No, that was hilarious. You should have seen your face."

They walked back out to the great room and Callaghan had the NNN special cued up on the TV ready to play. Taylor's gut twisted. She sat on the sofa between Cail and Gray. "Would anyone like a drink before we start?" Callaghan asked.

"Tequila would be good," Taylor answered.

"You've never had hard liquor before," Cail said.

"Seems like a good time to start," she mumbled. "Before you start it, Callaghan …" Taylor took a deep breath in as everyone in the room turned their eyes to her. "I don't know what you want me to say about the book tour. It's been six months since the media began hounding me. I can't go anywhere without them shoving their microphones and cameras in my face and asking the same stupid questions over and over. I can't get away from it."

"We can keep you in seclusion, under police protection, until the trial is over," McIntyre suggested. "Your only exposure would be coming and going from the courthouse. The reporters that are present in the court room are obliged to behave in an appropriate manner. They can't shout out their questions inside the courtroom."

"They're still going to keep hounding you until you answer some of their questions," Chris put in. "Even if you just give them a few minutes after the trial, it might be enough to get them off your back. I know it's been hard for you having your past pushed in your face for the last six months, Taylor, but if you can hold on until after the trial, I think it will die down."

"God, I hope so."

Chapter 5

The NNN special began with a memorial to Taylor and Cail. Photos and videos of Taylor and Cail played over the screen throughout the commentary. The memorial ended with the limo being shot up then exploding before fading into a live shot of Cheryl Starr.

"Such a tragic loss, two of the city's fine new police officers with so much life and potential ahead of them. Caillen Worthington was a star player in Junior Hockey and many felt he would have made it to the NHL, but he put those opportunities aside and followed his dream to go to Law School, attending McGill University in Montreal." An image of Cail in his hockey gear floated behind Starr.

"Taylor was a gifted artist, which most people didn't know. She kept her drawings personal and for good reason. A source told us Taylor often draws her darkest memories, memories that would horrify anyone who saw them. She draws her happier memories as well, but even those she keeps ... kept ... close to the vest." Starr's voice cracked when she realized she used the present tense. The image of Starr was replaced with a slide show of Taylor's drawings. The first was one she'd done of Cail when he'd been out in the backyard at Gray's shirtless, tossing a football with Callaghan. It was followed by one of Gray and Callaghan, then one of Chris and Kate and the last one pissed her off the most. They were displaying one of her darker drawings.

"Oh. My. God. Where'd they get that? How would they get those drawings? They were all in Cail's apartment." And the only people who knew about her drawing were in this room, Taylor thought.

Kate was in a panic. "My parents can't see that drawing."

"You haven't told them yet," Cail realized.

Kate had yet to come out to her parents or anyone else for that matter. She'd told Cail only because he'd come right out and asked her. After spending quite a bit of time with Taylor, Cail, Gray and Callaghan, Kate was relaxed about her relationship with Chris with them, but no one else knew she was gay. Her eyes quickly flashed to Lane, a long-time family friend of the Worthington's, and Kate wondered if Lane would tell her mother now that she just blabbed it. "No and now everyone I know is going to find out from that drawing."

"It's not like you're having sex or anything," Cail said. "It just looks like two friends hanging out."

It wasn't that simple, Kate thought. Everyone knew Chris was gay. Not only did she not hide it, she was well known for speaking to high school kids about her experiences with bullying and being ostracized because of her homosexuality. She often counseled teens on how to deal with coming out and embracing their homosexuality. Anyone seeing that drawing of the two of them would naturally assume they wer partners.

"Someone's going to have to check your apartment to see what's missing," Callaghan interrupted.

"Yeah, we will," Taylor said, fuming at the invasion of her personal space.

"I meant a forensics team."

"Oh, hell no. I'm not having a bunch of strangers going through my drawings."

Their focus was drawn back to the TV as Cheryl Starr began talking about Taylor. As media photos of her flashed in the background, Cheryl stated, "To see her walking down the street, you'd never know the haunting background that terrorized her through much of her life. Tall, strikingly beautiful, confident, strong, graceful – Taylor Sinclair doesn't … didn't … exude the air of a victim. But a victim she was – a victim of the most horrific crimes imaginable, perpetrated by a very sick, evil woman out for revenge. Revenge wrongly targeted against an innocent.

"Tonight you'll hear shocking accounts from Sarah Johnson, the woman who allegedly orchestrated the repeated, often gruesome attacks on Taylor Sinclair beginning when she was just ten years old and continuing into her teens. And you'll hear from Darryl Johnson, who often did Sarah's bidding in her evil, twisted ventures right up to a recent attempt to take Sinclair's life."

Starr pivoted as the camera angle changed. "We begin with an interview with Darryl Johnson. DNA evidence confirmed Darryl Johnson is Taylor's blood uncle. Taylor was his brother Gregory's illegitimate daughter and Gregory Johnson was married to Sarah Johnson before he died in a tragic accident along with Taylor's mother. Darryl Johnson has pled guilty on all charges against him including attempted murder for his attack on Taylor this past August. He's been sentenced to life in prison and now resides at the Palmerton Correctional Facility in Palmerton, Ontario."

The screen faded to a shot of Darryl Johnson sitting in what appeared to be an interview room wearing the prison jeans and blue shirt of Palmerton Correctional. His light brown hair appeared clean and brushed and he was clean shaven, unlike most of the times Taylor had been in his company. He was average in height and thin as a rail.

Cheryl Starr sat next to him looking completely out of place in her red power suit, full makeup and her honey blonde hair styled to perfection. "Darryl, you've told the police Sarah Johnson, your sister-in-law, forced you to participate in the abuse against Taylor Sinclair. Can you explain that for us?"

Darryl moved his hands when he began to speak and the sound of his handcuffs rattling on the table drowned him out. He cleared his throat and started again. "I was an addict back then. You name the drug, I'd take it. Heroin was my drug of choice, but I'd take anything I could get my hands on. One night, I was jonesing for a hit. I was sick, really needed a hit. Sarah came to me and said we needed to talk, so we took a drive in her car. She knew I was hurting and she told me she could help me out with money for drugs if I helped her. She took out this picture of a little girl with dark hair and wild green eyes. Her eyes were just like my brother's ... just like Greg's. Sarah told me she was Greg's daughter and that she was just like her crack whore mother who killed Greg.

"Greg was everything to me. I blamed that woman for killing him and I blamed that little girl with Greg's eyes. I think at the time I saw her as the mother, as the same person as her mother."

"Millions of people struggle with drug addiction, but they don't all go around sexually assaulting little girls because of it."

"It was my situation. I needed heroin. You don't understand unless you're in that state that you'd do anything to get your next hit."

"Tell us about the first time Sarah took you out to abduct Taylor."

Darryl went on to describe some of the gruesome details of Sarah's attacks on Taylor, downplaying his role in the attacks. Gray kept glancing at Taylor to see how she was handling the interview. Her face was tucked between Cail's shoulder and the back of the sofa, both of her hands gripping Cail's. Her ponytail quivered down her back.

"That went on for a few of years," Darryl explained. "Then everything changed."

"Oh, Jesus," Taylor muffled into Cail's shoulder. She knew what he was about to say and she thanked God she told Cail the little bit she had. Cail's hand slid up Taylor's arm to her neck with her hand still fiercely gripping his. He turned into her so he could wrap her in his arms. Taylor's cheek rested on his shoulder, but she kept her head turned towards the back of the sofa.

"We grabbed her off the street this one day and took her into an abandoned building, into an empty apartment. Sarah was angry ... furious. You could tell Taylor was pregnant. She was all skin and bones, you know, except for this round belly, like she swallowed a soccer ball or something."

Fighting back tears and anger, Gray glanced over at Taylor again. Her body was stiff and the trembling was worse. She burrowed herself into Cail and hung on for dear life. Gray desperately wanted to turn the TV off and spare her the misery, but she promised herself she would leave that call up to Taylor.

"Sarah started throwing things around the room, yelling and swearing. She was raging. She said Taylor was nothing but a crack whore like her mother. She kept calling her a slut, over and over again." Darryl's cuffs rattled again as he leaned down and rubbed his eyes with his fingers. "She beat Taylor. I mean really laid a beating on her. We left her there for dead."

Gray reached a hand over and placed it on Taylor's back. Taylor flinched at her touch and let out a whimper, but Gray didn't let it stop her from rubbing her back.

"What happened?" Starr asked Darryl. "Can you tell us what Sarah did to Taylor?"

"No," he responded and Taylor let out a sigh of relief. "I couldn't watch. I didn't want to see. You have to ask Sarah."

"Oh, God," Taylor groaned. Her stomach felt like someone was wringing it out like a dish cloth.

"There are no medical records we've been able to find indicating Taylor was pregnant. How do you explain that?"

"I don't know. We left her there for dead. Sarah put feelers out on the street in case she showed up at school or at any of the shelters. There was nothing for about four or five months then Sarah came to me again. But it was different after that. Something changed with Sarah."

"What changed, Darryl?"

"She comes to see me again, asking for my help. But, Taylor was growing, getting stronger and faster. God, she could run like the wind. It wasn't as easy to find her or to take her, but when we did get her, it was different. Sarah would make me tie Taylor up and then she'd give me some cash and tell me to disappear."

"Why don't you pause it here, Patrick, and give Taylor a break?" McIntyre asked, watching Taylor trembling in Cail's arms.

"No," Taylor muttered, her voice cracking. "Just get the damn thing over with."

"What was Sarah doing to her during those times?" Starr asked.

"I don't know. She never told me."

When they switched to Sarah Johnson, she was in a similar interview room. Her hands were cuffed and shackled around her waist. At forty-five, she was a good fifty pounds overweight with mousy blonde hair and a pasty complexion, her brown eyes dull and just a bit too close together.

"She looks like she's not doing so well," Chris said. "She's lost weight and she looks older."

Taylor peered up from Cail's shoulder and looked at the screen. She turned back into him and listened as Starr took her through many of the same questions she'd put to Darryl. Sarah described the abuse against Taylor in excruciating detail, always pointing the blame directly at Darryl. She insisted she had no part in it, but knew all of the details from what Taylor and Darryl told her.

When Cheryl began questioning her about Taylor's pregnancy, she became very agitated. It was obvious she hadn't expected Starr to ask about it. "She was a ... bleep ... crack whore slut, just like her mother. Who the hell gets pregnant at thirteen? No good ... bleep ... sluts. God knows who the ... bleep ... father was."

"You don't think the father may have been Darryl, Taylor's uncle?"

"How the ... bleep ... should I know? That kid probably spread her legs for anyone to get her hands on some drugs, just like her mother did."

"Ms. Johnson, you were present with Taylor in the emergency room on numerous occasions when her blood was drawn and tested for substance abuse. As her case worker, you would have had access to the results of those tests. Did you ever know Taylor to test positive for any illegal substances?"

"Well, no, but that doesn't mean she wasn't a crack whore like her mother."

"Did you know her mother?"

"No, why the hell would I know her?"

"You seem to know enough about her."

"I know what Darryl and Taylor told me."

"There are no medical records indicating Taylor had a baby or was treated after being beaten while pregnant. Do you know where she may have been treated or where she had the baby?"

"How the hell should I know?"

"You said Taylor and Darryl told you everything."

"Maybe he was scared she'd die in that hole he took her to. Maybe he wanted to make sure he wasn't associated with her, so he took her away from the city."

"Why would he be scared he'd be associated with her?"

"I don't know. Maybe he was worried they'd find her dead in that apartment and there would be evidence there."

"Did he tell you what happened to the baby? Did Taylor tell you?"

"I don't know what the hell happened to it. What would she have done with a baby on the streets? She was still a kid herself." Sarah looked around the room, thinking, eyes darting all over the place. "Maybe Darryl gave her an abortion."

Taylor was seized by a gruesome flashback that put her right back on the dirty floor of that apartment. She felt the searing pains as Sarah hit her repeatedly with an iron frying pan she found in the kitchen. Darryl stood by, getting a vicious kick in whenever Sarah backed off. Taylor curled into a ball, desperately trying to protect her unborn child from the assault. She threw up what little food was in her stomach before the edges of her vision greyed and she passed out.

Another flashback followed quickly. She felt the pain spear through her abdomen as if her womb was contracting right at that moment. Then she saw something she hadn't remembered until she was gripped by that agonizing flashback. She was holding her tiny child in her arms, staring down at a beautiful little face. He looked just like a doll as he lay lifeless in her arms.

Taylor tried to stand and nearly fell over with dizziness. Cail stood and held her. "Sit back down, Tay."

She shook her head, making it spin. "I'm going to be sick," she whispered.

Cail picked her up and ran her through to the small washroom off the laundry room. "Do you need anything?" he asked after depositing her in front of the toilet.

"Water," she croaked. As soon as he was out the door she crawled to it, locked it and crawled back to the toilet before heaving violently. Her little boy. Darryl's little boy. God, that's just sick. That would make the baby her cousin too, wouldn't it? Her son was also her cousin. Oh, Christ. She heaved again.

Chapter 6

"Tay? Open the door."

With her head hanging over the toilet, she groaned. "I need a few minutes." She knew Cail would be desperate to get through the door and make sure she was okay, but she just wasn't ready to be around anyone.

"Taylor?" McIntyre's voice called gently through the door.

Crap, Taylor thought. "I'm fine. I just need a few minutes."

"Give her some time," McIntyre said to Cail. She took his arm and led him back to the great room.

"We shouldn't leave her in there by herself," Cail looked back over his shoulder.

"She's not going to do anything stupid," McIntyre soothed. "She wants some time alone, let's give it to her." Gesturing towards the sofa, she said, "Sit down."

Once Cail was seated, McIntyre took her seat again and addressed the group, "Obviously, this is going to be difficult for Taylor to deal with, but I think it's also difficult for everyone in this room."

"That shit can't be true," Chris said, but she knew it was. She'd seen where both Darryl and Sarah were lying and she'd seen where they were telling the truth. Chris's arms were crossed, her hands buried under her arms so no one could see them shaking.

"Five months." Gray's voice was barely audible as she leaned into Callaghan, his arms tight around her. "This afternoon when I said I was five months, she had a flashback. She must have been five months."

"Babe, you've had way to much stress today," Callaghan brushed his lips over Gray's temple. She closed her eyes and concentrated on his lips, calming her.

"Did they kill her baby, or does she have a kid out there somewhere?" Chris sat forward, raking her hands through her hair as Kate's arm came around her.

"We should really check on her," Cail said, glancing over his shoulder again.

"Give her a few more minutes," McIntyre said. "She'll want to pull herself together."

"She won't want to talk about it," Cail informed them. "This is too hard for her to talk about."

"She talked to you about it," McIntyre stated, but it was more of a question.

"Not the details. It was hard enough for her just telling me she wouldn't have kids." Turning to Chris, he pleaded, "Don't ask her to talk about it. Don't even ask."

"She can't have kids?" Chris turned to look at Cail and watched Taylor walk into the great room and start up the stairs.

Taylor stopped, her head hung low as everyone's eyes turned to her. "I'm okay. I just ... need some time ... alone." She continued up the stairs and disappeared into her room.

Cail leaned forward, rubbing his hands over his face and exhaling a deep breath. He couldn't do it. He couldn't sit there while she was up there alone. He stood and ran up the stairs. When he got to the bathroom door in Taylor's room he found it locked. He used a coin from his pocket to unlock the door and found Taylor standing at the sink, brushing her teeth, her eyes red and puffy. She removed the toothbrush from her mouth, glaring at him.

"That door was locked."

"I just need to make sure you're okay."

"I'm fine. I just need to take a shower. I need some time alone."

"You just had a shower, Bean."

Here we go, she thought. She prepared herself for the fight over her scrubbing herself clean. "I need to do it. I need to get it off."

"Get what off, Tay? Explain it to me."

Her voice was barely a whisper, tears stinging her eyes again. "The filth ... his ... hers. I need to feel clean again." She couldn't look at him. She turned back to the sink, the heels of her hands bearing her weight on the counter.

"Okay," he said gently and her head jerked around to him. "I'll be right out here if you need me."

Taylor watched him close the door. Where was the lecture about hurting herself? Where was the lecture from everyone about the excessive working out, about not sleeping? Were they all walking on eggshells around her because of the news coverage they'd seen during the tour?

Cail sat on the bed, listening to the shower turn on and let his tears fall. Gray came in behind him with more clean clothes and sat next to him. "Oh God. Sorry," he said, wiping his tears.

"Don't be. It's better to let them out," she soothed, running her hand up and down his back.

"I can't handle seeing her hurt like this."

"I know."

Chris and Kate were the next ones through the door, followed by McIntyre and Callaghan. They sat quietly, waiting. It was nearly forty minutes later when the bathroom door opened and Taylor stood in the doorway wearing a towel, her skin red and raw. "What's everyone doing in here?" she frowned.

"We just want to make sure you're alright," Gray answered as she tried to study the rawness of Taylor's skin without being obvious.

Taylor pushed back the tears that threatened again and nodded.

"I brought you some clean clothes. Just sleep pants and a tank top." She handed a tube to Taylor, adding, "And the cream for your skin."

"Thanks," Taylor's voice broke. "I'll do my laundry in the morning."

Gray stepped towards Taylor to give her a hug and sighed a breath of relief when Taylor embraced her. "You okay?" she whispered.

"Yeah." She squeezed her eyes shut against the tears. "I'm okay."

Stepping back, Gray cupped Taylor's face in her hands, studying her. "Okay." She smiled then kissed Taylor's cheek. "We'll give you some privacy."

As soon as Gray stepped away, Chris was there, embracing Taylor. "We're here if you need anything, kiddo."

"I know. I appreciate it."

She was followed by Kate, McIntyre and Callaghan, all whispering words of support as they hugged her. It helped, more than she could have imagined. She felt a little lighter as they walked out the door and Callaghan closed it behind him. Taylor turned to Cail. "I'm sorry."

"What have you got to be sorry for?" he asked, taking the tube of cream from her. She watched as he unscrewed the lid and started massaging the cream into her skin, starting with her arms.

"I shouldn't have shut you out."

"You needed the time," he said, working his way up her arms. "I understand that. I'm trying to understand everything, Tay." Seeing her raw skin was enough to make him ill. He hated seeing her like this, but he knew reacting to it in anger only made matters worse. He understood it a bit better now and he knew from past experience she needed his support, not his anger or condemnation. He massaged her shoulders until he felt her begin to relax before releasing her towel and letting it fall to the floor. Working his way down her back, he smiled when Taylor's head fell back with a moan. "I love all of this muscle you put on. I love all of the contours, the peaks and valleys."

"It doesn't make me look too much like a boy?"

With a laugh, Cail replied, "You could never look like a boy. You're too damn sexy for that."

"I like the way it makes me feel."

"How does it make you feel?" Cail asked as he worked his way up her long, lithe legs then up her rippled abs to her chest.

"Strong, like I can protect myself if I need to. I feel safer, almost like I feel when I'm wrapped in your arms." The cream cooled the burning of her skin, but his hands were sending out shock waves through every nerve in her body. By the time he finished applying the soothing cream, her insides were on fire.

Taylor covered his hands with hers. "Make love to me," she whispered.

His eyes met hers and he saw the tears pooling against her glowing green eyes. "Are you sure?" He didn't want to send her over the edge. She seemed so fragile right now and her skin was so raw. "Doesn't it sting?"

The burning sensation only confirmed she was clean again and she welcomed it. It was Cail's hesitance that scared her. She was sure that hearing the things Darryl and Sarah described had been enough to turn him off her even though he already knew most of it. The detail Sarah had gone into was enough to make her sick, never mind anyone else. "Do you still want me?" She asked the question, but wasn't sure she could handle his answer.

"Tay." Cail's hands slid up to cup her face. He tilted her head up and waited until her eyes met his. "I'll never stop wanting you."

Taylor touched her lips to his and whispered, "Show me." She kissed him gently, her lips barely brushing his. "Make me forget, so there's only you and me."

This was something Cail could give her to help her forget the ugliness of her past and focus on their love. He could have spent days exploring all of the nuances of her newly formed muscles, relearning every inch of her. They took their time, driving each other dreamily towards that peak with slow and delicate touching, tasting ... loving.

And after, she fell asleep wrapped in the safety of Cail's strong arms. With her head resting on Cail's shoulder, listening to the rhythm of his breathing and the beating of his heart, she fell asleep.

* * *

McIntyre was the first to come down the stairs in the morning. On the sofa, Taylor closed the sketch pad she'd been drawing in and said over her shoulder, "I made coffee."

"Great, thank you." She went straight into the kitchen to pour herself a cup then came out to the great room and sat in the chair next to Taylor, eyeing her sketch pad on the coffee table. "Did you get any sleep?"

"About four hours," Taylor answered.

"Nightmares?"

"I woke up at the start of it."

"Are you telling me that so I don't put you on Prazosin?" McIntyre asked with a smile.

"I wouldn't lie to you. I'd tell you the truth if I'd had a nightmare and I wouldn't go on Prazosin."

"Four hours isn't enough."

"It's more than I usually get."

McIntyre sighed, took a sip of her coffee and set it on the table. "Do you want to talk about the flashback you had before you were sick last night?"

Taylor looked down at her hands as she flicked at her thumb nail. "Sometimes they're more real than my memories."

"It was a bad one. You've never mentioned being violently ill after one of your flashbacks."

She was still flicking at her nail when McIntyre's hand covered hers and Taylor's chest rose, filled with emotion. Damn it, she didn't want to cry again. She waited a few moments before continuing so she could push the emotions back down. "You know what the flashback was. You know the whole story, don't you?"

"Yes," McIntyre answered softly.

Gray found herself in an awkward position at the top of the stairs. She didn't want to interrupt, but she felt like she was intruding as she heard Taylor talking to Lane. She was about to back up into her room when Taylor said, "It's alright, Gray. You can come down."

Taylor hadn't even turned around, so she must have sensed her there, Gray thought. "If you need some privacy –"

"No, it's alright," Taylor repeated. She waited until Gray got a cup of coffee and sat next to her on the sofa. With her head still down, she continued, "I don't remember a lot of what happened after they beat me." She felt Gray's tension beside her and thought she was an idiot to lay this on Gray right now. Taylor closed her eyes. "I'm sorry. You don't need to hear this." She felt Gray's hand on her cheek and covered it with her own as she welled up again.

"Let it out, hon. You'll feel better." Gray choked back her own emotions.

A few tears escaped before Taylor was able to gain control again. She lowered Gray's hand to the sofa, but kept a firm grip on it. "I didn't remember holding the baby … holding my son."

When Gray felt her own baby moving, she placed Taylor's hand on her belly. She wasn't sure if it was a good idea or a really bad one. Taylor felt the movement and cried out. The flood gates opened and her tears ran unrestrained as she covered her mouth with her free hand. Gray wasn't sure what to do, but Taylor kept her hand there so she didn't move it.

When she could talk again, Taylor said, "You've been worried about her. You and Callaghan have been worried because of all the stress I've caused you."

"That's not your fault, Taylor."

Taylor shook her head, but continued, "She's okay. She's strong and healthy. You know that. You can feel her, sense her, just as she's sensing you."

"I knew she was good when she was doing her little dance on my bladder at two in the morning." Gray gave Taylor a slow smile.

Taylor and McIntyre let out a little laugh then McIntyre said, "It's the greatest feeling in the world, isn't it?"

"Yeah, it is," Gray answered before her smile slowly vanished. "You know what it feels like, don't you, Taylor?"

Taylor felt that damn lump in her throat again. She squeezed her eyes tight and nodded.

"When did you know?"

She knew Gray was asking her when she realized she was pregnant. Taylor swiped her arm across her wet face. "In some ways I knew right away. I'd never even had a period, but I was scared all of a sudden, worrying about what I'd do with a baby on the streets. I was only thirteen. I just turned thirteen."

Like it wasn't enough the poor kid was all alone, on the streets, being terrorized by a psycho bitch, Gray thought. "What happened to the baby, Taylor?"

Taylor spared a quick glance at McIntyre before answering, "I'm not sure. I can't remember. I'm just getting flashes."

"I want to see them suffer for what they did to you, Taylor."

"Do you still want to talk to them?" McIntyre asked Taylor.

"Yes."

"Talk to who?" Gray asked. "Sarah and Darryl?" She was shocked.

"It's something that I need to do," Taylor explained. "Gotta change my laundry over," she said when she heard the dryer buzz. She got up and left the room thinking 'saved by the bell'.

"Taylor's very lucky to have you," McIntyre said.

"We're lucky to have each other." Gray said automatically, her mind still stuck on Taylor talking to those monsters.

"Chris feels like she's become a part of your growing family also."

Gray smiled and took a sip of her decaffeinated coffee. "She has. She doesn't say much about her past, but I get the sense that she's been alone for a long time, too."

"Mmm. You know I can't say anything. She's one of my patients."

"She's more to you than just a patient."

"Yes, she is."

"You'll have noticed that her relationship with Kate is on a different level, let's say, than her past relationships." When McIntyre kept tight lipped, Gray added, "She told me about her habit of ending her relationships when they get too serious."

"And you don't think she's going to do that with Kate?"

"I hope not. I think Kate's very special to Chris. To be honest, I don't think Kate will let her sabotage the relationship."

"I hope you're right," McIntyre said, lifting her cup to Gray before taking a sip.

"The reporters are going to drive Taylor mad asking what happened to her baby." Gray felt sick just thinking about it. "Do you think she can't remember or do you think she just can't talk about it?"

McIntyre let out a sigh. "Taylor's my patient, too. Let me just say this, it's not uncommon to repress traumatic memories."

"But she hasn't repressed the rest of her traumatic memories."

"We don't know what she's repressed," McIntyre answered, but Gray got the sense McIntyre knew a lot more than she could say.

* * *

When Taylor came out of the laundry room, Gray was sitting on her own with a book. "Where's Lane?"

"She's gone up for a shower."

"Oh." Taylor had been waiting for the opportunity to catch Gray alone. "Wait there for a minute," she told Gray and ran up the stairs to her room. She tiptoed past Cail, still in a dead sleep, and picked up her fifth suitcase which remained unopened. She tiptoed out of the room again and carried the case down to the great room, setting it on the table in front of Gray. "I got a little carried away," she said, unzipping the case and flipping the top open to reveal the ton of baby clothes she'd picked up on her travels.

"Oh my God, did you ever." Gray had wanted to talk to Taylor about going to see Darryl and Sarah, but this just didn't seem like the time. She tried to put it out of her mind for now.

"Look at this." Taylor pulled out a tiny sleeper with 'My Aunt Rocks!' printed on the front and they both giggled. "Oh," Taylor said as she rooted through the case. "We were driving through downtown L.A. and I saw this in a store window. I yelled for the driver to stop and I think the car was still moving when I jumped out. I had to get it." She pulled out a gorgeous white sundress with tiny flowers embroidered into the material. It was a perfect match to the sundress in Taylor's painting.

"Oh, Taylor." Gray's bright blue eyes pooled.

"No crying. Look at these." She pulled out miniature Nike running shoes, getting Gray laughing again. "Wait, they go with these." She picked up a tiny pair of workout shorts and a cropped tank and Gray doubled over laughing. Well, doubled as far as her baby bump allowed her. The two of them sat there for nearly an hour going through all of the clothes, bibs, soothers, plush toys, rattles, and more. There was even a set of silver baby spoons and a Beatrix Potter baby mug, plate and bowl.

"I could have bought so much more, but I had to limit myself to stuff that fit in a suitcase."

"Taylor, this is the best gift ever. I had so much fun going through all of it." She leaned over and planted a big kiss on Taylor's cheek.

"Me, too. I think I needed that. Can I go shopping with you when you go to get your baby furniture and stuff? It's so much fun looking at all of the tiny little things."

"I'd like that," Gray smiled.

"I've got something else for you, too." Taylor pulled a box out of the pocket inside the bottom of the suitcase and handed it to Gray.

"You didn't have to do this," Gray said.

"I wanted to."

Gray opened the box to find two matching bracelets of sterling silver beads and spacers with four sparkling sapphires on each. The larger bracelet had square sterling beads spelling out 'GRAY' and the little one spelled 'GRACIE'. "Oh, they're gorgeous."

"I think of her as Gracie, but when you name her, we can order the beads to spell out her name. You can also add different charms and things to them and Gracie's has an extension chain for when she grows." Taylor was looking at the bracelets as she talked. She glanced up at Gray and saw her eyes pooling. "No, no crying."

"Sorry. They're beautiful." Damn it, she wasn't going to hold back the tears. She let them flow. "They're such a beautiful gift."

"Crap." Taylor leaned in and hugged Gray until her tears ebbed.

"Gracie?"

Taylor sat back up and watched Gray brushing her thumb over the beads. "Sometimes I get 'Faith'. But Gracie's my favourite."

"It would be kind of weird to name my daughter after myself, wouldn't it?"

"No, men do it all the time."

"Name their daughters after themselves?"

Taylor chuckled. "No. You know what I mean."

Gray couldn't fathom how this kind, thoughtful, beautiful woman could be the same woman described in that show last night. How could she have lived through the horrors she had and turn out to be such a wonderful, giving woman? Chris was right when she'd said that the way Taylor turned out was a miracle. "I love them, Taylor. Help me put it on."

Taylor helped her secure the bracelet to her wrist and said, "The sapphires match your eyes … and Gracie's."

"If you keep calling her that, I'm going to have to name her Gracie."

Chapter 7

After breakfast, they all sat around in the great room. Gray and Lane were reading. Kate and Chris played a game of backgammon with Taylor and Cail snuggled up together watching them. Going through the baby things lightened Taylor's mood considerably. Callaghan came in from outside and announced, "It's a beautiful day out there. I don't think we should waste it sitting in here."

"What did you have in mind?" Gray asked.

"A hike. I bet Lane hasn't had a good tour of the area."

"That sounds like a wonderful idea," Lane said.

"Ah, we've got a little issue with Cail and Taylor being seen in public," Chris reminded them.

"Who's going to see them on a provincial trail in November?"

Chris studied Callaghan as she thought it through. "Alright, let's do it."

"Yes." Taylor grinned, jumping up to go and get ready.

They all got bundled up and gathered in the foyer just as Maggie came in the door. "Maggie, we're going on a hike. You should come," Taylor said.

"Oh, God no. My hiking days are over, honey. You have fun though." She walked towards the kitchen and turned back again. "Gray, have you got a minute before you go?"

"Sure," she answered and followed Maggie into the kitchen. "Everything okay?"

"That's what I was going to ask you. I watched that awful show last night. How is she?"

"She had a rough time near the end of the program, but she's coming around. You know her. She takes everything pretty much in stride."

"Yeah, and that worries me some."

"She'll be okay, I think. She's talking to Dr. McIntyre."

"Inviting Dr. McIntyre up here was a very thoughtful thing to do. Go on now. I'll make a nice hot lunch for when you all get back."

"Thanks Mags," Gray said, kissing her cheek. She walked back out to the foyer and began to do the zipper up on her jacket. "Oh, shit."

Everyone was watching her and burst out laughing. She couldn't do her jacket up for the baby bump. "Wear one of Callaghan's jackets," Kate suggested.

Callaghan took Gray's face in his hands with a wide grin and laughter in his eyes. "I love you, Mrs. Callaghan... and the bump," he said before giving her a heartfelt, passionate kiss.

"Keep that up and we won't be going for a hike," Gray waved a hand in front of her face. "I love you, too. Can I borrow a jacket?"

"Damn, that was hot," Chris laughed, earning an elbow from McIntyre.

Callaghan retrieved a down-filled jacket from the laundry room and helped Gray into it, making sure it zipped up over her baby bump. "Are we ready then?"

Taylor and Cail rode with Gray and Callaghan, while Lane rode with Chris and Kate and they drove to a provincial hiking trail on the opposite side of the lake from Gray's. "It's a seven and a half K," Callaghan announced. "Is everyone okay with that?"

"I assume you're aiming that question at me," Lane said with a sly smirk. "Seven point five K is walk in the park."

"Alright, then. Let's go for a walk in the park." He handed a backpack to Cail and put the other one on himself as they started down the trail. "There's an awesome lookout point at the top of the trail. We'll be able to see the house from there."

They'd been walking for about an hour and a half, chatting and laughing along the way, when Taylor started shushing everyone. She pointed into the bush and they all stopped, looking in the direction she was pointing. No one saw or heard anything. Chris snorted at the absurdity of them all standing there in complete silence staring into the bush. "I don't see anything," she whispered. "What are we supposed to be looking at?"

"Shhh," Taylor said quietly. She pulled her cell phone out and started recording video just as a deer walked out of the bush towards them. He was a young buck, with developing fuzzy antlers and a beautiful sheen of sandy fur.

"Oh, shit," Chris whispered and took a step behind Kate.

Kate snorted and whispered to Chris, "What are you going to do? Feed me to it to save yourself?"

Chris beamed devilishly. "Seemed like a good plan to me." She wasn't expecting Kate to lean back and kiss her, right there in front of everyone. It pissed her off and she hoped that everyone's eyes had been on the deer.

"Uh-oh," Kate whispered when she caught Chris's glare.

The deer stopped in a clearing and bent its head down to graze. It looked up at them, grazed some more then walked off into the bush again. "That was so cool," Taylor said.

"How did you see it? I didn't see it until it walked out to the edge of the clearing," Callaghan said.

Taylor looked at him and smiled. She'd been tuned into her surroundings, more so than usual, mainly because she was worried about someone wanting to kill Cail, but she didn't let anyone know that.

"Oh, yeah," Callaghan registered she sensed the deer long before she saw it. "You're handy to have around."

"He was beautiful," Gray said. "I've seen a few in the backyard, but never that close up."

"You'll have to send us copies of the video, Taylor," Lane said.

"Yeah, sure."

"Just post it on Facebook," Kate said.

"I don't do Facebook."

"Sure you do. You've got a page on there."

"Oh, Emma takes care of that."

"Get out." Kate couldn't believe it. "You've never even seen it? You don't write the responses on there? Emma does it?"

"Yeah," Taylor answered. "I saw it when she first set it up."

"You know that you have over a hundred thousand fans on there, right?" Kate asked.

"Holy crap. Really?"

"I bet they'd be pissed knowing they were actually following Emma."

Taylor frowned. Kate was right. She should be going on there herself if people were following it for her. Besides, how did she know what Emma was putting on there if she didn't take an active role in it? One hundred thousand was a hell of a lot of people to misrepresent yourself to. "I guess I better change that," she said.

"Shall we stop here for a break?" Callaghan asked. "I've got water in the packs."

"I've got a problem," Gray announced, swaying back and forth.

"What?" Callaghan looked at her, worried.

Taylor laughed. "You need to pee."

Gray smiled then started laughing when Callaghan pulled a roll of toilet paper out of his backpack. "Come on, sweetness. I'll take you for a walk in the woods."

The rest of the crew settled in the clearing. Taylor sat next to Cail on a log and said to Chris, "Don't you recognize this place?"

Chris looked around her and then up a tree. "Oh, yeah. Isn't this the tree we climbed?"

"Yeah. That was a hoot, wasn't it?"

"No," Chris said, but she let out a short laugh. "You freaked when I wrapped that rope around us."

"You practically tied yourself to my back."

"It was better than explaining to Callaghan and Gray how I let you fall out of a tree."

"When and why were you out here climbing trees?" Cail asked.

"When Taylor came out on the Ralph Morse search with me," Chris answered. "We were looking for where he was watching Gray's house from and Taylor got the idea to climb a tree to get a better view. We were about seventy feet up that sucker."

"I didn't know you were part monkey," Cail said to Taylor. She elbowed him and took a swig of her water.

When Kate sat next to Cail and grabbed a bottle of water out of his backpack, Chris went to sit next to Lane about twenty feet away. "Don't be angry with her," Lane said quietly.

"Why not?" Chris snapped.

"Everyone else is openly affectionate, why shouldn't Kate and you be?"

"It's not the same."

"Only if you make it that way. Everyone here loves you and accepts you for who you are. There's no need for you to hide your feelings when you're with them."

Chris picked up a stick and started doodling in the dirt. "Maybe I'm not comfortable with making out in front of people."

"You're pretty comfortable when it's someone else kissing," she said, referring to Chris's reaction to Callaghan and Gray's kiss in the foyer. Then referring to Kate's kiss again, she said, "It was a sweet, chaste kiss. What's wrong with that when you're surrounded by people who care about both of you?"

"It's not like we're not affectionate around them."

"I'm not saying you should do anything you're not comfortable with. I'm just saying, don't be angry with her."

Chris sighed and threw the stick down.

"Did you really tie yourself to Taylor's back?" Lane asked with a laugh, hoping to get Chris out of her funk.

"Pretty much," Chris answered with a smirk. "She nearly shit her pants because my body was touching hers."

"She's come a long way."

Chris looked across at Taylor, Cail and Kate laughing about something. Taylor leaned into Cail then he turned and brushed his lips over her temple. "Yeah, she has." She picked up another stick and started doodling again. "And I'm still stuck in the same spot."

"That's not what I said or what I meant. You're doing fine, Chris. Give yourself some credit."

She looked across the clearing again and caught Kate staring at her. Kate smiled, shot her eyebrows up and down twice in quick succession. Christ, Chris thought. How could she be angry with her? She shot her eyebrows up and down right back at her with a lusty grin.

When Gray and Callaghan got back, they grabbed a bottle of water each and watched as Taylor started climbing the tree. "Don't go too high," Gray called up to her.

"Yes, mom." Taylor laughed and kept climbing. When she got to the spot she wanted, she called down to Chris, "This is where we were."

"Holy shit. It looks a lot higher from down here. Climb down again. You're freaking me out."

Taylor took a good look around before climbing down. When she got to the bottom Cail was waiting for her. "You are part monkey." Taylor laughed as he pressed his lips to hers.

"I love you," she whispered and sunk into the kiss.

"Alright, you two, break it up. We're supposed to be hiking," Gray called out to them as they made their way back to the trail.

When they got to Callaghan's lookout point, Chris and Taylor shared a quick look. "This is where Morse was watching the house from," Taylor said to Gray. They stood on the rock ledge, staring out across the lake towards Gray's house.

"I think about what you did for me every day," Gray said.

Taylor put her arm around Gray's shoulder. "Don't you dare start crying on me."

Callaghan stood next to Gray with a serious look on his face. "I've known about this spot most of my life. Why the hell didn't I look for him here?"

"You may not have personally checked this spot, Callaghan," Chris said. "But you had it searched before I got here. It was marked off on the map."

"But I should have come back."

"You can't look back and say I should have done this or that. Hindsight's twenty-twenty."

They stood in a row, looking out over the lake and surrounding area. Taylor took out her phone again and took a video of the view before turning it on everyone standing in a line. The mood seemed almost somber when Gray broke the silence. "I need to go again."

The whole line broke out in laughter.

While Gray and Callaghan went for another detour into the woods, Taylor slowly circled around behind Cail, swept up a pile of leaves and dumped them on his head. When he spun around and looked at her, she was unsure for a moment. She wasn't sure if he was angry or playful. A smile slowly stretched across his face right before he charged her. Taylor screamed as she turned to run then broke out laughing. Cail scooped up some leaves on the run and grabbed Taylor, holding her still while he shoved them up her sweatshirt. She screamed again, laughing hysterically. "Cail, that's cold." She tried to brush the leaves out then grabbed another fist full and the chase was on again. He hid behind trees, dodged behind Lane and was sprinting between two rocks when she caught up to him and stuffed the leaves down the back of his jeans.

"Oh, Christ. They are cold." She hid behind Chris when he got the leaves out of his pants.

"Don't get me involved in this." Chris tried to step out of the way. Cail faked a grab at Taylor and stuffed the leaves down the front of Chris's pants. "Jesus fucking Christ. Okay, now you're in for it. Two against one." She nodded at Taylor as they both scooped up leaves.

"Kate? Even up the odds, babydoll," Cail called out as he ran and dodged.

Kate grabbed some leaves, faked she was going to help Chris then shoved the leaves up the front of her jacket.

"Oh, you bitch."

While Chris went after Kate, Cail grabbed Taylor, lifted her up then set her down on top of a pile of leaves and started shoving them up her top, down her pants and anywhere he could squeeze them in as Taylor screamed, delirious in laughter.

Gray and Callaghan stepped in next to Lane watching the fall frenzy. "It's good to see them laugh," Lane commented.

"I've never seen Taylor laugh that hard," Gray said with a look of concern on her face.

"It's a good thing, Gray."

"I just worry with the bouncing back and forth between the low lows and high highs." She turned to Lane and saw her biting her tongue. "I know. You can't talk about it."

"Let me just say this, she's doing as well as can be expected."

"You're not concerned about her talking to Sarah and Darryl?" Gray asked before catching herself. "I know, I know. Let me put it this way then, I'm worried about her talking to them."

McIntyre took Gray's hand and gave it a little squeeze of reassurance. "Like I said, she's lucky to have you. If it makes you feel better and Taylor agrees to it, you could come with us when she goes to speak with them."

"Yeah, I'd appreciate –" Gray was rudely cut off with a pile of leaves to the face.

"Whoops," Taylor grinned.

A smirk appeared on Gray's face. "Get her for me, won't you, honey?"

"My pleasure." Callaghan grinned before taking off after a screaming Taylor.

"How is it you haven't gotten a face full of leaves yet?" Gray asked Lane with a raised eyebrow.

"Don't even think about it. You're five months pregnant for goodness sake."

They played in the leaves for a while longer before beginning the trek back. Taylor rubbed her cheeks, sore from laughing. "Oh my God, that was fun. I think my boobs are frozen."

"What boobs?" Chris laughed, sticking her hands, cold from the leaves, in her pockets.

"Like you've got anything to brag about." Taylor gave her a shoulder bump.

"I don't know," Kate said. "I think they're worth bragging about."

"See," Chris bumped Taylor back. "Who's bragging about yours?"

Progress, Lane thought with a smile.

"Someone might be, if he wasn't peeing behind that tree."

"That's gotta be cold." Chris laughed. "I bet his hands are freezing."

Chapter 8

When they got back to Gray's, Maggie announced, "I've got hot minestrone soup and fresh bread right out of the oven. Just head into the dining room when you're ready."

Everyone spread out to different washrooms, before congregating in the dining room. "How many people pulled leaves out of their pants when they went to the washroom?" Taylor snickered.

"I don't want to hear that story," Maggie said with a disturbed look on her face, making everyone break up again.

After lunch, Taylor brought her laptop down and snagged Kate to show her how to sign up for a Facebook account. Then she called Emma, to ask her to add her as an admin on her Facebook Page. "I watched that program last night, Taylor," Emma said. "Are you okay, hon?"

Taylor closed her eyes, trying to put the images out of her head. "Yeah, I'm good. I want to take a more active role on the Facebook Page, but apparently I need to be set up as an admin."

"Okay, I'll take care of it right now. How are the nightmares? Are you getting any sleep?"

Ugh, Taylor thought. "Yeah, I got some sleep. I'm good, fine, okay, no problems."

"Sounds like you're trying too hard to convince me. You sure you're okay? I mean that was pretty graphic, the things they said on that program. Is that all true?"

Taylor felt a headache coming on. "I'm sure I'm okay. Listen, I've got to go, so could you set that admin thing up?"

"Yeah, I'm doing it right now. It'll only take a sec. Do you still want me to update it daily or do you want to do that yourself?"

"I'll take care of it for now and if it's an issue, I'll let you know."

"Okay, great. We'll pick you up at twelve-thirty on Tuesday. Call me if you need anything."

"I will. Thanks Emma." Taylor hung up before Emma could say anything else then closed her eyes and rubbed her temples. "She's starting to sound like a reporter."

Gray's eyes quickly went to Taylor. "She could be the leak about your drawing."

"The drawings they had were in Cail's apartment."

"Our apartment," Cail corrected. "And she could have told someone where to look."

"I can't see it," Taylor said as a sharp pain shot across her head. She winced then started massaging her temple again.

"When you think about it, she was privy to everything about you, including that nightmare she woke you up from," Gray said.

"She's one of Tony's top publicists. He trusts her and she's worked for him for years," Taylor countered.

Chris came down the stairs and took a seat next to Taylor. She glanced at Taylor's laptop on the coffee table and asked, "Taylor, what are you doing?"

"I had to create a Facebook account so I can manage my Facebook Page thing."

Chris tensed and sat up straight. "Close it down. Close it down now for fuck sakes."

"Why?" Taylor asked.

"You're supposed to be dead." Chris picked up the laptop and studied her profile page. "You've got over fifty friend requests already. Shut the damn thing down."

"Oh crap, how do I shut it down?"

Kate moved over to sit on the arm of Chris's chair and walked Taylor through deleting the account. "You'll have to call Emma back and ask her to take over your page again."

"Crap." Taylor dialed Emma's number again and explained the circumstances. "Oh okay, I thought maybe that situation had been cleared up. I put a notice on their yesterday. You know, a kind of memorial."

"I'll let you know when I'm not dead anymore and we'll try again."

"Sure," Emma said with a laugh. "It's kind of weird talking to a dead person."

"Yeah, I guess it would be. I'll talk to you later," Taylor hung up just as another sharp pain shot across her head.

Chris watched her visibly wince then rub her brow. "Migraine?"

"No. I've got a bit of a headache, but I'm fine."

"Why don't you take some Advil and lie down for a while," Gray suggested. That was twice now she'd seen Taylor wince and rub her temple. All the highs and lows, she thought. All of the stress.

"Yeah, maybe I will." She took the laptop from Chris, closed it and set it back on the table.

As she headed for the stairs, Cail asked, "You want some company?"

"Only if you feel like lying down for a while."

Cail followed her up and made sure she took the Advil as Taylor stripped down to panties and a tank top and settled into bed. "I'll stay with you until you fall asleep, if you want."

"Would you?" She was still apprehensive about falling asleep and having Cail there seemed to do the trick the night before. He climbed into bed with her and pulled her in close. Knowing it would relax her, he brushed his lips over her temple until the rhythm of her breathing deepened. Then he laid there with her for another few minutes just to be sure she was sleeping soundly.

* * *

Chris went up to her room to make calls to Detectives Boone and Pierson to get an update on the limo attack. Then she called Detective Blake to see if she'd been able to track down any medical records of Taylor giving birth. As she was coming out of her room, Chris thought she heard Taylor whimpering or crying. When she got closer to Taylor's room she heard her cry out, 'No'. Shit. All she needed was for McIntyre to find out Taylor was having a nightmare and she could probably kiss her hopes of working with Taylor goodbye. She let herself in and closed the door behind her. In the dim light, she saw Taylor's arms punching out, her legs kicking. "No! Nnnooo!"

Chris grabbed her shoulders, shaking her and in a loud whisper, said, "Taylor, wake up." She ducked out of the way of a right cross then gripped onto Taylor's wrists with great effort. Taylor was strong and fighting like hell. With clenched teeth, she tried again. "Taylor, wake up for fuck sakes." When that didn't work, she secured Taylor's wrists in one hand, keeping them down with all of her weight and gave Taylor's face a good slap. "Taylor."

Taylor shot up into a sitting position, gulping in air, eyes wide with fear like a spooked horse. She nearly sent Chris tumbling off the bed. Worried Taylor was about to scream, Chris clamped her hand over her mouth. "Shhh, for Christ's sake, don't scream." She kept her eyes focused on Taylor's. "It's okay, it was just a dream."

Taylor pushed Chris's hand away and looked down at herself as if checking to see if she'd been hacked to pieces. "O-oh, God." She sounded as though she was talking through a fan with the trembling in her voice. She wrapped her arms tightly around herself then brought her knees up to rest her head on them.

"Are you okay? You worked up quite the sweat." Chris laid a hand tentatively on Taylor's shoulder, making sure she didn't panic at her touch before rubbing circles around her back.

"Yeah, I'm okay. I'm okay," she said rapidly.

"Are you trying to convince yourself of that?"

Instead of responding, Taylor pinched her ear lobe and concentrated on the rhythm of Chris's hand circling her back to calm her heart rate and trembling. She took one last deep cleansing breath and asked, "Was I screaming?"

"No, but I don't think you were far off it."

Taylor turned her head to face Chris. "I'm done. Lane's going to make me take that stuff if I want to come back to work."

Panic was beginning to set in. She knew Taylor wouldn't take the prescription Lane wanted to put her on, but she wasn't willing to give up on working with Taylor. "No, let's not jump to that conclusion. You got some sleep and you woke up before it got out of control."

"Only because you woke me up."

"No one has to know that."

Taylor turned away again and rested her brow on her knees. She wouldn't lie to Lane about it.

"Look, you didn't have a nightmare last night, right?"

She'd started to, but she'd been able to wake up at the beginning of it, which had been normal for Taylor before the book tour. Instead of explaining that, it was easier just to say, "No."

"So all you have to do is make sure Cail's with you when you're sleeping."

"You think that will stop me from having nightmares?"

"Have you ever had one when he's been in bed with you?"

Taylor thought about it for a moment and was mildly surprise to find Chris was right. "No." She wondered if it made a difference to Chris when Kate was in bed with her. Assuming, of course, that Chris had nightmares and Taylor was sure she did.

"See." Chris grinned. "Problem solved. You come to work with me after the trial and all's well."

"Have you made arrangements for me to go and see them?"

Chris's grin disappeared with a sigh. "Yeah, Monday at eleven. You wanted to start with Darryl, right?"

"Yeah. So now we just have to hope that Boone sorts the mess out with someone trying to kill Cail by then."

"I've got some news on that if you want to come downstairs. I'll brief everyone at the same time."

"I'll be down in a few minutes."

"Alright," Chris said, getting up and moving to the door.

"Chris?"

She turned back to face Taylor.

"Thank you, for setting up the thing with Darryl and Sarah and for waking me up."

"No problem," she offered Taylor an awkward smile. She still thought it was a bad idea for Taylor to talk to Sarah and Darryl, especially Sarah, or as Chris like to refer to her, the fucking evil she-devil bitch.

As if reading Chris's mind, Taylor explained, "I have good reasons for wanting to talk to them."

"Do you want to share them?"

She didn't. Taylor didn't want to jinx it. "Not yet." When Chris rolled her eyes, Taylor asked, "You'll be able to hear what I'm saying to them, right?" She figured there was some sort of observation room where Dr. McIntyre would monitor her.

"Yeah."

"One of the reasons is I need to face them and put all of that crap behind me. The other you'll figure out when I'm talking to Sarah."

Chris stood there for a minute thinking about the strength it took to sit across from the person who terrorized and tortured you for years. She had her hand on the door knob and was staring at the door. "You know, as much as I think it's a bad idea, I have a lot of respect for you for having the strength the face them. I couldn't ..." she swallowed the lump in her throat, but it forced its way right back up and a sob tore out of her. "Shit." She opened the door and slammed it behind her.

Taylor squeezed her eyes tight, fighting back her own sob. She knew Chris trying to open up to her was probably one of the hardest things she'd ever done. She wished she could make it easier for her, but she also knew it was one of those things that would never get easier. She could make her feel a little better though. She cleaned herself up and dressed quickly then went down the hall and knocked on Chris's door.

"Yeah."

Taylor opened the door to find Chris sitting in a chair in the small seating area. "Sorry, I –"

Taylor cut her off. "No, don't apologize." She took a seat next to Chris and handed her a small black bag. She intended to give it to Chris as a Christmas gift, but what the heck. "I saw this in New York and had to get it for you."

Chris wasn't sure how to handle this. People didn't get her things. She sat staring at the bag in her lap.

"You're supposed to look inside it."

"I didn't get anything for you, not even when you graduated from the Academy and you've already given me those drawings."

"What's that got to do with anything?"

Chris shook her head and pulled a brown box out of the bag. Christ, what the hell did she buy her? She flipped the lid open and sat staring at the bracelet made up of little gold handcuffs linked together. In the middle of each chain connecting the sets of cuffs, sat a shimmering diamond. The matching set of earrings sat in the middle of the bracelet. "Please tell me those are cubic zirconias."

Taylor sat there with a slight grimace on her face.

"They're real? Taylor, for fuck sakes." They were probably worth a year's freaking salary.

"You don't like them?"

"I think they're awesome. I've never seen anything as cool as these, but I can't accept them if those things are real."

"Okay, they're fake," she said and grinned.

"What are you a fucking millionaire now or something?" When Taylor grimaced again, she said, "Jesus fucking Christ."

Taylor shrugged. "Rags to riches."

Chris had to laugh. If anyone deserved it, it was Taylor. She carefully removed the bracelet from the box and put it on, holding her wrist out for them both to admire. "It really is awesome." When Chris was able to pull her eyes away from the bracelet, she looked at Taylor and said, "I'm writing a fucking book."

"You should," Taylor exclaimed, completely serious. "I bet you've got tons of great stuff you could write about. You could write fiction, like Gray, using some of your cases for ideas. I'm sure Gray would help you and give you advice."

With a knit brow, Chris stared at Taylor until she finished her little rant. "That was supposed to be funny."

"Oh." Taylor smiled, slightly embarrassed. "You really should though."

"I think I'll stick with what I'm doing." She got up and put the bag and the box on the dresser. "We better head down so I can give everyone an update."

"Yeah." Taylor stood and headed for the door. She was halfway across the room when Chris stopped her, grabbed her face and gave her a big fat kiss square on the lips. "Thank you."

"Um …"

Chris nearly doubled over howling at Taylor's beetroot face. "That gets you back for laughing at me yesterday." She opened the door and waited for Taylor to walk out before following her.

"But I just gave you a really awesome bracelet and earrings."

"That's what the kiss was for."

"Thank God I didn't get you the necklace, too."

They were both laughing as they came down the stairs into the great room. "What have you two been up to?" Gray eyed them suspiciously.

"Just talking," Taylor answered.

"I would have been down sooner," Chris said. "But I'm still picking leaves out of my underwear."

"Dinner's almost ready," Maggie announced, shaking her head at the leaves comment.

"Have we got a few minutes so I can give everyone the updates from the limo incident?"

"Go ahead," Callaghan said.

Cail was sitting in one of the chairs nearest the fire, so Taylor cozied up on his lap. "You look like you're feeling better." He crooked a finger under her chin and turned her to him.

Taylor leaned her brow against his. "We'll see how I feel after Chris's briefing."

"Get a room," Kate snickered.

Cail displayed his pearly whites for her. "Best idea I've heard out of you in a long time, Katie girl."

"I've got some good news," Chris began. "Taylor and Cail should be back from the dead probably sometime tomorrow or Monday at the rate things are going."

"I told you, you're looking better." Cail beamed at Taylor.

Ignoring the banter, Chris continued, "Detective Boone has made one arrest in the shooting of the limo. Kevin Laurey has already sung for his supper and Boone's working on arrest warrants for several high level operators in Vincenzo DeCosta's organization, including DeCosta himself. Detective Pierson is also working on warrants based on Laurey's information. Vice has suspected DeCosta has been running a methamphetamine lab in the basement at his textile plant for years. They've had people working in the plant and never turned up anything. Laurey claims his accomplice in the shooting of the limo is also the accomplice who helped Carlos Spanner get his hands on over a million dollars' worth of DeCosta's crystal meth. He says they got it out of the basement at DeCosta's plant. Apparently, Spanner's accomplice is scared shitless and hiding out somewhere, but he knows how to access the basement and what's in it. He's also armed with a fully automatic assault rifle."

"So DeCosta did have a hit out on me," Cail said.

"Not just you." Chris turned to Cail. "They also suspect there was a hit out for your partner, Tara MacNeil."

"Is Tara okay? Where is she?" He should have thought of Tara as soon as he knew he was a target. If he was a target because of that bust, so was Tara.

"She's safe. She's been under protection since the limo blew up."

Because Taylor knew exactly who Kevin Laurey was, she asked, "Did Laurey give the name of this accomplice?"

Chris pulled a notebook out of a pocket on the leg of her cargo pants and flipped through it. "Guy's name is Troy Rappaport." She looked up at Taylor then followed her gaze to Callaghan and Gray. They were exchanging knowing glances and all looked a bit shocked. "What? Do you know him?" she asked.

Chapter 9

"Met him," Callaghan offered. "Once."

Taylor flashed back to the floor of Rappaport's apartment in downtown Toronto. 'Keep that gun pointed at her, Kev' Rappaport had said. Kevin Laurey.

Chris studied the three of them. Taylor's face had gone white as a ghost and not one of them would make eye contact with her. "What's the deal?" Chris's anger was rising. "All three of you know him." When no one said anything, she zeroed in on Callaghan. "For Christ's sake, if you know something about this guy, spill it."

"Don't get angry with him," Taylor said quietly as she stood and began pacing in front of the fire. "He only knows him because of me."

"You know him from the streets? Taylor, this guy is a known drug dealer. A violent one with ties to the fucking mafia."

Taylor knew just how violent he was. If it hadn't been for Gray and Callaghan coming to her rescue, she'd have been violently raped. "It's not like he was my buddy. You know how I feel about drugs."

"Do you know where he might be hiding out?"

"I don't know. There might be a few possibilities. I don't really have a specific address, so I'd either have to show you or draw a map."

"You'll do better than that. You're going back to work."

"You better clear that with Lane first," she muttered.

"If Tay's going to work this case, so am I," Cail stood, staring Chris down.

Kate stood next. "I was assigned to protect Cail and Taylor, so I'm in too."

"This isn't my case," Chris spat out, frustrated with them all.

"You just ordered Tay to work it," Cail pointed out.

Chris raked her fingers through her hair, telling herself to calm down. "I'll call your dad and see what I can do."

Kate smirked, licked her finger and drew a line in the air. "Score one for team Worthington."

"You have any objections to Taylor going back to work?" Chris asked Lane.

"Other than she's been working eighteen hours a day for over a month with little to no sleep and is having horrific nightmares and flashbacks?"

"I'll watch over her like a hawk." Chris wasn't going down without a fight.

"So will I." Cail was still standing. He walked to Taylor and put his arm around her waist in a display of solidarity.

Kate followed him and stood on the other side of Taylor with her arm around Taylor's shoulders.

Lane sat with her legs crossed, her foot bouncing up and down. "Taylor?"

"I'm good." Other than she was feeling a little anxious at being crowded. She didn't want to be rude and ask Kate to give her some space so she leaned into Cail.

Lane turned to Chris again. "When do you plan on going back? Tonight?"

"Tomorrow morning."

"If she sleeps well tonight with no nightmares, I'll allow it, but I want her in my office at the earliest opportunity for a complete physical."

"Eeuw." Kate winced. She patted Taylor's shoulder. "Can't help you there, babydoll."

"Some protection you are." Kate laughed at Taylor's comment then leaned in and kissed her cheek while Taylor did her best not to wince. "Are we done? I feel like a Worthington sandwich."

Cail got the message that she was uncomfortable and led her to the chair he'd vacated. He sat on the arm and entwined his fingers with hers.

"If you're done, dinner's ready," Maggie said.

Chris watched as everyone started to file into the dining room. As Taylor and Cail approached her, she said, "Taylor, I need to talk to you for a minute."

"Okay," she said, slowing down. Cail gave her a look that said 'everything okay?' When Taylor nodded, he gave her a quick kiss and continued on without her.

"You're worried about me having a nightmare tonight?"

"Well, yeah, but that's not what I wanted to talk to you about. Let's go into Gray's office."

This was more serious than she thought. She followed Chris into the office and closed the door behind her all the while wondering what was so important and private. Leaning back against the door, she asked, "What's up?"

Chris paced, trying to decide the best way to put this to Taylor. She was pretty sure she was going to piss Taylor off regardless, so why not just blurt it out. "Did Darryl and Sarah kill your baby?"

Taylor knew that questions about what happened to the baby would be coming, but it didn't make her any more prepared for it. She shook her head. The sharp stabbing pain that she experienced in the afternoon was back. She squeezed her eyes shut willing it to pass. When it did she opened her eyes and everything was blurry. Feeling dizzy, she gripped onto the doorknob for support.

"We know you weren't at school from that January through to the end of April, but we can't find any record of you giving birth, Taylor. What happened to the baby?"

"Can't."

"Can't what? Can't give me a statement?"

"Can't talk about that."

"I'll walk you through it, ask you questions."

Taylor squinted, trying to focus on Chris. "When is it going to be enough? You've got to stop investigating my past." Another sharp pain shot across her head. Her right hand went to her head to keep it from splitting apart and her left hand went out as if for balance. "Ugh." She was feeling shaky now, weak. The pain receded, but this time it didn't go away. She was left with a throbbing headache over her right eye.

With narrowed eyes, Chris watched Taylor. "Have you got a migraine?"

"No." It wasn't the same as the migraines she'd had in the past. This was different and she was more than a little scared.

Chris let it go, but kept a close eye on her. "Does Darryl know what happened to the baby?"

"Back off, Chris."

"You don't look so good. Are you alright?"

"I don't know." Another sharp pain took hold and Taylor cried out. Her left arm went out for balance but her body followed her hand and she started to go over. Chris was quick enough to catch her before she toppled into a side table next to the door. She lowered her to the floor. "No. No, no, no. Taylor?"

"Get up." Taylor couldn't see anything but a blur and her head was spinning. The sharp pain refused to recede this time. She struggled to her hands and knees.

"Stay down, Taylor. Where are your migraine meds?"

"My bathroom. Cail knows." She lifted her head and the pain took her down again. She bent forward so her head was supported in her hands on the floor. "Aah. Gotta get up. Gonna boot."

Chris grabbed the waste bin from beside Gray's desk and put it in front of Taylor. "Here, use this. You can boot in this." She watched as Taylor's arm came out blindly grabbing for the bin.

"Taylor, what's happening? Tell me what's happening."

"Headache. Sh-shoo-ting pain." She gagged covering her mouth.

"The bins right here. It's right in front of you."

She retched again, forcing it back as she waved her arm around searching for the bin. When she found it, she pulled it in and hung her head over it, heaving.

"I'm going to get Cail." She had to move Taylor over so she could open the door and then she screamed out as she ran into the great room, "Cail? I need you to get Taylor's migraine meds." She didn't bother going into the dining room to make sure he heard. Chris went straight back to Taylor, who was hanging over the bin in a cold sweat. "Taylor?"

"Hmm?"

"Talk to me."

"Gotta get up." She tried to push herself up from her hands and knees and wavered.

"Stay down, Taylor." She pushed her onto her side and cradled her head in her lap, brushing her hand over her forehead and scalp. "It's okay. Just stay down." Chris turned to face the door as Cail came into view. "Her migraine meds. Hurry for fuck sakes." Cail turned on his heel and raced for the stairs as everyone began to gather in the doorway.

She started heaving again and Chris lifted her, holding her over the bin. "My head." Her voice was getting weaker and weaker.

Chris looked up in great relief when Lane came through the door. "Where the hell were you?"

Lane studied the scene as she walked through the door and became very concerned. She turned to the crowd in the door. "Could someone run upstairs and bring down my medical bag? It's in the bedroom closet." Turning back to Chris and Taylor, she ordered, "Tell me what happened."

"She's got a headache. She said she's got shooting pain. She fell over, just toppled over." Chris demonstrated by bending her arm at the elbow with her hand in the air and then moved her hand from a vertical to a horizontal position.

"What was happening when she started getting the pains?"

"We were talking."

"About something stressful or just talking?"

"About something stressful." Chris pulled Taylor into her. "Did I break her? Taylor, talk to me."

"Can't talk about that."

"Put her on her side please, Chris." Lane ordered then knelt in front of Taylor taking her pulse. "Taylor, can you describe the pain for me?"

"My head. Make it stop." She curled into the fetal position, grasping her head in her hands and groaning. "Please, make it stop." Her voice was so weak the plea sounded heartbreakingly pitiful.

Gray stood in the doorway, a pained look on her own face. "Is it a migraine?"

"I don't think so," Lane answered. "Taylor, are you having flashbacks too, or just the shooting pain?"

"Please, make it stop," she pleaded again as Cail squeezed through the doorway with her migraine meds. He handed them to McIntyre and she studied the prescription label.

"Okay, I'm going to give you one of your Maxalts, Taylor. Are you having flashbacks or just the pain?" Lane repeated as she slipped the small wafer in Taylor's mouth.

"Pain."

"Is it like the migraines you normally get?"

"Different. Sharper."

With a sigh, Lane said to Chris, "She really should be seen in emerg and go for a CT scan."

"Can't we just wait and see if her meds work? They're supposed to be dead. If we take her in, it would put her and Cail at risk."

Kate came in with Lane's medical bag and Lane busied herself with taking Taylor's blood pressure.

Cail brushed his fingers over Taylor's cheek then brushed his knuckles back and forth over her temple as Taylor's hand wrapped around his.

Cail turned to Lane. "What's wrong, Lane? You don't think this is just a migraine."

"She's been under a lot of stress, Cail. She's been dealing with too much," Lane answered.

"I think she's starting to relax a bit," Cail observed as he continued to brush his knuckles over her temple. He'd been watching a vein in her neck pulsing, pulsing.

Taylor tried to focus on Cail, but she was having a hard time keeping her eyes open and everything was still blurry.

"Do you hurt anywhere else, Taylor?"

"No. I gotta get up."

"We'll get you up soon, honey. Is the pain any better?"

"No, not yet."

Lane took Taylor's pulse again then her blood pressure. "Taylor, are you having any flashbacks?"

She didn't like that question. How was she supposed to answer it without making it sound like she was totally messed up? "No more than normal."

"What's normal?" Cail asked. "How often do you get them?" He knew she had flashbacks, but he thought they were rare.

Taylor wasn't prepared to answer Cail's question. She was just going to end up digging a deeper hole that would end up with everyone worrying about her even more than they already were. "The pain's a little better."

Lane took Taylor's pulse and blood pressure again. Satisfied that her heart rate and blood pressure were coming down, she turned to Cail. "Can you carry her up to bed?"

"Yeah," he answered and carefully scooped Taylor up in his arms.

"I'll give you a hand," Gray offered and followed him up.

Chapter 10

When Cail and Gray came back down, they joined everyone in the great room.

"Do you want to tell us what you think caused that headache?" Cail asked Lane.

"I believe Taylor is suffering a reaction to acute psychological stress. Her heart rate and blood pressure were significantly increased and I believe the blood vessels in her brain constricted, resulting in the severe pain. Without a proper exam and CT scan, I can't confirm that, but it's my professional opinion. The good news is she'll be fine."

"Oh, thank God." Chris felt the weight of the world lift from her shoulders.

"I'd like to explain a few things that might help everyone to understand what Taylor goes through on a daily basis. I'm sure you'd all agree that, considering everything Taylor has been through, she handles it very well and is very well-adjusted." She waited for the nods of assent. "And you'd all be wrong."

"She holds everything in," Gray said. "It's not healthy to hold it all in."

Lane smiled at Gray. "You're right about that," She glanced at Chris and was met with a scowl. "I would have insisted Taylor go to emerg, but it may very well have made matters worse."

"Hospitals are one of her triggers," Gray explained. "They trigger horrible flashbacks."

"Right again." Lane shot Gray another warm smile. Here was a woman who knew Taylor very well, she thought. "Taylor is an expert at concealing them. You could be standing right in front of her, having a normal conversation and not have any clue horrific images from her past are flashing through her brain."

Cail's colour completely drained from his face. He always figured he knew when she was having one and that they were few and far between. Again, he asked, "How often does she get them?"

"I'm walking a fine line here." Lane sighed, struggling with what to reveal. "You all know what she's suffered through. Unfortunately, there are triggers just about everywhere she looks – household items, certain vehicles, everyday sounds, songs, smells, common words, certain times of day, different places around the city. She can't escape them. They're all around her. Add to that that Taylor is hyper aware of her surroundings. She's constantly looking, listening, smelling, sensing. If there are any triggers, she finds them. And that's without taking into consideration the media throwing her past in her face everywhere she goes."

"How can we help her?" Gray asked. "How can we make things easier for her?"

"This is my fault," Chris groaned. "I put pressure on her when she was already dealing with too much. She just seemed so good today."

Gray took Chris's hand and said, "It's holding everything in that took her over the edge. She has to learn to get it out."

"So, what we need to do is try to get her to talk to us?" Chris asked. "She won't. She worries about what knowing about her past, having that in our head, does to us. So, what are we supposed to do, Lane?"

"I'd like to suggest that we try a few group sessions. I know it didn't go over very well yesterday, but, in time, she may come around."

"I'm in," Gray said. "Just tell me where and when and I'm there."

"We'll all do that for Taylor," Chris began, "But, what can we do in the meantime? She's got a hell of a lot of stress coming at her with going to see Darryl and Sarah, the trial coming up, and I'm sure she's worried sick about Cail being in danger."

"There's no question the next few weeks or so will be incredibly stressful for her. The only thing we can do is be there for her. She needs rest, first and foremost. I could ask you to keep her emotional stress to a minimum" Her eyes flashed to Chris again. "But, I know that in some cases that's impossible at the moment."

A now familiar battle raged in Chris's head. How could she keep forcing Taylor to do something that she didn't have the guts to do herself? She stood with the intention of pacing, but found herself walking right out the front door, consumed with anger at herself. She stood on the porch, looking out at the dark, cold night, wishing there was something handy she could punch.

"Chris?" Kate stepped out onto the porch with their jackets. She handed Chris hers and shrugged into her own. "What's going through your head?"

"Nothing. I'm just … frustrated … angry. You're better off stepping back inside. Let me cool off."

"You'll do more than cool off if you don't put that jacket on."

She put the jacket on then raked her fingers through her hair. Turning to Kate, she said, "It's on. Go back inside."

"Why not just talk to me? You hold more stuff in than Taylor does."

Chris spun back around, glaring at Kate standing there – drop dead gorgeous with her long black curls, the glow of the moon lighting up eyes bluer than blue. Don't do it, Chris told herself. She bit her tongue, turned back around and leaned her weight on her hands on the porch rail. When Kate stepped up next to her, leaning her back against the rail, she had to tell herself to hold her tongue again. "You're being pretty fucking brave, right now."

They stood there in silence for several minutes, Chris staring out at the patterns over the gravel driveway from the moonlight shining through the trees while Kate stared down at her feet giving Chris time to cool. Kate broke the silence with barely more than a whisper, "Who hurt you, Chris?"

Her knuckles turned white as her grip tightened on the rail, her anger spiking to the boiling point. She spoke very slowly, jaw clenched, "Back. Off."

"You see on a daily basis what holding it in is doing to Taylor. What makes you think you're not going to just fall to pieces one day, or combust or something?"

"You don't know what the fuck you're talking about. Back. The fuck. Off."

"She looks up to you, respects you. Maybe it's time you give her something to respect."

The cap on Chris's temper blew off. "Who the hell are you to talk to me about holding shit in? Have you told your family that you're gay? Have you come out to anyone but the people inside that house?" She stabbed her finger towards the front door. "I'm a private person. I don't like to tell people my business, but at least I don't go around pretending to be something I'm not."

"Bullshit," Kate fired back. "You go around pretending you're not a victim." She pushed off the rail and went back inside, slamming the door behind her.

"I'm nobody's fucking victim," Chris rasped, choking back the tears trying to claw their way up her throat. She stood there a moment, a solitary vein pulsing at her temple. Pushing off the rail, she marched off the porch and got in her car, gravel spitting out from beneath her spinning tires as she drove off.

* * *

Slowly everyone wandered off to bed until it was just Kate and Lane left in the great room. Kate sat directly across from Lane in one of the chairs with her elbow resting on the arm, propping her head up in her hand.

"You look exhausted, Kate. Why don't you go and get some sleep? I'll wait up for her."

"Where would she go? You don't think she went back to Toronto, do you?" Kate tried texting and phoning Chris God knows how many times, but she wasn't responding.

"She's probably off sulking somewhere. She'll be back once she cools off."

"You've known her for a long time."

"Yes, and she's a patient."

"I know. Confidentiality laws, blah, blah, blah."

She'd known Kate a long time too. Lane's husband had been very close to Cal Worthington and Lane's kids grew up with Kate, Cail, and Dave. "Would you like to talk about you?"

"You could get into choppy waters since it involves Chris."

Lane moved over to the sofa, so she was sitting kitty corner to Kate. "We could talk about you being afraid to tell your parents that you're gay."

"I'm afraid to tell anyone," she said with a quick laugh. "Everyone here knows, but not because I told them. Well, except for Cail, but he came right out and asked me."

"What made him ask, do you think?"

"I think he asked me because Taylor told him she thought I had the hots for Chris."

"If Taylor saw it, what makes you think your parents haven't?"

"Taylor's got that ESP and incredible intuition."

"I've known you since you were five years old, Kate. I've never known you to have a boyfriend. You don't think your parents would have picked up on that?"

"I had a couple of boyfriends."

"Have you had a sexual relationship, male or female, before Chris?"

Kate's face flamed red. "Oh my God."

"I'll take that as a no. You're nearly thirty years old for goodness sake. How much have you passed up in life because you've been hiding in the closet? Come out. Live. Love. Laugh."

Kate laughed. "It's not that easy."

"Sure it is. You suppressed your sexuality until very recently. I'm curious, why Chris?"

After ranting to Chris about holding everything in, she couldn't very well shut down now. She ran her thumb nail down the seam of her jeans. "I think I fell in love with her about four years ago."

"Tell me about it," Lane said with a smile.

With a roll of her eyes, Kate thought back to the first time she'd seen Detective Sergeant Chris Cain. "I'd heard about her. She had a hell of a reputation as being this cold, authoritative, tough, bitch. I was partnered with Jenn Mosby at the time. We were first on scene at this domestic dispute. This two hundred and thirty pound guy is beating the crap out of his hundred pound wife, so we separate them and send the wife off in an ambulance. We didn't even see the kid until after we sent the mother off. She just sort of blended into the sofa, white as a ghost and scared shitless. I think she was eleven, if that. Jenn tries to get her to stand up and she won't budge. She's sitting there in her pyjamas, shaking like a leaf with her hands between her legs. We thought maybe she peed herself. I sat down beside her and asked her what her name was. She wouldn't talk, so I just kept talking away trying to make her feel safe. I finally got her to laugh and she moves her hands …" Kate shook her head, shaking off the emotions. "The bastard was nearly two hundred and fifty pounds and here's this little thing … Jesus. No friggin' wonder she was bleeding."

Kate took a deep breath and continued, "Anyway, we call dispatch and ask for Sex Crimes and Child Services to attend. They call back and advise Detective Hicks and Detective Sergeant Cain are en route. Jenn tells me to stay with the kid, she'd wait outside. She was afraid of Cain. It kinda scared me because Jenn doesn't shy away from anything. So I'm sitting there trying to talk to the kid and in walks Chris wearing a beat up leather jacket and those cargo pants she wears. I have to say she looked intimidating as hell. I don't know if it was from all the hype or she's just that way. She pulled me into the kitchen, says 'Report' and I give her the story.

"She didn't say a word, just let me give my report then nodded and walked back into the living room. I followed her in and leaned against the wall. She walks toward the kid real slow, speaking softly as she went. When she got close, she crouched down so she was at eye level. Five minutes and she had that little girl wrapping her arms around her neck and laying her head on Chris's shoulder as if she was her mother. She carried her out, took her to the hospital herself."

Lane grinned with pride. "So at what point during all that did you fall in love with her?"

Kate huffed out a laugh. "The second she walked in the door."

"You're breakin' my heart, kiddo," Chris said, leaning against the wall by the foyer.

Startled, Kate slapped her hand over her heart. "Chris, how long have you been standing there?"

"Long enough. I'm going to bed." She weaved a little on the way to the stairs then began the climb. "Night."

Her hand still over her heart, Kate's eyes welled up. She wasn't sure what to do. She just confessed her love for this woman and was snubbed. It hurt.

Lane took her hand. "She's been drinking. I'm sure she didn't mean to hurt you."

"Don't make excuses for her. Getting drunk doesn't give her the right to humiliate me." She pulled her hand out of Lane's. She wanted to run off somewhere to be alone, but she didn't know where to go. She didn't even have her car there. "I'm going … to make a tea." She didn't want a damn tea but the kitchen seemed like a good place to retreat to.

Lane sat for a minute, disappointed in herself. Kate was right. There was no excuse for Chris treating her like that and the fact Lane had defended her was a bit disturbing. She got up and went up the stairs, stopping at Chris's door. Lane raised her hand to knock then let it drop to her side. No, she'd wait until the morning when, hopefully, Chris would be hung the hell over then she'd tear a strip out of her.

* * *

Taylor lay in bed watching Cail sleep. God, he was beautiful. Was it a bad thing that she wanted to kiss him awake and climb on top of him? She wondered what Lane would have to say about that and stifled a giggle. She watched him for a few more minutes then placed a soft kiss on his lips before sliding out of bed. She dressed in a pair of sleep pants and a sweatshirt then searched through a couple of sketch pads until she found one with blank pages in it, grabbed her pencils and headed downstairs to make some coffee.

She stopped in the kitchen doorway when she heard crying and there was Kate, sitting at the breakfast bar. "Sorry, I thought everyone was in bed," Taylor said from the doorway, not sure if she should go in or not.

Kate hadn't heard her coming. It must be her night for people sneaking up on her. She swiped at her face, mopping up the tears. "Sorry, I'm a bit of a mess." She glanced over at Taylor again. "Aren't you supposed to be resting?"

"I did. I was going to make coffee. Would you like one?"

"Sure, why not? Doesn't look like I'll be sleeping." After the way Chris brushed her off, she didn't think she could go up to their room. Was she supposed to go and slip into bed beside Chris as if nothing had happened? She couldn't do it.

"Need a shoulder to cry on?" Taylor walked to the breakfast bar covering a long yawn with her hand on the way.

"Are you sure you should be out of bed?"

"No, but it was either that or I was going to jump Cail in his sleep."

Laughing again, Kate assured Taylor that Cail probably wouldn't have minded.

"You're probably right, but the boy has to sleep sometime." She placed her art supplies on the bar and made her way to the coffee pot.

Kate eyed the infamous sketch pad. "Mind if I take a look?"

Turning to look at the pad, Taylor bit the side of her lip. "Um … there's a few rather intimate one's of Cail in there, but if you don't mind that, have at it."

A little thrill of excitement shot through her. She was getting the opportunity to browse through one of Taylor's guarded sketchbooks. This was awesome. Flipping it open to the first drawing she found there were indeed some very intimate drawings of Cail. "Oh, wow."

"You can skip by those ones if you want."

She laughed. "Hell, no."

Taylor loved hearing Kate laugh. She was always so full of fun and laughter. She got the coffee brewing and walked around the bar again to take a seat beside Kate. "You're still on the first one."

"I don't understand how you can draw these so perfectly from memory. You've even got that little scar on his chin. He got that in a hockey game when he was playing for the Canadian Junior team. We were so proud of him. He could have gone on to play in the big leagues but he figured he wanted to play in the courtroom."

This could be fun, Taylor thought. She enjoyed listening to Kate tell stories of all of them growing up. They got a few more pages in when Kate came across a drawing of her and Chris. They had their arms around each other, lips a fraction apart as they contemplated a kiss. When Taylor had seen them, they reminded her of the first time she saw Callaghan and Gray gaze into each other's eyes with that unmistakable look of love and passion passing between them.

"Oh, wow again. When was this?"

"The weekend we were all up here after the Academy graduation in August."

Kate's whole family had been up that weekend. If Taylor had caught them in an intimate moment like this, it was entirely likely her parents had at some point, too. Kate remembered the moment it happened. They thought they were completely alone, otherwise neither one of them would have been so openly affectionate.

"Would you like to keep it?"

"You'd give it to me?

"Sure. Just rip it out of the pad."

Taylor made them each a coffee as Kate continued through the sketch pad. When she sat next to her again, Taylor asked, "Did you have a fight with Chris?"

With a sigh, Kate shrugged. "I'm not sure what it was. We said a couple of things to piss each other off and then she went out and got drunk."

Oh, snap. Taylor didn't like the idea of Chris running off and drinking. She felt about over indulging in alcohol the same way as she did about drugs. It made people do horrible things, in her experience. "I'm sorry. I know you probably don't want to hear that, but as far as I'm concerned getting drunk is a bad way to deal with your feelings." A cowardly way to deal with them, Taylor thought. "Is that why you're sitting down here?"

"I just don't feel like I can go up there right now."

"There's another guest room. I could make up the bed for you."

"No, you don't need to do that. You're supposed to be resting, anyway. I know where to find the linens." She was grateful for Taylor's offer. She'd been contemplating curling up in a chair in Gray's office. Flipping another page in the sketch pad, she said, "I'm really happy you and Cail found each other. You're very good for him. I've never seen him dote on anyone with the possible exception of my mother. He's just so attentive and caring towards you. It's lovely to see. I didn't think either one of my little brothers had it in them."

"I didn't think I had it in me to have a relationship with anyone. I fought it for a while, but he just wouldn't give up on me."

"I have to admit when he first told me he was dating you, I was worried. I mean, the guy finally finds someone who means more to him than a wham, bang, thank you ma'am and–" Kate stopped herself, realizing how she must sound.

"I understand. He's your brother and you love him and want to protect him. You wanted someone better for him." It didn't hurt Taylor that Kate felt that way. She often wondered what Cail saw in her, too.

"He told me that he watched you walk into Tryst that night and he knew you were *the one* the moment he laid eyes on you. I thought he was attracted to you for your looks. Well, I'm sure he was, but I thought he only cared about the fact that you're outrageously beautiful and didn't consider all the other stuff." She winced, thinking that didn't sound right either. "Maybe I should quit before I really embarrass myself. What I mean is that you are beautiful, Taylor, but not just on the outside. He's really lucky to have you in his life. We all are."

Taylor took a long sip of her coffee as she tried to think of how to respond to that. "I think I'm the one who's lucky," she whispered between sips. "If Cail hadn't been so persistent, I would have really lost out. That's what you need to do with Chris. Don't let her push you away, Kate. You're good for her in the same way Cail's good for me and vice versa."

"I know she has a habit of dumping her girlfriends when things get too serious. I think that's what she's doing now. She knows I'm in love with her and that's the end of the line for her."

"She's in love with you, too. She's just not willing to admit it yet."

It startled Kate, hearing Taylor say those words. Her brow knit and Taylor saw the pain in her eyes. "You really think she loves me?"

"I'm no expert on relationships, but I see the way she looks at you and the way she is with you and I know that look of love in someone's eyes. I've seen it between Callaghan and Gray and I see it between you and Chris. You can see it in that drawing."

A wave of emotions soared up Kate's chest and she blew out a deep breath when they rolled up to sting her eyes. She picked up the drawing Taylor had given her with a weak smile. "Thanks, Taylor. I'm glad we talked." She felt a little better now and her steely determination was building. She'd be damned if she let Cain push her away. "I'm going to go up and make up that bed." She'd let Chris wake up alone with her hangover and then sometime tomorrow they'd have a serious talk whether Chris liked it or not.

They embraced in a warm hug and Kate thanked Taylor for the drawing. As she walked out of the kitchen, she stopped and turned back to Taylor. "He went back to Tryst every night, hoping to find you there again. Then he saw you on the news and I've never seen him so happy. His plan was to do his training at the Academy and then he was going to track you down. When he ran into you at registration, he said he knew it was fate. That you were meant to be together." She smiled then disappeared out the door.

Taylor sat there for a while then made another coffee and took her drawing supplies out to the great room, got comfortable on the sofa and began to draw.

Chapter 11

Lane couldn't sleep for worrying about Kate. She decided to get up and see if she was still downstairs. When she walked out into the hallway, she saw the light on in the great room below and peeked over the railing. Rolling her eyes, she headed for the stairs. "Taylor, you should be in bed."

Taylor closed the sketch pad and waited for McIntyre to come around the sofa and sit next to her.

"If you want me to clear you for work, you really need to rest."

"I'm okay, Lane. It was just some weird headache." Taylor was prepared to fight to be able to go back to work.

"The weird headache was a result of the acute psychological stress you're under. If you keep pushing it, you'll have a lot worse than severe pain in your head."

"I'm doing everything I can to relieve some of that stress. It's one of the reason's I need to speak with Darryl and Sarah. If all goes well, by the middle of the week I should be under a lot less stress."

Lane narrowed her big, brown eyes. "What are you up to?"

"I don't want to say quite yet, but you'll know in a few days." Taylor put her hand on Lane's. "I want to go back to work in the morning. I can help them find Rappaport."

"Even if I thought you were up for it, I'm not sure Chris is going to be in any shape to work in the morning."

"Yeah, I heard she went out and got drunk." There was no sympathy in Taylor's voice. She wasn't sure what went down between Chris and Kate, but she was angry at Chris for putting their relationship in jeopardy. She knew deep down their relationship was unlike any Chris had in the past. Chris was just as in love with Kate as Kate was with her and she was too stupid to realize a great thing when she had it.

"This is all very stressful for her, too."

"She really hurt Kate." Taylor didn't know if it was all of the stress she was under or the upset between Chris and Kate or what, but she felt such a heaviness in the air. She felt unbelievably melancholy, such a strange feeling for someone who'd gone so long without being able to feel anything.

Not being able to comment on Chris's behaviour and the reasons behind it was becoming frustrating for Lane. She was sure everyone understood Chris sabotaged her relationships for a reason, but she knew no one understood or knew what those reasons were. "I know there is no excuse for how she treated Kate tonight. I'll talk to her in the morning."

"She pretty much left Kate stranded down here with nowhere to go. I think she was planning on sitting in the kitchen all night because she couldn't go up to Chris's room."

Once again Lane was angry with herself. She was the one who abandoned Kate down here. She should have thought that she wouldn't have been comfortable sharing Chris's room after what happened. Pinching the bridge of her nose, Lane said, "I'm just making a mess of things. Where is she?"

"She's in another guest room." Taylor saw the guilt in Lane before she heard her statement. "Why do you feel like you have to protect Chris from everyone and everything?"

"Because no one ever has." It was out of Lane's mouth before she thought it through. She took one look at Taylor and could have throttled herself. How could she say that when Taylor had been in an even worse situation with no one looking out for her? At least Chris had the support of the government, a roof over her head, food, clothes, and a little pocket money. Taylor had been denied all of that.

"You can't save them all, Lane."

It was as if Taylor read her mind and Lane was sure she had at least sensed what she was thinking. "When did you become the psychologist?" She smiled at Taylor, took her hand out from under Taylor's then patted Taylor's hand. "Some are just not ready to be saved," she said of her meetings with Taylor so long ago.

Taylor assumed Lane was referring to Chris. "She's investigating what happened to my son."

Lane's eyes widened then her lips pursed in thought. "She won't find anything, Taylor."

"I know, but she'll keep battering me with questions about it."

"Do you want me to ask her to lay off."

"She'd listen to you."

"I'll talk to her in the morning." She patted Taylor's hand again and went back up to bed.

Taylor sat quietly for some time. She wasn't sure if she just insulted Lane by telling her she couldn't save everyone. There seemed to be so much turmoil around all of them right now. Three more days, she thought, and things should be much better. All she had to do was convince Lane to let her go back to work. She picked up her sketch pad again and finished her drawing of Kate as she'd seen her sitting hunched over the breakfast bar weeping. When she was satisfied with the drawing, she tore it out of the pad and made her way upstairs. Quietly opening the door, she tip-toed into Chris's room and laid the drawing up against the pillow on the vacant side of the bed.

When she went back downstairs, she settled back onto the sofa with her sketch pad. She wanted to do a drawing from their leaf fight during the hike. She sat there thinking about it for a few minutes then came up with an idea that made her smile.

* * *

Gray came down the stairs to the aroma of fresh coffee that she always looked forward to when Taylor was home. Coming down the stairs in the morning and seeing Taylor there always made her feel good. Gray headed straight into the kitchen to pour a cup of decaf and then walked out to the great room. Taylor had just stuffed a mouthful of spaghetti into her mouth when her eyes met Gray's. She watched Gray's eyes light up and a half smile spread across her face. "Um … I wuz hungwey," Taylor said with spaghetti dangling from her mouth then tried to stifle a laugh.

"I take it you're feeling better." Gray took a seat beside her on the sofa and studied Taylor.

"Mm," Taylor finished chewing, swallowed and then said, "I'm fine." She got the raised eyebrow and a stern look in response. "It was a weird headache. Everyone's making a big deal out of nothing."

"Taylor, Lane–"

Taylor cut her off. "It could have been from flying on God knows how many airplanes over the past month."

Gray pursed her lips in frustration as Taylor took another mouthful of spaghetti. "Were you having flashbacks while you had the pains in your head?" She knew Taylor would deny it, knew she would brush it off and say she was fine.

Taylor waited until she swallowed again. "To tell you the truth, all I can remember is the pain. It was worse than those migraines I had in the spring."

"I'm worried about you, Taylor."

At the sound of fear in Gray's voice, Taylor set her bowl aside then slid her hand over Gray's belly. "I know you're worried and I don't want you to be. Another few days and the stress factor everyone is so worried about will be gone … or significantly reduced … hopefully."

Taylor referring to the stress factor reminded Gray about Taylor facing her attackers. "I'd like to come with you when you go to see Darryl and Sarah."

"What does Callaghan think about you going?"

"Why are you worried about what Patrick thinks all of a sudden?"

"Because I feel terrible about all the stress I'm causing and I know he's very worried about you and Gracie."

Gray couldn't help but smile.

"What?"

Her hand covered Taylor's on her belly. "I don't know. It just does something to my heart to hear you call her by that name like you're best friends already."

A sparkle lit in Taylor's eyes that matched her grin. "Maybe we are."

When both of Gray's eyebrows shot up, Taylor was taken aback. She was so used to Gray raising one eyebrow. It was like her signature move. Well, that and handing out slaps. She reached out, touched a finger to one eyebrow and tried to push it down. When Gray slapped her hand away, she laughed. "Want to know how she's doing today?"

"What am I going to do when you go back to Toronto and I won't have you here to do this?" Gray was going to miss it. It was like having a direct line to the baby.

"She didn't dance on your bladder last night and you're worried."

Gray frowned then nodded. "It's weird how you do that."

"I know, but I like doing it with Gracie. It's the only time that I do."

"Were you able to do this with your own … oh, my God. Taylor, I'm sorry. I'm sorry." Gray's hand covered her mouth and she closed her eyes while she told herself what an idiot she was. When she opened them again, Taylor saw them glistening.

"Don't. Don't cry. It's fine. It's a natural question to ask. No, I wasn't able to do it. When I first realized you were pregnant, that was the first time I've had any sort of experience with this." She offered Gray a warm smile then to change the mood said, "She didn't dance on your bladder last night because you didn't sing to her. Can't dance if you ain't got music."

Gray was still in a funk with blurting out that question. She'd known Taylor didn't start having visions until the past spring when she was helping to find Ralph Morse, the man who abducted, raped and killed Taylor's sister before abducting Gray over sixteen years ago. Gray had been able to escape and her testimony put Morse in prison. When he escaped from prison, Taylor knew he was going back for Gray and did everything she could think of to warn Gray and get the police on the right track. It bothered Gray she just blurted the question out without thinking of how it would make Taylor feel or if it would give her a flashback.

"Wanna try something?" Taylor asked with a mischievous grin.

It was the mischief in her that concerned Gray, just a bit. "What?"

"I want to see if I can get her to kick, to let her mommy know she's okay."

Gray's response was a half laugh, half huff. "Go for it." She sat back to watch. Taylor kept her hand over Gray's belly and closed her eyes concentrating on picturing the baby kicking. Almost immediately, they both felt the little flutter of a kick. Taylor let out a little gasp before her smile cut her face in half.

"Okay, that could be a fluke," Gray said, not quite sure whether or not to believe Taylor had made the baby move.

"Okay, try singing to her."

"I have a terrible singing voice," Gray announced with a shake of her head.

"All the crap you've been through with me and know about me and you're worried about singing in front of me?"

Her eyebrows drew together then, with a sigh, she began singing the chorus to 'You Are My Sunshine'. There was no movement while she sang, but as soon as she stopped Taylor let out a howl of laughter as Gray's belly fluttered away. "It's not my singing she likes," Gray laughed. "It's when I stop."

"Let me try." Leaning down over Gray's belly, Taylor sang the same verse Gray sang. As soon as she stopped, the flutters began and Taylor let out a whoop of laughter again.

"What are you two doing?" Callaghan asked, fresh out of bed. He stood at the bottom of the stairs with his dark curly hair a mess from sleep, scratching his head.

"We're making Gracie dance." Taylor peered at him over the back of the sofa. "She's rockin' out."

Callaghan came around the sofa to sit next to Gray. He gave his wife an enthusiastic good morning kiss that had Taylor looking away then spread his hand over Gray's belly. "Make her dance, then."

"You've got to sing to her."

Gray smiled, entertained that Taylor would make him sing.

"You are my sunshine?" he asked. That's what he heard Taylor singing in her sultry, smoky voice.

"Yeah."

He kept his hand over Gray's belly and sang the verse. He was about to complain she hadn't moved when he felt the series of flutters. His face lit up and he sat there for a moment trying to think of another song to sing. With a smirk he began singing the chorus from Tim McGraw's 'My Little Girl'. Sure enough, at the end, he felt several little flutters across Gray's belly.

"I think you may have started something that could make me crazy, Taylor. Everyone's going to be singing to my baby bump and I'll be the one who needs diapers." Saying that, Gray pushed herself up and headed off to the washroom.

"That was so cool." Callaghan beamed at Taylor.

"I know, eh?" Taylor grinned back. "That was a really sweet song."

"I've always loved that song. Now I'll have good reason to sing it." Callaghan stood and headed for the kitchen. "Wake that man of yours up. I'll be making a full Irish breakfast in a little while."

* * *

Chris woke with a moan, running her tongue over fuzzy teeth with her face half buried in the pillow. She slid her hand over and found a cold empty spot on the bed where Kate should be. Opening one eye, she confirmed Kate's side of the bed hadn't been slept in. As everything from the night before drifted back into her mind, she groaned. "Ah, fuck."

Her eyes were dry and gritty when she tried to open them and her mouth felt like a litter box. She thought about sitting up and knew her head was not going to appreciate it.

"There's a glass of water and some Advil on your nightstand." Lane sat in a chair with her feet up on the coffee table, arms crossed in front of her.

Chris lifted her head to look over at her and then dropped it back down on the pillow with another groan. "Oh, fuck. This just keeps getting better. What the hell do you want?"

"I want to whoop your ass, but I think you might be a little old for that." She walked across the room and threw the curtains open, letting in the bright sunshine.

"Would you fuck off," Chris snarled, her hand coming up to cover her eyes. "Just get the hell out and leave me alone."

Lane strolled over to the bed, picked up the glass of water from the nightstand and dumped it in Chris's face. With a gasp, Chris bolted upright then grabbed her head. "Jesus. I could have used that water." She ran her tongue over her teeth again. "I feel like I've got little sweaters growing on my teeth."

"Talk to me like that again and you'll be looking for a new therapist."

Oh shit, Chris thought. She'd never heard Lane threaten to dump her as a patient. Did she do something to piss her off that she didn't remember? She used the duvet to wipe the excess water from her face. "What is this? The tough love technique?"

"If you want to drown yourself in your sorrows and push everyone out of your life, Chris, you go right ahead. You're going to wake up one morning and find yourself lonely as hell with no one to swear at but an empty bottle. You had a real chance at something good with Kate and you may have thrown that away. What you did to her last night was inexcusable."

"Do you have to be so fucking loud?" What the hell did she do that was inexcusable? She remembered tip-toeing into the house, trying to sneak up to bed without anyone noticing she was shit-faced. She remembered finding Kate telling Lane about the first time they met and then Kate saying she fell in love with her the second she walked in the door. She'd been touched by Kate's story. So much so that she just wanted to escape, so she ran up to bed. What was she missing?

"I came in here to tell you to smarten the hell up before it's too late." She was reaching for the door knob when she stopped herself and turned back to Chris. "You've lived your entire life without knowing love, Chris. Don't deny yourself when you have a real chance at it."

"That's not true," Chris mumbled into her up-drawn knees. "You loved me."

With a warm smile, Lane's hand brushed over Chris's soggy hair. "Like one of my own."

With that she walked out the door, leaving Chris soggy and drowning in sunlight with a throbbing headache.

And alone.

"Fuck." She turned to see Taylor's drawing resting against the pillow and picked it up to take a closer look. Damn it, Taylor, stay the fuck out of my business, she thought as she touched the tip of her finger to the tear running down Kate's face. That's a hell of a way to tell someone they fucked up. It might have helped if she'd told her what the hell she did to make Kate so upset. Maybe she should have drawn a picture of that. Chris frisbeed the drawing across the room and dropped her head back to her knees. If the bed wasn't soaked, she would have laid back down and covered her head with the duvet. Instead, she sat there brooding. "She could've at least left me enough water to take the damn Advil," she bitched. Now she had to get all the way into the bathroom to get more water. The thought of standing up and having that rush of pain sear through her head wasn't appealing.

* * *

Kate sat awake all night in Gray's sixth bedroom, the sheets she brought in still sitting folded on the end of the bed. Her determination not to let Chris push her away faded with each tear. She didn't think she had the strength to hurt like this again. She could hear people moving around, voices and laughter drifting up from downstairs, and she didn't want to face them. How could she face them when they all knew she was the latest victim of Detective Sergeant Love 'Em and Leave 'Em?

She splashed cold water on her face in the bathroom and tried to gear herself up to go and get her things from Chris's room so she could take a shower and change into clean clothes. It would be even more embarrassing to go downstairs with the same clothes she wore yesterday. Okay, she told herself, just go in there, pack up your stuff and get out. Piece of cake.

She walked down the hall to Chris's door and stood there with her fist raised to the door. Yeah, piece of cake, she thought, blowing out a shuddering breath. She trotted back down the hall then turned and headed back again. Just go in there and get your stuff for God's sake. She wrapped three times on the door.

"What?!"

Pleasant as ever, she thought. "It's Kate. I just need to get my stuff." She hoped she sounded a lot more confident than she felt.

"So get it."

Why did that hurt so much? She sounded completely indifferent, as if Kate hadn't mattered. Kate gritted her teeth and went through the door. She caught Chris sitting on the bed with her head on her knees in her peripheral vision. She damn well wasn't going to give her the satisfaction of looking at her. God, she had great skin, so silky and soft. That long bare back ripped with muscle. Damn it. She gathered up her clothes, stuffing them in a duffle bag then headed into the bathroom to gather the rest of her stuff.

As soon as she rounded the corner into the bathroom, she doubled over bracing her hands on her knees and tried to breathe. She felt like she had the wind knocked out of her. Was she an idiot because she just wanted to cry on her mother's shoulder right now? And as soon as she thought of her mother a great sob burst out of her.

Shit. Chris slid out of the bed and into sweat pants and a t-shirt thinking if she booted it would be Kate's fault. She picked up the empty glass and the Advil and dragged herself into the bathroom. There she was, leaning on the counter in a full out bawl. Normally, the sight of a grown woman crying like that would have made her sick, but for some reason she felt nothing but sympathy for Kate. Chris set the glass and Advil down and placed a cautious hand on Kate's back. "Kate?"

Kate shot up and took a step back from Chris with no shame over her tears. "Don't. Just let me get my stuff and get out of here."

Chris raked a hand over her pounding head. She must have given Kate her walking papers. Why didn't she remember that? "Look, it has nothing to do with you," she tried to soothe.

That did it. Kate's temper kicked in and she spewed out everything that popped into her head. "What?! Is that the standard line you give all of your dumpees? Do you really believe that shit? If it has nothing to do with me then why the hell do I feel like there's a car sitting on my chest? Why the hell do I feel like my heart's been torn to shreds? I knew better. I knew your reputation, Detective Sergeant Bump 'em and Dump 'em. Do you even know how many names they call you behind your back?"

"I don't give a shit what people think of me" Chris glared, reaching for the Advil. Why did everyone have to yell when you were hung over?

"It's pretty obvious you don't care what I think of you. You could have at least had the decency to give it to me straight instead of getting blasted and making me feel so humiliated. You could have at least given me that."

Chris got the Advil down her throat with a shudder and prayed it stayed there. "If you knew my reputation, you should have known it was coming."

"You cold, heartless bitch. How could I have been so wrong about you? You were right about me yesterday. I've been living a lie my entire life. I couldn't even admit who I was to myself. I don't know what the hell possessed me to think that a relationship with you was a good idea. If I had known how much it was going to hurt, I would have stayed the hell away from you. I should have stayed the hell away from you," she cried.

As Chris stood leaning over her hands on the counter taking Kate's assault, Kate dumped the rest of her things in her bag. She started to storm out and stopped herself, turning back to Chris and staring at her as she leaned there with her head hung low. She hadn't been wrong, she thought. There had been love there. Right up until last night. Could she just turn it off? It didn't seem possible. Her voice hoarse from yelling and the sobs clawing up her throat, Kate whispered, "Look me in the eye and tell me you don't love me."

Chris continued to stare down at the counter, pissing Kate off even more. With gritted teeth she growled, "Look at me and tell me you don't love me."

Chris's bloodshot eyes, a kaleidoscope of gold flecks over deep brown, met Kate's striking blues. Her short hair was messy from sleep and wet from having the glass of water thrown in her face. She was planning on staring Kate down and saying she didn't love her. They stood there, eyes locked, for what seemed like forever to Kate. Chris's jaw clenched in anger and she hissed, "I can't." Unable to hold the intimate contact of their eyes, Chris dropped her head again, leaning heavily on her hands. "I can't," she repeated, more to herself than Kate, shock and fear coursing through her veins.

"Then why?" Kate whispered, still weeping.

"Just go."

"If I walk out that door, it's done. I can't go through this again." The longer she waited for Chris to respond, the heavier the pressure on her chest became. Her heart breaking all over again, she stormed out of the room and flung the bedroom door open to find the rest of the house standing in the hall. She dropped her bag and threw herself into Cail's arms.

Cail held her tight, feeling her pain right to the core of his being. "It's alright, babydoll. I've got you. I've got you."

Chapter 12

When Chris finally made it downstairs, there was silence in the great room. Great, this is going to be awkward. She went straight into the kitchen and stared at the empty coffee pot. Shit. She got a filter and began measuring the coffee out when Maggie came in and saved the day. "Let me get that for you."

"God bless you." Chris took a seat at the breakfast bar and laid her head down on her hands.

"Feeling a little rough today?"

"Yeah. My own fault," Chris mumbled. She shouldn't have closed her eyes because now she was finding it too hard to open them again.

"Mm … you made quite the impression in town last night."

"What impression? I sat at the bar and drank. I don't think I even talked to anyone."

"I think it was the amount you drank that turned heads."

"I'm beginning to understand why Gray has an aversion to small towns."

Maggie laughed. "At least you had the good sense to get Matt and Joey to drive you and your car home."

"I think it was more them insisting after I fell off my bar stool."

Maggie laughed again. When the coffee was ready, she fixed a mug for Chris and set it in front of her. "Do you remember everything from last night?"

Chris slowly lifted her head, which seemed to weigh about fifty pounds more than it did yesterday. "Pretty much. I guess I've made an impression here, too." Chris lifted the mug to her lips, sipped and moaned. "God, that's almost orgasmic."

Maggie ignored the last comment. "Maybe when you fell off that bar stool, you landed on your head." She poured herself a cup of coffee then turned to face Chris again and raised her cup to her. "You fucked up royally, kiddo."

"Apparently I'm renowned for fucking up royally. So why is everyone suddenly all freaked out at me for doing it again?"

"If you don't know the answer to that, you really did hit your head. I'd call the doctor, but someone had to drive that poor girl home."

Chris's eyebrows shot up. "What? She didn't leave, did she?"

"Yes, she did."

"With Lane?" Lane was hers. Why the hell was she driving Kate home? She should be here helping her though this, not trotting off with Kate.

"Yes."

"Fuck." Chris set her mug down with a bang and headed for the great room with more energy than she'd been able to muster all morning. She aimed her glare at Cail. "Why the hell did you let her go? She's assigned to protect you for fuck sakes. She's on the clock."

"She's been declared unfit for duty. If you've got a problem with that, Detective Sergeant, you can contact Dr. McIntyre."

"Don't take that fucking tone with me."

"Then change your own fucking tone, Cain. Don't come in here and breathe fire down my neck and not expect me to fire back. You're also charged with protecting us and I don't think that drinking yourself under the table falls under the protocol for acceptable behaviour." He stood now and stalked over to Chris. "She's my sister and the way you treated her makes me sick. So, you just watch your step because I'm not above kicking the shit out of you right now."

Taylor stepped between them. "To your corners, kids."

Chris stomped off and headed out the front door again. Taylor ran after her, opened the door and screamed out at her. "That's great. Run away again like a damn five year old."

Skidding to a halt in the gravel, Chris whirled on Taylor. She had no idea where the hell she'd been going. All she knew was that she had to get away from everyone before she punched someone or broke something. Before she could yell anything, Taylor shouted, "Pull yourself together, Detective Sergeant."

"Oh, you've got a hell of a lot of nerve pulling that on me."

Closing the distance between them, Taylor said, "If you need to get your anger out, get it out. Scream, shout, kick, punch ... swear your head off if that makes you feel better. But, get it out of your system and pull your crap together so we can go back to work." Taylor was pretty sure she could see steam coming out of Chris's ears. "Cry already. Let it out before you freaking explode."

Chris just stood there glaring at her, fists clenched at her side, her entire body shaking with anger.

Taylor gave up. Before she turned back to the house she quietly asked, "What the hell did she do to deserve to be flicked off your shoulder like she was nothing to you?"

Chris swung her fist at Taylor's head like she was looking for a knock out, but Taylor was fast and blocked the punch with her forearm. Pain shot down her arm to the tips of her fingers and she shook her arm and hand out in an attempt to relieve the singing pain.

Sickened by what she'd nearly done, Chris sunk to her knees then doubled over, her chest heaving in sync with her sobs while Taylor danced back and forth, blocking Cail from getting to Chris.

"Go back inside before things get even more out of control. Please, Cail. Go back inside."

Callaghan got to him before he was able to dodge around Taylor. "You can go back inside or I can put you down and cuff you," he huffed as Cail struggled in his hold.

"She needs help, not fists," Taylor pleaded quietly.

Cail raised his hands up in surrender. "Okay, okay," he panted, forcing his body to relax. "Help her then."

Leaning into him, Taylor touched her forehead to Cail's and breathed a sigh of relief.

"You okay?"

"I'm okay," Taylor answered.

He kissed her gently. "Go on then. Make sure she's okay."

Taylor sat on the gravel beside Chris, wrapped her arm around her and pulled her in, rocking back and forth with her.

Chris was crying too hard to apologize, years of built up pain and emotion flooding out unrestrained. Why the hell did Lane have to desert her when she needed her the most? She'd been so worried about Taylor going over the edge and here she was completely over the top. It was ages before she cried herself out. By the end of it she was exhausted. She could have fallen asleep right there in Taylor's arms out on the cold driveway. How did you pick yourself up with an ounce of dignity when you'd sobbed like a spoiled kid in a candy shop? She knew she had to start with an apology to Taylor. "Sorry," she croaked.

"It's okay," Taylor whispered. She was freezing and couldn't keep the shiver out of her voice.

Chris heard it and pulled away from Taylor, wiping her tears away with her sleeve. It took all her strength to pull herself up to her feet. Taylor followed her up and they walked silently back towards the house. At the porch steps, Chris said, "Come into Gray's office with me." They slipped into the house and straight into the office. This was becoming a regular habit, Chris thought. She hoped it turned out better than their last meeting in this room. She closed the door behind them.

"I don't know what to say," Chris began. "There's no excuse, nothing I can say to change what I just did."

"You didn't do anything, Chris."

"I did. If you hadn't blocked my punch ..."

Gray knocked gently on the door then popped her head in. "Everyone okay?"

"Yeah," Chris answered, pacing. Gray started to close the door when Chris quietly said, "Stay."

Their eyes met and Gray saw the pain and guilt in Chris's red rimmed eyes. She closed the door and took a seat next to Taylor.

Still shivering, Taylor wanted nothing more than to go out to the great room and sit by the fire.

"Kate tried to get me to talk last night out on the porch." Chris blew out a breath trying to fight back the tears again. "Said I hold things in more than Taylor." A half laugh rushed out of her. "She said I was going to combust or something." Taking a seat on Gray's desk, she added, "I guess I did."

Taylor and Gray sat quietly. If Chris was trying to open up, they'd give her the floor.

"I don't know how to make things right. I don't know if you can ever forgive me, Taylor. You're the last person I would want to hurt."

Taylor shook her head. "It just seems like we're all under a lot of stress." That heaviness she felt in the air seemed to be effecting Chris as much as it was her.

Chris shook her head. "There's no excuse for what I nearly just did. I don't care how stressed I am, there's no excuse."

Taylor said nothing. She didn't know what to say. They sat there in silence for a few minutes. Both Taylor and Gray could see Chris's wheels turning, could see her fighting to stay in control.

When she began talking again, Chris's voice was hoarse. "When I was eleven, my mom went into the hospital to have surgery. I don't even remember what she was having done or how long she was in there." Another few minutes of silence went by. "While she was gone, my dad … started coming into my room at night." Chris swiped her face with her sleeve again and cleared her throat. "He kept coming … even after she came home again." She glanced up at Taylor when she heard her sniffle then dropped her eyes down again.

Taylor buried her face in her hands, trying to hide her tears.

"I was fourteen when I had my first girlfriend. I went home after school one day and just decided out of the blue I'd tell my mom I'm gay. I just blurted it out. She slapped my face so hard you could see her angry red hand print on my face for hours afterwards. My brothers thought it was hilarious.

"When my dad got home, I was in my room. Sulking probably. He came up, grabbed me by the hair and dragged me downstairs to my mother and made me tell him what I'd told her. Then he started beating the living shit out of me while she stood there and watched. I don't know what made me do it, but I started screaming at my mother that she knew what he'd been doing to me and asking her why she hadn't stopped him. She called me a lying little bitch and told me I was dead to them." Chris huffed out a laugh. "He threw me out the front door. Best thing he ever did for me. I had nothing but the clothes on my back. No shoes. No jacket. I walked around for a while in the cold. I think I was in a bit of a daze. I don't remember a lot of it, but I ended up walking into a cop shop. I figured someone there could help me find a place to stay or they might let me sleep in the lobby. They put me in an interview room and I sat there by myself for a long time, scared shitless. Then this woman comes in and sits down, starts talking to me." Her sleeve swiped across her face again with a sniff. "She didn't ask what happened right away. She kind of tried to gain my trust first, gave me something to eat and drink. I didn't tell her what happened. I was too scared of what my dad would do to me, but she took me to the hospital herself, stayed with me."

"The lady was Lane," Taylor said.

Chris nodded then blew out again, fighting off the tears. "They checked me out from head to toe, stuck me in a CT scanner, the whole works. They found the old breaks, the new ones, the internal scarring. She stayed with me the whole time, explaining everything they were doing and why.

"It's not an excuse for what I just did to you," she nudged her head towards Taylor. "I don't know why I get so angry. I don't know how you can be so caring, forgiving … why you're not filled with this rage."

"I get angry," Taylor admitted. "I just try to run it out."

"Who are you angry at?" Gray asked. She'd sat quietly, listening; hurting for the little girl Chris had been, grieving for yet another shattered innocent.

"Myself, mostly."

"Why?"

"For not being able to get past it. For letting it affect my relationships, my life. I've never had friends before, not like the friendship I have with both of you. I'm angry that I've hurt you, both of you. I'm angry that I hurt Kate. I'm not even sure what I did, but I know it hurt her to the core."

"Maybe it's time you forgive yourself," Gray suggested gently.

"You think that Lane hasn't said that to me a hundred times?"

"So what's it going to take to get you there?"

"Nearly punching my best friend is one hell of an eye opener, one hell of a start."

Gray rose and went to Chris. Embracing her, she planted a kiss at her temple then leaned back and took Chris's face in her hands. "I think you need to see Lane. You've got a lot to talk about. I called her a little while ago, Chris. She's on her way back."

Chris's hands closed over Gray's as she shut her eyes to ward off the tears. Leave it to Gray to know just what she needed.

"You've made major progress today because of that eye opener." Gray gave her another kiss and then left to give Chris and Taylor some time.

"Feel any better?" Taylor asked after a few moments of silence.

"I don't know yet. I'm still sick about what I nearly did to you." She slid off the desk and dumped herself in the chair next to Taylor.

"Are you afraid to love and be loved because you're afraid you'll turn into your parents? Or are you afraid if you let anyone get too close they will abandon you, so you abandon them first?" A bit of both, Taylor figured.

"I think I just proved I'm my father's daughter."

"Like hell you are. You're comparing yourself to a man who molested his own little girl and a woman who stood by and watched it happen. You don't stand back and watch it happen, Chris. You do everything you can to put the bastards who do that to little girls away so they can't do it anymore. You're not them, Chris. You're the opposite. Don't throw Kate away because you're afraid you'll lose her. You're losing her anyway by pushing her away."

Taylor's words made her think of the drawing Taylor left on her bed. She'd caught so much more than the tears in the expression on Kate's face. That's what made Taylor so good at reading people, she thought. One glance and she picked up on all of the subtleties in one's expression. She hadn't even meant to do it, to be so cruel to Kate, but she'd seen in Taylor's drawing she made her feel ashamed, humiliated, heartbroken, and she'd seen the pain. Then she'd seen it in the broken woman wailing in her bathroom. She didn't blame Kate for not wanting to feel like that again. "It's a little late for that. Kate's done with me."

Chapter 13

Chris stayed in Gray's office, wanting to be alone, when Taylor came out to the great room and headed straight for the fire. Cail was on her like a magnet on metal wanting to make sure she was okay. "Give me a minute to warm up," Taylor pleaded.

"You're freezing," Cail said when he touched her hand. "I should have brought your coat out or a blanket." Standing behind her, Cail wrapped his arms around her waist and her hands covered his as she leaned back into him. She loved it when he held her like this. Something about his strong arms circling her made her feel so safe.

"I'll warm up in a sec. It's not like I haven't been cold before," Taylor recalled many miserable nights in the dead of winter searching for warmth on the cold, cold streets. She'd always been smart, resourceful and it had kept her alive. They stood there like that until the chill was out of her. Then, turning into Cail, she whispered, "Don't be angry with her."

Her warm breath brushed his neck and he touched his brow to hers. "I understand she's hurting, Tay, but what she nearly did to you …"

"You have to find it in your heart to forgive her. She's beating herself up about this more than anyone else will. I know it was wrong, but it forced her into a breakthrough that's probably been a long time coming."

One corner of Cail's mouth rose as he considered Taylor's words and he let out a sigh. "I'm trying not to be angry, Tay, but, Jesus, if she landed that punch…"

"She didn't."

"Dr. McIntyre's on her way in from the gate," Maggie announced.

Gray met Lane at the door and whisked her into the laundry room to give her an update on Chris since she called her.

"Okay," Lane said as she processed everything Gray told her. "Let's see how she's doing?" She headed for Gray's office. When she stepped inside, Chris was pacing back and forth with one hand in the front pocket of her cargo pants and the other holding her cell phone to her ear. Lane closed the door behind her and took a seat to wait for Chris to finish her call.

One glance at Lane and Chris knew she was going to lose it, so she kept her eyes on the floor as she paced. She tried to focus on her conversation with Detective Ian Pierson. "Alright, thanks Detective. I'll give you a call as soon as we're back in the city." She ended the call and slipped the phone back into its holder on her belt before letting her eyes drift to Lane. "I fucked up," she managed before her eyes began to burn.

Lane was on her feet, closing the distance between them before a tear could spill. Chris's head dropped into Lane's shoulder as they embraced. "It's about bloody time," Lane said. "I've been waiting for you to have this breakthrough for years."

"I could've really hurt her for Christ's sake." Chris pulled away and took a seat, rubbing her face with her hands to wipe away the tears.

"Do you still feel angry?"

"No I feel sick, and ashamed for what I nearly did to Taylor. And I'm not even sure what I said to Kate that hurt her so much. I don't remember telling her I was done. I remember coming home and hearing her tell you that story. I was wasted. I just wanted to pass out. I can't remember anything after going upstairs to bed."

With a sigh, McIntyre took a seat next to Chris. "She'd just professed her love for you. Something I'm sure she wasn't ready to tell you because she was afraid you'd dump her if you knew. You announced you were going to bed and wobbled up the stairs, saying good night on the way. She felt like you dismissed her. She felt humiliated for baring her heart and then being dismissed."

"I didn't mean anything by that. I didn't mean for her to take it that way. Christ, after what you said to me this morning and then her coming in to pack up her stuff, I thought I'd dumped her." She raked her hands through her hair then looked up at Lane. "I should talk to her. Explain what happened."

"She's not here, Chris."

Chris didn't understand. Kate was with Lane, how could she have not come back with her. "You didn't have time to take her all the way back to Toronto and come back."

"No, she refused to come back. She insisted I drop her at a restaurant off the highway. David and Rose were picking her up."

All Chris could think of in that moment was Kate telling her if she walked out of the room, she was done. Damn it, why hadn't she said anything? Why had she let Kate go? "She's not going to talk to me, is she?"

"She's going to need some time."

"You didn't even say goodbye. You just left with her." God, she couldn't believe how incredibly selfish she sounded.

"I stopped by your room when I came up for my bag, but you were in the shower."

"Would you talk to her for me? Explain that it was all a misunderstanding?" Chris pleaded. But she knew what Lane would say. It was up to her to talk to Kate. It was her mess to clean up. "Could you at least tell her I really need to talk to her?"

"You saw how much this hurt her, Chris. You may not have intended to end the relationship last night, but how long would it have been before you tossed her aside? You end all of your relationships when they start to get serious. You've told me that yourself time and again."

"I always thought I did that because of abandonment issues. I thought if I ended the relationship before it got too serious, I was avoiding them dumping me. But, Taylor asked me if I'm afraid to love and be loved because I'm afraid I'll become my parents. What I did to Taylor today makes me afraid that I'm just like my father."

"I'm not going to say that you don't have some anger issues, but you sure as hell are not your father ... or your mother. You know that. Could you do to someone what they did to you?"

"No." Chris didn't even have to think about it when the question was put that way. "I'm sick of being angry. I don't want to be angry anymore." Chris rubbed her hands over her face then dragged them through her hair again. "Maybe I need to do what Taylor's doing, so I can put it all behind me."

"You want to meet with them?"

The thought of seeing her parents had her stomach in knots. "Shit, I don't know. No. I want to stop being angry, that's all."

"Well, you can think about it. Wait for a little while to see how you feel now that you've been able to talk about it with Taylor and Gray. Now that it's out on the table, they'll be able to help you through the difficult times and you'll be able to talk to them if you need to. Taylor especially because of the similarities.

"Your anger issues have a lot to do with the environment you were raised in. You grew up in a household where anger and rage were expressed daily, usually targeted towards you in the form of violence."

"That's what's scaring the shit out of me. I've never become violent like that before. Now, I'm just like him."

"No, you're not. You threw a punch in anger and frustration and that was wrong, but you knew it. You didn't keep trying to hit her. You didn't want to hurt Taylor. So let's look at why you were angry and frustrated."

"I don't know. I was angry at myself for hurting Kate, frustrated at everyone telling me I'd been an idiot."

"It goes further back than that. This started last night, before you went off to drink your face off. Why were you so angry last night?"

"I was angry at myself for what I've put Taylor through. I keep making her face things that I can't face myself then I send her over the edge trying to get her to tell me what happened to her baby."

"And you went out to the front porch. Kate followed you out before you drove off."

"She kept pushing me, making me even angrier. I tried to tell her to go back inside, but she wouldn't back off. She told me I hold more shit in than Taylor and she asked me who hurt me. She wanted me to talk to her."

"So where's the root of the anger you've been feeling?"

Chris raked her fingers through her hair, getting frustrated. "I don't know. I don't know where it comes from, I'm just sick of feeling angry all the time."

"Are you angry that Kate was nearly successful at getting through your barriers?"

"I don't know! Christ, you're giving me a headache." Chris dropped her head into her hands, covering her face. "She called me a victim."

"Ouch," Lane said quietly. "And your response to that was to drink yourself silly?"

"Go on, say it. I know it's been killing you. Turning to alcohol is not an appropriate behaviour." When Lane didn't respond, Chris felt like pulling her hair out. They sat there in silence for a few minutes before Chris spoke again. "Maybe it's time I transferred out of Sex Crimes."

"You've worked Sex Crimes for a long time. The Johnson case has been harder on you than any of your previous cases. Why do you think that is?"

"I don't know, maybe because I've gotten so close to Taylor. None of the other victims I've worked with have been attacked by the media like Taylor has been. It's made it so much harder for her to deal with. Watching what it has done to her, knowing I'm responsible for it, has made it hard on me."

"I'm going to ask you stop your investigation into what happened to Taylor's child."

"If Sarah Johnson was responsible –"

"She wasn't. I can't tell you any more than that."

"If you know what happened –"

"Chris." McIntyre waited until Chris raised her head and looked into her eyes. "Let it go. Please."

She wasn't sure why Lane was asking her to drop it, but she'd never interfered with one of Chris's investigations before. Was it because Lane cared about Taylor, too? Did she think Taylor couldn't handle what she would dig up?

They talked for a while longer. Just as they were about to go out to the great room, Chris said, "It's different, Lane."

"Hm? What is?"

"With Kate. It's not like any of my other relationships. I don't want our relationship to end. I don't want to screw it up."

Lane smiled then placed a hand on Chris's face. "I know you love her, Chris. I hope Kate is able to get past the hurt."

"I didn't have to give her walking papers for her to think I did, because everyone was expecting me to do it."

"Yes. How many times have I heard you say 'it's what I do'? Even you expected it of yourself."

Chris frowned at that because she realized it was true. But, for the first time in her life she didn't want her relationship to end. Things were changing. She was changing. It had a lot to do with her friendship with Taylor and Gray. She owed a lot of the growing she done over the past six months to Taylor. Who knew someone with such a tortured soul would be the one to teach her not only how to love, but to want to love. It wasn't something she learned in her home life, that was for sure.

At the entrance to the great room, all eyes turned to Chris. She stuffed her hands in her front pockets and announced, "We need to get back to Toronto. Vincenzo DeCosta and Antonio Mallamo, his second in command, are in custody. There will be a press conference at Headquarters at nineteen hundred hours to announce Taylor and Cail weren't in that limo. The Chief wants you both there, in uniform."

"What about Rappaport?" Taylor asked.

"This isn't my investigation, but Detective Pierson is welcoming the help. We'll go into a briefing with him after the press conference and go from there."

They gathered up their gear and loaded up Chris's car. As they were about to head out the door, Callaghan pulled Chris aside. "Rappaport is a danger to Taylor. He'll want to hurt her, or worse. Make sure that doesn't happen."

Chris eyed him suspiciously. "You want to give me the history?"

"That's Taylor call, if she wants to go there."

Chris was trying to put it together in her head and it just didn't fit. How the hell did Taylor, Gray and Callaghan get caught up with Rappaport? It had to have been something that happened since Taylor came to Gray's. She pictured the first time she met Taylor and Gray. Taylor's face was pretty bruised up, but they were well on their way to healing. She remembered having to wait for them to come back from Toronto to interview them. Something happened while they were in Toronto, but what? "Okay," Chris said with a nod. She took a step towards the door and turned back. "Thanks, Callaghan."

With a half-smile, Chris walked out the door. Gray was at the car with Taylor and Cail saying her goodbyes. "You're going to see them tomorrow for Christ's sake," she said to Gray.

Gray pulled back and placed a quick kiss on Taylor's cheek. "I'll bring the rest of your luggage to Chris's in the morning."

"Don't lift them yourself," Taylor warned. "Get the driver to put them in the car for you and I'll take them out when you get to Chris's."

"Yes, little mother," Gray said and grinned.

Taylor slid her hand over Gray's belly. "See you tomorrow, Gracie."

Chris asked Cail to drive so she could catch up on some work, but the real reason was she still felt like crap and it wasn't just the hangover. She gave Gray a hug and climbed into the back seat. Gray leaned into the car. "Don't be too hard on yourself, Chris."

Tears threatened again, so Chris didn't say anything. The glassy eyed nod she gave to Gray said it all. She didn't inquire about Rappaport on the drive home. She spent most of the drive staring blankly at her iPhone while her thoughts filled with everything Kate. For a while she sat watching the interaction between Cail and Taylor. If they weren't holding hands, his arm was resting on her headrest while he played with her ponytail. Several times his fingertips brushed her long neck in just the right places because she watched Taylor rise a bit in her seat every time. Cail got a chuckle out of it then turned his focus back to the road.

It would have annoyed her before, she thought. She would have teased them about their playfulness, had some sarcastic comment at the ready. But, right then, all she could do was think how much she wanted that with Kate. She had that with Kate, she corrected herself. Weren't they doing the exact same thing on the drive up? How the hell did Taylor Sinclair, with the nightmare past, fall into love, into a healthy relationship without seeming to have any idiotic neuroses? Chris let out a quick laugh to herself thinking it was because she had enough for both of them.

They unpacked the car when they got to Chris's little house in Toronto. Taylor and Cail couldn't go back to their own place until after the press conference. Even then, Chris suggested they stay at her place until the media attention died down. Chris dropped her bag in her room and rooted through her closet for her beat up black leather jacket. She slipped into it as she headed down the hall through the living room towards the front door. "I've got a couple of things to take care of. I'll be back to pick you up in time to make the press conference."

Taylor watched Chris pass through the living room and out the door. She hadn't even looked at them. "I'm worried about her," she said to Cail.

"I know," he said as he brushed his fingers over her cheek. "I get the feeling she's had a rude awakening. Maybe you're right. Maybe it was just what she needed."

"You think she's gone to find Kate?" Taylor was sure she was, but wanted Cail's take on it. He knew Kate better than any of them.

"Yeah. I don't know if she'll like what she sees when she finds her though. Kate's strong. I've never seen her hurt like that and she's not the type to set herself up to be hurt again."

* * *

Chris banged on Kate's apartment door several times before using her key to let herself in. Kate hadn't come home. Her duffel bag wasn't there. That only left one other place she could be. Chris raked her hands though her hair as she stood in Kate's quiet apartment, trying to build up enough courage to go to Kate's parents' house.

When she pulled into the driveway, she took several long deep breaths before heading for the door. She knocked then took another deep breath and rolled her head, trying to relax the tension in her neck and shoulders. It was Kate's mom, Rose, who answered the door. She was a five foot three bundle of energy and the most nurturing woman Chris had ever met. All three of her kids had her colouring with the jet black hair and deep blue eyes.

"Chris," Rose greeted with a smile.

"Hi, Rose. Is Kate here? I just wondered if I could talk to her."

"She's not feeling very well at the moment. Why don't I go up and ask her if she's up for a visitor?"

While Rose scurried off up the stairs, Chris stood nervously at the door praying that Kate would talk to her. The look on Rose's face when she started back down the stairs told her she was out of luck. She suddenly knew how Kate felt the night before when she thought Chris was giving her the brush off. A stab of pain shot straight through her heart.

"I'm sorry, Chris. She's just not up for company."

"I know that she's hurting," Chris began, not sure how to say what she wanted Rose to convey to Kate without giving away that she was the one responsible for Kate hurting so much.

"Looks to me that you're both hurting," Rose said quietly and placed her hand in Chris's, giving it a little squeeze.

The tears Chris was bound and determined not to shed burned like fire in her eyes. "She told you." It was barely more than a whisper.

"No," Rose responded. "We've had our suspicions for a long time, but we wanted her to tell us when she was ready." She patted Chris's hand in hers. "We only had to see you together to know, Chris."

"She's been so afraid to tell you."

"I know. Still, I felt it best to let her do it when she was ready. It's taken her up until recently to admit it to herself. She wasn't ready to tell us what she couldn't accept herself." Cupping Chris's cheek in her hand, Rose softly encouraged, "Give her some time."

Chris shook her head. "I hurt her. I didn't mean to hurt her. I'm scared she won't talk to me again, that she won't let me explain."

"It only hurts because you love each other. Whether that love is enough to get you both through this remains to be seen. But, I'll talk to her."

Chris covered Rose's hand with hers and closed her eyes against the tears. It was more than she deserved. "Thank you," she whispered then hurried out the door before she broke down. She sat in the car and let her tears flow. She'd never cried like this in her entire life, never felt such despair. She could take her father's constant beatings, his constant abuse of her small body, she could take being kicked to the curb by the people who were supposed to love her, but she was pretty sure she couldn't take much more of the overwhelming sense of loss and emptiness that Kate's absence seemed to fill her with.

Chapter 14

Moments after Chris pulled out of the driveway, Rose greeted Lane at the door.

"How is she?" Lane asked as Rose took her coat.

"Miserable. Heartbroken."

"Is she talking to you about it?"

"Not really. She wants to know why I didn't tell her love could hurt so much." Rose covered it well, but Lane could see her heart was breaking for her daughter. She was hurting as much as Kate. Rose hung Lane's coat in the closet then turned to face her. "Chris was just here, but Kate refused to see her."

"So, you know Kate is gay."

Putting her arm through Lane's, Rose led her into the living room as she talked. "We've suspected for some time. Then seeing them together … well, it was pretty obvious."

"I thought you must have known," Lane offered her reassuring smile. "No one knows their children better than a mother."

"Maybe we should have talked to her about it, but we thought it was best to let her do it in her own time."

"You knew?" Kate stood at the bottom of the stairs with red, puffy eyes, her fair skin blotchy. All this time she'd been scared to death of what her parents were going to think of her and they knew. "You could have said. You could have helped me to understand it myself." She walked to the sofa and took a seat next to her mother. "All these years I've been fighting this battle inside me, not knowing how to deal with it."

"I'm so sorry, Kate. We weren't quite sure how to approach it and we didn't think you were ready to talk to us about it."

Kate let herself fall into the back of the sofa. Would she have been open to talking to her parents about it? She wasn't sure herself. She turned her focus to Lane. "You talked to her?"

"Yes."

"Did she hurt Taylor?" All she knew was that Gray called Lane asking her to turn around and come back. She heard Lane ask if Taylor was okay, but all Lane would say when she got off the phone was that Chris needed her.

Lane hadn't come to talk about Taylor, but how could she avoid this question? "No."

"You're not going to tell me about it, are you?" The one word answers to her questions told Kate she was treading on ground Lane didn't want to cover, or couldn't.

"That's not the reason that I came by. I wanted to make sure you're okay and, if you're up for it, to talk to you about Chris."

"You can't do that, can you? Confidentiality and all that."

"She asked me if I would talk to you. There's a lot I can't say, but she wanted me to tell you that she desperately wants to talk to you about what's happened." Lane waited while Kate thought about what she said.

"She asked you to talk to me because she wants to get back together? Is that what you're saying?"

"Yes."

"Why does she want to get back together? It's not her pattern."

"Last night, when Chris made you feel like she dismissed you, we both mistook it as she was giving you the brush off. We assumed that because we both know her history. But, your relationship with Chris is not like any of her past relationships. She's never been in love before."

"No offence, Lane, but I gave her the chance this morning and she didn't take it. If she wanted to explain why she's behaving the way she is, she should have told me herself. She shouldn't have sent you to do it for her."

"Would you talk to her?"

"I'm not ready to talk to her yet. I'm not sure that I want to."

"Do you know why she went out drinking last night, Kate?"

"No. We said some things to each other on the porch. I know she was angry."

Lane knew she had to tread lightly or she'd just make matters worse. "Did you push each other's buttons, make her angrier?"

Chris's warnings for Kate to go back inside and back off rang through her head. "I know she was abused at some point. I can see it in the way she is with the victims she works with, especially the kids. I guess I just wanted her to get it out so that she doesn't end up like Taylor."

"What happened at Gray's this morning between Taylor and Chris forced Chris to have a breakthrough I've been waiting years for. She's never been able to talk about what happened to her, Kate. For the first time in her life, she's ready to talk, but the last thing she wants is to be seen as a victim. I know you're in terrible pain, Kate and I'm sorry for it. I just want you to know Chris is hurting just as much as you are."

At that, Lane made her exit, hoping Kate would come around in time and let Chris back into her life. Kate waited for Rose to come back into the living room after seeing Lane out. Rose sat next to her and Kate rested her head on her mother's shoulder. "Why didn't you say anything?"

"We weren't sure what to do," Rose answered. "It's taken you a long time to come to terms with it yourself. Maybe we should have gone to Lane a long time ago and asked her advice."

"I thought you'd … I don't know … I guess I thought you would think less of me."

"Oh, Katie. We love you. We'll always love you. We want you to be happy and you looked so happy and content when you were with Chris."

"I don't know what to do, Mum. I didn't know it could hurt this much and I don't want to go through this again."

"It hurts so much because you love her," Rose repeated what she told Chris. "You're both hurting. Give yourself some time to figure out what you want then I think you owe it to yourself to at least sit down and talk with Chris."

* * *

Taylor and Cail sat in full uniform in a meeting room down the hall from where the press conference was taking place at Toronto Police Headquarters. Chris leaned against the wall in the corner, lost in her thoughts when Chief Madison Clarke walked in, closely followed by a young constable. Taylor and Cail got to their feet and stood at attention, but Taylor's focus was on the tall, rail thin constable. This guy had to be close to seven feet tall with light brown hair cut in a military precision buzz cut. He might have been good looking if it weren't for the acne scars dotting his long, thin face. Taylor couldn't place where she'd seen him before, but he looked oddly familiar.

Chief Clarke, in her mid forties, was young for a Chief of Police. Her dark brown hair was cut in a stylish bob and the crisp white shirt and uniform looked good on her five foot eight, fit frame.

"At ease," Clarke waved her hand at them. "It's good to see both of you alive and well."

"Not half as good as it is to be alive and well," Cail said. "I believe we're about to come back from the dead."

"Yes." Clarke glanced at her watch. "In about fifteen minutes." She pulled out a chair across the table from Taylor and Cail and they all sat again except for the Chief's aide who stood stoically by the door.

"We still have the matter of Troy Rappaport, who I understand is someone you've been acquainted with, Sinclair."

"Not in a friendly manner." Taylor didn't want Clarke thinking she'd been friends with the creep.

"But you have some ideas about where he might be hiding out?"

"Possibly. There are a few places that might be worth checking."

"And you know about these places how?"

Taylor's face turned red with a mixture of shame and embarrassment. Her voice was low when she answered, "I know a lot of places to hide."

To her credit, Clarke didn't flinch at her stupidity. Instead, she rose, keeping eye contact with Taylor. "You're an asset to the department, Sinclair. I thank God you weren't in that limo." At the door, she looked over her shoulder with a grin. "You too, Worthington."

"Who was that guy?" Taylor asked after Clarke and her shadow were gone.

"Brandon Moody," Cail answered. "He's the Chief's aide. Why?"

"I don't know. Bad vibe. He gives me the creeps."

Chris raised an eyebrow at Taylor's comment, but said nothing.

The next to come through the door of the meeting room was a media relations officer, Constable Gayle Reynolds. She explained when they were to make their entrance, where to sit, and what they were cleared to say. They waited until the press conference began then made their way down the hall to wait outside the door for their cue.

"They're making a big deal over this." Taylor sneered, more than a little nervous.

With a quick laugh, Cail brushed his lips over Taylor's temple. "It's good publicity for the department. Everyone loves you."

Inside the conference room, Chris found a spot to lean against the wall and watch the spectacle that was about to take place. The room was filled to bursting with reporters from every news media. Chief

Clarke took the podium and gave the updates on the investigation into the shooting of the limo. She talked about the arrests of DeCosta and his right hand man, Antonio Mallamo, and stated the investigation was ongoing and more arrests were pending. At the end of her briefing, she stood quietly waiting until she had the attention of every reporter in the room. "The remains of the driver, Jonathan Graham Williams, were recovered from the limousine. No other bodies were found in the wreckage." As that sunk in, Cail and Taylor walked behind the table set up at the front of the room and stood behind the two empty seats next to the podium. Gasps and shouts of surprise filled the room. Taylor couldn't help but think the Chief set it up like this for a reason. She just couldn't imagine what that reason was. Maybe she just enjoyed shocking the media, but it was a bad idea, in her opinion, to incite the media like this. And incite them it did. Pandemonium broke out with every reporter in the room shouting.

When the hairs on the back of Taylor's neck stood up, she turned to look behind her for the cause of her sudden unease. The Chief's aide was staring at her, but quickly averted his gaze when she turned. I know you, she thought again. It was irked her to not be able to place him.

Clarke raised a hand and waited until everyone calmed down. "I know you have a lot of questions and I'm going to try to address some of them, but this is an ongoing investigation. You know the deal with divulging certain details and information on an active case.

"That being said, I can tell you that Constable Sinclair's publisher arranged for a second limo to be in the underpass leading from the airport towards the 427. It was that limo the news helicopters followed down the 427 to the 401. His intention was to give Constable Sinclair a break from the unrelenting media attention she experienced on her recent book tour."

Mumbling continued to fill the room even as the Chief of Police explained what happened. Before opening up the floor to questions, she said, "I expect all of you to show consideration and professionalism with your questions. The moment one of you fails to do so, this conference ends." She stood in silence for a moment, her eyes wandering the room until she was sure she had made her point. "Okay, any questions?"

Once again the room filled with shouts. Chief Clarke pointed to Cheryl Starr from the National News Network to get the questions rolling.

"Taylor, where were you at the time of the attack on the limo and how did you find out you were supposedly killed?"

"We were on our way up to Balton for the weekend. We heard about the incident when we arrived there." They should be asking Cail, she thought. It was his case.

"Sarah Johnson's trial is scheduled to begin in three days. We know you're scheduled to testify. Will you be in court for the entire trial?"

Here we go. They just can't keep off that damn topic. With a long sigh, Taylor answered, "Yes, I'll be present for the entire trial."

"Cail, will you be there to support Taylor?"

"I can't take too much time off work, but I'll be there to support Tay as often as I can."

"There are still arrests pending in the case against the people who tried to kill you in that limo. Are you worried there will be another attempt on your life or that Taylor is in danger?"

"I don't believe there will be another attempt. The key players have been taken into custody. It's just a matter of tying up the loose ends now. As for Taylor, I'm always worried about her safety, but that comes with loving a cop."

"Ditto," Taylor whispered with a smirk.

"When are you going to ask her to marry you, Cail?"

Taylor's eyebrows rose while Cail laughed. "Before we die again."

At the end of the question period, Chief Clarke keyed a remote and a picture of Troy Rappaport filled the projection screen behind her. "The Toronto Police are requesting the help of the citizens of Toronto in locating the man you see on the screen behind me. Troy Evan Rappaport is wanted in connection with the limo homicide and in the Carlos Spanner case. Rappaport is five foot nine, one hundred and eighty pounds with brown hair and brown eyes. If you see this man, call nine-one-one or Crime Stoppers. Do not approach. He is considered armed and dangerous."

All in all, Taylor thought the press conference hadn't been that bad. She wasn't sure if the questions steered away from the abuse she suffered because of Chief Clarke's threat or if they were all so shocked that Cail and Taylor were alive that they forgot about it. Whatever the reason, she was relieved not to have sat through the nightmare of hearing some of the questions most reporters insisted on asking her. She was sure there would have been questions about what happened to her child, but, to her relief, they never came.

They grabbed some coffees and met Chris in a briefing room in the

Vice department. Handing her a coffee, Taylor whispered, "You okay?"

"Fine," Chris glared at her with a clenched jaw.

Taylor understood she was pissed that Taylor asked her that here, in a room full of cops. She also understood they weren't friends here. Chris was Detective Sergeant Cain and Taylor was Constable Sinclair. She took a seat next to Cail and sipped her coffee while they waited for the briefing to begin. "What do you know about the Chief's aide?" she whispered to Cail.

"Not much really. He's a bit of a geek, but he plays hockey in the force's league. He's been with the Chief since she took the top spot about five years ago."

A knock at the door had Taylor turning her head. She watched Detective MaryAnn Blake pop her head in and nod to Chris. Taylor didn't like Blake, but the feeling was mutual at least. Chris got up and left the room. When she came back in a few moments later, she was carrying a file folder. She sat down, opened it and began reading the papers it held as Taylor continued to watch her.

"Alright," Detective Ian Pierson commanded attention from the front of the room. "Some of you are just joining this investigation so I'll give a quick overview. Carlos Spanner, the nephew of Vincenzo DeCosta, was arrested last week and over a million dollars' worth of crystal meth was seized from the trunk of the vehicle he was driving. One of the shooters in the limo case, Kevin Laurey, informed us that Spanner's accomplice in stealing the meth from DeCosta was also the second shooter in the limo case. Troy Evan Rappaport is one of a select few individuals reputed to know how to access DeCosta's meth lab in the basement of his textile plant. We've executed a warrant at that location and were not able to access the lab. I want Rappaport. Word is he's gone to ground. He's hiding somewhere in the city and we haven't been able to locate him.

"Constable Sinclair, I understand you may know where he's hiding out."

Getting to her feet, Taylor replied, "There are a few locations I know of that we can check." Nodding toward the white screen displaying an image from Google Earth, Taylor asked, "May I?"

"Go right ahead," Pierson said, moving off to the side.

Taylor showed them four locations, three of which it was just a matter of giving the address. The other, she explained, she'd have to show them.

Pierson took the front of the room again as Taylor returned to her seat. "We'll break into two teams. My team will take the first two locations. Detective Sergeant Cain's team will take the other two with Sinclair. You find him," he gave Chris a stern look. "I want to know asap."

Chris was still studying whatever was in the file folder. "You will," she said without looking up. She'd sent Detective Blake to every hospital, clinic and doctor's office in the city looking for medical records from Taylor's pregnancy. Blake found a small clinic run by a Dr. Carla Sanchez. Taylor's file was under her first name only and gave her birth date simply as the month and year, which made sense because, up until Chris was able to obtain Taylor's IDs, Taylor hadn't known the exact day of her birth. Taylor's last visit to Sanchez had been just days before she left on the book tour. She'had blood work to test for communicable diseases and had been given an injection of Depo-Provera, a birth control shot that lasts up to three months. As Chris read through the file, she found Taylor was seeing Sanchez every three months like clockwork for the injection and every six months for blood work. Flipping to the last page in the folder, Chris's eyes hardened. Dr. Sanchez's notes from Taylor's first visit when she was thirteen years old described a frightened child flat out begging to be sterilized. The date on the report was at the tail end of the four month period Taylor had been absent from school when she was thirteen. Chris snapped the folder closed and stormed out the door.

"Where the hell is she going?" Cail wondered out loud. Taylor had a feeling it had something to do with the Sarah Johnson case. She tried to put it out of her mind as Pierson continued.

"I don't think I have to remind you that Rappaport is armed and extremely dangerous. Vests are mandatory. I want everyone going home to their families safe and sound tonight." Once he made his point, his gaze moved to Cail. "Worthington, I thought Cain was bringing in three officers to assist."

"The third's off sick." He didn't offer any more of an explanation. It wasn't anyone's business but Kate's.

"Alright," Pierson nodded. "My team, get ready to head out. We'll meet in the garage in fifteen."

Chris came back in without the folder, looking pale, just as Pierson was heading out. Taylor wanted to ask if she was okay, but she knew she'd just face another steaming glare. Taking command, Chris studied the two locations they'd been assigned. "We'll start with the Queen Street Station."

"Lower Queen Street Station," Taylor corrected. When Chris looked at her with a confused expression, Taylor elaborated. "It's below the Queen Street Station. It was supposed to be an underground street car station, but it was never completed. They built the street car line on Bloor instead."

"How do you know all this?" Chris asked, dumbfounded. She had no idea there was a station below the Queen Street Station. When Taylor just looked at her, Chris clued in that it had probably been one of the places Taylor lived when she was on the streets. "Shit, never mind." She shook her head wondering what the hell was wrong with her. Keep your mind in the game, she told herself. "Are you getting a sense of where he might be?"

"No," Taylor answered immediately and Chris knew that it was her way of saying she wouldn't use her ESP.

"What's the other location we're assigned?" Cail asked.

"It's the abandoned warehouse near the docks," Taylor answered.

"Okay." Chris straightened. "We start with the Lower Queen Station." She hated going into subway stations, hated being underground. It always made her feel claustrophobic, like the walls would cave in and bury them alive.

"Your vest," Taylor said, noticing Chris wasn't wearing her police issue Kevlar vest.

Chris narrowed her eyes at Taylor. "Like that would stop a bullet from an automatic assault rifle." Again, she got a dead stare from Taylor. "It's in the car. Relax for Christ's sake." As they walked out of the briefing room door, Chris mumbled something about who's in charge. At the elevator she punched the down button and stared at the doors until they opened. Once inside, Taylor reached over and pressed 'G' for the garage before Chris could punch that, too.

"Are you going to be this pleasant all night?" Taylor asked once the doors closed.

Chris ignored the question. She was too busy thinking about going into an underground station that had subway trains running above it. Really, what was to stop the train from coming through the roof? "Why's an asshole like Troy Rappaport playing around in subway tunnels? Did he live on the streets at some point?"

"Not that I know of," Taylor answered as the doors opened to the garage.

"How does he know about this station under a station?" They walked to Chris's car where she popped the trunk and grabbed her vest.

"He's a drug dealer," Taylor said. "Sometimes people owe him money and when they don't pay ... well ... they need a place ... where no one will hear the screaming." She stumbled upon just that kind of screaming when she'd been looking for a safe place to sleep. It was one of the few hiding places the Johnsons never found, but once she realized Rappaport was using it, she'd never gone back. Taylor suspected Rappaport found it by following her at one time or another.

"Jesus. Sounds like a great guy." She unlocked the doors, putting her vest on before she got behind the wheel. Cail rode shotgun while Taylor climbed in the back.

It only took a few minutes to drive to Queen and Yonge, but Chris had to park over a block away. When they started walking toward the subway station, Chris hung back a bit and let Taylor lead. She watched her scanning every direction and using the reflection in store windows to check behind her. When there was a doorway or an alley between buildings, Taylor moved to the outer edge of the sidewalk, approaching them with caution. She checked every vehicle parked along the curb and if one was occupied, she moved closer to the buildings as she approached. Sarah Johnson had been in jail for months, yet Taylor continued to be extremely wary of her surroundings. Chris figured it was so ingrained in her by this point that she'd probably always be hyper-aware of her surroundings on the streets of Toronto.

Taylor took them down below the tracks to a pedestrian underpass. Halfway across, she stopped at a locked door. She noted a young guy leaning against the wall in baggy jeans and a brown hoody typing away on his Blackberry. "He could be a lookout," Taylor said as she nodded in the kid's direction.

"I was thinking the same thing," Chris said just as the kid looked up from this phone. He pushed off the wall and headed up the stairs on the opposite side from where they entered the underpass.

Taking two thin picks out of her coat pocket, Taylor said to Chris, "You might want to look somewhere else for a minute."

Chris glared at her then rolled her eyes. She eyed Cail, who shrugged and the two of them watched Taylor crouch down and expertly unlock the door in seconds. "You ever think you might be in the wrong business?"

Taylor let out a short laugh as she removed her flashlight from her duty belt. "You know me well enough to know I couldn't steal.

Besides, you're the one who wanted me to be a cop." Taylor quietly opened the door and held it open for Chris and Cail. When they were all in, she closed the door quietly behind her and relocked it. Cail had his flashlight aimed down the stairs and they made their way to a shallow platform where Taylor described the room they were going down the tunnel to check.

"God, this is freaky." Chris felt the darkness all around her as a chill ran up her spine.

"Shhh," Taylor said, shining her light in her face as she pressed a finger to her lips. She nodded toward the tunnel and led the way.

Every few minutes a train rumbled along the tracks somewhere above them. The cinder block walls were reinforced with large steel I beams. Above them, pipes and vents ran in every direction. Apparently, they'd never gotten around to adding the tracks because the floor was fairly even cement.

They walked for about ten minutes then Taylor stopped, shining her light on herself again. She nodded toward the wall on the right with a grey metal door. Drawing her gun, she took one side of the opening as Cail took the other.

Chapter 15

Cail reached for the door knob and waited for Chris's go ahead. At her nod, he threw the door open and followed Chris through the door with Taylor right behind him. They didn't need their flashlights as a single bulb hung from the ceiling. The eight by ten foot utility room featured an old, disgusting mattress on the floor and take out containers and garbage spread all over the place. It smelled of old urine and Chris was pretty sure something was dead somewhere under all the garbage.

Rappaport wasn't here, but someone was. The girl was around seventeen, Taylor figured, with long, curly red hair and a slim build. She scrunched up in the corner of the mattress, her knees pulled in, arms wrapped around her legs, and bundled up in a puffy, white down-filled jacket and jeans that were dirty and torn in a couple of places. She whimpered as Taylor crouched down beside her.

Chris had been about to do the same thing, but stood back and observed when Taylor went to her. Before Taylor could say anything the girl said, "You're Taylor Sinclair." She was trembling, Taylor noticed, but her voice was strong.

"Yeah. What's your name?" Taylor asked softly. She could see a bruise forming under the girl's right eye and brushed her fingers over her cheek to move a few stray hairs from her face.

"Rebecca Knightley. I saw you on the news. You were in that limo."

"We were in *a* limo, just not the one you saw on the news," Taylor explained.

"Troy said 'give Sinclair a message for me'. I didn't know he was talking about you. He knew you were coming. The guy that followed me onto the train came in and told him the cops were at the door on the underpass. He said 'Sinclair's on the underpass'."

"What was the message, Rebecca?"

"He said to tell you he hasn't forgotten about your unfinished business. Something like that."

A chill ran down Taylor's back as she remembered Rappaport's fists raining down on her as she held on to her jeans for dear life. "How long ago was that?"

"About ten or fifteen minutes. I'm not sure."

"Do you know his full name, Rebecca?"

Nodding, Rebecca stared at Taylor with big eyes. "Rappaport, Troy Rappaport. My boyfriend owes him some money. It doesn't have anything to do with me. I don't even do drugs."

"I need to ask you some hard questions, Rebecca."

"He didn't get the chance," Rebecca said, shaking her head. "We just basically got here when that guy came back and said you were coming."

"Who? Who is the other guy?"

"He followed me into the College-Yonge Station then I feel a sharp pain in my side. He held a knife to my ribs and made me take the southbound train. I was supposed to go northbound to get home. I was scared. He was creeping me out and made me get off the train at the Queen-Yonge Station. Troy called him something … Spades … no, that's not it."

"Blades?" Taylor said more to herself than to Rebecca as she flashed back more than thirteen years.

"Yeah, that's what Troy called him – Blades. He made me walk down here. I kept falling and he would haul me up again. I recognized Troy when we got to this room and I knew it had something to do with drugs. I don't do drugs. I'm not sure that Mick does, but Troy said Mick owed him money for meth and he was going to take it out on me to teach him a lesson. I was so scared."

"Can you show me where he held the knife on you, Rebecca?" Taylor watched as Rebecca pushed her finger into the side of her jacket. She examined the puffy, white jacket and couldn't see so much as a nick.

Chris covered her mouth and nose with her sleeve. How could anyone stand the stench down here? Cail made it worse, stirring it up by sifting through all of the garbage wearing black nitrile gloves. It was times like this that she was grateful as hell she had rank. She'd just be adding to the stench by booting all over the place if she had to dig through that shit.

Something wasn't playing right for Taylor in Rebecca's story, something more than the fact she knew Blades wouldn't have lured a young girl down here. "What's Mick's full name?"

Rebecca looked at her with fear in her eyes. "Is he going to be in trouble? I don't even think he does drugs. Maybe that's naive of me, but wouldn't I know if he was doing something like meth?"

"He's not going to be in trouble, Rebecca. I need his name and address to make sure he's safe."

"Oh, God. They could have him, too. I didn't think of that." Tears pooled in her sea green eyes. "Why didn't I think of that?"

"It's okay," Taylor soothed. "He's probably fine, but I need to check."

"Michael O'Hara. He lives on Carlton Street near Yonge. I can't remember the street address."

"When was the last time you saw Mick?"

"When I left his apartment around eight thirty."

"So Blades followed you onto the train at the College Station?"

"Yeah. He must have followed me from Mick's. Can you call and check on him? There's no cell signal down here. I tried to text Mick."

"Let's get the hell out of here," Chris suggested through her sleeve, still covering her nose. "We can call when we get to street level."

"Got something," Cail called out from the other side of the small room. Standing, he held up an iPhone encased in black then tried to get into it. "Password protected."

"We'll get Brice to work on it. Bag and tag, Worthington. Great job."

"Do you think you can walk out of here?" Taylor asked Rebecca.

"Yeah. I think it's just scrapes and bruises," Rebecca said as she looked down at her torn and dirty jeans.

Taylor helped her to her feet and wrapped her arm around her until she was confident Rebecca was steady.

"Is there a quicker way out of here?" Chris hoped.

"The quickest way is the way we came. We could go in the other direction, but it's about a thirty minute walk."

Chris gave Rebecca the once over. Her injuries seemed to be limited to scrapes and bruises, but they'd get her checked out just to be safe.

Cail found himself wondering if Taylor stayed down here. It was one hell of a revelation to think about. He'd read her book, knew that she lived under horrid conditions for most of her life, but this really made it hit home. The raunchy smell was making his eyes water. His gaze met Taylor's and he saw she knew exactly what he was thinking. "Tay—"

"Don't," she cut him off before turning to stomp out of the room. She was glad for the darkness so they couldn't see the shame in her face.

When they got back up to street level, Chris called Detective Pierson and gave him an update. Pierson's team completed the search of their first location with no signs of Rappaport. They turned Rebecca over to a patrol unit with instructions to take her to the emergency department at Toronto General while they went to check on Michael O'Hara. The mood in the car was very somber.

"Impressions?" Chris asked as she eyed Taylor in the rear-view mirror.

"Her story isn't adding up. She said she felt a sharp pain in her side when Blades held the knife to her ribs, yet she's wearing that big, puffy jacket and there are no cuts in it. I don't get why Troy would have left her there with her phone. Why didn't she try to get out? She just waited in there for us. The other thing that's bothering me is her reaction when Cail found that phone. She was more scared by that than she was when she realized her boyfriend might be in danger."

Chris had a smirk on her face. God, she was going to love working with Taylor.

"One more thing," Taylor said. "Blades would never lure a young girl to the likes of Troy Rappaport."

"How do you know that?"

Because he found me on the floor of an abandoned apartment and saved my life ... and my son's, Taylor thought. "Because I know. I know Blades." Taylor turned to stare out the window and push back the tears.

O'Hara wasn't in his apartment and he wasn't answering his phone. A neighbour told Chris she saw Mick leaving with Rebecca at around eight thirty pm. Chris showed her a picture of Rappaport and asked if she saw him around Mick's apartment. She stated that she didn't recognize the man in the photo. They stopped by the emergency room where Chris questioned Rebecca again. She revised her story to say Mick walked her as far as the subway station. Chris's instincts told her Rebecca was lying. Taylor was right. Something wasn't adding up.

Their next stop was the warehouse on the shores of Lake Ontario. Chris pulled her car up in front of the building, noting there were no lights on inside. They got out of the car and Chris headed for the front door.

"I usually come and go from the roof," Taylor said, gesturing towards the side of the building.

Chris raised an eyebrow. "Usually?"

Should have just picked the lock, Taylor thought. It would have saved her the embarrassment of having to explain. "I ... slept here. Before," she said awkwardly, avoiding Chris's and Cail's eyes by staring down at her feet, shifting back and forth.

Chris stared at her dumbfounded for a moment then shrugged. "Okay, lead the way."

Taylor took them around to the west side of the building then dragged a wooden palette and propped it up beneath the ladder attached to the side of the building that began about six feet off the ground. They made quick work of climbing the ladder and crossed the roof to a black wooden door. Taylor pulled her flashlight from her duty belt and opened the door, leading the way down a metal staircase to the second floor level.

"Any lights in here?" Chris asked. It was going to be a pain in the ass searching the place with just their flashlights.

Taylor wasn't sure if the lights even worked. She never used them when she stayed there because she didn't want to draw attention to the fact she was there. She found the light switches on the wall and, surprisingly, the overhead fluorescent lights buzzed, crackled and then flickered on.

The last time Taylor had been inside this building was in the spring, before she drove up to Balton on a mission to stop Ralph Morse from getting to Gray. It wasn't until she stood there, scanning around the space, that she realized she wanted a home just like this. It was mostly open space with scarred wood plank floors, massive windows, and exposed brick. For reasons she couldn't explain, she felt comforted here, felt a warmth and a sense of belonging.

Chris was surprised at how tidy the place appeared to be considering it was used by the homeless as a place to crash. Towards the back of the space were several doors that appeared to be offices. The first two rooms were empty. The third had to be where Taylor had been sleeping. There were four or five blankets stacked on the floor that created a makeshift bed. An old, battered, metal desk stood below the window with a rickety wooden chair pushed into it. The only other object in the room was a wooden crate turned on its side with the remnants of a candle sitting on top.

This room was also tidy, with no garbage littering the floor and no foul odours lingering in the air. Chris realized she'd been too quick to assume that a bunch of homeless people crashed here. It was only Taylor who'd been using this place. "Is there running water in here?" she asked, and then added, "Heat?"

"No." Taylor shook her head. "There's no one here, but we should check downstairs anyway."

The main floor wasn't nearly as tidy as the second floor. It was very dusty and bits and pieces of construction materials scattered around the entire open area as if the job had been abandoned part way into gutting it. Near the front entrance, Chris opened a door that revealed a cinderblock wall. Turning to Taylor, she asked, "Is there a basement?"

"No, I don't think so."

If there was, Chris thought, someone had taken care to block off access to it. "What did Rappaport use this place for?"

Taylor shrugged. "Nothing really. I think he just used it for a place he could go to kind of get away from everything and clear his mind. He'd sit up on the roof, looking out over the lake." It was the same thing Taylor had first used it for.

They made their way back to Headquarters to meet in the briefing room. Pierson led the debriefing then asked Taylor, "Is there anywhere else you can think of that he might go?"

"No, I don't think so. I mean he could go anywhere. He knows enough people in the city that he could be staying anywhere."

"Why don't we call it a night and we'll regroup tomorrow at eighteen hundred hours," Chris suggested. That would give her plenty of time to convince Taylor to use her ESP to find this asshole and throw him in a cage. She also wanted to know what Taylor's unfinished business with Rappaport was all about.

"Alright, we meet back here at eighteen hundred hours," Pierson confirmed.

* * *

Chris climbed into bed and pulled Kate's pillow to her face. The knock at the door startled her.

"Chris?"

Oh God. What the hell did Taylor want? She took a deep breath and hoped she didn't sound over emotional. "Yeah?"

"I can't find my Advil. Have you got any?"

She took one more deep breath, inhaling Kate's intoxicating scent and slipped out of bed. "Yeah, just as sec." In her en suite, she found a bottle of Advil and went to her bedroom door. Opening it, she handed Taylor the bottle. "Do you need anything else?"

"Nah, I'm good." With a frown, she added, "Are you okay?"

"Yeah, fine."

Taylor knew she wasn't, but she also knew Chris wasn't about to open up to her about it. "Okay. Well … if you need anything …"

"I'm fine, Taylor. I'll see you in the morning." Chris closed the door, anxious to get rid of Taylor before her emotions took over again.

Chapter 16

In the dream, Taylor awoke in a room completely devoid of colour. Everything was white from the bedspread, the carpet, the walls, the furniture to the silk negligee she was wearing.

Taylor sat up in bed. Weird, she thought, wondering where that dream came from. She laid back down, listening to the rhythm of Cail's breathing for a while as she watched him sleep. Then, leaving a soft kiss on his lips, she slid quietly out of bed and donned a pair of sweat pants and a tank top. She headed for the living room, armed with a sketch pad and her pencils and was surprised to find Chris on the sofa, feet up on the coffee table, in the dim light from a small table lamp. "Hey," Taylor whispered. "Can't sleep?"

Swiping her arm over her face, Chris tried to hide her tears. "No."

The sketch pad and pencils were laid carefully on the coffee table before Taylor took a seat next to Chris facing the fireplace. Above it hung the drawings Taylor gave to Chris when she and Cail graduated from the Police Academy. In the corner, a flat screen TV was tuned to NNN with the sound muted. They were running a replay of last night's press conference at Police Headquarters. "Want to talk about it?" Taylor asked.

"There's nothing to talk about. It's done. She won't talk to me. Probably serves me right."

"She loves you, Chris, just as much as you love her. Maybe she just needs a little time to process everything." Taylor took a closer look at Chris. She looked pale, her eyes already beginning to show dark circles beneath them.

On the silent TV, Chris watched as an image of Taylor and Cail embracing filled the screen. Again, Chris found herself wondering how someone who'd been through so much worse than she had could end up in such a loving relationship. "How did you go from not being able to stand anyone touching you to that?" she asked, nodding towards the screen.

Taylor turned back to Chris with a rosy blush in her cheeks then turned her eyes to gaze at the fireplace. "He touches me and everything else fades away." A warm smile washed over her face as her thoughts turned to Cail. "He makes me forget."

Chris found herself on the verge of tears again. She had to ask, didn't she? She couldn't just keep her mouth shut, leave it alone. No, and now Taylor was pulling out her emotions again with that mixture of honesty and innocence that the whole world had fallen in love with.

Taylor turned to Chris again and asked, "Does Kate make you forget?"

Chris released a quick laugh. "I've never really associated what my father did to me with sex. It's not like my partners have a penis." Chris laughed again when, even in the dim light, she saw Taylor's face turn deep red. "Oh shit, I forgot how much fun it is to make you blush."

Taylor smiled at hearing Chris's laugh, at seeing the Chris she remembered, but that wasn't where Taylor meant to take the conversation, so she tried to steer it back on course. "But, it's different with Kate, isn't it? Compared to your past relationships, I mean." Until Cail, Taylor had never had consensual sex, but she was sure no one else could touch her and evoke the intensity of sensations and emotions that his touch generated in her. She watched the grin disappear from Chris's face and was sure she stepped where Chris had no intention of going.

That ache that had been so intense while Chris lay in bed, hugging Kate's pillow, slowly seeped back into her cells as she was suddenly struck by the realization that what made everything with Kate so much more intense was love. That single emotion she avoided like the plague in the past had crept up on her. She hadn't even realized how much she loved Kate until Kate asked her to look at her and tell her she didn't. But, how could Taylor know that? How could someone who's only ever had one relationship understand the difference between casual sex and sex with someone you love deeply? "How could you possibly know that?" she blurted out then immediately cursed herself for saying it out loud.

Now that was somewhere Taylor had no intention of going, but she'd opened the can of worms. While she tried to think of how to answer, Chris said, "I'm sorry. I didn't mean–"

"No, it's okay," Taylor cut in. "I asked the question. I guess I just know that no one else could make me feel the way he does. I see the way you are when you're with Kate and I know you share that something special, like what Gray and Callaghan have, like there's no one else you're meant to be with."

"I'm a complete idiot." Chris sunk further into the sofa. "I've avoiding feeling for anyone most of my life because I know we hurt the people we love the most. I can't take back what I did to her or to you."

"If they hadn't happened, you wouldn't have progressed to where you are now. You wouldn't have had that breakthrough. Maybe those things had to happen so you could allow yourself to love and be loved."

"Have you been taking lessons from McIntyre or something?" With a weak smile, Chris turned to Taylor. "Are you going to draw something?" She nudged her head towards Taylor's sketch pad.

Taylor knew Chris was trying to change the subject. "Probably."

"So what, you woke up from a nightmare and now you're staying up the rest of the night?"

"Yeah," Taylor answered, although it hadn't really been a nightmare. It was nothing like the terrifying ones she usually had. Trauma nightmares, Lane liked to call them as they were all related to the traumas of her past. The dream she just had didn't have anything to do with her past. Since Chris seemed to be so open, Taylor asked, "Did you have a nightmare?" Taylor waited for Chris's reply and when none came, she assumed Chris wasn't going to answer. She picked up her sketch pad and opened it to a blank page then carefully selected a pencil from her set of sixteen graphite pencils. Gone were the days when she was satisfied with a regular 2H.

"No," Chris stated.

Taylor almost forgot what the question was. She spared a glance at Chris, noticing she looked a little pissed off.

"I never went to sleep."

"Oh." That had Taylor wondering if she didn't go to sleep because she was worried about having a nightmare or if she just couldn't sleep.

"How do you do it? You sleep like two or three hours a night, if that, and function like you had a good eight hours."

"I guess it's just what I'm used to."

"How do you wake yourself up at the start of a nightmare?" Chris had been staring off into space, but she turned her gaze to Taylor who sat cross legged with her sketch pad in her lap.

"I don't know. I just do … most of the time, anyway." When Chris continued to stare at her, she explained, "When I started having nightmares, it was dangerous. You don't want to draw attention to yourself in the middle of the night on the streets. I just started waking up at the start of them."

"Someone got to you. When you were screaming from a nightmare."

Taylor narrowed her eyes. "Where's this going?" The last thing she needed was Chris going off on another investigation into her past.

"Nowhere, I'm just trying to figure it out." Raking her fingers through her hair, Chris continued, "It's got to be your subconscious mind. The survival instinct, right? Nightmares equal danger, therefore your subconscious mind tells you to wake the fuck up."

"I don't think my subconscious mind says it quite that way, but yeah, it sounds logical."

Chris laughed. In so many ways, Taylor was still so innocent. Swearing was an example of that innocence. She couldn't do it, not even in her subconscious mind.

"Are you worried you'll have a nightmare if you go to sleep?" Taylor risked pissing Chris off even more.

"No, I just couldn't sleep." She'd gotten so used to having Kate beside her over the last few months. She laid there breathing in Kate's scent from her pillow, staring at the empty space beside her and the ache for her was so intense she had to get up.

"You're missing Kate," Taylor stated, knowing what it felt like missing Cail when she was away on the book tour. She began flipping through the pages of her sketch pad, stopped at a drawing of Chris and Kate together and ripped it from the pad. She'd drawn them sharing one of those looks that made their love for each other unmistakable, caught in the expression of their eyes and the slight smirks on their faces, as if they shared an amusing secret. "Maybe if you remember the better times, you'll be able to sleep." She handed the drawing to Chris. "She loves you. Don't give up on her yet."

Eyes burning, Chris studied the drawing. Saying nothing, she got up, leaned over to press a kiss to Taylor's brow then continued down the hall to her room.

* * *

Gray arrived at Chris's with half an hour to spare before they needed to leave for the Palmerton Penitentiary. Chris made her a tea and they sat in the living room waiting for Taylor to finish getting ready.

"Is she okay?" Gray asked.

"You know Taylor, she won't complain." Chris smiled then rose to open the door when she saw Lane's car pull into the driveway. Lane joined Gray in the living room as Chris went to the kitchen to make her a cup of coffee. She set the mug in front of Lane then sat next to her on the sofa. "It's going to be a hard day for her," Chris said quietly, her eyes glancing down the hallway towards the bedrooms.

"Yes," Lane answered, but she was more concerned with the hard day Chris had the day before at the moment. "Are you feeling any better today?"

"I don't know how to fix it if she won't talk to me."

Lane reached out and took Chris's hand, giving it a little squeeze of encouragement. "Give her a little time to sort out her feelings. Being in love is a new experience for her, too."

"I don't want to give her a little time. I need to talk to her, sort this out sooner rather than later." Chris sighed then turned towards the hallway as she heard Taylor's heels clicking on the hardwood floor.

Taylor's hair was swept up in a French twist. She wore a form fitting black sweater dress under a layer of black lace. Black heels and stockings finished off the look. She'd put some concealer under her eyes, added a little blush and some lip colour. A long black leather coat hung over her arm.

"Wow, you look ... hot." Chris couldn't take her eyes off her.

Taylor frowned. "That's not exactly the look I was going for."

"You look beautiful – classy and elegant." Gray went to her and kissed her cheek.

"How's Gracie today?"

Gray's hand absently circled her belly. "I think she's exhausted. Patrick has been singing non-stop." With brows drawn together, she added, "Thinks it's funny."

"Sorry." Taylor chuckled. "I shouldn't have shown him."

"Yeah, you should have left that one for the adults. I'd like to kick his bladder."

Chris laughed. "That'd teach him."

"I guess we should head out," Taylor said with a glance at the clock.

"You okay?" Gray asked her quietly.

With a quick nod, Taylor replied, "Yeah, just a bit nervous."

It was cold, damp and overcast as they started out for Palmerton. The closer they got to the penitentiary, the more Taylor's fingers drummed away on her thigh, as her leg bounced up and down on the ball of her foot. Gray's hand covered hers and she stopped tapping. "I can't help it."

"Take a few calming breaths."

Taylor closed her eyes and took five deep, cleansing breaths. Just as she opened her eyes, the penitentiary came into view. The dismal grey of the building matched the dark, ominous clouds in the sky. It was surrounded by trees, stripped of their leaves. The high, gusty winds made the denuded branches appear to be waving in a dreary greeting.

Once they cleared through several security checks, they stood in an observation room, staring at Darryl Johnson through the glass. His short brown hair was unruly and his five o'clock shadow left him looking unkempt, in stark contrast to his appearance on the NNN special. He was average in height, a few inches shorter than Taylor, but Taylor knew he was deceptively strong. His wrists sported handcuffs which were attached to a steel ring on the table. Taylor prepared herself for this day, she knew what she wanted to say, what she wanted to accomplish.

"I'll be right here, watching," Lane told her. "If you need a break or need to talk at any point, just go to the door and we'll take you out."

"Okay." Taylor closed her eyes and did some more deep breathing. "Okay."

When she walked into the room, Darryl was stunned. "You're the last person I expected to see."

Taylor took the seat across from him, not sure if it was the stale air inside the room or her nerves that had her chest tightening. Everything she prepared to say flew out of her head. They sat staring at each other for a moment before she found her voice. "You lied about the baby. Why?"

His big brown eyes glossed over as he answered. "The truth was too brutal, too sickening."

"Why tell them at all?"

"I wanted them to know what she did to you."

"What you both did to me. You're as responsible as she is." The pain in his expression caught Taylor off guard. "You tried to kill your own child."

"What kind of life would it have had?"

Taylor was surprised by how calm she felt now, by how calm their words to each other were.

"She changed," Darryl's eyes darted all over the room; everywhere except for Taylor. "Sarah changed after that. For a while, we thought you were dead, but then you turned up at school again. It was different. She made me bring you to her and tie you up then she sent me away. What did she do to you? What was she afraid of me seeing?"

Taylor ignored his questions, but took a moment to try to shove the memories away. "I want to know about Greg. Was he a drug dealer?"

"Yeah. Crack mostly but he was getting into meth at the end."

"Did he cook his own meth?"

"Sometimes. Sarah wouldn't let him do it at home, so it depended on if he could find a place."

All the years that Sarah accused Taylor's mother of killing her husband and deep down Taylor had known it wasn't true. "Greg was cooking the meth. My mother didn't kill your brother. He killed my mother."

The pained expression on Darryl's face deepened. "I know," he whispered, tears pooling in his eyes again.

"Is that why you pled guilty?"

"Partly."

"Why did you try to kill me?"

"It was Sarah. She wanted me to kill you. She wanted you to die a painful death. She thought if I killed you, she would get out of jail."

"Yet you waited until you were sure you'd been identified as her accomplice. You tried to kill me to keep yourself out of jail. Why didn't you finish it?"

"I couldn't. Your eyes ... Greg's eyes were staring up at me. I couldn't do it."

"And all this time I thought you couldn't look me in the eye because you're a coward. They didn't stop you from raping me all those times, did they? Knowing I was your brother's daughter, knowing I was your niece, didn't stop you from raping me."

"I was strung out on drugs back then, Taylor. I know it's no excuse, but I believed all the crap she was telling me. I was so wasted most of the time that I didn't know what the hell I was doing. I just went along with it." He bent over and wiped his shackled hands over his face. "Did you come here for an apology? Is that what you want?" Glancing up at her, he said, "I'm sorry. I'm sorry for everything I did to you."

Taylor didn't want his apology. "All that stuff you wrote on your apartment wall–"

"No," Darryl cut in. "Sarah wrote all of that. You can do a handwriting analysis. It's her writing."

"You think blaming everything on her makes you any better than she is? You sick bastard. You deserve to rot in prison for the rest of your life. You deserve to be treated the way they treat child molesters in prison." It pleased her when she saw the fear in his eyes. She got up, walked to the door and waited for it to open.

Behind her, Darryl Johnson repeated, "I'm sorry," over and over.

Turning back to him, Taylor asked, "Did you love your brother?"

"Of course," he answered. "He was my big brother. I idolized him."

"What would he think about the way you treated his daughter?" She turned to the door just as it opened, listening to him shouting behind her.

"What was she afraid for me to see, Taylor? What didn't she want me to see?" Taylor didn't look back.

She took two steps down the hallway to be sure she was out of Darryl's sight and then leaned into the wall. The lights seemed too bright, so she closed her eyes just for a moment to steady herself. Was that the lights buzzing or her ears? Opening her eyes again, she looked straight into Lane's big brown eyes. Right behind her stood Gray and Chris. She hadn't even heard their footsteps.

"You're shaking." Lane laid a steadying hand on Taylor's arm.

"I had it all planned out, what I wanted to say. As soon as I stepped into that room, I forgot. I can't do that with her." Darryl didn't really matter as he'd already pled guilty. She wanted to make sure he knew she held him just as responsible as Sarah. But, Sarah was a different matter altogether. If she didn't play it just right, she had a lot to lose.

"You did fine, Taylor. You came across very calm and confident. Why don't we find you a seat?" Lane put her arm around Taylor's waist and began to lead her down the hall. Gray fell into Taylor's other side while Chris followed along behind.

"I'm fine, really. A little fresh air and I'll be good as new." There just didn't seem to be enough air inside this wretched building. She felt like she could only get half a breath into her lungs. On top of everything else that concerned Taylor about coming face to face with Sarah, she now worried that she'd get into a room with her and completely forget everything she needed to say.

They drove back into downtown Toronto to the jail where Sarah Johnson was awaiting her trial. The setup was surprisingly similar to the penitentiary. Taylor looked through the glass of the observation room where Sarah Johnson was handcuffed to a chain around her waist and her ankles were cuffed to a D-ring on the floor. Her sandy blonde hair fell in loose curls to just above her shoulders. She looked pale, as if she'd been in jail for years. The way the room was setup, Taylor would be facing the observation room. She'd hoped it would be the other way around, but she'd have to make do.

Taylor turned to Chris before she left the observation room. "I might say some things in there that will offend you. I just want you to know up front that I'm only doing it to push her buttons."

Chris grinned. "If it pisses her off, you can say things that offend me all day long."

Chapter 17

Sarah shot to her feet as soon as Taylor stepped into the room, her beady brown eyes narrowed, boring into Taylor's, full of hate. "What the hell do you want, slut?"

Taylor smiled. "Sit down, Sarah." She knew her tone came across as authoritative and she gave a silent nod to her training at the Academy. Sarah held her ground for a moment then sunk back into her chair. Taylor elegantly took the seat across from her and took a minute to primp. Her eyes then went to Sarah and studied her from head to waist. "I have to say, you look exceptional in bracelets. They really suit you." She grinned.

"Fuck you! What the hell do you want?"

"I was in the neighbourhood and thought I'd stop by to see how you're doing," Taylor answered with a sarcastic bite.

"You're nothing but a slut like your crack whore mother."

"You don't want to talk about my mother, Sarah. She was a hell of a lot better than you." She paused for effect. "Your husband knew that."

Sarah shot out of her seat again. "Fuck you, you little bitch."

Taylor didn't flinch, but that familiar stab of fear jolted through her. She refused to let Sarah see it and gave her a smile instead. This wasn't going as Taylor planned. She'd have to tone it down to keep Sarah from getting too agitated. "Why sexually molest me? Why didn't you just kill me?"

"Are you that stupid, slut? Don't you understand? You had to pay for the sins of your mother, *with* the sins of your mother. When your file was dropped on my desk and I saw your name and your photograph ..." Sarah dropped her head and laughed. "It was fate. All those years I blamed Greg's drug abuse for me not being able to get pregnant and when I saw your file, I realized that it wasn't him at all. It must have been me. Your mother didn't have any right to bear his child. You had to pay for her sins."

"You took your anger and frustration at not being able to conceive a child out on me. After you calmed down from your rage at seeing me pregnant, you realized it was your opportunity to have the baby you've always wanted. I bet you went back, didn't you?" For the first time, Taylor saw pain in Sarah's eyes. "I bet you freaked when I wasn't there." Taylor allowed herself a quick laugh at the irony. "You totally screwed up your chance at my child by losing your head." The look of pain in Sarah's eyes quickly faded. Her face reddened and the veins in her neck swelled out, pulsing wildly.

"Or maybe I have it all wrong," Taylor continued. "Maybe it wasn't really anything to do with me or my mother. Maybe you just like molesting little girls. Is that why your husband spent so much time in my mother's bed?"

"Fuck you. I don't have to put up with this shit," she yelled. "I don't have to listen to your bullshit, slut."

"It's alright. I know the answer. It's not men who turn you on. I bet you fit right in here, Sarah. I bet there are a few girls in here who want you for their bitch. Have they got to you yet, Sarah?" She leaned in and whispered, "Have they come to you in the night and raped you yet?"

"Shut the fuck up. You don't know what you're talking about."

Taylor leaned in closer, whispering again, "All those things you did to me were probably things you like, weren't they, Sarah? Would you like me to make up a list and give it to your girlfriends in here? I'm sure they'd be more than happy to oblige." Taylor sat up straight again with a grin.

"Fuck you."

"You'd like that, wouldn't you? Even if I was gay, I'd find you repulsive. Your own husband couldn't even stand you in bed. Were you thinking of little girls when he had sex with you, Sarah?"

Sarah was on her feet, yanking at her chains. "I'm going to fucking kill you, slut. You're nothing but a crack whore's bastard slut. Say it, slut. I'm the bitch of a fucking crack whore slut. Say it." Sarah stomped her feet, screaming, "SAY IT!"

Taylor had been expecting it. She didn't even blink. Her eyes stayed focused on Sarah's and she tried to tune her mind out. Even then, she wanted to curl up in a tight little ball and hide in the corner, but she'd be damned if she gave Sarah the satisfaction of seeing her flinch. "I was conceived out of pure love. I was conceived out of the coming together of two people who loved each other. Is that why you hate me so much, Sarah, because he loved my mother more than you; because he loved me more than you?"

"He didn't love you, slut. You were conceived from two fuck ups high on crack. Your mother was a whore, selling her body for crack."

"And what does that make your husband?" Taylor wondered out loud.

Yanking at her chains again, Sarah screamed, "Fuck you, slut. Fuck you."

"Temper, temper," Taylor smirked. She leaned in close again and whispered, "Fighting the restraints is only going to make it worse." It was a phrase Sarah Johnson said to her repeatedly over the years and it did exactly what Taylor thought it would do – it pissed Sarah off. So much for her strategy of keeping Sarah calm.

"I'm going to fucking kill you when I get my hands on you. Wait until I get out of here, slut. I'm coming for you."

"By the time you get out of prison, if you get out, you'll be too old and weak to do anything to me. But, don't worry." Taylor's lips curled up into a smirk. "I'll be thinking of you locked up in your little cell. When you get to the Federal Penitentiary, I'm sure there will be days when you won't be raped. Not many, but I'm sure there will be the odd day. You do know how much they hate child molesters in prison, don't you? You know what they do to pedophiles like you?"

"You think you're something, but you're still that snotty nosed, street rat, slut. You'll always be that."

"No," Taylor said. "I'm a hell of a lot more than that. My life is good ... no, my life is great. I've got everything I could possibly want. A man who loves me for who I am, friends and family who love me just as much, a career I love, wealth ... should I go on or am I boring you?"

"You don't deserve any of those things. I should have killed you when I had the chance."

"Hindsight's a bitch, isn't it?" Taylor started laughing. "I can't believe how stupid you are. So desperate for your fifteen minutes of fame and you end up in here. Then you dribble bits of information to the cops and get yourself in even deeper."

"It's was all Darryl."

Taylor leaned in close again so Sarah blocked her from being viewed from the observation room. She lowered her voice to a whisper. "Have you wondered why I didn't go on NNN with Cheryl Starr and spill my guts? Have you wondered why I didn't put anything about you in my book? I'm saving it all for the trial, Sarah. I have no problem getting up on the witness stand and telling them everything. Everything, Sarah. They show the news in prison, don't they? All your girlfriends will hear what you like to do to little girls."

Chris, Gray and Lane couldn't see Taylor for Sarah. "Can you hear what she's saying?" Chris asked. "I can't hear her."

Taylor continued in a low whisper, "After the trial, I'll talk to Starr and I'll tell her all of it. You think I won't do it. You think I'm too scared and humiliated, but I'm not. Actually, I'm looking forward to it. I can't wait to see your face when I get up there in the witness box and can't stop talking."

"Fucking bitch. You and I both know you're bullshitting." Sarah leaned over and was nearly spitting in Taylor's face. "You liked it. You *need* it. Or have you forgotten that you came to me to give you what you need. Who's going to do that for you while I'm locked up? Who? Can Caillen Worthington give you what you need, Taylor? I don't think so."

Taylor kept her voice low enough that only Sarah would hear her, although it was rich with fury. "I don't need anything, especially from you. And if I did, surely you're not stupid enough to believe you're the only one who possesses that particular skill."

"You're no better than that crack whore who spat you out from between her legs. You're a street rat and you always will be. Pretending to be some glamorous chick doesn't change what's underneath. You can't just turn off the kind of needs you have."

"Nothing's changed underneath. That's true. I'm still the same person. I'm just where I belong, finally. And you're exactly where you belong." She stood and stared down her nose at Sarah Johnson. "You're pathetic," Taylor said with a smile. She was about to walk away then leaned over and whispered in Sarah's ear, "See you in court. I'll be the one talking up a storm." Taylor straightened and walked to the door. Behind her Sarah Johnson was ripping at her shackles, yelling and screaming profanities. The door opened seconds later and Taylor stepped out, taking a few steps down the hall.

As soon as she heard the door secure behind her, the trembling began again. Gray, Chris and Lane rushed out of the observation room as Taylor braced her hand against the wall then slid down to a crouching position, hugging her legs. Her entire body was flooded with pins and needles. The walls spun around her, the floor ebbed and flowed, the darkness closing in on her.

The guard, who'd just secured the door, brought a chair to Taylor. Chris and Lane eased her into it and Taylor dropped her head between her knees.

"Breathe," Lane ordered, crouching next to her.

Taylor started her deep breathing, embarrassed half to death. She focused on the rhythm of Gray's hand circling her back to calm herself. Chris leaned against the wall, a little unstable herself. Taylor said she'd understand the second reason why she needed to see Darryl and Sarah, but Chris hadn't been able to hear half of what Taylor said to her. She was still trying to figure out what Taylor's goal had been. What was the point if you were going to feel like shit when you stepped out of the room?

"Okay, I'm okay," Taylor said as she slowly sat up. "Let's get out of here."

"Sit for a minute," Lane said. She made Taylor sit for another few minutes before getting to her feet.

"Were you trying to get a confession out of her?" Chris asked. "We can use some of what she said in there."

"No," Taylor answered. "I don't care what she said in there. It doesn't matter. A lot of what I said was lies. I have no memories of Gregory Johnson."

"What do you remember from when your mother was still alive?" Chris asked out of curiosity as they made their way through security.

Taylor didn't answer right away. There were too many ears around. She thought back to the night she told Cail some of her memories from back then. When she thought back to her early years, most of her memories were of Leila.

Once they got back to Chris's car and were under way, Taylor stared out the window and began, "I remember my mom sleeping most of the day while Leila was at school. I was always hungry and lonely. There was always this blue haze in the trailer." Even the thought of that smell of stale cigarette smoke and drugs in the air made her stomach queasy.

Feeling her cell phone vibrate in her coat pocket, Taylor pulled it out and read the text from Cail. "Cail's going to the apartment after work to get a few things. What time are we supposed to meet Pierson? I want to see if there are any more of my drawings missing."

"Eighteen hundred," Chris answered, which was the same time Cail finished his shift. "Why don't we swing by there right now?" She wanted to get a look herself. Someone obviously broke in to Cail's apartment to steal Taylor's drawings that were shown on the news and Chris wanted to know who.

"The place will probably be surrounded by reporters." Taylor didn't want to expose Gray to that, especially with her carrying precious cargo.

Chris met Taylor's gaze in the rear-view mirror. "You've got the code for the garage, right?"

"Yeah."

"So we'll just go in that way."

"They'll see us going in."

That gave Chris another thought. The building had been swarming with reporters since before Taylor got home from the tour. Someone had to have seen who went inside the building to break into Cail's place. "Maybe it's time I had a little chat with them. I'd like to get my hands on the buildings video surveillance tapes, too, if they have them."

"Okay," Taylor agreed. "But let's go up to the apartment first and see what's been taken."

When Cail's building came into view, Taylor was surprised to see just a handful of reporters out front. "They must know we're not staying here," she thought out loud. Chris pulled into the garage, turning at the bottom of the ramp. A police cruiser was parked near the door leading into the building. "That's Cail and Tara's squad."

"I thought you said he was coming here after work." Chris eyed Taylor in the rear-view mirror again.

"That's what he said in the text message." Something just didn't seem right and Taylor got that sick feeling in her gut. She didn't text him to let him know she was on the way up. She wanted to surprise him, to see what he was up to.

Outside the apartment door, Chris warned them not to touch anything until she had a chance to look around.

"We might be too late for that." Taylor frowned as she turned her key in the lock. To the left of the entranceway, a wall of windows opened up to a view of downtown Toronto and Lake Ontario beyond it. The dining room was just on the left, the kitchen on the right. Beyond the kitchen were the living room and the hallway leading to the master and two spare bedrooms. One of the bedrooms was set up as Taylor's art room.

Constable Tara MacNeil leaned against one of the dining room chairs as Taylor stepped into the apartment. The only downside to having Caillen Worthington as a partner, in Tara's opinion, was Taylor Sinclair. She was completely intimidated by Taylor. Aside from being drop dead gorgeous, six feet tall and ripped, Taylor was smart and more observant than any other police officer she'd met. At five foot seven, Tara wasn't exactly short and she worked hard at keeping herself in shape, but she never seemed to be able to get that extra ten pounds off. Staring up at Taylor as she entered the apartment, Tara felt self-conscious. "Hey, Taylor. I think Cail's in your ... um ... art room." Tara saw the anger rise in Taylor's face before she started across the room towards the bedrooms, her long, black leather coat flowing out behind her.

Taylor turned into the art room, seeing the Ident Officer dusting black powder over one of her sketch pads and turned her rage on Cail. "What the hell do you think you're doing?"

"Tay?" Cail's surprise at seeing her was evident. He looked like he'd just been caught with his hand in the cookie jar. "I didn't want to upset you with this. You've got enough on your plate."

The Ident Officer sensed trouble and decided it was a great time for a break. He scurried out of the room before he got caught in the storm. Taylor waited until he past her in the doorway, her rage mixing with the pain of betrayal. "You know how I feel about anyone seeing my drawings."

"That's why I'm standing here. He's only dusting the outside of the sketch pads, Tay. I wouldn't let anyone look inside them."

Taylor stepped into the room, examining the black dust all over her art desk, the shelving units and all of the various sizes of sketch pads on the desk and on the shelves. The pads that were on the shelves had been stacked from largest to smallest, the edges perfectly aligned. They were scattered now and Taylor had a strong urge to straighten them.

"I'll clean it up when they're done," Cail offered.

"No. You won't touch anything. I'll do it." She reached a hand to line up the pads on the shelf and had to force herself to pull it back again. There were two sketch pads on the angled desk – the ones she had been drawing in before she went on the tour. A large sketch pad sat against the wall beside the desk. "You should have told me."

"I'm sorry. I didn't want to upset you."

Trying not to be too obvious, Taylor walked to the side of one of the shelving units and took a quick peek behind it before turning back to Cail. "They're all here. They must have picked out the drawings they wanted and taken them out of the sketch pads. You know how private my drawing is. You had no right to do this without letting me know."

Cail caught her fingers in his. "Someone broke in here and went through them, Tay. Someone knew about them. Nothing else in the apartment was touched. Did someone you knew on the streets know about your drawings?"

"No." She'd never been close to anyone on the streets. She kept to herself for the most part. As far as she knew, no one had seen her drawing and she was always careful to destroy them afterwards.

"Then it had to have been Emma."

"She's been working with Tony for fifteen years and he trusts her. I can't see her telling anyone." Seeing the black dust everywhere and everything out of place was stressing Taylor out. She desperately wanted to put it all back in order. "How much longer before Ident's done?"

"He's almost finished. I'll get him back in here."

Taylor stayed and watched the Ident Officer like a hawk until he finished dusting for prints. "Find anything?" she asked as he packed up.

"I've got a few good prints, but they could be yours or Cail's. We'll let you know if we get a hit on them."

As soon as he was out the door, Taylor headed for the cleaning supplies and went back into the art room, closing the door behind her.

"She okay?" Chris asked Cail. They'd all gathered in the kitchen, sipping coffee and tea. Chris, Gray and Lane occupied stools at the breakfast bar, Cail was leaning on the counter facing them and Tara leaned in the doorway.

"She's pissed at me for not giving her a heads up."

"You're sure nothing else in the apartment was touched?"

"No, everything was just as I left it on Friday morning."

"Is it possible someone went through her art work before Friday morning?"

Cail thought for a moment before answering Chris's question. "No, I went in there before I left for the airport. I don't know why? Just to make sure it was ready for her coming home, I guess. All of her sketch pads were perfectly aligned where she keeps them on the shelf. She's funny that way. She can't stand if they're not lined up exactly."

"And they weren't lined up when you came in this afternoon?"

"No, not perfectly. They were a little off."

"Like someone tried to put them back how they found them but not with the precision Taylor would have done it?"

"Yeah, exactly."

"Okay, what apartment is your super in? I'm going to go and pay him a visit." Chris slipped off the stool.

"We'll come with you," Cail offered. "We have to get back to work." Tara fell in behind Cail and they headed out while Gray and Lane went to check on Taylor.

Gray tapped on the door before opening it. Taylor stood over the art desk, flipping through the pages of a sketch pad. Most of the black dust had been cleaned up and there was a stack of sketch pads on the shelf, lined up to precision. "Do you know how many drawings they took?" Gray asked.

"I'm not sure. I think it was just the ones they showed on TV," Taylor answered, not looking up from what she was doing. She finished flipping through the pages then set the sketch pad on the shelf with the others, lining it up carefully.

"You mind if I take a look at some of your drawings?" Lane asked. She'd been down this road with Taylor before and always got a flat out no. But, it was worth another try seeing as she was right here.

Taylor knew which ones Lane wanted to look at. She wasn't interested in Taylor's more pleasant memories. She gave Lane a hard stare. "It's not going to help anything."

"It will give me a better understanding of your flashbacks and nightmares."

"The stuff I've done recently is all at Chris's."

"Maybe I can have a look at those when we get back there."

Taylor stood staring down at her desk. She decided to pick up a shredder as soon as she could and shred the darker drawings she did on a regular basis. It had been easier to destroy them when she was on the streets, easier to find a place to burn them. Now she had too many of them hanging around and if they were hanging around, someone could find them. She made a rash decision to let Lane see some of her darker drawings before she destroyed them. She went to the shelving unit and pulled a sketch pad out from behind it then laid it on the art desk. "Knock yourself out," she said. "I'm going to get changed." She didn't want to be there while Lane looked through them.

As Lane settled herself into the chair at the art desk, Gray wasn't sure what to do. Did she even want to see the drawings? "Would you like another coffee?" Maybe if she just kept herself busy she wouldn't be tempted.

Lane glanced over her shoulder. "No, thank you."

Gray stood by the door watching Lane flip through the pages. "How do you deal with it? You care about Chris and Taylor, so how do you deal with what was done to them?"

"Are you having problems dealing with it, Gray?"

"Ha, now you're really sounding like a therapist." Gray hadn't meant for the question to be turned on her. Lane just smiled and continued to flip through the pages. "I don't think we'll ever really know the extent of the terror Taylor lived through," Gray said idly.

"No," Lane said in agreement. "There's a lot that she won't talk about, that she can't talk about."

"Is that why you want to see her drawings?"

"Partially," Lane answered, distracted. The detail in Taylor's drawings was unbelievable. In one of the drawings you could see a billboard across the street through a window. The ad on the billboard was for a local news program and featured a very popular anchor. Taylor would have been about twelve when that anchor was on the air and yet she'd drawn the woman to perfection. "Oh, dear Lord. She's got an eidetic memory," Lane whispered to herself. It was bad enough to have the kind of past Taylor endured, but to remember every sound, every sensation, every emotion, every expression, every word spoken in minute detail was its own kind of torture.

As Lane continued to study the drawings, she noted, "She draws her nightmares more than her flashbacks."

"Maybe she relives it enough in her mind that she doesn't need to draw the flashbacks. Her nightmares, on the other hand, may give her some insight into what she experienced."

Lane looked up from the drawings. She almost forgot Gray was there. "You think she's trying to make some sense out of what happened to her?"

"I think Chris's investigation has given her some sense of why it happened, but I don't think she'll ever be able to make any sense out of what they did to her. It doesn't make any sense. It's madness."

"A strong argument for the defense, perhaps."

"God, I hope not," Gray responded. The idea of Sarah Johnson being found not guilty due to diminished mental capacity just didn't sit right with her. "Do you think they'll focus on her state of mind as a defense?"

"No, Sarah Johnson is insistent that she had nothing to do with the assaults on Taylor. She blames everything on Darryl."

"Do you think Taylor will get through the trial?"

Lane closed the sketch pad and went to place it behind the shelving unit where she'd seen Taylor pick it up. "She's strong, but you saw how she was during the NNN special. It will be difficult for her to say the least." Glancing behind the shelves she saw at least six more sketch pads. "How long ago did you give Taylor these art supplies?"

They bought Taylor the art desk and a ton of art supplies at the end of August, when they discovered they missed her birthday in July. Taylor's birthday had been the day they went to the fundraiser for the Secret Garden and she hadn't said a word. "About two and a half months ago. Why?"

"And she's been gone for one month. She's doing a heck of a lot of drawing." Lane placed the sketch pad behind the shelves and brought out another one.

At the sound of a knock at the door, Gray escaped from the art room. She opened the front door to Chris. "Lane's in the art room. I'm just going to go and check on Taylor." She knocked softly on the bedroom door then popped her head in. Taylor sat on the bed in a tank top and underwear, her back to the door. "You okay, Taylor?"

Taylor shook her head. "They took more than the drawings."

Gray rounded the bed and took a seat next to her. "What did they take?"

Taylor nodded towards the dresser. Sitting on top were two silver picture frames, one containing a picture of her with her sister Leila and the other an old police photo of her mother. Between the frames sat a small pewter box with the lid open, the inner lining of blue velvet visible. Gray felt her heart sink. She knew what Taylor kept in the pewter box. She'd given the box and the frames to Taylor as a gift. She stood, shocked, and peeked inside the box to be sure. "No. Oh God, no."

"What's up?" Chris asked from the doorway.

"Taylor's bracelet and Leila's locket." Gray turned to Chris. "They're gone."

"Did you take them with you on the tour?" Chris crossed the room to look in the box.

"No," Taylor answered quietly. "I was worried I'd lose them."

"Anyone who read your book would know what they mean to you." Turning, Chris caught the look of defeat in Taylor's murky eyes.

"They wouldn't have had to read it to know."

She was right, Chris thought. The title of the book, *Leila's Locket*, had reporters all over the continent asking its meaning. It was common knowledge what that locket meant to Taylor. Chris crouched down in front of her. "What's your gut telling you? Who do you think would take them?"

"Someone who knew what that bracelet meant to me before I even wrote the book." Taylor glanced up at Gray then her eyes locked on Chris's. "Troy Rappaport. He knows I'll come for them."

Chapter 18

They sat in the living room while Taylor related the story of giving her bracelet to Troy Rappaport to hold until she returned the Jeep she borrowed from him. She needed transportation to Balton to warn Gray Ralph Morse was coming after her when he escaped from prison. Troy called Taylor at Gray's and demanded she bring the Jeep back along with the two hundred dollars she agreed to pay for the loan of the vehicle. She didn't have the money yet. She returned the Jeep and tried to arrange to pay Rappaport back once she was able to earn the money. Rappaport became violent.

When Gray realized Taylor had gone that morning, she convinced Callaghan to drive her to Toronto to find her. They arrived at Rappaport's apartment just in time to save Taylor from being raped, but she'd been badly beaten. Gray took her to her suite at the Grand Hotel while she got back on her feet then took her back up to Balton.

"The guy who was holding a gun to my head while Troy ..." Taylor shook her head, unable to say the words. "The guy with the gun was Kevin Laurey."

"And you think Rappaport broke in here and took the necklace and bracelet to get you to come to him?" Chris asked.

"Unfinished business," Taylor said, reminding Chris of Rebecca's warning. "Troy Rappaport wouldn't have shot at that limo if he thought I was in it. He's wanted me for a long time. It just doesn't make any sense."

"I want you to use your ESP to help us find him," Chris said. No use in beating around the bush at this point. She already received a text message from Detective Pierson stating his team was following up on a lead so they wouldn't be meeting as previously arranged. That's fine, Chris thought. We'll be following our own lead.

"If we wait, he'll contact me. He wants me to meet him."

"If you're right, Rappaport either broke in here on Friday or had someone do it for him. I've got the building's CCTV recordings from Friday on disk. When we get to the office, we'll go through the video to confirm it was Rappaport. Then I need you to help us find him. I'm not going to wait until he makes contact."

"I don't understand why he'd break in here and steal them when he thought I was dead," Taylor said. "What if the theft of the drawings isn't connected to the bracelet and locket?"

Chris narrowed her eyes, thinking it through then stood and headed for the door. "I'm going back down to see the super. We need the surveillance tapes from last night and today." Son of a bitch, she thought. The bastard broke in here after he found out Cail and Taylor were still alive.

* * *

At Headquarters, Chris followed Taylor into the change room and took a seat on the bench as Taylor opened her locker. "You never finished your story from when your mom was still alive."

Taylor eased her coat off then hung it inside her locker. "What does it matter?" She didn't feel like talking about it. She'd been in a mood since finding Cail and the Ident Officer in her art room.

Chris shrugged. "I always thought you had good memories from back then."

"She loved us," Taylor offered a thin smile then turned back to stare in her locker. "She just loved drugs more."

"I doubt she loved drugs, Taylor. She was addicted."

Taylor shimmied out of her jeans then pulled her sweatshirt over her head. She folded her clothes neatly before placing them in her locker and reaching for a uniform shirt. She knew enough about addiction to know her mother wasn't able to tackle the problem on her own. But, as a young child she hadn't. She figured since they were talking about it anyway, she may as well finish it. "There were always people there, partying with my mom. Different people all the time, I think. There were a few who would come back regularly, but for the most part I think they were strangers. Sometimes things would get out of hand and Leila would take me into the closet in my mom's room. I don't know. I don't remember a lot from back then, but I think we spent a lot of time in that closet. I used to crouch up in a tight ball, make myself as small as I could."

"You still do that." Chris half smiled, sitting with her legs stretched out and her hands tucked in her pockets. "When you're overwhelmed."

"Huh," Taylor breathed out with a slight laugh. "It's a comfort thing, I suppose." Kind of like Gray using the name her mother called her instead of her full name, Grace, Taylor thought. "You read *Leila's Locket*. You know most of what I remember from back then - Leila and I coming home from school and the trailer blowing up when we were about twenty feet from it. I don't know how many times in my life I wished I had just hurried the hell up. We would have been inside if I hadn't been so slow."

Shit, Chris thought. Why the hell can't I learn to keep my mouth shut? "You don't feel like that now, do you?"

"No." Taylor shook her head as she secured her duty belt around her waist. Taking her boots from the bottom of her locker, she sat on the bench directly across from Chris. She had so much more to live for now.

"Do you think you had ESP even back then? Is that why you were dragging your heels maybe?"

"I don't know." It was an interesting thought. Taylor continued, "We stayed with a neighbour that night. When we got to school the next morning, Child Services were waiting for us."

"Sarah Johnson?" Chris asked, cursing herself for wanting to know.

"No," Taylor answered. "I didn't meet her until after Leila went missing." She huffed out another short laugh. "Those five years were the best years of my life up until now. Those years Leila and I were together in a foster home."

The air was thick with the unspoken question – What would Taylor's life have been like if Leila had lived? They were doing fine, right up until Leila was abducted. Would they have continued to thrive? Would Leila's dream of finding a job, getting them an apartment of their own and continuing their education have come to pass? They sat there in silence for a moment, both of them pondering the same thing.

"I've got to stop by to pick Brice's brain. I'll meet you in my office in ten minutes then I'll get you set up at your desk." Chris stood and started to leave thinking Taylor probably needed a few minutes.

"I have my own desk?" Taylor asked just as Chris pulled the door open.

With a grin, Chris turned back quickly. "Yeah, you do."

Taylor was thrilled with the idea of having her own desk, right up until she realized she would be sitting facing Detective MaryAnn Blake. Her dark curly hair was up in a ponytail, leaving her long face unframed. Dark eyes flitted up from the computer monitor to glance at Taylor.

"Here's your user IDs and passwords," Chris said, handing Taylor a piece of paper. "Change your passwords then you can start going through the surveillance tape from your apartment for last night and today. Blake's already started on Friday's tape."

"They'll be carrying a tube or a portfolio," Taylor said to Detective Blake. "The drawings didn't look like they'd been folded, so you should be able to pick them out easily enough when they exited the building."

Blake looked up from her computer again, meeting Taylor's gaze. "Thanks."

Taylor nodded then busied herself with logging into the system and changing her passwords. Just as she loaded the disk to view the video, she sensed Cail behind her. "Is that the video from Friday?" he asked, brushing a kiss over her temple.

Taylor glared up at him, annoyed at the display of affection in the middle of the department. "No, it's last night and today."

"Hey, Cail," Blake nodded.

"MaryAnn. How's it going?" Cail flashed his gorgeous smile, annoying Taylor even more.

"No complaints. You?"

"All good." He turned his attention back to Taylor. "Why are you looking at last night and today?"

Taylor kept her eyes on her computer screen, studying the images of people coming and going from the building. "Because the drawings weren't the only thing missing," she replied quietly. She wasn't entirely comfortable having this conversation with Blake right there. Although, Taylor knew Blake had been involved in the Sarah Johnson investigation. There probably wasn't a lot Blake didn't know about her. Maybe that was part of why Taylor disliked her.

"What's missing?" Concerned now, Cail rested his hip against Taylor's desk.

"My bracelet and Leila's locket."

The look of concern stayed on Cail's face. "You don't think they were taken on Friday?"

"It's possible, but my gut tells me Rappaport took them sometime after the press conference last night."

"What the fuck, Tay?" Cail spat out a little too loudly. "What the hell's going on? I think it's time you told us what the hell this guy has against you."

As her blood began to boil, Taylor's eyes met Blake's over their computer monitors. She quickly dropped them back to her monitor again.

"Worthington," Chris called out from her office door, her mouth a tight white line and her brows drawn in.

Cail looked over his shoulder at her and caught the nod toward her office. "Shit," he whispered under his breath as Taylor breathed a little sigh of relief. Pushing off Taylor's desk, Cail walked to Chris's door and took a seat inside when she gestured towards one of the two chairs facing her desk.

Chris closed the door and asked, "What the fuck do you think you're doing?"

"Checking in and trying to find out what the hell's going on?"

"You think making a scene out there is the way to go about that? Are you even thinking about what that might do to Taylor?"

"Maybe if you'd tell me what the hell's going on, I might have an idea what it would do to her."

"Rappaport tried to rape her. That's the unfinished business."

Cail sat staring at Chris, his face red as he tried to keep his temper from raging and listened as she went through the whole story.

"This stops now, Chris. I'll be damned if I let him lure her to him with that bracelet and locket."

"I need to convince her to use her ESP to help us find him. Do you know where her migraine meds are?"

"Yeah and that's another reason I stopped by. I don't have a key for your place."

Chris took out her keys, removed her house key and handed it to him. "Stay in uniform and I'll make sure you get paid. Pick up her meds and get back here."

Cail stopped at Taylor's desk before heading out. "I'm going to Chris's. Do you need anything?"

"You're coming back?" Taylor clicked pause on the video and looked up at him.

"Yeah, I'll be back in a bit."

Taylor knew he was up to something, but now wasn't the time to get into it. Not with Blake sitting right there. "Can you grab some Advil? I thought we'd be going back to Chris's before we came in."

"Do you have another headache?"

"It's not bad. I just need something to take the edge off."

"Sinclair," Blake called out before tossing a small bottle of Advil to her.

Taylor grabbed it one handed, midair. Was this some sort of peace offering? she wondered. "Thanks." She spilled two out into her palm and tossed the bottle back.

"I'll see you in a bit then." Cail smiled and brushed a kiss over her temple again. He let out a chuckle at Taylor's glare and walked away.

"Must be rough," Blake said with a sigh then went back to studying her monitor. The man was a God. She was pretty sure there wasn't anyone as sexy and hot as Caillen Worthington.

Taylor clicked play again and blocked Blake out as she studied the video. She didn't hear the CD tray on Blake's computer open, but she caught the movement out of the corner of her eye and watched Blake walk into Chris's office and close the door behind her.

Chris looked up from her computer as Blake shifted back and forth from foot to foot. "You need to take a look at this, Sarge."

"Did you find something?"

"I'm not sure, but you need to take a look at it."

Chris pulled up another chair beside hers and gestured for Blake to take a seat. Blake slid the CD into Chris's computer and cued up the camera and time she wanted to show Chris. They both watched the monitor as a woman entered the main entrance of the building with a key. When Chris didn't recognize her, she frowned. "Who is she? Am I supposed to know her?"

"Lisa Harmon. She's Cail's ex. Sort of."

"What do you mean, sort of?"

"Word is they've been sleeping together since high school. Not in a relationship ... more of a booty call type of thing. If neither one of them has someone on the go, they hook up."

"Friends with benefits. Enough that she has a key to his building."

"And his apartment."

"Maybe she just stopped by for a visit."

"For a couple of hours?" Blake asked, scrolling to the point in the video where the woman exits the building. She watched the expression on Chris's face turn to shock as she recognized the person walking out arm in arm with Lisa Harmon.

Chris pursed her lips, narrowed her eyes. She didn't want to believe these two had anything to do with the theft of Taylor's drawings.

"They're not carrying the sketches."

"Could be under that long coat." Blake pointed at Lisa Harmon on the monitor.

Chris raked her hand through her hair and sat for a moment as she gathered her thoughts. Just because they entered the building after Cail left for the airport and departed a couple of hours later didn't prove they were responsible for the theft of Taylor's drawings. "Keep looking," she said as she took the CD out of the tray and handed it back to Blake.

Detective Blake took the CD and started for the door. Turning back, she said, "I've known the Worthington's for years. They're all very close and very protective of each other."

Chris glared up at her. "Keep looking, Detective."

Taylor watched Blake slip back into her chair. She knew something was up and didn't like the fact they were keeping whatever it was from her. She'd just started studying her video again when Chris came out and announced she was heading to the E-Division and would be right back.

That left Taylor with no one to report to when she found what she was looking for. She was damned if she would share it with Blake. She pulled out her cell phone and sent Chris a text message.

Nearly twenty minutes later, Chris barrelled around the corner. "Show me," she called out to Taylor. Taylor had already printed stills and had the video cued up ready to go.

"Jesus," Chris muttered as she looked over the stills. "Sure as hell doesn't look under duress, does she?"

"No, she doesn't," Taylor agreed as she clicked play. They watched as Troy Rappaport used a key to unlock the back entrance door to Cail's building. Pulling the door open, he let Rebecca Knightley enter before him. They walk off down the hall with Rebecca wrapping her arm around Troy's waist. It made Taylor sick that he had been in Cail's apartment, in Cail's bedroom. She switched over to the parking lot camera where a dark coloured pickup truck pulls into the lot, parking in a resident's spot.

"Any chance we can get the plate?" Chris asked.

Taylor zoomed in on the front of the truck. "Alpha, Tango, four, two, three, two."

"Run it," Chris ordered. "I have a feeling it belongs to Mick O'Hara."

"Why?" Taylor asked as she began to enter the plate number into the system.

"Briefing in Meeting Room A. Fifteen minutes. I'll pull it all together then." Heading towards her office, Chris called over her shoulder, "Bring what you have, Sinclair."

* * *

Taylor walked into the meeting room carrying the stills and the CD containing the surveillance video from Cail's building. "You were right. The truck is registered to Michael Allan O'Hara." She stopped in her tracks, seeing Chris wasn't alone.

"Detective Boone, Constable Sinclair," Chris said in introduction.

Detective Warren Boone rubbed his hand down the thigh of his jeans before extending it to Taylor and offering her an admiring smile. "Sinclair. Pleasure to meet you."

Taylor returned a firm handshake. "You too." She'd seen him around Headquarters and caught a glimpse of him during one of the news broadcasts on the limo shooting. He wasn't quite as tall as Taylor's six feet, but close enough, and lanky. His short cropped hair was the silver of birch bark, a sharp contrast to his dark tan.

Cail walked into the room carrying a tray of coffees with Blake right on his heels. They were laughing about something, which annoyed Taylor once again. Chris was the first to grab a coffee. She added cream and sugar then she returned to writing on the whiteboard. Taylor studied the board, realizing Chris was putting together a time line since the shooting of the limo – a time line of Rappaport's movements. Above the timeline, Chris had posted police photos of Laurey and Rappaport.

Cail greeted Boone like an old friend and had Taylor wondering if Cail knew every cop in the city. They settled into chairs with their coffees.

"Okay," Chris began. "I'm not going to bother with the details of the limo shooting and the arrests of DeCosta, Mallamo and Laurey. I think everyone is up to speed on that. Kevin Laurey gave up Troy Evan Rappaport as his accomplice in the shooting and Rappaport reportedly went into hiding."

"Rappaport wouldn't have shot at that limo if he thought I was inside," Taylor blurted out and then sank back in her chair at the glare she got from Chris.

"Why's that, Sinclair?" Boone asked.

Taylor's eyes went to Chris for approval before she answered. "I've known him most of my life. He wants me. Alive."

"Why would Laurey give him up as the second shooter?"

"I don't know. Kev and Troy are partners. Troy brought Kev into his business off the streets and made him very wealthy. They've been inseparable for most of the time I've known them."

Boone wasn't convinced. He nodded at Cain for her to continue.

"We checked several locations for Rappaport last night and, apparently, just missed him at a location beneath the Queen and Yonge Subway Station. At that location, we found seventeen year old Rebecca Knightley, who claimed to have been abducted from the subway by a subject known as 'Blades'." Chris put a photo of Knightly next to Rappaport's then followed it with another photo. "Justin Ripkin, aka 'Blades'," Chris said as she fastened his photo to the board. "So named for his preference of knives. Rappaport pays Justin Ripkin to give people a not so gentle reminder of their debts.

"Rebecca stated she left her boyfriend's apartment and got on the train at the College Station. Her boyfriend, Mick O'Hara, left her outside the station, or so she stated. A neighbour collaborated Mick left his apartment with Rebecca Knightley at approximately twenty thirty hours. He hasn't been seen since." Chris paused while it sunk in.

Taylor glanced briefly at Boone. Now she knew why the homicide detective was here. "Whose phone did Cail find?" she asked.

"Mick O'Hara's. He was in that room and Rebecca Knightley led him there." Chris picked up the CD Taylor brought in and inserted it into a laptop connected to a projector. "Why don't you do the honours, Sinclair?" Taylor went to the laptop and brought up the camera she wanted then scrolled to the correct time.

As soon as Cail recognized it was Rappaport walking into his building, rage hit him like a fist. "That fucker was in our apartment. Jesus Christ, Tay. He was in our room?"

It was at that moment Taylor realized Chris had told Cail what Rappaport had nearly done to her. Her eyes met his for an instant before she dropped them to the laptop screen. If they hadn't been staying at Chris's ... God, she couldn't even think it.

"Worthington." Chris gave Cail the evil eye, a warning to keep his temper in check.

Biting back his anger, he met Chris's glare with one of his own.

"Care to fill the rest of us in, Cain?" Boone asked.

Taylor hit play as Chris began to explain. "At oh two seventeen this morning, Troy Rappaport and Rebecca Knightley let themselves into Constable Worthington and Constable Sinclair's apartment. We have reason to believe they stole two items – a bracelet and a locket – with the intention of luring Sinclair to him."

"Why would he do that?" Boone asked.

Taylor felt everyone's eyes on her. Instead of waiting for Chris to answer, she blurted out, "He has unfinished business with me." Her eyes skimmed over Blake then Boone before locking on Cail. "He tried to rape me in the spring. He wants to finish what he started. He wouldn't have shot at that limo."

"Missing Persons has already been contacted with regards to the disappearance of Michael O'Hara," Chris went on. "But, the vehicle Rappaport and Knightley used last night was O'Hara's. I've put out a BOLO on the vehicle – a 2014 black Chevy Silverado."

"So now we've got Homicide, the Drug Squad, and Sex Crimes all running after the same perp," Boone stated. "Have you heard from Pierson tonight?"

"Not yet," Chris answered. "They were running down a lead. He didn't fill me in on the details."

"What's your next step, Cain?"

"If we can pick up Rebecca Knightley and Justin Ripkin, they may lead us to Rappaport. I'm also tugging another line on Rappaport, but I'll have to get back to you on that."

Taylor was getting frustrated that no one was listening to her about Rappaport. She also knew Blades had nothing to do with O'Hara's disappearance, but she was honour bound not to give the reasons why she knew he was innocent.

"Would you mind if we took Knightley and Ripkin? I'd like to question both of them on O'Hara's disappearance and Rappaport's location."

Chris raked her hand through her hair. She knew Boone's question was merely a courtesy. Technically, they had nothing to do with Sex Crimes. "Okay," she conceded.

Boone stood. "I appreciate the heads up Detective Sergeant. If you would keep me in the loop, I'll do the same for you."

"Done," Chris nodded and watched Boone walk out.

Taylor stayed seated behind the laptop, unsure if Cail's temper had ebbed. She watched Chris's cheeks puff out before she blew out a long breath. "Ripkin isn't involved in this, Chris. They're trying to set him up."

"If that's the case, he'll be cleared. We need him picked up and questioned to be sure."

"Where does that leave us?" Taylor asked.

"It leaves us tugging another line." Chris looked Taylor in the eye. "I need you to use your ESP."

It was Taylor's temper that flared now as she glared at Chris. "We've gone over this enough that you should know my answer by now."

Cail banged his fist on the table. "Damn it, Tay. Would you rather wait until he gets to you?"

Taylor's heart leapt into her throat at the sound of his fist hitting the table. She knew she had visibly jumped and hoped everyone's eyes had been on Cail when they heard the bang.

Chris dragged a chair next to Taylor and sat facing her. "He's out there with God knows how much meth, armed and dangerous. He's already killed two people, Taylor. Cail was right. What if you had been home last night? What if he finds out where you're staying? It wouldn't be much of a leap for him to figure it out."

Taylor was suddenly grateful Gray was staying at her suite at the Grand instead of her home in Balton. She thought briefly that she and Cail could go to stay with her at the Grand, but then what would happen if Rappaport went to Chris's looking for her?

Chris stared at Taylor, waiting for an answer when she felt Cail's hand on her shoulder. "Give us a minute," Cail said quietly.

What the hell, Chris thought. Cail might have a better chance of convincing Taylor to use her psychic ability than anyone. Taylor wouldn't want him worrying about her and she may do it to ease his mind. Nodding, Chris rose and gave a nod to Detective Blake. "We'll be in my office," Chris announced before stepping out.

Cail took the seat Chris vacated and, leaning forward, he gripped lightly onto Taylor's fingertip. The simple contact was enough to ignite the fiery connection between them. Taylor closed her eyes, feeling his pulse, the beating of his heart, and the many emotions stirring within him. She felt his fear and worry, felt his anger, but most of all she felt the deep love and desire. And the love she felt for him was just as deep, just as strong.

"It scares you," Cail said, locking his eyes on hers.

"It terrifies me." Taylor knew he was referring to using her ESP, but the answer also fit her thoughts on their feelings for each other.

"Because of what you saw with Astra?"

Taylor thought of the little girl who'd been abducted and raped while Cail and Taylor were at the Police Academy. They took part in the search for Astra and Taylor had been overwhelmed by a vision of

Astra's ordeal. It was as if she experienced everything Astra experienced – not only the fear and terror, but the rapes themselves. On the other hand, she'd been able to save Astra by using her ESP to help find her. "Mostly, yes."

"If I could get the time off work and be with you twenty-four seven until this is over, it'd be different. But, I have to work these shifts that I traded to get the weekend off, Tay. If he gets to you …"

"I'm not going to let that happen." Taylor tried to soothe him, but she knew they only had tonight. Tomorrow she had to come in for her physical and then she and Gray had a book signing in the afternoon. The day after that, Sarah's trial began. Unless, of course, her plan worked and there wouldn't be a trial. She wondered when and if she'd hear anything. And why hadn't Rappaport contacted her? What was he waiting for? "He's going to contact me. Why else would he take the bracelet and locket?"

"Your book signing is advertised, Tay. Everyone knows you'll be at that library tomorrow. And everyone knows you'll be in court on Wednesday."

"It's too much of a risk. There are too many people at those things, too many eyes."

Cail let out a deep sigh of frustration and leaned in, resting his brow on Taylor's. "We could get him in custody tonight. Finish it."

"I've got enough images in my head from my own life, Cail. I don't want to take on anyone else's. If I open myself up to it, I might see a hell of a lot more than what I intend to."

"At least I'll still have you. You're everything, Tay. Being away from you this past month was harder than anything I've ever experienced. Like the air I breathe, I can't survive without you."

"That's totally unfair," Taylor said, closing her eyes again. He didn't have to survive with all of the images in his head, all of the feelings and sensations. She let out a long sigh of frustration, then, "If Detective Boone can't get anything out of Knightley, then I'll do it."

Chapter 19

Taylor leaned against the wall in Chris's office with her arms crossed in front of her listening to Chris's pleading. "Even if they find Ripkin and Knightley tonight, there's no guarantee they'll talk. What's to stop Rappaport from walking into the library tomorrow afternoon with an assault rifle and taking out a ton of people with you?"

"Metal detectors," Taylor answered dryly.

"Ugh," Chris raked a hand through her hair. "Taylor, we're trying to protect you."

Oh, for crying out loud, Taylor thought. She took several cleansing breaths then leaned her head back against the wall. She brought an image of Troy Rappaport into her mind and tried to focus on his surroundings. Seeing nothing but darkness, she changed her focus to concentrate on Rappaport himself. She could smell the spicy cologne he wore mixed in with male sweat and stale cigarette smoke. Suddenly, he was lunging forward out of the dark and Taylor's eyes flew open with a gasp. "Where's Kate? Where the hell is Kate?"

"She's at my parents' place," Cail answered, taking Taylor's hand when he read the terror in her eyes. "She's safe."

"Call her," Taylor demanded.

Chris was in a panic now. As Cail frantically dialed his parents' number, Chris surged to Taylor. "What did you see?"

Taylor shook her head. If she could have taken a step back, she would have. "Does Kate have a key to your place?"

"Yes. What did you see, damn it?"

"He was in your house … waiting in the dark." Everyone's focus turned to Cail as he talked to his mother on his cell.

"I need to talk to Kate, Mom. No, no … everything's fine. I'll try her cell." He hung up and dialed Kate's cell. "She's heading over to your place, Chris."

All eyes remained trained on Cail as he waited for Kate to answer her cell. Chris stuck her hands in her pockets to keep them from shaking and started pacing. *Pick up. Pick up, damn it.*

"Kate, it's Cail. I need you to phone me as soon as you get this message. If you're on your way to Chris's, don't go in. We think someone may have broken in and he's armed and dangerous. Call me." Before he could disconnect the call, Chris grabbed her jacket and ran out the door with Taylor, Cail and Blake right on her heels.

"Dispatch, this is Detective Sergeant Cain. I need a unit at my personal residence ten eighteen. Suspect wanted in connection with the limo shooting may be inside the house. Possible ten seventy-nine. Flag Alpha Victor. Use extreme caution." Chris called out her home address as she ignored the elevators and charged into the stairwell.

"Ten-four Detective Sergeant. Dispatch to twenty-eight fourteen. Respond to one ten Orchard View Boulevard. Suspect Troy Evan Rappaport believed to be on scene. Possible ten seventy-nine. Subject is believed armed and violent. Use extreme caution."

"Ten-four, Dispatch. Twenty-eight fourteen responding, one ten Orchard View Boulevard. ETA is two minutes."

When they burst out into the garage, Chris called out, "Worthington, you're riding with Blake. Sinclair … with me."

Taylor jumped into the passenger seat and was still closing the door when Chris shot out of the parking spot towards the exit. Taylor clicked into her seat belt and, as soon as Chris cleared the garage exit, she activated the lights and sirens.

* * *

After two days of brooding, thinking and talking things out with her mother, Kate decided the root of her misery was she missed Chris. Despite the hurt, she wanted Chris. The least she could do for both of them was to sit down and have a civilized conversation about where they wanted to go from here. She dressed in a plain pair of jeans and a sweatshirt. If all went well, it was what she wore under them that would show Chris just how much she missed her.

She stopped at the liquor store and picked up a nice bottle of wine. A glass or two while she waited for Chris to get home would give her a little confidence to say what she wanted to say. Then, knowing Chris's fridge would be empty save for a case of beer, she stopped at a grocery store and picked up some bare necessities.

The musical tone of her cell phone sounded from her purse just as she pulled onto Chris's street. Kate ignored it until she pulled into the driveway. Fishing her phone out of her purse, she checked the call display and wondered what Cail wanted. She stuck the phone in her pocket, resigned to giving him a call once she got inside, put the groceries away, and poured a glass of wine.

Kate shifted all of her bags to her right hand as she climbed the porch steps, selecting Chris's house key from the key ring in her dominant left hand. She unlocked the dead bolt, pushed the door open then closed it behind her. She'd barely taken a step towards the kitchen when an arm wrapped around her neck and jerked her back. The keys and bags dropped to the floor as her hands clasped around the arm, desperately trying to relieve the pressure on her throat. Terror seeped through her when she stomped the heel of her boot into the asshole's instep and he didn't even flinch. She thrust an elbow into his ribs then tried to turn and aim her elbow at his face. It was like fighting a rock. The cold steel of a hand gun pressed to her temple and Kate stopped struggling. "You son of a bitch." Her voice was strangled and raspy.

"Do you want to live?" a deep voice whispered into Kate's ear. Her stomach twisted with the scent of his overbearing cologne and sweat.

Kate tensed as the barrel of the gun ran down her face, her neck and she felt the hard length of him grinding into her ass. Her lungs burned as she tried to get a breath. She cried out a weak scream when the gun slid over her breasts then down her torso until he rubbed it between her legs.

* * *

Lights flashing, sirens blaring, Chris raced up Yonge Street, weaving in and out of traffic. Taylor turned up the volume on the police radio.

"Twenty-eight fourteen requesting ten fifty-two. Female victim, late twenties, with breathing difficulties. Suspect fled on foot heading west towards Eglinton Park."

Chris didn't say a word. She didn't have to. Taylor could see it all in her expression. There was nothing she could say to comfort her, so she stayed quiet, thinking. Tilting her head back, she closed her eyes and tried to conjure an image of Troy Rappaport.

Chris squealed around the corner onto her street where lights flashed from two squad cars and an ambulance. She screeched to a stop in front of her house and they were both out of the car and running, only Taylor headed west towards the park.

"Sinclair," Chris screamed, but Taylor didn't slow down. "Fuck," she murmured. Coming to a halt she grabbed her cell phone and dialed Detective Blake's number. "Sinclair's on foot, westbound on Orchard View heading toward Eglinton Park. Catch up with her and back her up."

"We've got her on the radio, calling in her position to Dispatch," Blake responded.

"Great, get to her." Chris hung up and climbed the steps to her small porch, approaching the officer who stood guard at the door. He'd been on the force for years and Chris recognized him, but couldn't put a name to his boyish face. The black Velcro strip displaying his surname on the right breast of his Kevlar vest saved her the embarrassment. "Constable Kline, report."

"She's conscious, DS. The medics are with her. My partner is on foot, pursuing the suspect through the park."

"Get an update from your partner and call in back up. I want the bastard in custody." Chris stepped through the doorway and saw Kate sitting on the sofa. When she saw the bruises forming around Kate's neck, it was all she could do to keep her rage at bay. She stood staring down at the broken glass, wine and groceries littering the floor, unsure if she should go to Kate or keep her distance.

Kate looked up at Chris while a medic took her blood pressure. "I'm okay," she rasped.

"Report," Chris ordered.

It reminded Kate of the first night she met Detective Sergeant Chris Cain. Although she sounded cold, Kate saw the emotions in the expression on Chris's face and in her eyes. She related what happened with professional precision. "When he heard the sirens, I think he panicked. He pushed me to the floor and took off."

"Okay," Chris sighed in relief, raking a hand through her hair.

* * *

Taylor ran straight through the park, down a side street and came out on Avenue Road, her breaths steaming out in plumes with the cold night air. She scanned all around and headed north, calling an update of her location into Dispatch as she ran. As she approached Roselawn Avenue, she caught sight of Rappaport getting into the passenger side of a black BMW sedan. Picking up her pace, she managed to get close enough to read the plate number before the sedan sped off. "Twenty-seven twelve to Dispatch, suspect has been picked up in a black BMW sedan, licence bravo, victor, bravo, six, niner, six, four heading northbound on Avenue Road at Roselawn."

"Ten four, twenty-seven twelve. Patrol units responding."

Taylor watched as two squad cars lit up about two blocks south of her and followed them with her eyes until they were well north of her. She started to turn to head back to Chris's and found herself being shoved violently into a brick wall. Her upper back hit the wall with such force she felt pins and needles right down her arms to the tips of her fingers. Cail's hands gripped her upper arms as he gave her a good shake.

"What the fuck do you think you're doing?" he shouted.

It took a minute for Taylor to catch her breath and get her bearings. She glanced at Detective Blake over Cail's shoulder and felt like she was drowning in shame. She dropped her eyes before responding, "My job. I followed procedure."

"Procedure? You should have stayed with Cain and I'd be checking on my sister right now instead of chasing you down." Cail gave her another shove before turning to Blake. "Let's go."

"Come on, Sinclair. I'll give you a ride back," Blake said.

"Fuck that. She can walk back. It will give her time to think about the damage she's done by stalling on using her fucking ESP. Kate wouldn't have been hurt if she hadn't been so fucking selfish." Cail got into the passenger seat of Blake's car and slammed the door.

Taylor bent forward, one hand splayed over her stomach as if she physically felt the blow Cail just threw her, and the other braced on her knee. Choking back the knot of tears crawling up her throat, she waved Blake off. "It's alright. I could use the walk."

"He's out of line, Sinclair." Blake looked back and forth between Cail and Taylor. "Cain will kill me if I don't bring you back."

"I'll back you up with Cain. I really need to blow off some steam." Taylor started at a jog down the sidewalk, leaving Blake no choice.

Across the street, Blades stop recording the action on his cell phone and rolled his car window back up.

* * *

Once Taylor was sure Cail and Blake were out of sight, she crossed Avenue Road and hailed a cab going southbound. Once inside, she pulled out her cell phone and sent a text to Chris.

Need the rest of the night off

She was waiting for a text in response, but her phone started ringing instead. After two calming breaths to stave off her emotions, Taylor answered.

"Where the hell are you?" Chris asked.

"On my way back to HQ."

"Why? Are you coming back here?"

"No."

"For fuck sakes, Taylor, tell me what's going on."

"Is Kate okay?"

"Yeah. She's shaken up and has some kick ass bruises, but she's going to be fine."

"Tell her I'm sorry," Taylor whispered through her tears and hung up.

"Taylor?" Chris yelled. "Damn it." She pressed end and then redialed. When it went straight to voice mail she knew Taylor had turned her phone off. Her next call was to Detective Blake. "Did you track Sinclair down?"

"Yes. We're just pulling up to your place now."

"But you don't have her with you," Chris stated.

"No," Blake squirmed in her seat. "We'll be right in, Sarge."

"What's going on?" Kate asked. She'd been cleared by the medics and was curled up on the sofa sipping a beer.

"Damned if I know," Chris scowled. When Cail and Blake walked in, she stood glaring at Blake with her hands fisted on her hips.

"She's running back," Blake explained. "She should be here any second."

"She's not coming back. Care to explain to me what the fuck's going on."

Blake glanced at Cail, who ignored them both and went straight to Kate. "You okay?" he asked, sitting next to her and taking her hand.

"Yeah, I'll be fine. The sirens scared him off. If it hadn't been for Taylor ..." Kate sobbed at the thought.

Cail saw the bruises on Kate's neck and brushed his fingers over them as pure rage burned inside him. "If it hadn't been for Taylor, you wouldn't have gotten hurt."

Kate was shocked. If Taylor hadn't used her ESP, she was sure she would have been brutally raped and probably murdered.

"How the hell do you figure that, Worthington?" Chris fumed.

"If she hadn't stalled ... if she'd just used her ESP when you first asked her ..."

"Jesus Christ. Did you tell her that?" Now Chris understood why Taylor seemed so upset. "You fucking idiot."

Cail shot to his feet and got in Chris's face. Kate jumped up behind him and tried to get between them.

"She could have prevented this. We would have caught Rappaport inside the house and Kate wouldn't have been attacked."

"Cail, she saved me from being raped or worse for Christ's sake. What's your problem?" Kate yelled, her voice still hoarse.

"Stand down, Constable." Chris glared at Cail.

Cail gave her a shove then headed for the door. "Give me a ride back to Headquarters, MaryAnn," he ordered and stormed out the door.

Blake turned to Chris. "He was pretty hard on Sinclair. Roughed her up a bit."

"Jesus." Chris raked a hand through her short hair yet again. By now it was sticking up in all directions.

"She caught up to Rappaport just as he was picked up in a black BMW on Avenue Road just south of Roselawn. The plate came back to Beverly Jeanne Knightley. They dumped the car near Lytton Park and the patrol units lost them. They've set up a perimeter and they're bringing in K-nine."

"Shit," Chris sighed. She paced back and forth for a minute then nodded towards the door. "Give Worthington a ride back. See if you can get him to cool down."

"What about the other thing … from the video?"

"I want the rest of that video checked, but you can get back to it in the morning."

When Blake went out the door, Chris dumped herself onto the sofa. "What a clusterfuck."

Sitting beside her, Kate said, "I'm sorry. He gets a bit unreasonable when he's angry."

"Ya think?" Chris raked her hands through her hair again then stood. "I'm going to get my car and pull it into the driveway. Then I need to find something to patch up the window." Rappaport had broken the window on the back door to gain access to the house. She had that mess to clean up and the broken wine bottle at the front door. While Chris went out to get her car, Kate got a broom and dustpan and started cleaning up the broken bottle and spilled wine. By the time Chris got back with a thick piece of cardboard and some duct tape, Kate was putting the groceries away.

"You shouldn't be doing that."

"I need to do something," Kate responded. She closed the fridge door and leaned back against the counter. "Need some help with that?"

"Nah, I'm just going to cover the hole and I'll get someone in to

173

replace the glass tomorrow."

"You really should get an alarm system."

"Yeah, I think I will." Chris taped the cardboard over the hole in the glass then grabbed a couple of beers from the fridge, passing one to Kate. Leaning back on the counter, she took a long drag on the bottle then stared down at the floor. "I'm sorry about the other night. I didn't mean to brush you off. I was drunk and I heard you tell Lane that you were in love with me. It freaked me out a bit. I just wanted to escape. When I woke up the next morning, Lane was there giving me a piece of her mind and I figured I must have given you your walking papers and didn't remember."

Kate thought she knew exactly what she wanted to say to Chris, but she was drawing a complete blank. They stood side by side staring down at the floor.

"I didn't realize how much I cared for you until you asked me to tell you I don't love you," Chris continued. "It scared the hell out of me." She let out a short laugh then took another swig of her beer. "I want you to move in with me, Kate."

Kate's head whipped up and she stared into Chris's gold flecked eyes. "Why do you want me to move in?"

Chris shrugged. "I don't like going to bed when you're not here. I don't like waking up and you're not here. I don't like coming home and you're not here."

"You want me to move in because you don't like it when I'm not here?"

Chris took another swig of beer and continued to stare down at her feet. "You're going to make me say it, aren't you?"

"Damn right," Kate grinned.

"I've never said it before."

Which made it all the more special, Kate thought. "You're stalling."

Chris took a deep breath and set her beer on the counter. Turning into Kate, she took her hands. "I want you to move in because I love you."

"That didn't hurt too much, did it?" Kate asked, leaning her brow into Chris's.

"Kate," Chris sighed. "You know I'm all kinds of messed up, right?"

"Someone hurt you. I know that. It doesn't stop me from loving you, Chris."

"I'm not a victim. Not anymore. I was when I was too young to protect myself, but I'm sure as hell not one now."

"No, you sure as hell aren't. I'm sorry I said that. I guess I can be unreasonable when I'm pissed, too."

"I'll tell you about it, just … not tonight. I don't want to think about it right now."

"I don't want to think about it right now either," Kate whispered, her eyes flicking between Chris's eyes and her full lips.

"So … are you going to move in?"

"That depends."

Chris straightened, looking into Kate's eyes. "On what?"

"On whether or not you put in an alarm system."

With a grin, Chris slipped her fingers into the waist band of Kate's jeans and tugged Kate to her. "First thing in the morning,"

Chapter 20

At Headquarters, Taylor showered and changed back into her street clothes. Then taking a seat on the bench across from her locker, she turned on her iPhone and went online to search for psychics in the Toronto area. She didn't know why she hadn't thought of it before. She scanned through half a dozen names, but kept going back to Quinn Paylen. She clicked on the link for the psychic's blog, then clicked the 'About Me' link. A picture of Quinn Paylen filled her cell phone screen. Her gorgeous mocha skin, fine features, and smoky grey eyes alluded to Paylen's mixed race heritage. Taylor quickly read through the bio then clicked on the link for Paylen's contact info and dialed the number.

She was taken aback when a low, raspy voice answered with, "I've been waiting for your call, Taylor."

It took her a second before she responded, "Then you know what I want."

"Yes. I can help you. Come to me. You know where."

The line went dead and Taylor frowned thinking that had to have been the weirdest conversation she'd ever had. Her next thought was that she had no idea where to find Quinn Paylen. She walked out of the Headquarters lobby into the cold, dark night, turning the collar up on her long black leather coat. She looked up and down the street before turning west into the cold wind with a shiver.

Half an hour later, her cheeks and ears red and numb with the cold, Taylor stared up at a red brick apartment building off Dundas. In the front entrance, she rubbed her hands together in an attempt to warm them as she scanned the board next to the intercom system for Paylen. When she found the apartment number, Taylor took the elevator to the seventh floor, turned to her left out of the elevator and found Paylen's door. As she raised her hand to knock, the door opened and she stood staring into the smoky grey eyes of Quinn Paylen. Her bio had given her age as forty-nine, but Taylor would have sworn the woman that stood before her was in her thirties. "Why didn't you just give me your address?"

Paylen's deep laugh was as smoky and sultry as her eyes. She was a good six inches shorter than Taylor, but dozens of small braids swept up on top of her head added to her height. Taylor expected her to be wearing some sort of colourful smock, but she wore faded jeans and a sweater that accentuated her curves and matched the grey of her eyes. "You need the practice, troubled one. If you're going to master your gift, you must use it."

Taylor frowned at being called 'troubled one'. Quinn took her hand and led her inside. The living room was a kaleidoscope of rich, earthy colours. The sofa and chairs were dark rust, a sharp contrast to the deep, dusty blue of the carpet. Candles flickered throughout the space, giving it a warm glow. Quinn took Taylor's coat before they settled onto the sofa. A cup of steaming coffee sat on the dark wood coffee table in front of Taylor. Quinn nodded to it, saying, "Two sugars and cream, just the way you like it."

It was unsettling that this woman seemed to know so much about her. Taylor wondered if she was making a mistake then quickly put it out of her mind. "Thank you." She picked up the mug, wrapping both her hands around it to soak up its warmth.

"You've had the gift your entire life, Taylor," Quinn began. "A very powerful gift, but you chose to tune it out, ignore it … for the most part."

"Gift?" Taylor asked. "Or curse?"

"You see it as a curse because it has only caused you grief, until now. As a child, you saw what the future had in store for you and Leila, so you chose to block your abilities."

"I don't remember that." Taylor sipped at the hot coffee, nearly moaning as she felt its heat slowly make its way right down to her belly.

"I know. You blocked that out too, and who could blame you?"

If she was able to block that out, Taylor wondered, why couldn't she have blocked out everything else? Why did she have to remember and relive every horrid moment?

"Soon you can put it all behind you." Quinn patted a hand on Taylor's thigh. "And maybe that will be enough."

Taylor felt her emotions rising to the surface and forced them back.

"In the meantime, we start with learning to accept and use your gift the way you're meant to use it."

* * *

Taylor knocked on the door to Gray's suite at the Grand Hotel. When Gray opened the door with a smile, Taylor tried her best to return it. "Sorry I didn't call."

Gray took her hand and led her inside. "You don't need to call, Taylor. Is everything okay?" That was all that it took to release the flood gates on Taylor's tears. When she was able to speak coherently again, she told Gray about Rappaport, Kate, and Cail.

"This isn't the first time he's said hurtful things to you when he's been angry," Gray said. "But, he also made you feel humiliated in front of Detective Blake. Neither one of those things is okay, Taylor. Did he hurt you physically?"

Taylor shook her head quickly and turned away.

"Taylor?"

With a sigh, Taylor answered, "It's just a couple of bruises."

"Christ." Angry now, Gray said, "Take off the sweatshirt. Let me take a look."

Taylor slid away from her, raising her hands in defense. "It's just a couple of bruises. It's not a big deal."

"Jesus, Taylor. It starts off with a couple of bruises and before you know it he's beating the shit out of you on a regular basis."

"I wouldn't let him beat me for crying out loud. I wouldn't put up with that." Taylor brought her knees up, curling into a ball and rubbed her hands over her face. "One minute he's telling me he can't survive without me and the next … I just don't know what the hell to think."

The shrill ring of the room phone pierced the air and Taylor's stomach twisted in knots. "That's either Cail or Chris," Gray announced, watching Taylor for a reaction.

"If it's Cail, please don't tell him I'm here. I don't want to deal with him tonight."

With a nod, Gray picked up the phone. She didn't even get a chance to say hello before Cail's voice boomed, "Is she there?"

"If you want to talk to me, Cail, you'll lower your voice."

She heard a long sigh, then, "I'm sorry. It's just that I can't find her."

"She's not here, but I've talked to her and she's okay, despite the verbal and physical assault." There was absolute silence on the line and Gray started to wonder if his cell phone lost the connection.

"Cail?"

"I didn't hurt her," he said with barely controlled fury.

"You put bruises on her. What would you call it, Constable?"

"Gray," Taylor whispered. Pissing him off was just going to make matters worse.

"I didn't mean to hurt her, Gray. I was angry because Kate had been assaulted. Taylor could have prevented it."

"Oh, my God. Do you really believe that? It's Taylor's fault that both she and Kate were assaulted? I'm hanging up now." Gray set the phone back onto the base and unplugged it. "Jesus."

Gray had it wrong. Taylor knew it *was* her fault Kate was assaulted. It was her past history with Rappaport that had him lying in wait. She put Kate in danger just by being associated with her. "I'm sorry," Taylor said as she uncurled her legs and stood. "I shouldn't have come here and put you in the middle of this. It's just upsetting you and the baby."

"Where do you think you're going?"

"I'm going to go downstairs and get a room. That way when Cail shows up, you can let him look around to see that I'm not here then kick him out."

"That's just crazy. Sit your ass down and if he shows up, we'll deal with it. If you walk out that door, I'll really be stressed." Gray marched into the kitchen, announcing, "I'm making you a hot tea."

With her hand on the door knob, Taylor leaned her brow against the door. She didn't know what the hell to do. Pulling her phone out of her pocket, she took a deep breath then turned it on. Seventeen text messages from Cail and three from Chris waited for her. She opened Chris's first and found Cail was calling Chris every five minutes demanding to know where the hell she was. She typed:

Sorry for the harassment. I'll see that it stops.

Cail's messages were all along the lines of 'where the hell are you?' She sent a message stating she was somewhere safe, stop harassing Chris and Gray, and she'd talk to him tomorrow. Seconds after she hit send, her phone was ringing. Taylor took another deep breath before hitting talk.

"Where the hell are you? We need to talk."

Taylor closed her eyes with her head still leaning into the door. "I don't want to talk to you right now. Leave Chris and Gray alone and I'll talk to you tomorrow."

"Are you telling people I assaulted you?"

"No, it's not like that," she sighed.

"Do you have bruises on you?"

"Do you think I care about some bruises? It was what you said, Cail. It was how you said it and how you made me feel."

"Damn it, Tay. You could have prevented her from being hurt."

It hurt that he blamed her for Kate's injuries even though she knew it was true, but not in the sense Cail was implying. "If I hadn't done it when I did, it would have been so much worse."

"You don't know that."

"I saw what he was planning to do. I felt what he was planning to do," she choked back a sob. "Did you stop to think that maybe the timing of it made all the difference? If I'd tried earlier, I may not have seen him waiting in the dark and I may not have seen Kate." Taylor flinched when she felt the hand on her back then relaxed again when she realized it was Gray.

"Jesus, Tay. Tell me where you are. I'll come pick you up."

"No. I need some time. I'll talk to you tomorrow." Taylor didn't wait for a response. She hung up and turned the phone off again. Turning into Gray, she let her tears fall once again.

* * *

When Gray went off to bed, Taylor stayed curled up in a tight ball in the corner of the sofa. There was too much circling through her mind for her to settle into sleep. She bounced between wondering what to do about Cail, her anxiety over the trial, the curse of the visions and using her psychic ability, blaming herself for Kate being hurt, Rappaport still being on the loose, worrying about her physical with Lane, and dealing with sporadic memories of her baby boy lying in her arms. She was startled when she felt Gray's hand touch her shoulder and surprised when she looked up and it was daylight.

"You haven't even tried to sleep, have you?" Gray asked in a gentle voice.

Rubbing her hands over her face, Taylor asked, "What time is it?"

"Nearly seven." Gray put caffeinated coffee on thinking Taylor could really use the caffeine and turned the kettle on to make herself a tea.

"I need to pick up my car from Cail's then go over to Chris's for some clothes."

"Why don't I just come with you," Gray offered. "We can get Emma to pick us up at Headquarters after your physical."

Taylor unfolded her legs and went to the breakfast bar, sliding onto a bar stool. "You don't need to do that, Gray. I'll be fine."

Gray took a couple of mugs out of the cupboard then turned to Taylor with a sigh. "I want to go with you. There's nothing wrong with having a friend tag along for support."

Taylor's elbows slid down the counter and she laid her head on the back of her hands. "I guess I could use it. I'm terrified of this stupid physical. I don't see why it's necessary." She had no idea why she suddenly burst into tears. How could she go sixteen years without shedding a tear and now she seemed to be crying all the time? Gray came around the counter to comfort her, circling her hand over Taylor's back.

* * *

When they got to Chris's, a man was installing an alarm system just inside the door as another wandered throughout the house installing contact alarms on all of the windows and exterior doors. A third man had just finished installing new glass on the back door and passed Taylor and Gray on his way out.

Gray and Taylor stepped inside to find Chris sitting on the sofa wearing an olive green shirt, cargo pants, and hiking boots, her feet up on the coffee table as she typed away on a laptop. "Hey," she called out as she continued typing. "Come on in. I'm just finishing up my report from last night."

"Any news?" Taylor asked, but she knew Rappaport was still out there. She was trying to keep herself open to her psychic abilities and practicing what Quinn taught her. She couldn't forgive herself if Rappaport got to Kate again, or to Chris or Gray.

Chris wasn't sure if she was asking about Rappaport or Cail then decided Taylor would be able to get an update on Cail directly from the source if she wanted. She opted not to tell her Cail had already dropped by looking for her. "Boone picked up Justin Ripkin last night. He was questioned and released. Rebecca Knightley has yet to be found." She turned her attention back to her laptop, adding, "There's coffee in the kitchen if you want it. I'll put the kettle on in a minute if you want some tea, Gray."

"I can get it. You keep working on your report." Gray smiled when Kate came bounding down the hall wearing jeans and a red turtle neck sweater, her long jet black curls bouncing. She stopped quickly to lean over the sofa and wrap her arms around Chris, planting a quick kiss on her cheek. "Morning, Kate," Gray greeted.

"Morning," she grinned. "I'm glad you're both here. My parents have invited you over for dinner tonight. Six o'clock."

Taylor felt that familiar twisting in her gut, but she offered a weak smile before Kate wrapped her in a tight hug. "Thank you for what you did last night."

"You okay?"

"A few bruises, but otherwise I'm great." Leaning back, Kate studied Taylor's face, the red, puffy eyes with dark circles underneath. "You look like shit."

"Kate." Chris turned from the laptop then saw Kate was right. Taylor looked like she'd been up crying all night. "You do look like shit."

Taylor's response was a frown. "Mind if I take a shower?"

"No, go ahead." Chris waited until Taylor went into the spare room then turned towards Gray in the kitchen. The look of concern on Gray's face didn't surprise her. She knew Taylor was angry with Cail, but she hadn't expected her to look quite so upset. "She had a rough night."

Gray glanced at the man working on the alarm system then moved to the sofa, sitting beside Chris as Kate came around the sofa to join them. Quietly, Gray explained, "She just had a shower an hour and a half ago."

They sat in silence while Taylor came out of the spare room and crossed the hall into the bathroom. "Is this because of what happened last night?" Chris whispered.

Gray raised her hands then dropped them to her knees. "I don't know. She's dealing with so much right now, I'm not sure you can narrow it down to just one thing. She's been up all night and she's very emotional. I really don't know what to do for her."

"Did Cail hurt her last night?" Kate looked pale as a ghost when she asked the question she wasn't sure she wanted the answer to. "Detective Blake said he roughed her up a bit."

Chris laid a hand on Kate's thigh as she watched the two men who were installing the alarm system gathering up their tools at the front door.

"You're all set," the older man called out. "Do you need a quick tutorial?"

"No, I think I've got it." Chris already had the manual with the codes written in it and it wasn't like she wasn't familiar with alarm systems. "Thanks for the quick service."

"No problem, Detective Sergeant. Let me know if you have any issues." He nodded and the two of them stepped out, closing the door behind them. As soon as it closed, both Chris and Kate turned back to Gray who was looking more and more pregnant by the day. She wore a pair of dark blue maternity slacks and an oversized blouse in a light shade of blue that set off her deep blue eyes.

Gray wasn't altogether comfortable discussing this with anyone, never mind Cail's sister. "I think humiliating her in front of another cop was much more damaging than a few bruises." Gray felt for Kate as she watched her sink into the back of the sofa, twisting the hem of her sweater between her fingers.

Chris dropped her legs and set the laptop on the coffee table. "Maybe I should give Lane a heads up."

"No," Gray said, patting Chris's leg. "Leave that to Taylor." She got up as the kettle came to a boil, leaving Chris and Kate on the sofa.

"You okay?" Chris whispered. When Cail stopped by earlier, he swore to Kate he hadn't hurt Taylor.

"I could kill him right now. What the hell was he thinking?"

* * *

Taylor didn't see Tara MacNeil sitting in the corner of the waiting room of Dr. McIntyre's office flipping through a magazine. She walked straight to the receptionist and was taken right through to an exam room while Gray took a seat in the waiting room.

The small exam room was painted a soft green. A small counter and sink took up one corner with an exam table along the long wall and a computer station and two chairs along the opposite wall. Taylor felt like she was in a hospital.

"Take everything off and put this on with the opening to the back," the receptionist told Taylor as she handed her a gown. "Dr. McIntyre will be in to see you in a few minutes." She closed the door behind her and left Taylor alone.

Taylor set the gown on the exam table and sat in one of the chairs, bouncing her legs on the balls of her feet and tapping her fingers on her thighs. She had her hair up in a French twist and was wearing her long black leather coat over black skinny pants and an oversized grey shirt. Black leather ankle boots adorned her feet. She leaned her head back and took several calming breaths to settle her nerves.

Lane walked in several minutes later, frowning when she saw Taylor fully clothed looking terrified. "You were supposed to put the gown on."

Taylor's eyes flicked quickly up to glance at Lane then she stared straight ahead again. "I can't do this," she whispered.

With a sigh, Lane sat at the computer station. "Will you at least let me take your blood pressure?"

"There's nothing wrong with me, Lane."

"Then you won't mind me taking your blood pressure." McIntyre watched Taylor closely. The colour had drained from her lips now too and her breaths were quick and short.

Her eyes flicked to Lane again. "It smells like a hospital in here."

"Okay, we'll go into my office." Lane took Taylor's arm as she stood and led her through to the office where Cail sat waiting in uniform on one of the leather chairs. Ignoring him, Taylor took the seat Lane led her to then bent forward, hiding her face in her hands.

Cail was shocked by how frail she looked as he watched her tremble.

Lane went back into the exam room and returned with a blood pressure cuff and stethoscope. Sitting next to Taylor, she said, "I'll need you to take your coat off and roll up your sleeve."

Taylor stood and shrugged out of her coat. "He needs to leave." She wasn't going to be able to push the sleeves up far enough which meant she'd need to take her shirt off and she wasn't prepared to do that with Cail sitting there.

Cail was out of his chair, forcing Taylor to raise her hands in defense and take a quick step back in retreat. "Goddamn it, Tay. You're going around telling people I assaulted you. If you've got some bruises you'll fucking well show me."

Lane stepped between them and addressed Cail in a stern voice. "Sit down or I'll ask you to leave."

"I'm not telling people you assaulted me," Taylor defended quietly.

Cail's fists balled at his sides, his face red. "You told Chris, Kate and Gray."

I haven't even talked to Chris or Kate about it. I talked to Gray last night, but I haven't told anyone that you assaulted me."

Lane raised her voice, "This is the last time I'm going to say it, Caillen, sit down."

With gritted teeth, Cail backed off and sat down. Taylor wrapped her arms around herself and paced back and forth, trying to release some of her nervous energy.

"Why don't you tell me what happened, Cail?" Lane asked while she took her usual seat. "Starting from when you approached Taylor on Avenue Road."

Cail glared at her.

Lane didn't explain how she knew. "You were angry with Taylor."

"She could have prevented Kate from being hurt if she hadn't stalled on using her ESP. Damn right I was angry."

"What makes you think Taylor could have prevented what happened to Kate?"

"She could have seen what was going to happen. If she'd done it when Chris first asked her, we could have gotten to Chris's before Kate got there. We would have Rappaport in custody."

"The limited experience Taylor has had with these visions makes it impossible for anyone to predict what she might have or might not have seen. To my knowledge, she's only ever had one vision that dealt with something that would happen in the near future. Most of her visions have been of things that have already happened. Cail, it's unrealistic to blame Taylor for what happened to Kate. If anything, her vision prevented a much worse scenario."

Cail knew Lane was right. He'd known it from the moment Taylor explained to him the night before that the timing of her vision may have been key. He needed to blame someone and Taylor had been convenient.

"Go on," Lane encouraged softly. "Tell me what happened last night."

"I yelled at her for going off on her own after Rappaport. Blake and I had to track her down instead of going to check on Kate."

Lane watched him as his fists remained clenched at his sides. He was staring at Taylor now instead of keeping eye contact with her. "Did you put your hands on Taylor?"

Cail answered with a clenched jaw. "I may have grabbed her arms, but I didn't hurt her."

Taylor let out a breath that almost sounded like a laugh. She continued to pace, staring down at the floor. Her emotions were right there, balled in her throat ready to leap out at the slightest motivation. She wished the hell she could feel anger instead of all of this hurt. Biting back her tears she quickly started unbuttoning her shirt. As soon as she got it off, she sank into one of the chairs and covered her face with her hands, feeling humiliated all over again.

Lane's jaw clenched at seeing the dark hand prints on both of Taylor's upper arms. She glanced at Cail who sat staring at Taylor's arms before dropping his head in shame with tears in his eyes. Lane got up to sit on the arm of Taylor's chair and got a peak at the mottled bruises on her upper back and shoulders, disappearing under her black tank top. She touched her fingers softly to the bruises, letting Taylor know she'd seen them. "Are there any more?"

Taylor shook her head.

Lane turned back to Cail. "When you grabbed Taylor's arms, did you push her into anything?"

"I was angry. I just remember grabbing on to her and trying to shake some sense into her. We were standing in front of a wall, but I don't remember pushing her into it."

"Cail, how do you think Taylor felt with you physically and verbally assaulting her in front of another officer?"

Cail's anger spiked again and he glared at Lane.

"What would you call it?" she asked calmly. "You're a police officer. What do you call the way you treated Taylor?"

"I didn't mean to hurt her," he growled through gritted teeth.

"No, of course not," Lane responded. "Has he ever hurt you before, Taylor?"

Taylor just shook her head again.

"I'll go to anger management," Cail offered. "I'll do whatever needs to be done … just don't leave me, Tay. I really didn't mean to hurt you."

"It's not the bruises that hurt so much," Taylor responded. "I told you that last night. I've got nothing else to say to you right now."

"Goddamn it." Cail pressed the heels of his hands to his eyes then reeled on Lane. "Goddamn MaryAnn Blake sent you a fucking report."

"No," Lane responded. "Although she should have filed a report." She got up and went to her desk, turning the iMac monitor around to face them and clicked play on a video. "This was sent in by a concerned citizen late last night."

Cail watched himself grab Taylor and slam her into the wall and felt sick. He pushed her with such force her feet came right off the ground before she hit the wall. The video played out, capturing the entire incident in both audio and video. "Christ. I'm so sorry, Tay."

Taylor felt as sick as Cail. She looked up at Lane with terror in her eyes. "Please tell me that didn't go to the media."

"No. At least, not that I'm aware of."

"What happens now?" Cail asked.

"You're to go and see Sergeant Nadle. When you're done with him, your father would like to see you in his office."

"What about us, Tay?"

Taylor felt sick for him, but there was nothing she could do at this point. She knew he would be turning in his weapon and his badge to Sergeant Nadle pending a disciplinary hearing. As far as their relationship went, Taylor didn't know what to do. "I need some time to think things through," she said quietly.

Cail looked defeated. He slowly got to his feet. "Okay. I love you, Tay. I meant what I said about not being able to survive without you." With that, he crossed to the door and walked away.

Taylor wasn't sure if that meant he was going to kill himself if she didn't go back to him or what. She looked up at Lane with tears in her eyes. "Lane, you don't think he would ..."

"No, he's trying to make you feel guilty enough to take him back. He's not going to hurt himself, Taylor." She took a seat next to Taylor, sliding her arm around her back as Taylor dropped her head into her hands again.

"I've recommended he participate in anger management counseling. If you want to continue your relationship with him, Taylor, I think it would be a good idea for both of you to come and see me together for a while."

"I need some time to think this all through. I don't know what to do, Lane. I just don't know what to do."

"You take all the time you need. Don't let him bully you into taking him back."

"We just heard," Chris said from the doorway, flanked by Kate and Gray.

Lane looked up at them, annoyed. "From who?"

"Inspector Worthington," Chris answered. "Is Taylor okay?" The three of them stood in the doorway. From their vantage point, the bruises on Taylor's back and left arm were visible.

"Come in and close the door," Lane said.

Taylor kept her face buried in shame. Gray sat on the arm of Taylor's chair and began rubbing her back. Once again, the rhythm of the slow circles helped Taylor to calm herself.

Chris and Kate sat across from them in silence.

"We can cancel the book signing," Gray offered.

"No," Taylor shook her head. "It'll be fine."

Chris was itching to see the video. She glanced over her shoulder at the iMac screen then turned back to a scowl from Lane. God, the woman could read her mind. "We've got a security detail set up for the signing this afternoon. I've got Kevlar vests for both of you, plus one for Emma."

"You think that's necessary?" Gray asked.

"Yes," Chris answered quickly. "Same deal for tomorrow at the court house."

Taylor felt sick again at the mention of the trial tomorrow. She hoped to have heard something by now. The more time that past, the more she figured Sarah Johnson hadn't taken the bait. The urge to run was nearly unbearable, but she didn't have the time. "I need to clean myself up a bit," she said.

"Let me just get this done," Lane said as she secured the blood pressure cuff around Taylor's arm. "It's going to put some pressure on those bruises," she warned as she began to pump it up.

It hurt, but Taylor didn't show any signs that she felt pain nor did she complain. She sat quietly with her free hand covering her face until Lane removed the cuff then she grabbed her shirt and headed for the washroom. As soon as she was out the door, Chris made her way to the iMac and clicked play on the video.

"Chris," Lane admonished. She made her way quickly to the desk, but it was too late. They'd already seen Cail thrusting Taylor into the wall. Lane turned the monitor around and closed out the program.

"Oh, God." Kate wasn't expecting the level of violence she saw on the video. She was downright shocked at her brother's behaviour. She sat there open mouthed even after Lane turned the monitor.

Chris raked her hand through her hair. "Holy shit." Now she wished she hadn't played it.

"Repeat what you just saw and I'll make damn sure you're disciplined," Lane sternly advised.

"You know me better than that, Lane. I'm nosey as hell, but I don't have a big mouth." Chris frowned at the glare she got from Lane.

Taylor told Gray what Cail said, but even she wasn't prepared for the force with which Cail slammed Taylor into that wall. "What happens to Cail?"

"He's being suspended pending an investigation and disciplinary hearing," Kate answered. When her father told her she thought they were over-reacting. After seeing a few seconds of the video, she understood why he was being disciplined, but she still couldn't believe it.

Chapter 21

A black Cadillac Escalade pulled to a stop in front of Police Headquarters. "There's Emma," Taylor nodded towards the glass door.

They made their way out to the car and piled into the back. Chris gave Emma a quick briefing and helped her into a Kevlar vest as Taylor stared silently out the window. As they rolled up on the library, Taylor saw the mass of reporters filling the sidewalk and the line of people waiting outside in the cold. "Take Gray in first," Taylor said to Chris. "I don't want all those reporters pushing and shoving her."

"Okay," Chris nodded. "You're up, Gray. We'll take you in as well, Emma." She waited for the two body guards to open the door then stepped out. She turned to help Gray and Emma out and Kate followed them. They circled Gray and led her in among shouts and screams from both the reporters and the people in the line.

While she waited, Taylor listened to the crowd chanting her name and it almost made her laugh. What the heck made all these people crave her? She couldn't figure it out. Chris, Kate and the two body guards made their way back to the vehicle and formed a tight circle before opening the door. As soon as Taylor stepped out, everyone went wild. The pushing and shoving started immediately, nearly knocking Kate off her feet. The crowd was screaming and calling out to her. It was nearly enough to drown out the shouts of the reporters, but not quite. Most of the questions were about the baby. Everyone wanted to know what happened to her baby. She did her best to ignore them, but just before they made it through the door to the library, someone called out, "Is it true you and your boyfriend have a list of sexual acts that you refuse to perform?" Her face reddened in both embarrassment and anger, but she didn't look back to see who asked the question.

Inside, she pulled Chris aside. "Have you told anyone about that sex book you found when you packed up my room at the Academy?"

Chris heard the question, too. "Taylor, you asked me not to say anything about it, so I haven't. Besides, you never told me you made a list. You just said that Cail needed to know what was going to set you off."

Taylor paced back and forth like a caged lion. "Jesus, Chris. How could they find that out? It had to have come from Cail."

"Not necessarily. Where's the list? Did you write it out or put it on your computer?"

"Oh, God." Taylor stopped pacing because she was sure her knees were about to give out. "It was in the back of the book, in the night stand in Cail's room."

"I'll call Cail and ask him to check."

"No, it's alright. I'll do it," Taylor said. She walked further down the hall for privacy. When Cail didn't answer she left a desperate message. "I need you to check that sex book in the night stand in your room. I need to know if the list is still there. Cail … a reporter knows about that list. Please, check and call me back." Turning, she walked back towards Chris. "I need a few minutes," she said in passing. She headed inside the library as Chris, Kate, and Gray watched after her.

"What's going on?" Gray asked.

"A reporter asked a question that upset her," Chris responded, keeping her promise not to say anything about the book.

Gray found her in the back corner of the library in a whimsical sitting area. The corner was filled with lush green plants. Plush chairs circled a centre water feature. As she listened to the water fall, Gray watched Taylor tucked up in the corner chair with rays of light from the skylight shining down on her dark hair. "You've spent a lot of time here," Gray said, smiling.

"Ha," Taylor choked back a sob. She couldn't afford any tears now. "I read all of your books sitting right here."

Gray smiled as Cail stepped up quietly behind her. Studying Taylor curled up in her little sanctuary, he thought he'd never seen her look so beautiful. He took out his phone and captured her photo so he'd never forget how she looked at that moment. "I just got your message." It nearly broke his heart when she looked up at him with her bright green eyes so sad.

"I'll give you some privacy," Gray said. She took one last look at Taylor then turned and walked away.

Taking the seat next to Taylor, Cail reached for her hand. She stared down at their hands with their fingers interlocked then closed her eyes, feeling all those familiar sparks and emotions. "Would you go and check for me?"

"I'll go." He lifted her hand to his mouth, brushing his lips over her knuckles. "Tay, I'm so sorry."

"I know," she whispered gently. Her eyes were burning, but she held back the tears. "I'm sorry, too." When he leaned in and brushed his lips over hers, she felt the desperate need he always brought out in her. With her core muscles clenching she closed her mouth over his and took, savouring the taste of him. They were both desperate for more, when Taylor pulled away. Her hand covered her forehead as she asked herself what the heck she was doing. She just couldn't control the desire he stirred in her. If she was going to take the time to really think about their relationship and the effects of his anger, she'd have to stay away from him or she'd just cave.

"You look like an angel, sitting here," Cail whispered. "My angel." Leaning in again, his lips caressed her temple.

"Cail." She couldn't handle his comfort at that moment, so she turned away from him.

Cail let out a sigh, knowing he had a lot of making up to do. "Let me walk you back, then I'll go to the apartment and check the book."

With a nod from Taylor, they stood and Cail kept his hand firmly locked in hers. He led her out to the front of the library where the tables and displays were set up. Gray's latest book, *Strength of Innocence*, wasn't due out for another week, but fans here had the opportunity to purchase the book pre-release. Emma had set up a display to the right of the tables showing the cover of the book and a life size photo of Gray. To the left of the tables, next to a life size cardboard cut out of Taylor, the cover of *Leila's Locket* was displayed with the title written in the top third in big, block letters. Dangling from the E in 'Locket' was a gold chain and heart shaped locket. Taylor was perched beneath the title, sitting with her legs curled up to her chest, one hand around her lower legs and the other extended out in front of her, palm up, cupped just under the dangling locket.

Chris stood with her arm around the cardboard Taylor, laughing. "This is your last signing, right? Can I take this home?"

"What the heck would you want that for?" Taylor asked.

"Sure, you can take it," Emma offered.

"I'm going to put it in my living room. If I ever get pissed at you, we can use it as a dart board."

"Lovely." Taylor smiled then took her seat at the table, shaking her head.

"There's a box of books at your feet," Emma whispered to Taylor.

"Thanks, Em." She looked over at Gray settling in to the seat next to her. "You ready?"

"Hang on," Gray said as she opened a hard cover book and began writing. When she closed the book, she leaned over and passed it to Taylor. "I want you to have the first one."

Taylor found herself fighting back tears again. "Thanks, that means a lot to me." She opened the book to the page Gray signed. The dedication printed on the page read, 'To my dearest friend and sister, Taylor Grace. Thank you for inspiring this story.' Below it Gray had written, "You're the strongest person I know and the most beautiful soul I've ever met. Thank you for gracing my life with your friendship. With all my love, Gray.'

Oh crap, Taylor thought as she swiped at the tears. "I should have read that later." If she didn't get herself under control, she felt like she was going to completely lose it again. When Chris danced past the front of the table with cardboard Taylor, she saved the day by making Taylor laugh. "Put that back," Taylor ordered, but she was nearly doubled over.

"Doing some reading today, Taylor?" Taylor recognized the voice before she turned to see Annie standing behind her. She stood quickly with a wide smile and embraced the librarian she'd known since childhood.

Annie was taken aback at Taylor's hug. Everyone who worked at this library for any length of time knew Taylor shied away from being touched and they were always careful not to get too close to her. The Taylor standing in her arms was a new, more confident Taylor than she'd known. "We're so proud of you, Taylor," Annie cried. "But we sure as heck miss you around here."

"I'll try to stop by more often."

"Susan wants to thank you for the donation you made to the library. She'll see you after the signing if that's okay."

Gray raised her eyebrow at hearing about the donation. It was just the kind of thing Taylor would do and not say a word about.

"I'd love to see her," Taylor said and took her seat again just as Emma announced the doors were opening.

Two hours later they were still busy signing away. Gray leaned over and whispered, "This book's either going to be on the best-seller list by the time we're done here or my hand is going to drop off."

"Believe me," Taylor answered. "You're hand drops off first." She sent Gray a smile just as a vision flashed into her head. She saw a man striking a woman, but it was gone as quick as it had come. Taylor searched the line for the faces she'd seen, but found no match. She turned her attention to the young girl standing in front of her. "Hi." Taylor recognized the signs of someone who lived on the streets. She figured the girl was about fourteen. Her jet black hair was a bit too oily, her clothes worn and dirty. Taylor was pulling a book out from under the table as the girl started to speak.

"I don't have a book or anything. I just wanted to meet you."

"What's your name?"

"Kelsey."

"You're on the streets," Taylor said as she signed the book. "Are you in school?"

"Yeah, I'm in grade nine. I wasn't going to bother going back this year, but I heard about you."

With a smile, Taylor handed her the book. "Here Kelsey, I want you to have this. There's a card inside with my cell number on it. You can call me if you ever want to talk."

"Seriously?" Kelsey asked, wide eyed.

"Seriously," Taylor responded.

"Cool, thank you."

"You're welcome. Stay in school."

As Kelsey walked away, Emma leaned over and whispered, "That never gets old."

"I know, right?" Taylor smiled then just about jumped out of her skin when something brushed against her neck. Cail's voice whispered in her ear.

"It's there. It's still in the back of the book."

Taylor whipped her head around, staring up at Cail as another vision ripped through her. She saw the same couple. The man punched the woman in the face before throwing her on the bed and climbing on top of her. Taylor whipped around again and studied the crowd for the busty blonde she'd seen in the vision.

"What do you want me to do?" Cail whispered again.

"Did you leave it in the book? We need to destroy it."

"Is everything okay?" Gray asked.

"No, not really." Taylor got Chris's attention and gave a slight shake of her head and a shrug of her shoulder.

Knowing what Taylor was referring to, Chris took Cail's arm and pulled him aside. "Have you told anyone about that list?"

"No," he answered. "Well … Kate and Dave, but they wouldn't have known where it was and they wouldn't have told the damn media."

Chris had a sinking feeling in her gut. "You're sure they wouldn't have told anyone who might have passed it on?"

"They're my brother and sister. They wouldn't have told anyone."

"Okay," Chris soothed, but she moved away, pulling out her cell phone to call Detective Blake.

Taylor had several more ugly visions before she saw the woman standing in line with big, dark sunglasses on. She leaned over to Emma. "Can we take a break now?"

"Sure." Emma stood and announced to the crowd that Ms. Sinclair and Ms. Rowan would be taking a short break.

"Thank God," Gray smiled. "Gotta pee."

Taylor laughed as Gray toddled off to the washroom with Kate as an escort. She turned to Annie. "Is there a private room I can use for a few minutes?"

"Sure. You can use the break room. You know where it is."

"Thanks." Taylor moved down the line, closely followed by a body guard and Chris. She approached the buxom blonde who clutched a copy of *Leila's Locket* to her chest. "Hi, I'm Taylor."

The woman smiled. "Yeah, I figured that. Mel."

"Do you have a few minutes to talk?"

Mel's brow furrowed and she took a step back. "About what?"

"It's alright. I just want to talk," Taylor tried to soothe. She held her hand out and, reluctantly, Mel took it and followed her to the break room. Taylor closed the door behind her, shutting out the body guard and Chris. She gestured to a chair and waited until Mel sat then took the seat next to her. "You've probably heard that I get these visions … ESP kinda thing."

Mel squirmed in her seat. "I guess."

"I saw, Mel. I saw what he does to you."

Mel turned away from her, but not before Taylor saw the flash of anger and the humiliation in her eyes.

"Do you want help? Do you want to get away from him?"

"He'll kill me," Mel whispered. "He's waiting outside. He'll kill me."

"I can get you out of here right now and get you to the Secret Garden where you'll be safe. You can stay there until you get back on your feet." Taylor knew exactly how Mel felt as she sat and watched her tremble. "It's up to you, Mel."

"I want out, but I'm scared. What will happen to Mike?"

"He'll be arrested and charged. I'll send a female detective to the Secret Garden to interview you."

"Oh, God." Mel shook, still clutching the book to her chest. "He'll kill me."

"He won't be able to get to you, Mel." Taylor sat quietly watching Mel tremble and knew she was trying to convince herself she could do this.

The way things had been going, Mel was sure it wouldn't be too long before Mike took things too far and she'd be dead. "Okay, okay. I'll do it. I need to do it."

"Wait here for a minute while I set it up, okay?" At Mel's nod, Taylor stepped outside the room.

Chris was waiting with the body guard, her arms folded in front of her. "What the hell are you doing?"

"Her husband is parked outside in a white Chevy Cavalier. Can you have him picked up? I'm going to see if Gray can arrange for her to go to the Secret Garden. I told her a female detective will come and interview her there."

"What are their names?" Chris asked as she took out a notebook.

"Melanie and Michel Gallant. He goes by Mike."

Chris wrote in her notebook then grabbed her phone and called Kate, asking her to bring Gray over. When she got there, Taylor took Gray inside. "Mel, this is Gray Rowan."

"Oh, wow. I've read a lot of your books."

"Nice to meet you." Gray smiled at Mel then looked to Taylor wondering what was going on.

"I was hoping you could call the Secret Garden and see if they can take Mel in right away," Taylor explained.

Without another word, Gray pulled out her phone and made the call. Taylor stepped out again to get one of the body guards to bring the Escalade around to the back of the library. She escorted Mel out and got her settled into the vehicle. "Is there anything you want to pick up before you go?"

Mel shook her head. "No. No. I just want out."

"Okay." Taylor smiled and nodded to the book. "Would you like me to sign that?"

"Ha. I guess that's why I came here."

Although she let out a quick laugh, Taylor could see Mel was close to tears. She wrote quickly in the book and handed it back to Mel. "Good luck, Mel. I stuck a card in there with my cell number on it. You can call me if you ever want to talk or anything."

With watery eyes, Mel reached out and took Taylor's hand. "Thank you."

"My pleasure." Taylor closed the door and watched them drive away before making her way back inside the library. Chris stood watch outside the door and was on Taylor as soon as they walked back in.

"Michel Gallant is on his way to lock up. Any reason you've got your spidey senses on alert?"

"My spidey senses?"

"You know what I mean. Are you opening yourself up to seeing other people's shit because you blame yourself for what happened to Kate last night?"

"I've got to get back to signing."

"Damn it, Taylor. Talk to me."

"I don't have time for this right now."

Chris let it go, but she'd damn well make her take the time later. Taylor and Gray settled back into their seats and for the next two hours signed hundreds of books. Taylor was rolling her shoulders and shaking out her hand under the table when Gray leaned over and whispered, "I can see the end of the line."

"Hallelujah," Taylor sung and laughed. She glanced down the line to the last person, locking eyes with Gabriella Atwood. She had to be in her late forties, but Taylor thought she looked great with her long dark curls and big brown eyes. She had gorgeous olive skin similar to Taylor's. Taylor gave her biological aunt a quick smile. The last time she'd seen her father's sister was at their swearing in ceremony at Police Headquarters. Gabriella hadn't stayed to talk. Taylor knew she was waiting for her to make contact. She also knew Gabriella felt some responsibility for what her brother, Darryl Johnson, put Taylor through.

When Gabriella finally made it to the table, she set four copies of *Leila's Locket* in front of Taylor. Behind Taylor, Chris took a step forward, feeling protective over her when it came to Gabriella Atwood.

With a grin, Taylor asked, "Afraid you'll lose one?" She pulled the books in front of her and opened the first one.

"One for myself and one for each of my kids – Nate, Greg, and Arianna," Gabriella explained. "They'd really like to meet you, Taylor.

We were wondering if you and Cail are free for dinner tonight."

"Oh," Taylor said in surprise.

"I'm sorry. I've dropped a bomb on you."

"No, it's just that we already have plans."

"That's alright," Gabriella soothed. "I should have given you more warning."

Taylor didn't want to commit to the next night. She wasn't sure how she'd feel after the first day of Sarah Johnson's trial. "How about Thursday night?"

Gabriella's eyes lit up and a gorgeous white smile spread across her face. "That would be great. I'll make reservations at Buca on King West. Would six thirty suit you?"

"Sure, that's fine." Taylor finished signing the books and slid them back to Gabriella.

"Taylor, I ..." Gabriella started then had to bite back tears. She shook her head quickly and smiled again. "I'll see you on Thursday." She turned and rushed towards the exit.

Taylor took a deep breath. "That was a bit awkward," she said under her breath as Gray grabbed onto her hand and gave it a gentle squeeze.

"I'm going to run to the ladies room before I talk to Starr," Gray announced. Taylor glanced over to where Cheryl Starr had set up for interviews. She and Gray were each expected to give her five minutes.

As Gray headed for the washrooms, Emma leaned over and whispered in Taylor's ear. "Cheryl Starr would like to interview you with Cail. Is that okay for you?"

That twisting feeling in her gut returned. Taylor glanced up at Cail, who stood behind her with Chris and Kate during most of the signing. "Give me a minute, Em." She stood and went to Cail, relaying Starr's request.

"She's going to ask about the list," Cail realized, taking Taylor's hand.

If she was going to ask about it, Taylor would rather have Cail next to her than deal with it on her own. She let out a shuddering breath, leaned back into the end of a row of book shelves and closed her eyes for a moment. "Why can't they just leave us alone?" When she felt Cail's lips brush over her temple, she could have cried again. She couldn't wait for this week to be over and all of the stress behind her. She hated feeling so emotional which was ironic when she'd spent most of the last sixteen years wishing she could feel something.

Kate returned from escorting Gray to the washroom. She stepped in beside Chris as she watched Taylor and Cail. "How can he be so sweet with her most of the time yet so aggressive when he's angry?"

"Anger can make you do horrible things," Chris answered in monotone. She stood watching Cail for a minute then turned to Kate and brushed her fingers down Kate's cheek. "Things you'll always regret." The show of affection in a public place had Kate's heart swelling and a sharp pang of desire shooting through her.

When the bright lights came on, they all glanced over to see Gray standing with Cheryl Starr. "We've only got a few minutes," Taylor said to Cail. "How are we going to handle this?"

Cail felt Taylor's trembling and wished he could take it all away. "It's no one's business but ours, Tay. I have no problem telling Starr that."

"It had to be whoever took the drawings. I can't see Rappaport doing this."

"Chris," Cail called out. "Did you find anyone on the security tapes from Friday?"

Shit, Chris thought. She wasn't ready to discuss this with any of them. "Nothing conclusive. We didn't find anyone carrying the drawings out. What about fingerprints?"

Cail shook his head in answer. "Just mine and Tay's."

Taylor knew Blake saw something on the video, but this wasn't the time or the place to discuss it. She studied Chris and knew she was holding back.

"You're up," Emma said to Taylor when Starr was finished with Gray. Cail led her over keeping her hand gripped in his. Taylor stood on the mark Starr pointed to on the carpet and Cail stepped in behind her, wrapping his arms around her waist. Taylor nearly laughed when she realized Starr had been standing on a stool for her interview with Gray.

"Give us a minute, Brian," Starr said to the cameraman. She waited until he was out of hearing distance. "I wanted to say this off camera and off the record," Starr began. "A freelance reporter by the name of Kyle Sledmore claims the two of you have a list of sexual acts that Taylor won't perform."

Taylor forced out a quick laugh. "What does that have to do with anything?"

"He claims to have the details of what's on the list that he got from the same source who gave him your drawings." Starr wasn't surprised when she watched the colour drain from Taylor's face. "Personally, I don't think your sex life is anyone's business but your own, but my producer has ordered me to ask you about the list."

Taylor was grateful Cail was supporting her when her knees buckled. Cail didn't flinch. He just tightened his grip on her until she got her legs back. "We appreciate you giving us the heads up, Cheryl," Cail said. "And you're right. It's no one's business but our own."

Starr motioned to the cameraman that they were ready and she climbed up on the stool. At the look she got from Taylor, she laughed. "You're even taller than Gray. If I didn't stand on the stool, I wouldn't be in the frame." Turning to the camera, she began, "With me are Taylor Sinclair and her boyfriend, Caillen Worthington. First off, I'd like to congratulate you, Taylor, on a successful book tour and for a fourth straight week on the New York Times Best-Seller List with *Leila's Locket*."

"Thank you," Taylor blushed.

"In *Leila's Locket*, you talk about the time you spent in Toronto's Public Libraries. You refer to them as sanctuaries, as places you could go to escape from the terrors of the streets. Obviously, Toronto's libraries hold a special place in your heart. Is that why you chose this library for your last signing?"

"Yes, this library in particular. It feels like coming home. I felt safe here and I was able to lose myself in the books I found here."

"Is that why you've made a generous donation to this branch?"

"This library and the people who work here gave me so much more than a place to sit and read. It's the least I can do to try to repay a debt of gratitude."

"I've been watching while you signed copies of your book for close to two thousand fans here this afternoon. You gave several copies of your book away to young people who are living on the streets or in severe poverty. Can you tell us why you do that?"

"The people I wanted to target the book to are not always in a position to afford it. Kids living on the streets are the people who will benefit the most from reading *Leila's Locket*, so I want to make sure they have access to the book."

"And that's also the reason you have donated copies of *Leila's Locket* to every Public Library here in Toronto, as well as to high school libraries?"

"That's right."

"I had a chance to interview a couple of the people you gave a copy of your book to today, Taylor, and they both said you've already been an inspiration to them. Hearing your story has made a difference in their lives. How does that make you feel?"

"I'm not a fan of all of the media attention I seem to attract, but if it has made a difference in even one person's life, I guess I have no reason to complain. I'm grateful my story inspires people to try to better their lives."

"Tomorrow marks the beginning of Sarah Johnson's trial. How are you feeling about it?"

Taylor sighed. "I'll be glad when it's over."

"Both Sarah and Darryl Johnson had a lot to say on the special aired on NNN last Friday evening. Did you watch the special and do you have any comments on it?"

"It sickens me that you've fed her desire for the spotlight. This whole mess began with her grasping at a chance for fifteen minutes of fame. She got more than she bargained for, but by giving her exactly what she wanted, you've probably set her up to profit from her crimes."

"How do you think she's going to profit, Taylor?"

"She knows people are interested in the details of the horrors she's committed. Why wouldn't she write about it? She's going to have plenty of time on her hands."

"Why don't you beat her to it? You've already shown your talent for writing."

With a shrug, Taylor said, "I can't say I haven't thought about it. If it would get the media off my back, it might just be worth it. No offence, Cheryl."

Starr smiled. "None taken. I know this is a difficult topic for you, Taylor, but do you have a child out there somewhere? Did your baby survive the beating?"

Taylor knew it was coming, but she wondered why Starr had given them a heads up about the sex list and blindsided her with the baby. "No comment," she replied with a hard stare.

By now, Starr knew Taylor well enough to know that the look she sent her was a warning to drop that particular topic. She turned her attention on Cail to give Taylor a moment to recover. "What are your thoughts on Taylor writing about the sexual abuse she's suffered, Caillen?"

"She might be right. It may help to alleviate some of the media pressure and it also could be very therapeutic for her."

"Cail, I know you've said you have obligations to your job, but will you be in court to support Taylor tomorrow morning?"

"I've had some changes to my schedule, so I will be there to support Tay." He smiled at Taylor when she turned to glance back at him then pressed a kiss to her temple.

"You seem to have a very close and loving relationship. Do you have any comments on reports coming out this afternoon about a list of sexual acts Taylor refuses to perform?"

"All I've got to say about those reports is Tay and I have a very healthy and active sex life. We're not going to discuss any details of a part of our lives that's very personal and private."

"Is there anything you'd like to add to that, Taylor?"

"No, I think Cail put it very eloquently."

"Congratulations again, Taylor, and I wish you both all the best."

"Thank you," Taylor and Cail said in unison.

Chapter 22

Cail wrapped his arms around Taylor and held her tight. Her arms circled his neck. Even with everything that had happened the night before, she still felt secure in his arms. The world around them dissolved until all she could hear was the slow rhythm of his breathing and all she could feel was his heart pounding against hers, his strong arms cocooning her.

"You okay?" He whispered into Taylor's ear.

"Yeah, fine."

"Come back to the apartment with me. We can talk until we have to go to my parents'."

Taylor turned into him with a sigh. "I need some time to sort out my thoughts, Cail."

"There's so much I need to say to you. I'm scared to death you're going to leave me, Angel."

Taylor rested her head on Cail's shoulder, feeling his hands running slowly up and down her back. "I still don't understand how you make me feel the way I do. Anyone else touches me and it makes my skin crawl. You touch me and it fires up all these sensations I'd never felt before. It's like I just can't get enough."

"You do the same to me."

Lifting her head, she stared into his eyes wondering how that was possible. "I need some space so I can sort out my thoughts. I can't think when you're close to me."

Cail dropped his brow to hers. "Please, don't leave me."

"I don't think I could even if I wanted to. I just need some time."

"Okay, I can live with that. Just don't take too long."

Taylor went back to the Grand with Gray. When they got to her suite, Gray asked, "Do you need to talk?"

"No, you look exhausted. Go and put your feet up for a while before we have to go to the Worthington's."

"You should do the same," Gray said as she studied Taylor's face. "You haven't slept."

"I think I will." Taylor went into the spare bedroom, stripped down to her underwear and tank top, and carefully hung her clothes in the closet. Setting the alarm on her iPhone, she climbed into bed and curled up under the duvet. She didn't expect to sleep with all of the thoughts running through her head, but felt good to cuddle up in the warmth of the bed.

Gray felt like she just dozed off when she woke to the sound of Taylor's screams. She made her way quickly into Taylor's room, throwing on the overhead light. Taylor's body was bowed in the bed, her fists clenched at her sides as she screamed through gritted teeth. Gray leaned on the side of the bed, putting her back towards Taylor to protect her baby bump, and shook Taylor's shoulder as she shouted, "Taylor, wake up. It's just a dream."

Taylor shot up with a gasp. Her hands splayed across her abdomen as she looked down at herself. With a groan, she pulled her knees up and curled into a ball.

"You're okay," Gray leaned over and wrapped her arm around Taylor's shoulder. "It was just a dream."

"Sorry," Taylor whispered.

"You're shaking like crazy."

"It'll stop soon."

"Why don't you lie back down? Get back under the covers. I'll stay with you if you want."

"What time is it? Don't we have to get up?"

"Taylor, you've only been in here for about five minutes."

Taylor glanced at the bedside clock with a scowl. How could she have gotten that deep into a nightmare in just a few minutes? She scooted over to the far side of the bed and lay back down.

Gray turned off the light and climbed in beside her. "What were you dreaming about?" When Taylor didn't answer, she reached over to rub her back and found Taylor still shaking like a leaf. Gray circled Taylor's back, slowly feeling the trembling ebb, until she drifted off to sleep.

When the circling stopped, Taylor listened to the rhythm of Gray's breathing to calm herself the rest of the way.

About thirty minutes later, Gray woke feeling refreshed. She glanced over to see Taylor in the dark, pushed back against the headboard, curled up in her tight little ball. "You awake?"

"Mm-hmm."

"Want to talk about it?"

"About what?"

"Any of the number of things that are weighing on you right now."

Taylor decided to tell her about the one she'd be seeing on the news tonight anyway. "Some reporter wrote a blog post stating Cail and I have a list of sex acts – a list of things that I won't do." Taylor took a deep breath and leaned her head back as she explained how the list came about. "Cail and I were in bed one time at the Academy and I freaked out. I didn't know what he was doing and I panicked. He decided he needed to know what was going to set me off, so he bought a book about sex and we went through it, wrote a list of the things I wasn't comfortable with. The list is in the back of the book, in Cail's night stand. It was there when Cail went to check this afternoon, so the reporter doesn't have the list, but someone told him about it."

"Do you think it was the same person that took your drawings?"

"I don't know. Maybe. We never should have written it down."

"What kind of things are on the list?"

Taylor's cheeks puffed out before she blew out a long slow breath. She passed her cell phone to Gray. At the questioning look she got in return, Taylor explained, "The reporter's blog post has gone viral."

"Oh, no." Gray sat up, taking the phone from Taylor. She scanned quickly through the list. "It's a pretty long list," Gray murmured. "Do you need to be in control, Taylor?" She didn't really expect Taylor to answer, knowing how embarrassed she was talking about this kind of thing.

"Not necessarily. I guess I prefer being in control, but I'm okay when Cail is. He knows what my boundaries are and he doesn't push them too much. The thing is, what that reporter put in his blog isn't accurate. He's got stuff on his list I've never even heard of. Someone may have told him about the list, but it looks like he pretty much made up what he put on it." Taylor figured Gray was probably the only person she could have this kind of a conversation with, but she was still incredibly embarrassed.

Gray handed Taylor's iPhone back to her. "What kind of things are on your list? Is it a long one?"

"There are things on the real list that I'm okay with now. It was just that I didn't know what to expect, I guess."

Gray figured as long as Taylor was talking she'd keep going. She asked, "Do you have orgasms every time you and Cail have sex?"

"Isn't that the point?"

With a laugh Gray said, "I used to think my sex life with Marc was amazing, but when I started sleeping with Patrick I found out a lot was missing in my relationship with Marc. Patrick's focus is on satisfying me. Not to say that Marc's wasn't, but there were times when he was only focused on himself."

"I guess Cail is more like Callaghan. He's slept with a lot of women. He knows what he's doing, which is probably a good thing because I didn't have a clue."

"So, despite this list, you're satisfied with your sex life?"

"Yeah, we both are." At least Cail had never given her any reason to think he wasn't satisfied with their sex life. He was always eager to make love and eager to please. Taylor thought maybe she should ask him outright, just to make sure. She wasn't sure why she was spilling so much out to Gray. Her thoughts turned to the reasons they needed a list. Maybe it would help to put some of it behind her if she talked about it, so she decided to fess up.

"I told Sarah Johnson I was going to get up on the stand and tell everything. I hoped it would be enough to get her to change her pleas. But, I think I would have heard by now. I don't think she took the bait."

"That's why you wanted to talk to her. You thought you could convince her to change her plea and there wouldn't be a trial."

"Yeah," Taylor answered.

"What did she do to you after the baby, Taylor?" As soon as the question was out of her mouth, the alarm on Taylor's phone sang out. She slid off the bed and into the bathroom without answering.

Gray lay in bed for a few more minutes. She worried Taylor was maybe slipping into a depression with everything that happened since she got home just four days ago. She got out of bed when she heard a knock at the door and went to answer it. Looking through the peep hole, she saw one of the bell-men carrying a long white box. She opened the door and the young man announced, "These were just delivered for Taylor Sinclair."

Gray took the box and gave him a generous tip. "Thank you."

"You're very welcome." He smiled at the tip then walked off down the hall. Gray set the box on the kitchen counter and went to get herself ready.

When she came back out, Taylor was curled up in a corner of the sofa, so she took a seat next to her. "I wish there was something I could do to help."

Taylor raised her head then unfurled her legs. "Sorry, I'm being Debbie Downer. I'm just trying to sort out my thoughts, but there's so much swirling around in my head I don't seem to be able to think straight."

"Well, take a break from thinking for a few minutes and open that box on the counter that came for you."

Taylor glanced up at the long white box. "I wasn't expecting anything." She made her way over to it and carefully lifted the lid to a dozen yellow roses. In lieu of a card, there was a letter from Cail. She took it back to the sofa with her while Gray searched for a vase.

"If I'm not mistaken, yellow roses mean friendship, but they also signify new beginnings."

"No one's ever sent me flowers before," Taylor announced as she curled up with the letter. She read through it as Gray arranged the flowers in a vase then set them on the coffee table. "You're good at that. They look beautiful."

"They smell lovely, too."

Taylor leaned forward and breathed in their sweet scent. "Mmm, they do."

"What does the note say?" Gray asked then quickly followed it with, "You don't have to tell me. I'm being nosey."

"He says he's glad someone sent in that video because he never would have believed how horribly he had treated me if he hadn't seen it. He apologized for hurting me and said he's made arrangements to see Dr. McIntyre for anger management counseling." Taylor folded the letter and slid it onto the table. "You can read it if you want."

"Does he want to start over, do you think?"

"I don't know. Maybe. He doesn't want to lose me."

"And you don't want to lose him." It was an easy deduction after seeing them together at the library.

"No, I really don't. Most of the time he's so caring and attentive, but when he gets angry, he scares me. I'm glad he's anxious to get started on therapy. But, in the back of my mind, I'll always be worried about what he'll do the next time he gets angry."

"Well, maybe that's not such a bad thing for now. It will keep you alert if his temper flares while he is learning to manage it."

* * *

They were the last to arrive at the Worthington's. Everyone was settled in the living room in front of the TV watching the news. Taylor wanted to turn and run in the opposite direction.

"Dinner will be a few minutes," Rose informed them. "Make yourselves comfortable." Gray took a seat next to Kate and Chris on the sofa while Taylor opted to lean against the wall. Cail crossed the room to her.

"Thank you for the flowers. They're beautiful," Taylor said.

"Not nearly as beautiful as you, Tay. They don't smell quite as delicious as you either."

"You're really turning on the charm, aren't you?"

"Can't blame a guy for trying," he grinned. He leaned against the wall next to her when Cal turned up the volume on the TV. Over the screaming and shouting, Cheryl Starr's voice boomed out, "We're here outside the Toronto Public Library in the heart of downtown where thousands of screaming fans await the arrival of New York Times Best-Selling authors, Gray Rowan and Taylor Sinclair. They'll be here signing copies of their books from noon to four on this cold afternoon." Cheryl shifted her stance so the camera got a view of the Escalade pulling up in the background. The two bodyguards jumped out of the front and converged on the back door. The camera focused on Gray as they piled out from the back of the vehicle and the noise level of the reporters and the fans surged. Taylor smiled. Gray glowed on camera.

"It appears that Ms. Rowan is under heavy security with two bodyguards and two of Toronto's finest surrounding her as she makes her way into the library," Cheryl announced.

They watched as the bodyguards, Chris, and Kate hurried back to the vehicle. As soon as Taylor stepped out, you could see the wave in the sea of reporters as the pushing and shoving to get close to Taylor began. The noise level went through the roof. "Perhaps this is the reason for the heavy security," Starr reported as she was visibly bounced around.

"Pause it," Taylor suddenly called out. "Pause it."

Cal hit the pause button on the remote and everyone's attention turned to Taylor. She pointed into the sea of reporters behind Cheryl Starr. "Right there. That's Blades. That's Justin Ripkin. Run it back a bit and you'll see him trying to get through the crowd."

Cal pressed rewind until Ripkin was out of the shot then pressed play again. It was obvious he was trying to get close to Taylor. When he wasn't making any progress, he looked angry. Giving up, he turned and disappeared out of the shot. Cal pressed pause again. "Pretty bold move to try to get to you in front of a mob of reporters."

"Maybe he figured he'd blend in. With all the extra security we had there, no one picked up on him until now. If he'd gotten through, it would have been a quick stab and he would have disappeared into the mass of people again. Did you sense anyone there watching you?" Chris asked.

"Oh, yeah. I sensed a lot of people there watching me." Taylor didn't mean to sound so sarcastic, but it was out before she thought it through. "Sorry," she winced. "I was just focused on getting inside, away from the questions. Anyway, Blades wouldn't hurt me. I told you he saved my life."

Everyone's attention turned to Taylor again, including Cail. "What do you mean he saved your life?"

She had to be careful what she disclosed. "He found me, beaten half to death. I would have died if he hadn't come along."

Cal pressed play again. Once Taylor was inside the library, the screen switched back to a shot in the studio. The news anchor flashed her white smile to the camera. "In other Sinclair news tonight, reports of a list of sex acts Taylor Sinclair refuses to perform has reportedly been distributed to several news reporters. Here's freelance reporter, Kyle Sledmore with that story. The screen faded to a shot of Kyle Sledmore standing outside the library.

Taylor pegged him at about forty-five with sandy blonde hair and a salon tan. He looked like the type of guy who kept himself in shape more out of vanity than anything. Taylor walked around the corner, out of the room and leaned against the wall in the foyer. She was too embarrassed to have everyone staring at her while Sledmore told the world about their 'No-Go' list. Cail followed her out and wrapped her in his arms as they listened to the commentary.

"A reliable source close to Caillen Worthington shared with me a list of sexual activities and positions Taylor Sinclair refuses to perform. According to the source, Taylor and Caillen created the 'No-Go' list together in an effort to make her more comfortable during sex."

"Kyle," the studio anchor began, "Why would you bring something like that to the attention of the media? It's obviously a very private matter between Sinclair and Worthington."

"Come on, Susan. You must know by now that everything Sinclair is newsworthy."

"As a journalist, I'm shocked that people who call themselves professionals sink to such a low level just to make a name for themselves." Susan Redman's producer screamed in her ear bud and she flat out ignored him. "Sure, the public has a right to know, but there has to be a line drawn somewhere and I think we've gone way past crossing it with Taylor Sinclair. Where's the professional integrity?"

It was obvious the producer pulled the plug on Susan Redman. The screen went to black for several seconds before an image of Cheryl Starr standing in front of the library appeared. "Uh … well," Cheryl stumbled for words. "Today's book signing here at the Toronto Public Library has been a great success. Both best-selling authors greeted over two thousand fans. A few times during the signing, I watched Taylor give away copies of her book to teenagers who couldn't afford the purchase price. Here's what Kelsey, a fourteen year old girl living on the streets, had to say about her encounter with Taylor Sinclair.

The studio rolled a clip that Cheryl Starr recorded earlier with Kelsey. "What brought you down here to wait in line in the cold to meet Taylor Sinclair, Kelsey?" Starr asked.

"I've seen some of the news coverage on Taylor. Most of the people I know on the streets are talking about her and what she's been able to accomplish. She's an inspiration to all of us and she's the reason I decided to stay in school. I don't want to spend the rest of my life on the streets. I want to be like Taylor and find a way out."

"Taylor gave you a copy of her book. Have you had a chance to read it yet?"

"No, not yet, but I'm super stoked. I couldn't believe it when she just gave me a copy. She made me feel like I'm someone, not just another street rat. She made me feel like I matter."

They rolled Starr's interview with Gray next. Taylor turned to peek around the corner at the TV. Starr asked about her latest book, her recent wedding, and the baby. Taylor watched with a smile as Gray answered Starr's questions with grace and class. She had a way of providing an answer without really revealing anything. When the clip of her and Cail began, Taylor turned back around and rested her head against Cail's shoulder.

When it was over and they went on to other news, Susan Redman had been replaced by a male anchor. Taylor stayed out in the foyer with Cail for a few minutes before Rose called them all to the dining room for dinner.

"You going to be okay to sit through this?" Cail whispered.

"I'm just incredibly embarrassed."

"Don't be. They don't have any details of our private life, Tay. The things that asshole wrote on his blog post are complete bullshit. Someone may have told him about the list, but they didn't tell him what was on it."

"Someone talked to that guy who knew we created it together, Cail. I never told anyone about it until today and you and I were the only ones who referred to it as the 'No-Go' list."

"Are you trying to say that I told people intimate details of our relationship?"

"I'm just stating the facts. I don't know who could have betrayed us like that."

With a long sigh, Cail pressed his lips to Taylor's brow and took her hand. "Come on. We better get to the table before Mum pitches a fit."

They were almost at the dining room when Taylor heard Rose's voice. "She was right. Digging into their sex life crosses a line."

"Oh, and putting Darryl and Sarah on TV for two hours talking about the horrors they did to her isn't crossing a line?" Kate asked.

Taylor stopped dead in her tracks feeling like she'd just been punched in the gut. She couldn't take any more. Didn't people have anything better to talk about? It took a second to get her breath and then she turned and headed for the front door.

Cail grabbed her arm to stop her. "Don't run, Tay. Please."

Pulling out of his grasp, she said, "I can't do this. I'll be at the track at HQ." She grabbed her coat out of the closet and ran out the door without putting it on. By the time Gray got to the front door, Taylor was pulling out of the driveway.

Chapter 23

"She's gone to the track at Headquarters," Cail announced. "She needs to run it out. I'll head over there and check on her after dinner."

Cail took his place at the table, staring down at his plate then glanced around the table. There were two empty place settings – Taylor's and Dave's. "Where's Dave?"

"He said he would be here," Rose answered.

He'd never known his brother to be late for a free home cooked meal. "Was he coming from work?"

"He's on night shift," Cal responded. "Maybe he slept in."

Cail stared down at his plate again. He picked up his fork and proceeded to push the peas around his plate. Rose watched him from the end of the table. It had been a rough twenty-four hours for all of them. Her heart ached for her oldest son. He just looked so despondent. "Maybe a good run would do you some good too, Caillen."

"Maybe we should all go for a run," Kate suggested.

"Have you ever seen her run, Kate?" Cail asked with a slight smile. Rose caught the glimmer in his eye and smiled herself.

"No."

"She moves like a cat, so graceful and fast. She's incredible to watch."

"Why don't we go then?"

"Finish your dinner," Rose ordered. "Then you can all go and Dad and I will clean up."

"You'll talk to Taylor about her testimony, Chris?" Cal asked from the head of the table.

"Yes," Chris responded. It was one of the reasons the Worthington's had invited them all to dinner. Cal and Chris planned to talk to Taylor about her testimony at Sarah Johnson's trial.

"What about her testimony?" Cail asked.

Cal's eyes focused on his son while he decided what to tell him. "The Crown Attorney's Office left several messages for Taylor to make arrangements to rehearse her testimony. She hasn't returned any of their calls."

Silence hung over the table like a thick fog. Cail continued to stare at his plate, pushing his food around aimlessly. "You're worried she's not going to be able to do it."

"That's why we need to talk to her," Cal explained. "If she doesn't think she can, we're going to give her the option of submitting the videos to the Crown Attorney." Cail knew they had videos of Darryl and Sarah assaulting Taylor, but he assumed they would have been admitted as evidence. His eyes shot up and locked on his fathers. "Darryl Johnson kept recordings of Sarah's assaults on Taylor," Cal explained. "For insurance."

"Jesus." Cail dropped his fork onto his plate and rubbed his hands over his face. "Why haven't you submitted them to the Crown Attorneys' Office? They'd probably get a confession and guilty plea out of Sarah if she knew about these videos."

"We didn't want to put Taylor through that. But, if she's not going to be able to testify, we may have to give them over. We want to give Taylor the option."

"Wait a minute," Cail said, feeling sick to his stomach now. "What do you mean by Sarah's assaults on Taylor? Did he record what they did to her when she was pregnant?"

"No. If he recorded it, he must have destroyed it when he believed they killed her. The videos he had all seem to predate the pregnancy. We decided we wouldn't put the videos into evidence unless it was absolutely necessary. You know what that would do to Taylor." Cal stared his son down.

Cail knew his father was right. If those videos got out it would destroy Taylor. "So what are you going to do if she can't testify and she doesn't agree to you releasing the videos? You know she won't agree to it."

"We'll present her with the option. It may give her some incentive and make it easier for her to give her testimony."

The room filled with silence again. No one was eating anymore, their appetites lost to thoughts of what was on the videos.

"As long as we're addressing uncomfortable topics, why don't we address the other elephant in the room?" Cal began. His gaze focused on Cail again. "Who knew about your list?"

Cail's face reddened.

When he didn't answer, Cal asked again. "Who's the reliable source close to Caillen Worthington?"

Cail glared at his father. "You think I have anything to do with talking about that list to the media?"

"Cut the crap, Caillen. Who knew about the list?"

"I don't go around telling everyone about our private lives. The only people I told anything to were Kate and Dave. I haven't told anyone we made the list, just that I needed to know what was going to freak her out."

"What about Lisa?" Kate knew she was risking sending Cail's temper off the scales, but she asked anyway.

"Katie," Rose admonished.

"She's a slut with a big mouth."

Cail turned his ire on Kate. "She's a close friend. One that I can trust."

"Really?" Kate let out a short laugh of disbelief. "You can trust her? She's been sleeping with both you and Dave since high school."

That was news to Cail. He'd been friends with Lisa since grade nine. They had an unspoken agreement that they would hook up when one or the other didn't have anyone else to hook up with – a friends with benefits deal that was more of a booty call than a relationship. That she'd have the same sort of deal with Dave had never occurred to him. The level of his anger raised another notch.

"Enough," Rose scorned. "Both of you."

Chris sat quietly listening to the accusations. She kept to herself what she'd seen on the surveillance tapes from Cail's building. She wanted to talk to the source first then broach the subject with Kate before she presented it to anyone else.

* * *

Taylor's first stop was Cail's apartment to pick up the sex book with the list still tucked in the back. Then she made a quick stop at a Sports Mart and picked up some new running gear. She kept a bag of gym clothes in her locker at Headquarters, but she wanted a shirt with long sleeves to cover the bruises on her arms and upper back. She changed quickly in the locker room and did some warm up stretching before starting at a jog on the red oval. Massive overhead lights lit up the auditorium, giving the impression of daylight. A couple of young men were jogging together, but otherwise the track was clear. When Taylor soared passed them, they unconsciously picked up their pace.

By her second lap, Taylor was going all out. The two young men stepped off the track and just watched her. It was about forty-five minutes later when Chris, Cail, and Kate began stretching beside the track. Gray and Callaghan took a seat in the stands to watch.

Taylor was relieved to see Callaghan with Gray, feeling guilty for ditching Gray at the Worthington's. She knew Callaghan was coming down for the trial, but she hadn't known when he would get in.

Kate stood at the side of the track watching Taylor blaze past. "You've got to be kidding me." She'd never seen anyone run so fast and Taylor made it look so graceful and effortless. Cail had been right, she was something to see.

"Are you coming?" Chris asked as she started out at a jog.

"I think she'll just embarrass me."

With a laugh, Chris turned and ran backwards to face Kate. "She embarrasses anyone who runs with her." Turning again, she fell into a rhythm as Cail sailed past her. Kate caught up and settled into the pace next to Chris.

"How long can she keep that up?"

"I think it depends how much she's got on her mind. I'd say she'll be at it for hours."

Callaghan heard all about Taylor's speed and grace on the track, but he'd never actually had the opportunity to sit and watch her. He sat with his arm around Gray as she leaned back into his shoulder. "Wow. That's all I can think of to say. Just ... wow." Before long, the seats around them began to fill with people dressed in everything from gym clothes to police uniforms and business suits. They watched for a while then the crowd thinned out again.

Taylor continued to run at a good fast pace, desperate to release some of her frustration and nervous energy. Every time she passed Cail, he tried to pick up his pace to run with her, but she just increased her pace until he was left behind her. She needed the space and it seemed like every time she turned around he was smothering her. She knew part of it was because he was worried about her, but the other part was that he was worried she'd leave him. She tried her best to ease his mind, but he just didn't seem able to give her the time and space she needed.

She started going over all of the things that were weighing on her and asking herself if there was anything she could do about it. There was nothing she could do about the trial at this point. She'd done what she could. Now, she'd just have to gear herself up for giving her testimony.

She couldn't do anything about her past or about it playing out in the media. She might be able to do something to stop the onslaught of questions about the abuse though, but she wasn't sure if it would stop the questions or just pour more fuel on the fire. She was considering either writing another book or giving Cheryl Starr the interview she wanted. Maybe if she gave them the answers they seemed so desperate to have, the reporters would finally leave her alone.

Breezing by Cail again, Taylor knew he was getting pissed off, but she kept going. The 'No-Go' list. Her stomach knotted at the thought of someone telling that reporter about the stupid list. She had no control over it now, but she'd love to get her hands on whoever was releasing this stuff to the media. Chris knew. Blake found something on the building surveillance video and Chris was holding back. Why? Because it was someone they knew? It had to be someone they knew, someone close enough to Cail for him to share something so personal. Who? Kate? She was up at Gray's when the drawings were taken. Dave? Why didn't she know any of Cail's friends? The more she thought about it the more frustrated she became. Did Cail still hang out with friends? He certainly knew enough people around the city.

Ugh! She'd come back to that one. Next up was Troy Rappaport. If he stole her bracelet and locket to lure her to him, why hadn't he contacted her? Did the same person who took her drawings take them? Why? Money? Did he, or she, think they could get a good price for them because they were Taylor Sinclair's? Is that why they took the drawings and spilled about the list, too? She was getting off track. Rappaport. She could do something about Rappaport. Where in the hell was he hiding and what was he planning? She would find some quiet time during the night and practice the things that Quinn taught her. She'd try to find Rappaport before going to Chris. As Taylor sailed past Chris and Kate she felt a little pang of guilt. Maybe she should go to Chris first.

Cail. What could she do about Cail? He'd already taken the steps to learn to control his anger and Taylor's gut told her seeing the video someone sent in had been a real eye opener for him. Would it be enough to stop him from getting physical when he was angry? Only time would tell. At this point, she loved Cail too much to just throw it all away. She had to believe the counseling would help and there was always the opportunity to reassess the situation if things got worse. If he continued to be abusive, she would have to let him go. After a lifetime of abuse, she couldn't live in an abusive relationship.

The baby. She couldn't answer the questions about what happened to her son. Funny, she thought. He would be the age now that she was when she had him – just a kid. Thirteen seemed so much younger than she felt when she had him. She couldn't think about him without her chest tightening. Her breaths were shortening, her lungs burning. So, pinching her ear, she tried to put him out of her mind and took herself to Gray's deck over the lake until she loosened up again.

When she looked at the overall picture, there wasn't a heck of a lot she could do about most of the things that were getting to her. So why was she letting them get to her? Because it's humiliating as hell, she answered herself.

Up ahead, Cail slowed to a walk. She considered slowing down and walking with him then kept running. She wasn't ready to stop yet. She came up behind Chris and Kate and slowed to their pace. "The video from Friday," she began. "Blake saw someone. Someone that is close to Cail. Who did she see?"

"We didn't find anything conclusive," Chris insisted.

"Bull! I want to see the video."

Chris's mind reeled for an out. "I can't show it to you."

"No, you won't show it to me, because it's someone we know; someone who is close enough to Cail he would talk to him or her about that list."

Kate didn't know whether to slow down and give them some privacy or keep going. Then she began to wonder if Taylor was accusing her of talking about the list to a reporter. "He told me he went through a sex book with you to determine what you were comfortable with, Taylor, but he didn't mention making a list and I didn't repeat anything he told me to anyone. I would never tell something like that to the media. I wouldn't do that to Cail and I wouldn't do it to you."

It pissed Taylor off that Cail told anyone about it. Sharing intimate details with his sister infuriated and embarrassed her, but she knew it wasn't Kate's fault and she believed her when she said she wouldn't repeat what he told her. "I know that, Kate. I didn't mean to infer you had anything to do with it. But, someone close to Cail did. That blog post has gone viral on the Internet and I want to know who the hell it was, Chris. You know. I know you do."

Chris slowed to a stop and Kate and Taylor followed suit. Taylor stood with her hands fisted on her hips, staring Chris down. "Give us a minute," Chris said to Kate.

"Sure." Kate nodded. She started off at a jog then slowed to a walk to cool down.

Chris waited until Kate was a ways down the track. "We didn't see anyone carrying out your drawings."

"But you saw someone both you and Blake recognized."

Chris raked her hand through her hair then used her sleeve to wipe the sweat from her brow. She needed more time to figure out how to handle the situation.

"Damn it, Chris," Taylor said in frustration when Chris didn't answer. "You're protecting someone who has completely humiliated me."

"Give me twenty-four hours. If I don't have it sorted out by then, I'll give you what I've got."

"Forget it," Taylor spat out as she started to run again. "I'll find out myself."

"Taylor. Wait." Chris started to run after her and couldn't catch up. She slowed down to a walk, swearing under her breath.

The conversation with Chris just made Taylor angry. She picked up her pace until she was running full out again to try to burn some of it off. If Cail told Kate, he probably told Dave as well. She didn't know enough about Dave to know whether he would do something like this or not. She didn't like Dave. He always gave her the creeps, like he was imagining what she'd be like in bed as he stared at her. She didn't trust him, but Cail did.

Taylor ran for another solid hour. She could see everyone waiting for her in the stands, but she didn't care. She wished they'd all just go home and leave her be. When she finally slowed to a walk, Cail came up beside her. He was just about to ask if she was okay, when Taylor said, "You told Kate about the sex book. Who else?"

"Why are you so worried about that stupid list? There's nothing we can do about it now."

"Who else?" Taylor asked more sternly this time.

Cail wished she'd just let it go. He didn't want to answer, but finally conceded. "Dave, but I didn't tell them about making the list, Tay."

"Would he tell anyone about it?"

"No. He's my brother. I trust him implicitly."

"Then who? They said it's someone close to you. You must have an idea of who did it."

"I haven't told anyone who I think would betray me like that."

Taylor stopped walking and glared at Cail. "You keep telling me I need to trust you, but how can I when you won't be straight with me?"

Cail's blood was beginning to boil again. Why the hell couldn't she just let it go? "Alright," he spat. "I've told one other person, but it's someone I completely trust, a close personal friend. She wouldn't have talked to anyone."

Taylor just stood there, dumbfounded, glaring at Cail. She? A close personal friend he trusts completely? "Has *she* been in your apartment?"

"Our apartment," Cail was quick to correct as he shifted back and forth from one foot to another, his hands clenched at his sides.

Taylor got the sense this close personal friend was much more than a friend. If she was so close Cail would tell her intimate details of their relationship, why hadn't she heard of her before now? Taylor dropped her eyes, no longer able to look at him. That sick, twisting feeling was back in her gut and her anger was beginning to flare again. Is that why he was content with their sex life? Was he getting the things she wouldn't give him somewhere else? On a sob she turned from him and began running again.

"Damn it," Cail whispered in frustration.

"Way to go, slick," Kate said from behind him.

Turning towards her, Cail yelled, "What?" He threw his arms up then let them drop to his sides.

"Are you still sleeping with this Lisa chick?" Chris asked with narrowed eyes.

"No, of course not!"

"Well, congratulations," Chris spat back at him. "Now she thinks you are."

Cail had no idea how they could come to that conclusion based on the conversation he just had with Taylor. He had just about enough for one day. Screw it, he thought and stormed off towards the change room.

"Cail?" Chris called after him. When he turned to face her, she asked, "Does she have a key to your place?" She watched as Cail's face turned a deeper red, full of rage. Without answering, he turned again and continued on to the change room.

Chapter 24

Taylor opted to spend the night at Chris's. Most of her clothes were there and it would give Gray and Callaghan some privacy. As soon as they arrived, Taylor headed straight for the shower, letting the hot water ease the ache of the bruised muscles in her upper back and shoulders. After brushing her hair out, she tied it up in her usual ponytail and changed into sleep pants and one of Cail's t-shirts. There were no messages from Cail on her phone, so she took her laptop out to Chris's living room where Kate and Chris curled up on the sofa watching TV.

The life-sized cardboard cut out of Taylor standing in the corner of Chris's living room had her stopping in her tracks with a furrowed brow. That's just weird, she thought before continuing on to the chair next to Chris's sofa.

"Wanna beer?" Chris asked.

"No, thanks." It was the most Taylor had said since they left HQ. She opened up her laptop and went online.

"You going to be okay giving your testimony at Sarah's trial?"

Taylor looked up at Chris with an annoyed expression on her face, shrugged her shoulders and turned her attention back to her laptop.

"I'm asking because there's another option," Chris said as she studied Taylor. She was getting frustrated with Taylor's lackadaisical attitude.

"What option?" Taylor's attention remained on her laptop screen.

"We could hand over all of Darryl's videos to the prosecuting attorney."

Taylor's head shot up and she glared at Chris.

Oh yeah, Chris thought. That got your attention. "It's up to you," Chris continued. "You can return the phone calls from the Crown

Attorney's Office and prepare for giving your testimony or we can turn over the videos."

Taylor's eyes went back to her screen, but Chris could see the anger in her red face. Her nostrils flared out as she sucked in air. Chris sat waiting for her response, but it never came. Instead, Taylor slapped the lid closed on the laptop, set it down on the coffee table then disappeared into the spare bedroom. Chris's eyes met Kate's. "That went well."

"What did you expect? You made it sound like a threat."

"She pissed me off."

"Maybe it's time someone cut her a break. God knows she could use one."

Chris sat with a scowl on her face staring at Taylor's laptop until she couldn't stand it anymore. She leaned over, picked it up off the coffee table and turned it on.

"Chris," Kate whispered, nudging Chris's arm.

"What? If she didn't want me to look she wouldn't have left it on my table." She opened up the browser and scanned through Taylor's browsing history. "Hmm."

"What?" Kate tried to look over Chris's shoulder, but Chris angled the screen away from her. "Oh, come on."

"One minute you scold me for looking and the next you're mad at me for not letting you see." Chris laughed as Kate crossed her arms in front of her and stuck her lower lip out. Turning the screen back, Chris said, "She's looking for an apartment."

"Shit. She's not going to take Cail back. Damn it. He's screwed up the best thing that's ever happened to him." Kate picked up her cell phone and immediately sent a text message to Cail saying they needed to talk.

"She's been on Cail's Facebook page, too," Chris announced. "She found Lisa on there … Lisa Harmon. Pretty girl."

"Shit." Kate deflated into the sofa. "We need to do something about this, Chris. He's not sleeping with her anymore. At least, I don't think he is."

"There's something not right there if he's been hiding his friendship with her from Taylor." Chris closed the laptop and put it back on the table. "Does Cail tell you all the details of his relationships?"

"Not so much with Taylor. Both Cail and Dave taught me everything I know about pleasuring a woman." Kate shot her eyebrows up twice in quick succession with a seductive smile. "How do you think I knew what to do when we first slept together?"

"I figured you knew from experience."

"You're the only person I've ever slept with."

"What? You can't be serious. You're twenty-nine years old for Christ's sake." Chris thought back to the first time they slept together and thought there was no way it was Kate's first time.

"I'm totally serious. The furthest I ever went before you was kissing my prom date and that wasn't a pleasant experience, believe me. I tried dating guys, but they just didn't interest me sexually. It took me a long time before I was able to admit to myself that I'm gay. I think it was right around the time I first met you and fell hopelessly in love."

Chris was stunned. She couldn't understand how she didn't pick up that it was Kate's first time. "Did they just offer up the details of their sex lives? They must have been pretty specific. I never would have guessed it was your first time and I've had enough experience to know."

With a giggle, Kate admitted, "I used to drive them crazy with questions until they offered up what they knew. It was harder with Cail, but Dave was all too pleased to give me detailed descriptions. Cail's more of a romantic, please her first kind of guy. Dave's into some serious kink."

"Would Dave take those drawings from Cail's and talk to the media about the list?"

"No. God, no. We're all pretty close. He wouldn't betray Cail like that."

"So you think it was Lisa Harmon?"

"I wouldn't trust her. I figured out both Cail and Dave were sleeping with her when we were all still in high school. Dave knew Cail was having sex with her, but Cail didn't know Dave and Lisa were going at it, too. I think Dave got some sort of kick out of it. Lisa was in Cail's grade, two years older than Dave."

"So Dave still hooks up with her?"

"Yeah, I think so. From what Dave's told me, I'm guessing she's into this whole kink scene, too." Chris put her feet up on the coffee table and was laid back in the sofa. Kate watched her, knowing she was thinking, trying to figure something out. "Are you going to tell me who you saw in the video going into Cail's apartment?"

Chris had butterflies in her stomach at the thought of telling Kate. It was Kate's reaction that was making her nervous and she wanted to talk to Dave first, but she hadn't been able to get hold of him and he wasn't returning her calls. Better to get it over with, she thought. "Lisa Harmon entered the building with a key approximately an hour after Cail left for the airport. Ten minutes later, Dave let himself in with a key. You can see the elevator's floor indicator on the lobby cam, so we know they both took the elevator to the twenty-first floor. A couple of hours later, they came out together, arm in arm. They didn't appear to be carrying Taylor's drawings, but Harmon was wearing a long coat. They could have been rolled up and concealed under her coat."

"That doesn't mean Dave was involved. They could have been going to someone else's apartment or maybe they just met at Cail's to have sex. That's something Dave would do. He'd get a kick out of having sex with Lisa in Cail's bed."

Taylor's head spun as she leaned against the wall in the hallway. She didn't know if she was going to be sick or pass out. With a hand on the wall for balance, she made her way back into the bedroom, quietly closing the door behind her. She had a bad feeling about Lisa Harmon. Taylor hadn't received any messages from Cail tonight, which was highly unusual for him especially when they were at odds. She had a horrible feeling that he was with Lisa Harmon.

* * *

Taylor felt Cail slide under the duvet and run a cold hand up her thigh then under her t-shirt, following the long curve of her spine up to her neck. With a gasp she turned into him. "Tay, I miss you. God, I miss you."

"I know," Taylor whispered, running her fingers through his short ebony curls. "I miss you, too." She pulled his head down to meet her lips and devoured his mouth as if she'd been craving it for far too long. The fires raged inside her as Cail's hands gently explored. "Now," she groaned.

As Cail moved on top of her, Taylor watched his expression change, his eyes widening in horror and the anger rising until his face was red, the veins in his neck pulsing. "What the fuck is this?" he raged.

"What? What's wrong?" Taylor trembled. She'd never seen him this angry and she didn't understand what was setting him off.

"This." His fist rammed into her stomach, doubling Taylor and knocking the wind out of her lungs. "You fucking slut. Whose baby is it?" Sarah Johnson glared down at her, dark eyes full of hate.

"It's mine. Just mine," Taylor cried.

"You're nothing but a slut like your crack whore mother. You're going to end up with a bunch of bastard children who don't have a clue who their father is, just like your whore of a mother."

"Noooo." As the first shocking pain ripped through her belly, Taylor screamed wildly, like the growling of an injured, terrified animal.

* * *

Chris and Kate sat bolt upright in bed at the same time. "What the hell is that?" Kate cried, her eyes wide in fear.

"Taylor." Chris jumped out of bed and rummaged through a drawer for a t-shirt and sweat pants before running across the hall. She flicked the light on to find Taylor's body bowed so far that she was nearly bent over backwards. Every muscle in her body was visibly tensed as she growled through a clenched jaw. Chris jumped on the bed and began shaking her. "Taylor, wake up."

With one last primal scream, Taylor's eyes opened and focused on Chris hovering over her, pinning her shoulders to the bed and shaking her. Overwhelmed with shame and humiliation, Taylor curled herself into a tight ball and turned away from Chris, burying her face in the pillow.

"Hey," Chris lowered her voice to a whisper, laying a hand tentatively on Taylor's shoulder. "You okay?"

"Just go," Taylor mumbled through the pillow, her voice low and hoarse from screaming.

"Taylor, you're shaking like crazy. There must be something I can do."

"Go. Please."

Chris didn't want to leave her alone like this, but she didn't know what to do to help. "Do you need a drink or something?" When Taylor didn't respond, Chris raked her fingers through her hair in frustration. "Okay. I'm just across the hall if you need anything."

Kate stood in the doorway, her eyes still wide as saucers. She could see Taylor's entire body shaking as she curled up in a tight little ball. She took a couple of steps back as Chris came towards her then closed Taylor's door behind her. "What the hell was that?" Kate whispered.

Chris took Kate's hand and led her back into their room. "Nightmare," she finally answered once their bedroom door was closed. "She had a nightmare."

Chris was as pale as new fallen snow and was shaking a bit herself. "Are you okay?" Kate asked. She'd never seen or heard anyone having a nightmare as terrifying as what she just witnessed. No wonder Chris was shaking. She felt a little shaky herself.

Chris paced back and forth like a caged animal. "You can't mention this to anyone. Do you understand? You can't tell anyone what you just saw."

"Okay," Kate agreed, remembering Lane's threat to put Taylor on some kind of medication if her nightmares continued. "Chris, you need to try to calm down."

"It just doesn't seem right to leave her in there by herself in the state she's in."

"Why don't we make her a tea? It will give us an excuse to go back in and check on her."

Chris stopped pacing. "Good idea."

* * *

Taylor pulled the duvet up over herself and stayed curled up in a tight ball while she calmed down. Cail had never shown up in one of her nightmares before and she didn't want him there. She didn't want him included in the dark parts of her life.

When Chris and Kate tapped on the door and came back in, Taylor pulled the duvet up over her head.

"We made you some tea," Chris whispered as she set a mug down on the bedside table. When Taylor ignored her, she added, "Chamomile, to help you relax." Still Taylor ignored her. Chris glanced over at Kate and shrugged her shoulders. "Are you not talking to me?"

"I just want to be left alone," Taylor mumbled.

"I can't leave you alone like this, Taylor. I'm worried sick about you." Chris sat on the edge of the bed with a long sigh. "Do you want me to call Gray?"

"I want you to leave me alone," Taylor snarled.

Chris glanced over at Kate again, hoping she'd have some idea of what to do. Kate nodded her head towards the door. Chris was reluctant to leave again. She touched a hand to Taylor's shoulder through the duvet to see if she was still shaking and gave it a squeeze. She felt a bit of a tremor, but nothing compared to the way she'd been shaking before. Rising, she left Taylor's room, closing the door quietly behind her.

Taylor waited until she'd completely calmed herself then sat cross-legged on the bed, closed her eyes and opened herself up to her psychic abilities as Quinn had taught her. She focused on Leila's locket and her bracelet first. Taylor could feel the weight of them, holding them between her fingers and rubbing her thumb over their surfaces. Just thinking about it had a calming effect on her and a slight smile appearing on her face.

Oh, how she wished she could have them in her hands while she sat in the courtroom. The only images she could conjure were of complete darkness. Were they in a drawer, or a safe maybe? A jewelry box? Wherever they were, there was no light seeping in.

With a sigh she moved on, picturing them inside their pewter box on the dresser in Cail's room. She heard laughing and shushing before she saw Rebecca Knightley and Troy Rappaport stumble into the room. Taylor's head began to swim with their drunkenness. No, she thought, not drunk – high. Rebecca was the first to discover the pewter box and called Troy over to it. "Here," she whispered. "They're in here." With gloved hands she picked up the necklace and bracelet and placed them in her palm.

"Those, baby, are the key to getting to Taylor Sinclair." He laughed then wrapped his hand in Rebecca's hair, jerked her head back roughly, and kissed her hard.

Taylor tuned herself out of the vision, the sight of them making her stomach turn. Next she focused on the sex book in Cail's night stand and she quickly found Kate was right about Dave taking Lisa to Cail's bed. Dave looked so much like Cail, it was eerie. Taylor desperately wanted to pull out of the vision, but she needed to know, she needed to see. They stumbled across the sex book looking for condoms. "Hmm." Lisa giggled when the list slipped out of the book onto the bed. Picking it up, she waved it in front of Dave's face. "What have we here?"

"Put it back," Dave ordered.

Lisa unfolded the paper, holding it away from Dave as she quickly scanned through the list.

While her focus was on the paper, Dave leaned over and grabbed it out of her hands before putting the list and the book back in the drawer.

It was enough. Taylor pulled herself out and rolled her head trying to ease the headache beginning to take hold. Quinn told her meditation was the key to controlling the headaches. It was important to clear her mind and relax her body. She folded her legs into the lotus position and began with some deep breathing. She tried to picture white all around her, like she was surrounded by a big, puffy cloud, to clear all of her thoughts, but she kept drifting to thoughts of Cail.

Her body tensed with a jolt as a vision of Cail burst into her mind … entwined with Lisa on the sofa in his apartment, wearing nothing more than the watch Taylor just gave him. Taylor barely made it across the hall to the bathroom, where she was violently ill.

* * *

By the time Chris and Kate woke, Taylor had already showered and fixed her hair. She left a fresh pot of coffee in the kitchen for them and closed herself off in the spare room again. By eight ten, Taylor was ready to go. She wanted to look fierce and confident, wanted Sarah Johnson to see someone who was anxious to get on the stand and give her testimony, even if she didn't feel it. She'd left her hair down and loose. It would be the first time in as long as she could remember that she'd gone out in public with her hair down. It was her way of saying 'screw you, Sarah Johnson'.

Taylor rarely wore makeup, but this morning her bright green eyes bore a smoky shadow. She didn't bother with mascara as her lashes were naturally thick and long. Her high cheek bones were rosy and a dark rose adorned her full lips. She'd chosen a black pant suit with a hip length jacket that hugged her body like a second skin. The deep V of the neck line plunged to reveal the lace and silk of a dark purple camisole. Her low heeled ankle boots finished off the outfit. Taylor sat on the edge of the bed doing her deep breathing exercises until she heard the SUV pull up out front.

With a final deep breath, Taylor rose and studied herself in the full length mirror one last time. Satisfied with what she saw, she took her long black leather coat out of the closet and slid into it just as a knock sounded at the door.

"Taylor? It's time to go," Chris called through the door. When Taylor opened it, Chris stood there in a black pant suit of her own, a cream turtle neck under it, her mouth gaping as she took Taylor in. "Wow," was all she could manage.

A little embarrassed, Taylor passed Chris in the doorway and headed out the front door. She was in the vehicle before Chris and Kate made it out to the porch. Taylor watched Kate come down the steps in a black knee length skirt and red sweater, her black coat open. When they settled into their seats, Taylor announced, "We're making a stop to pick up a friend. I gave the driver the address." With that, she put the ear buds of her iPhone in her ears, leaned her head back with her eyes closed, and listened to a mix of strong female voices, including Adele and Alicia Keys.

Chris and Kate watched Taylor as her legs bounced and her fingers tapped on her thighs. "Nervous," Kate commented.

"I wish she wouldn't tune us out. It worries me," Chris frowned.

"Maybe she's just trying to psych herself up for what's to come." Kate shoved her long back curls out of her face with a long sigh. The two of them sat silently watching out the window for the rest of the ride. It was a freezing cold November morning, overcast and windy. The weather seemed to match the mood in the car.

Quinn Paylen was waiting in the lobby when the Escalade pulled up in front of her building. She rushed out, not waiting for the driver to open the door for her and jumped in beside Kate. Taylor pulled her ear buds out to make the introductions. "Chris, Kate, this is Quinn." She offered no other explanation and Chris squirmed in her seat wanting to know who the hell Quinn was.

Quinn gave Kate a firm handshake and a smile then held her hand out to Chris. A quick gasp escaped Quinn's lips when she held onto Chris's hand. She hadn't been prepared for the violence of Chris's childhood. She nearly said something about it before she realized that Chris didn't talk about it. "A pleasure to meet both of you." Quinn recovered quickly with a wide smile.

"You too," Chris eyed her. "How long have you known Taylor?"

"Physically? Only a couple of days." Quinn grinned, enjoying the game. She'd expected Taylor to explain who she was. It amused her that Chris couldn't figure her out.

What kind of answer was that, Chris wondered. "And mentally?"

Quinn's deep, raspy laugh filled the car. Her eyes met Taylor's and her head cocked to the side. "Why are you so nervous, baby girl? You've only to look and you'll see that everything is going to work out fine." Taylor gave a quick shake of her head and Quinn picked up her thought. She was too scared to see, too worried about having to get up on the stand and say the things that were done to her in front of a courtroom filled with people. "Ah," Quinn nodded. "You need to trust in yourself, girl. You've already set the stage for what will happen today. Trust in yourself, baby girl."

"Okay," Chris scowled. "Who the hell are you?"

"It's killing you, isn't it?" Once again, the car filled with Quinn's laughter.

Chapter 25

For the second time in two days, Justin Ripkin found himself standing out in the cold surrounded by a bunch of reporters. If he didn't get to Sinclair this time, he might just give up. It was too damn cold for this. He learned something yesterday though and he spent a good half hour working his way through the crowd so he'd be as close to Sinclair's vehicle as he could get when she arrived. He pulled his wool hat down over his ears and waited.

Ripkin watched as a black sedan pulled up. Two cops and two bodyguards surrounded Gray Rowan as she stepped out of the car with her husband. He'd seen her yesterday at the library, but he was still struck by her beauty. That's one lucky man, he thought. When they passed by him, Rowan was within arm's length. Perfect, he smirked.

Inside the glass doors of the courthouse, Gray saw Cail off to the side watching out the window. "She's not here yet?"

"No," Cail answered with a shake of his head. He greeted Gray with a kiss on the cheek and Callaghan with a pat on the shoulder. "Have you talked to her this morning?"

"No. Chris said she's been locked in her room all morning." When she called Chris, Gray told her not to disturb Taylor. If Taylor was avoiding Chris and Kate, Gray figured she probably needed the alone time to prepare herself for the difficult day ahead.

"They're here." Cail gestured towards the black SUV pulling up at the curb. There was about seventy-five feet of courtyard between the entrance and the SUV and every inch of it was filled with reporters and people who just wanted to get a glimpse of Taylor Sinclair. Several uniformed officers lined up beside the vehicle, acting as a human shield against the throng of people now pushing and shoving, trying to get close.

Cail watched as a black woman he didn't recognized emerged first, quickly followed by Kate and Chris. Seconds later Taylor stepped out and the brisk wind immediately caught her hair and her long coat. Her loose dark hair flowed out behind her as she grabbed onto her coat and hugged it around herself. Cail's knees actually buckled when he saw her. Callaghan's hand came out to steady him, but he straightened himself quickly. The sight of Taylor had taken his breath away and brought tears to his eyes. She has no idea how beautiful she is, he thought with a smile.

"You okay there, bro?" Callaghan asked.

No, Cail thought. I'm a complete idiot and if she leaves me, I deserve it. "Yeah, yeah," he answered, brushing Callaghan off.

"I feel like that every time Gray walks into the room," Callaghan grinned. The comment earned him a wide grin and a quick kiss from Gray.

The sensation of her hair blowing in the wind was completely foreign to Taylor and she suddenly felt very exposed. She wrapped her arms around herself and lowered her eyes as they began the dreaded walk to the courthouse entrance amid the screams and shouts of the crowd. Dozens of reporters shouted out questions, most asking what happened to her baby. She sensed Blades struggling to get to her and, before she had time to react, he bumped into her, nearly knocking her off her feet, before he disappeared into the crowd again. "Blades." Taylor stopped, turned to try to follow him with her eyes, as someone grabbed her arm and pulled her. She turned again to see Chris gripping her, pulling her towards the entrance.

"Move," Chris ordered.

"Did you see that?" Taylor shouted over the din of the crowd.

Quinn quickly moved up beside her. "Check your pocket."

"What?" It had happened so fast, Taylor didn't know why he tried to get near her. They rushed inside the lobby doors and Taylor turned to Quinn. "What did you say?"

Quinn answered in a whisper. "He put something in your pocket."

"What happened? Why did you stop?" Chris asked.

"Blades. Justin Ripkin," Taylor answered. "Didn't you see him?" Taylor stuck her hands in her coat pockets. She felt her iPhone in one and in the other she felt a piece of paper. Her first thought was Rappaport sent a message through Blades, that he would lure her with the locket and bracelet. She left the paper in her pocket. "He bumped into me."

"Are you hurt? Take off your coat," Chris ordered.

"I'm fine. He just bumped me. I'm not hurt." Her eyes went to Quinn, pleading for her to keep her mouth shut.

"Where the fuck is your vest?" Chris yelled.

"I forgot. I didn't think –"

"You didn't think?" Chris cut her off. "This is life and death, Taylor." Damn it. Chris knew better. She should have damn well checked before they left the house.

"I had a lot on my mind. Sorry. Besides, Blades wouldn't hurt me."

"Tay?"

Taylor turned to see Cail in a pair of faded jeans and a tight shirt under a beat up leather jacket. He hadn't shaved and he looked so damn sexy with that dark shadow on his face. She didn't know what to think of her body still reacting to him. "Hey," she said in greeting as Cail's fingers ran through her hair.

"Everything okay?"

"Yeah, fine. I just got bumped around a bit. It's fine."

"Why don't we move inside?" Gray suggested. Where they were standing, they were on full display for the crowd outside.

"We've got a meeting room down the hall." Cal and Rose Worthington appeared out of nowhere. "This way," Cal said, gesturing down the long corridor. They had to go through security first, submitting their belongings and their bodies to scans.

Taylor hadn't thought about having to surrender their phones so no pictures could be taken inside the court rooms. She'd hoped to distract herself listening to music. She trailed behind the group, removing the note from her coat pocket and slipping it into her pants pocket. Once they were inside the meeting room, Taylor introduced Quinn to everyone as a friend before Chris was on her again. "Ripkin didn't bump into you for no reason. Did he hand you anything or put something in your pocket?"

"I don't know," Taylor lied. She held her arms out while Chris fished through her coat pockets.

"Leah Waitley, the Crown Attorney, was here with us. She got a call and excused herself, but I'm sure she'll be right back," Cal announced. "We need to talk about your testimony, Taylor."

"You don't have to worry about Taylor giving her testimony, Inspector," Quinn stated.

"I'll be fine," Taylor affirmed, though she didn't believe it.

Cal narrowed his eyes at Quinn. "Have you been helping Taylor with that?" he asked.

"You could say that." Quinn smiled. "Whatever happens, Taylor's ready."

Taylor wished she was as confident as Quinn. Every eye in the room was focused on Quinn, wondering who she was and how she was so sure Taylor was ready when the people closest to her were worried sick she wouldn't be able to handle it. Slowly the focus switched to Taylor for an explanation, but she didn't give it.

There was a light tap on the door and Lane stepped in. "They've got a couple rows of seats blocked off for us, but we should make our way up to the courtroom."

"All right then." Inspector Cal Worthington was disappointed Waitley hadn't returned. "This room will be locked, if you want to leave your coats here," he announced.

Gray put her hand on Taylor's shoulder. "Ready?"

Taylor only nodded as she removed her coat.

"You sure you're okay?" Gray whispered. She got another solemn nod from Taylor that only made her more concerned.

Taylor was sure her stomach was twisted into a thousand knots. Quinn told her over and over again everything was going to work out and tried to convince her to use her 'gift' to see, but Taylor couldn't make herself do it. On the way to the elevators, Cail slipped his hand into hers and Taylor took a step away from him.

"Tay?"

"We need to talk," she whispered, her eyes flicking towards everyone walking ahead of them.

"We will, but let me be here for you for now." His fingers brushed her cheek. "You're shaking. I can feel it through your hand. Just let me be here for you." Cail took a step towards Taylor and she stepped back again.

"You smell like alcohol." She could almost see it seeping out of his pores, the smell of it turning her stomach even more than it already was.

"I had a hell of a day yesterday. So what if I had a few drinks to wind down at the end of it?" Cail's voice was a controlled whisper, but Taylor could hear the anger in it. She took another step back just as Cal's big hand clamped down on his son's shoulder.

"Problem?"

"No," Cail glared at his father. "Can we have a minute of privacy to talk, please?" Cal's eyes met Taylor's and she gave him a quick nod before dropping her eyes. Cail waited until he made his way back to the rest of the group waiting at the elevators. "Why is it I seem to keep making things worse?" He rubbed his hands over his face and tried to start over. "I love you, Tay. I love you so much it hurts. I don't want to lose you, so just tell me what I need to do and I'll do it."

When he rubbed his hands over his face, Taylor noticed he wasn't wearing the watch she'd given him. She didn't know why, but it hurt that he didn't have it on. "This isn't the time or the place to get into this, Cail."

"Then let me just be here for you for however long we're in that courtroom today. After, we can go somewhere and talk."

"Okay," Taylor answered. It was the easiest way to diffuse the situation. She'd breathe through her mouth so she didn't smell the alcohol evaporating from him. Cail stepped towards her and hugged her tightly to him. Taylor closed her eyes for a moment, amazed that he could still make her feel so safe in his arms. She expected to feel revolted by his touch after what she'd seen in her vision the night before. Instead, she melted into him, absorbing the comfort he offered and letting it ease the tension she felt.

Inside the courtroom, Taylor sat between Cail and Gray, each of them holding one of her hands. The courtroom doors were closed and they sat there, waiting for what seemed like an eternity. Twelve people sat quietly in the jurors' box at the side of the room, but the tables at the front for the lawyers remained empty. At the front of the room, a court clerk worked away below the judge's raised desk of dark wood. Every seat in the gallery was filled. Taylor knew some of them were reporters, but she had no idea who the rest were. She kept her eyes focused on the front of the room, knowing that just about everyone in the room was staring at her.

The courtroom door banged open, making Taylor jump. Gray and Cail both gave her hands a quick squeeze. She took a deep breath as the lawyers, dressed in their black robes, made their way down the centre aisle and began setting up. The defense attorney gathered some papers together and approached the clerk where he was joined by Leah Waitley. Taylor watched as they whispered back and forth. She leaned forward so she could see Chris on the other side of Cail and whispered, "What's happening?"

Chris shook her head and shrugged.

It felt like they'd been sitting there for hours already and Taylor was getting more agitated by the minute. Finally, a side door opened near the front of the room and Sarah Johnson was escorted in, dressed in a pale grey skirt and white blouse. Her hair was swept up in a long clip at the back of her head. Sarah's eyes scanned the gallery until she locked eyes with Taylor. Taylor forced a smirk, made a little easier by the fact that Sarah looked pale and scared. She felt like she scored the first point when Sarah looked away first.

"All rise, the honourable Judge Joseph McNamara residing." The booming voice made Taylor jump again. Her legs were shaking so much she wasn't sure if she could stand and was relieved when Cail helped her up. Gray's hand ran up and down Taylor's back as they watched the grey haired, spectacled judge make his way to his throne high above them. As they took their seats again, the clerk set several sets of papers before the judge and they whispered back and forth. Taylor knew the first day or two of the trial would be filled with motions and opening speeches from both sides. She figured the documents the defense just submitted were all part of that. Judge McNamara looked up from the papers spread out before him, his gaze aimed towards the defense table. He received a nod from the lawyer then did the same with Leah Waitley at the prosecutor's table.

As the clerk returned to her seat, McNamara addressed the court. "In the case of the Crown versus Sarah Jane Johnson, a plea bargain has been reached between the accused and the Crown Attorney."

The noise level spiked with the murmuring of voices throughout the room. Taylor's head spun. "Oh, my God," she whispered. Shaking violently now, she dropped her head and tried to calm herself amidst the gasps and exclamations surrounding her.

The judge banged his gavel on the desk. "Quiet. Any more outbreaks and I'll clear the room. Understood?" The room fell silent before he continued, "In exchange for a plea of guilty on all charges, the Crown Attorney has agreed to a sentence of fifteen years imprisonment. Ms. Johnson, do you wish to change your plea on the charges presented to this court?"

Sarah Johnson rose to her feet, assisted by her attorney. "Yes."

McNamara began to list the charges. "Conspiracy to commit murder, multiple counts of child molestation ..." he took off his glasses and faced Sarah Johnson. "I don't think you need me to recite all of the charges against you, Ms. Johnson. How do you plead?"

"Guilty on all charges, your honour," Sarah replied in a barely audible voice.

Taylor's sob echoed through every corner of the room. She covered her mouth with her hand just as Cail wrapped his arms around her and pulled her into him. She buried her face between Cail's shoulder and neck, her shoulders heaving with muffled sobs.

"Very well," McNamara continued. "You're hereby sentenced to fifteen years in a Federal prison. The case of the Crown versus Sarah Jane Johnson is closed." With a final slam of his gavel, McNamara rose and fled the courtroom.

Taylor remained in Cail's arms, crying tears of relief as the din in the courtroom began to rise with spectators, reporters, and jurors all voicing their surprise. Sarah Johnson was led out of the room through the door she came in and, slowly, people began to file out of the main doors. Gray pulled tissues out of her bag and pressed them into Taylor's hand.

A few deep breaths expelled the last few tears, but Taylor was so embarrassed at her loss of control she kept her face buried in Cail's neck. "Get me out of here," she whispered with a raw voice.

Hearing her quiet plea, Chris advised, "Taylor, the media's going to go ape shit if you don't give a statement."

Cail turned his head so his cheek was against Taylor's, his mouth at her ear. "You can do it, Angel. It has to be a breeze compared to giving your testimony."

Taylor realized there were tissues in her hand and she began dabbing at the tears under her eyes. "At least let me go to the washroom and clean up a bit."

"There's a washroom in the back here I can take you to," Leah Waitley offered. "There's probably a crowd waiting outside the courtroom doors."

Another wave of embarrassment coursed through Taylor as she recognized Leah's voice. Cail helped Taylor to her feet and held her until her legs steadied then Gray's arm circled her waist. "Come on. I'll take you," Gray insisted. Taylor kept her head down with a hand across her forehead to block her face as Leah led them to the women's washroom.

Inside, Taylor gripped onto the counter and studied the damage. She dabbed some water over her face, dried it off, and reapplied some lipstick. There was nothing she could do about the puffy, bloodshot eyes.

Gray watched Taylor's reflection in the mirror with a smile. "How are you feeling?"

Eyes burning, Taylor fought back another wave of tears. Closing her eyes, she whispered, "Relieved ... just an overwhelming sense of relief."

"She'd been relying on you not being able to get up on the stand and talk. Convincing her that you could and would made all the difference. It was a very smart move, Taylor."

Taylor offered Gray a weak smile. "The funny part is that I couldn't have done it."

"You're stronger than you think, Taylor. You don't give yourself enough credit."

Taylor shook her head. "No, I couldn't have done it. I couldn't have gotten up there with all those people staring at me and said what they did to me."

The bathroom door swung open and Lane stepped in. She took in Taylor's white knuckles, gripping onto the counter, her head hung low and her long dark hair hiding most of her face from view. "Sorry to interrupt. I had to make sure you're okay, Taylor."

"Yeah," she nodded. "I was just so ... overwhelmed. I feel a bit better."

"It's already all over the TV, radio, and Internet. They're reporting the last minute plea bargain and that you broke down ... collapsed into Cail's arms."

"Don't waste any time, do they?" With a deep breath, Taylor lifted her eyes to the mirror again, ran her fingers through her hair to tidy it.

"They're setting up downstairs for a press conference," Lane announced. "Are you going to be able to handle that, Taylor?"

"Yeah," Taylor answered. "Yeah, I'll be fine. Can you just give me a few minutes alone to gather myself together a bit?"

"Sure." She crossed the room and rose up on her toes to press a kiss to Taylor's cheek. "It's all over," Lane smiled then rubbed the lipstick off of Taylor's cheek with her thumb. "Now you can start to put it all behind you."

As she walked out, Gray headed for a stall. "I'm just going to pee and then I'll give you some privacy."

Taylor laughed. "I'll bet you'll be glad when you're not peeing every five minutes."

"Oh, I don't know," Gray called out from the stall. "It's worth it being pregnant and feeling this little life moving around inside me."

Taylor smiled, thinking of little Gracie as she opened the note from inside her pocket.

I have a couple of things that belong to you and I want to make sure you get them back. You know you can trust me, Taylor. You know I'm on your side. Meet me tonight. There are some things I need to tell you.

It was signed 'Blades – xoxo' with a phone number written beneath. He was right about one thing, Taylor thought. She knew she could trust him. Taylor wanted to send him a text, but she would have to wait until she collected her phone from security on the way out. She folded the note and put it back in her pocket.

Chapter 26

The conference room was a large room with a podium and microphones set up at the front, facing rows and rows of chairs. At the present time, it was filled to capacity with reporters. Chris, Kate, Gray, Callaghan, Quinn, and the Worthingtons waited in a side room, watching on a monitor, as Cail led Taylor to the podium. He insisted on accompanying her, wouldn't take no for an answer. So Taylor laced her fingers through his and held on tight.

She stood staring down at the podium for a moment then gathered up her hair and dropped it behind her.

Cail just wanted to run his hands through it. Damn, she was sexy with her hair down.

As Taylor's gaze drifted over the sea of reporters in front of her, you could have heard a pin drop. "I'll take a few questions," she announced, her voice still a bit raw from crying and from screaming the night before.

The room erupted with the shouts of questions from every direction. Taylor pointed to Cheryl Starr. Might as well start with someone she knew. "Cheryl."

Starr waited a moment for the shouts to die down and, with a warm smile, she asked, "How do you feel … now that it's over?"

The right corner of Taylor's mouth lifted ever so slightly. "I feel a tremendous sense of relief, like the weight of the world just fell from my shoulders." She pointed to another reporter.

"Sarah Johnson has maintained her innocence from the beginning. Why do you think she suddenly decided to bargain for a deal?"

With a shrug, Taylor answered, "Maybe she finally realized she was sunk. Your guess is as good as mine."

"It's been a difficult time for you since you came off the streets.

Where do you go from here, Taylor? What are your plans?"

"I just want to get back to work and try to put the past behind me."

"What do you think about the controversy over this 'No-Go' list? NNN fired Susan Redman over her comments about the press crossing a line. What are your thoughts on that?"

"I have an incredible amount of respect for Susan Redman standing up for professional integrity and I think it's a disgrace that NNN fired her for voicing her opinion. I wonder how the producer who fired her would feel if his private life was brought out in the media, displayed for everyone to see? Susan Redman was absolutely right. There is a line that shouldn't be crossed. Maybe what journalists should be asking themselves before reporting stories like that is does it do any good or does it just do harm? Is there really a need for the public to know that kind of personal and private information?"

"Why did you write the list?"

Taylor's eyes locked onto Kyle Sledmore's. She wanted to wipe the smirk off his face. "Why did you pay someone a thousand dollars to tell you about it? Why did you pay someone five thousand dollars for my drawings?" The look of shock on his face was incredibly satisfying. "I could arrest you right now for receiving stolen goods, but it's not enough. If I find out you were in any way involved in the theft, I'll make sure you're tucked away in a nice little cell." Taylor's eyes drifted over the crowd again. "If you are paying for information, you better make damn sure it hasn't been obtained illegally."

When her eyes drifted back to Sledmore, his eyes were narrowed. "Is that a threat?" he asked through clenched teeth.

"If you weren't involved in the theft, if you didn't know they were stolen, you've got nothing to worry about, do you?" Taylor's eyes moved over the crowd again. "As for Mr. Sledmore's blog post, he was correct that Cail and I had made a list of the things I was not comfortable with. It was something Cail and I needed at the beginning of our relationship. However, the list Mr. Sledmore published was completely fictitious. Someone may have confided in him that we had made a list, but the list he published was completely fabricated." Taylor could feel her face burning with embarrassment, but she wanted to make it clear Sledmore was less than honest in his report. "Anymore questions?" she asked quietly.

A single hand slowly raised and Taylor was surprised to see Susan Redman stepping forward. "Not really a question," she began. "I just wanted to say thank you and I hope you get the peace and privacy you deserve."

Taylor smiled, feeling the anger and frustration begin to dissipate. "I should be thanking you. If NNN had been smart, they would have fired the producer and promoted you." With that, Taylor turned and began to leave the room, her hand entwined in Cail's again.

A quiet voice in the otherwise silent room echoed around Taylor. "What happened to your child, Taylor?"

Stopping in her tracks, Taylor dropped her head. If she didn't say something, this question would follow her everywhere. But there was very little she could share, even if she wanted to.

Cail released her hand and wrapped his arm around her shoulder. "Tay, you don't have to answer that. You don't owe anyone an explanation."

Taylor slowly turned away from Cail and stepped back up to the podium. While she tried to figure out what to say that would get the reporters to stop asking about her child without revealing too much, she stared down at the podium. The silence was deafening as dozens of reporters held their breath, awaiting her answer.

She didn't realize she was crying until she watched a fat tear drop hit the podium and splash outwards. It drew her out of the painful struggle with what she could say and she realized Cail was right. She didn't owe these people an explanation. It was none of their business. She slowly raised her head and began, "It doesn't matter how many times you ask me, or if you ask me with a quiet, sympathetic voice or with shouts, I'm never going to answer questions of how many times I've been raped, molested, tortured. Punished for sins I didn't commit. I'm never going to stop in the streets and suddenly tell you all of the details of what was done to me. Please," she pleaded quietly. "You have to stop harassing me with questions I'm never going to answer. What happened to my child is my business. It's my burden to bear. You're only causing me more pain by constantly throwing my past in my face. I understand you're doing your job, but Susan Redman was right. A line has been crossed and it's time for you to move on to the next story."

Taylor turned to leave and Cail was right there at her side. She hadn't even realized he'd rejoined her at the podium. His arm came around her waist and he led her out of the room.

When they walked into the side room, Chris said, "Well, that didn't go quite the way I expected."

"I need my coat," Taylor announced.

"Gray has offered to take us all out for a celebratory brunch," Rose said with a smile.

Sensing Taylor's discomfort, Gray gave her an out. "You don't have to come if you're not up to it, Taylor."

"You've got lots of time, baby girl," Quinn whispered from behind Taylor. "There's no rush and the people who love you need to know you're okay. Give them that."

It made Taylor feel a bit guilty for wanting to brush everyone off. "No, it's fine. Where are we going?"

* * *

The Grand Hotel had quickly set up a room and catered to Gray's party. Quinn bowed out gracefully, citing previous obligations, so they dropped her off on the way. Taylor excused herself and hid in a bathroom stall to enter Blades' cell phone number into her phone and send him a text. By the time she got back to the table, he'd already responded. Reading his text, she felt like an idiot for not just being straight with Chris in the first place. It read:

R u still at DS Cain's? (Sorry – Troy told me) I can talk 2 all of u. I'll meet you there at 10pm if you send me the address.

Taylor looked across the table at Chris. She was busy whispering something in Kate's ear then they both started laughing. When Chris finally met her gaze, Taylor nodded toward the door leading out to the hallway. Chris narrowed her eyes then nodded. Rising, she whispered into Kate's ear again and then headed for the door.

As Taylor got to her feet, Cail grabbed her arm. "Where are you going?"

Annoyed, she pulled her arm out of his grip and replied, "I'm going to talk to Chris for a minute. Is that all right with you?"

Cail put his hands up in defense. "I was just asking."

With her arm free again, Taylor turned and walked out to the hallway. Chris was on her as soon as she got out the door. "What's going on with you?"

"What do you mean?"

"You're all distant and bitchy. And how do you know what that reporter paid for your drawings and shit? And who's this Quinn lady?" Chris waved her hands in the air. "There's just too much weird shit going on with you."

Taylor just gave her a look of frustration and passed her Blades' note.

Chris read through it and narrowed her eyes at Taylor again. "You said he didn't pass you anything."

"It was in my pocket." Taylor pulled up the text from Blades and handed her phone to Chris. "He wants to stop by your place tonight."

As she read the text, Chris asked, "What's your gut telling you? Trust him or no?"

"I trust him. I know I can trust him."

"What if he's bringing the locket and bracelet to try to gain your trust then he sets you up or sets all of us up?"

"He won't, but if he does, I'll know."

"Oh, really? How are you going to know?"

Annoyed again, Taylor spun on her heel, turning away from Chris then spun back again with pursed lips. "Quinn's helping me to hone my psychic ability."

"She's psychic?" Chris glared at Taylor and then it dawned on her. "You're doing this because you feel responsible for what happened the other night." When Taylor began to turn again, Chris grabbed her arm and spun her back around. "No. You stand here and talk to me, goddamn it. I'm tired of you walking away, hiding out, and not saying a word. You're shutting down and you're blaming yourself for something that was beyond your control. Did you use your psychic ability to see who Kyle Sledmore paid for your stuff?"

Maybe it wouldn't have been beyond her control if she'd taken the time to figure out her psychic ability and learned to manage it instead of trying to suppress it all this time. She wasn't about to be pulled into an argument with Chris over it. She knew it wouldn't get her anywhere. She took a cleansing breath. "I'm not shutting down. I just need some time alone to sort out all of the crap in my head. And yes, I saw who stole my stuff."

"I've been trying to get hold of Dave, but he won't return my calls. Did you talk to him?"

"He didn't have anything to do with it. Lisa grabbed the drawings before he got there and hid them in her coat. They just happened to find the 'No-Go' list and Dave told Lisa to put it back."

"How did they 'just happen to find the list'? I thought it was in the back of the book in Cail's night stand."

Taylor rolled her eyes. "They were looking for condoms."

"I never use them," Chris laughed. "So, I don't know, do people usually keep a supply of condoms in the back of books?"

Taylor rolled her eyes again. "She saw the book, took it out and started fanning through the pages, probably just like you did when you found it in my room at the Academy. The list fell out onto the bed and Dave told her to put it back, but she read through it a bit before he could take it from her."

"Were you planning on telling me any of this?" Chris and Taylor whirled around to see Cail standing in the doorway with his arms crossed in front of him, anger smouldering in his eyes.

"Were you planning on telling me about *her*?" Taylor shot back. "And don't look at me like I'm crazy. You were with her last night."

"Okay, kids. Let's take this down a notch." Chris stepped between Taylor and Cail.

"She's just a friend," Cail explained through gritted teeth.

Taylor's eyes stung as she fought for control. In as calm a voice as she could manage, she asked, "Do you make out with all your friends?" She didn't wait for an answer. She stormed straight out the lobby doors leaving her coat behind and her cell phone in Chris's hand.

Chris glared at Cail. "I hope she's worth it. I hope this Lisa chick is worth losing Taylor over. You're driving her further away every time you stick up for that bitch."

"I'm not sticking up for anyone. She's just a friend."

"She's got a key for your apartment. You confide in her about yours and Taylor's personal matters, but you've never told Taylor about her. It makes you look like your hiding something, Cail. Can you really trust someone who's been sleeping with your brother for years behind your back? They had sex in your bed for Christ's sake and I'm willing to bet that wasn't the first time."

"You don't know that. Lisa said she hasn't been in the apartment."

"Jesus. Are you listening to yourself defending that slut? Would you like to come down to my office and see the video of the two of them entering and leaving your building? And why the hell were you with Lisa last night when Taylor could have used some support with the trial starting today?" God, was it any wonder she preferred women? How the hell did Taylor put up with his bull-headedness? Chris gave Cail one last glare and pushed past him to return to the table. She was just taking her seat as Cail grabbed his jacket from the back of his chair and started back out of the room. "Say 'hi' to Lisa for me," she called after him.

Cail's first stop was Dave's apartment. He found him passed out in bed, sandwiched between two women. Cail reached over a very well-endowed red head and grabbed Dave's arms, hauling him up to a sitting position. "Wake the hell up. I've got some questions and you are damn well going to give me the answers."

"Whoa, bro." Dave raised his forearm to cover his eyes. "What the fuck?"

Ignoring the two women beginning to stir, Cail yelled, "Were you in my apartment with Lisa on Friday?"

"Ah, shit." Dave rubbed his hands roughly over his face. "This is about that sex list." He looked up at Cail with bloodshot eyes. "I didn't know she talked to anyone about it until I saw that crap on the news. Seriously, I didn't know."

"Jesus fucking Christ. Why the fuck are you having sex in my bed?"

Dave squirmed, adjusted his position as if it would make the situation more comfortable. "Lisa likes to do it there."

"Who's Lisa?" The blonde stretched like a cat then draped her leg over Dave's.

Son of a bitch. How long has this been going on?

"About once a week, since the spring, since you met Taylor and called things off with Lisa."

Because he wanted desperately to pull his brother out of bed and slam his fist into his face, Cail turned and stormed out of the apartment, slamming the door behind him.

His next stop was the law firm where Lisa worked as a receptionist. When he didn't see Lisa at the desk, he assumed she must be on a break. "Hi," Cail said to the mousy blonde with thick, black rimmed glasses sitting at the desk. "I'm looking for Lisa Harmon."

"Oh," she exclaimed with a smile and pushed her glasses up her nose. "You're that guy. Taylor Sinclair's boyfriend."

He still wasn't used to people recognizing him. It always took him a little off guard. "Yeah, is Lisa around?"

"Oh," she said again. "I'm afraid Lisa doesn't work here anymore." Lowering her voice to a whisper, she added, "She was fired over a month ago."

Cail got back into his car and slammed his palms into the steering wheel. He wondered what the hell he'd been thinking. Just thinking about what he'd done last night had his stomach twisting – too many drinks at Delaney's, getting Lisa to meet him there so he could ask her if she told anyone about the list, going back to his apartment so they could have another drink and talk some more, then very nearly letting her lure him into his bed. Of course, she denied being anywhere near his apartment. Maybe if he hadn't been drinking he would have seen through her lies. If he hadn't been drinking he sure as hell wouldn't have made out with her in his living room.

* * *

The wind whipped wildly at her hair making Taylor wish she'brought a hair band with her. She considered dropping in to a drug store and picking some up then realized her debit card was in her coat pocket back at the Grand. Her eyes swept continuously, scanning for trouble as she jogged down the busy sidewalk. Store windows were already lit up with Christmas displays, despite it being only mid-November. It wasn't until Taylor was standing in front of the building she realized she'd been heading to Quinn's.

The warmth of the lobby had Taylor sighing in relief. She rode up to the seventh floor and found Quinn waiting at the door for her.

"Come. I've got a hot cup of coffee waiting for you. It will take the chill out of you." Quinn led Taylor into the living room and wrapped her in a warm fleece blanket as soon as she took a seat on the sofa. "You should have at least grabbed your coat, baby girl."

"Why do you call me baby girl?" Taylor asked. Reaching for the coffee mug, Taylor noticed the hair band sitting next to it. Her eyes met Quinn's.

"I've got tons of spares," Quinn said as she waved off Taylor's unasked question. She waited while Taylor secured her hair in a tight ponytail and watched her pick up the coffee mug, letting it warm her hands, just as she'd done the last time.

With a warm smile, Quinn remembered the first time she'd seen Taylor in a vision. "I think you were three the first time you came to me – such big, green eyes ... so sad. Even back then you were long and lean. You were sitting on the floor, cold and hungry. The TV was on, but you weren't paying attention to it. You were watching the rise and fall of your mother's chest as she slept on the couch, wishing she'd wake up and find you something to eat. Her eyes opened and she saw you sitting there staring at her. It was as if you willed her awake," Quinn smiled at the memory. "She reached a hand down and, caressing your cheek, she said, 'Hey, baby girl'. I didn't know who you were or how to find you, so I just called you baby girl."

Taylor didn't remember the exact scene Quinn described, but there were plenty of days like that when she was small. She had a vague memory of her mother calling her 'baby girl' though. "Did you see ... everything ... what would happen to me?"

"No, not at first. You came to me sporadically in the beginning. I'd just get quick glimpses every now and then, but I always wondered who you were, where you were. There was a long period when I didn't get anything and I thought maybe you were okay. I figured things had turned around for you and you were being taken care of. I moved over to England for a few years to be closer to my family. It wasn't until I came back that I began to see everything. You would have been twelve at that time."

"Do you see other kids?"

"Not really. Not like you. It was very frustrating. I wanted to help, but I didn't know how to find you. As hard as I tried, I was never able to figure out your name. I went to the police and I went to Child Services, but they all thought I was whacked. When I saw you on the news, I knew what my purpose was and I knew you'd be coming to me. I just didn't know when." Quinn patted a hand on Taylor's thigh. "But, that's not why you came here now. Why don't we talk about what's troubling you?"

"A lot of things are troubling me." But, that wasn't what she was here for either. "How do you stop yourself from seeing things you don't want to see?"

"Like your boyfriend making out with another woman?"

Taylor was beginning to realize that Quinn might know more about her than she did herself. "Yeah … stuff you don't want to see, don't want to know. Can you open yourself up, but block certain things out?"

"Why don't you want to know what he was up to behind your back?"

"I don't want that image in my head. And, I know deep down why he stopped himself, why he didn't go any further than he did." The coffee cup continued to steam in Taylor's hands as she stared into it. She'd yet to take a sip.

"You know that because of what you saw last night and what he was feeling. There is no one else who makes him feel the way you do. It's been like that since the first moment he laid eyes on you. There's no one else he wants."

Taylor knew in her heart Cail loved her as much as she loved him, yet how could she trust him if he couldn't be honest with her? "So there's no way to block certain visions?"

"I didn't want the images of what happened to you in my head. Not when there wasn't anything I could do to help. We can't always control what we see, baby girl."

With a long sigh, Taylor said, "I don't know what to do."

"Yes, you do." Quinn smiled, passing Taylor her phone.

Chapter 27

Taylor took her time walking out to the car when Cail pulled up in front of Quinn's building. It didn't matter what she did to try to calm her nerves, it just wasn't working. She got into the passenger seat with a belly full of butterflies. Before she was able to get a word out, Cail's tires squealed as he sped away from the curb. Taylor's hand shot out to the dashboard to brace herself as she struggled into her seat belt. "What's the emergency?"

"We're going to talk to Lisa. She'll tell you I'm not sleeping with her and she'll explain why she stole your stuff."

"I don't need to see her. I don't want to see her. I already have the image in my head of the two of you together last night, Cail, and I sure as hell don't want it there." Taylor braced herself again when he took a corner too fast. If she'd known he was this angry she never would have gotten in the car. "Slow the heck down or let me out."

Cail turned to the curb and slowed to a stop before dropping his brow to the steering wheel. "You used your ESP to see what I was doing last night." His fury was barely contained. Taylor felt it coming off him like waves crashing into shore.

"I didn't purposely try to check on you. I was trying to meditate, trying to clear my mind and it just popped into my head. I didn't want to see that, believe me."

"Meditate?"

"It's supposed to help with the headaches. I was using my psychic ability to figure some things out and then I was trying to meditate to clear my head."

"You used it to find out who stole your stuff and I just happened to pop in there because you were open to it?"

"Something like that. This isn't what I wanted to talk about. We're

247

getting off track. I need you to be completely honest with me. I want to trust you, Cail, but you're not giving me any reason to."

His head lifted from the wheel as he shifted the car back into gear. "Okay, we'll talk, but first we're going to pay Lisa a little visit."

The last thing Taylor wanted to do was come face to face with Lisa Harmon. She wasn't sure she could restrain herself from drilling the bitch in the face, but she followed Cail into the building. On the tenth floor, he unlocked Lisa's apartment door with a key and pulled Taylor inside. Didn't he realize having a key to her apartment was inappropriate? She yanked her arm out of his grasp with her own fury beginning to bubble. It was dark and quiet with all of the drapes closed. The place smelled like rotten garbage. Taylor got a whiff of something in the air that took her back to the blue haze filling the trailer she and Leila lived in with their mother.

"Lisa?" Cail called out. There was no response.

He checked the entire apartment, ending in the master bedroom, but there was no one there.

Taylor stood in the bedroom doorway, her attention focused on the wall where Lisa had pinned up four drawings – four of Taylor's drawings of Cail in very intimate moments. "Call your Dad," Taylor ordered. "I want a search warrant to make sure she doesn't have anything else that belongs to me."

He followed her gaze to the drawings. "Tay? Come on."

That he was still trying to protect Lisa, stabbed Taylor's heart like a knife. When he made no move to take out his phone, Taylor entered the room, grabbed the phone from the bedside table and called Chris.

"Why are you doing this?" Cail asked with contempt when she hung up the phone.

"Why are you trying to protect her?" Taylor didn't bother hiding the hurt she felt. She knew it was evident in her eyes, in her expression, in her voice, and she wanted him to see it, wanted him to know what it was doing to her. Leaning back against the wall, she shoved her hands in her pockets.

The words Chris had spoken were ringing in Cail's ears – 'I hope Lisa's worth losing Taylor over'. He asked himself why the hell he was sticking up for Lisa when what he wanted most was standing right in front of him. The only answer he could come up with was they had been friends for so long. What kind of friend sleeps in your bed with your brother? he wondered. What kind of friend steals personal items from your home and sells them to the media? He could have kicked himself for his stupidity. "I don't know why I'm making such a mess of things, Tay. I'm sorry. I just want everything to go back to the way it was. I miss you. I just want us to go back to how we were."

"I don't know if that's possible. How can we go back after everything that's happened over the past few days? You want me to trust you, but you haven't been honest with me. I don't understand how you could be so close to her that you'd share intimate, personal information about our relationship, yet you've never even mentioned her to me. Do you have other friends you talk like that with? How come I don't know any of your friends? Do I even really know you?" She glanced at the unmade bed, wondering how many times Cail slept with Lisa in it then pushed herself off the wall and started for the door. "I can't be in this room."

Cail followed her out to the living room where Taylor opened the curtains to let in some light. "Tay?" He hadn't realized he lost her trust to the point she questioned if she even knew him. "I never mentioned her because it was … I don't know. I guess I thought it would be awkward."

"You felt like you had to hide her from me. Isn't that a sign of guilt? Isn't that a sign that your relationship with her is inappropriate?" Taylor scanned the room and understood why the drapes had been drawn. The place was a pig sty with clothes and papers scattered everywhere. On the coffee table, there was a mess of dirty dishes, take out containers, beer bottles … and used needles, burnt spoons, lighters, and white residue.

"It's not inappropriate. I just didn't think you'd understand. I've been friends with Lisa for a long time." Cail followed Taylor's gaze again when he registered her disgust. "Jesus." He ran his fingers through his hair, leaving his hand on his head as he stared at the mess in disbelief.

"Cail, she went into your apartment and stole things that are very private and personal so she could sell them to feed her habit."

"Our apartment," he replied automatically. "She lost her job, Tay. That's why she needed the money."

"It's like you're wearing blinders where she's concerned. It wasn't rent money she was after. She needed the money to support her habit. Can you not see what's all over that table?"

"I saw it." His anger was beginning to rise again. "It doesn't mean it's hers."

"God." Taylor pressed the heel of her hand to her forehead and squeezed her eyes shut. She was getting a headache out of pure frustration. "You know what? I give up. I hope you two are happy together." She desperately wanted to run out the door and keep running, but Chris was on her way, hopefully with a search warrant.

"Don't do that for Christ's sake. You know how much I love you. You know you're the only one I want."

"I'm not the one bringing ex-lovers to *our* apartment and getting naked with them." It was a low blow, because she knew he only did it because he was drunk and Lisa was coming on to him like a house on fire. And she knew he stopped himself before it went all the way because he couldn't stop thinking about Taylor. The knock at the door had her sighing in relief. She started for the door when Cail grabbed her arm.

"I'm sorry, Tay. If I could take last night back, I would. I was a complete idiot. Forgive me. Please, forgive me."

Taylor pulled out of his grip again, pushing her emotions back and answered the door. Chris and Kate walked in, taking in their surroundings.

"Eeuuw." Kate screwed up her nose.

"A couple of uniforms are heading over with the warrant," Chris announced, dropping a large black case on the floor that she used for gathering evidence.

"Hopefully, you've got extra gloves. I sure as hell don't want to touch anything." Kate turned her attention to Cail and Taylor and thought, uh-oh. "Everything all right?"

"No," Cail answered. "Nothing's all right."

Taylor went to look out the window while she fought back tears again. Chris and Kate decided to divide and conquer. Kate took Cail through to the bedroom while Chris approached Taylor.

"Want to talk about it?"

Pursing her lips to keep them from quivering, Taylor shook her head and continued to stare unseeing out the window. Chris handed Taylor's iPhone to her and said, "Give Gray a call. She's worried."

A solitary tear spilled out and dribbled slowly down Taylor's cheek before she swiped it away then crossed her arms in front of her.

"Did he sleep with her?" Chris asked.

The image of Cail writhing around with Lisa on his sofa would be forever imprinted on Taylor's brain. "He stopped just shy of intercourse," Taylor's raspy voice whispered as a few more tears spilled. She had to get herself under control before the uniforms arrived. "I can't talk about this right now." She swiped at the tears again and then dropped the bomb on Chris. "The drawings she has in her room are from the sketch pads that I have at your house."

"What? That bitch broke into my house?"

"I'm not sure," Taylor answered. "But, that's where those drawings were."

"Can you use your ESP?"

"I've already got a pounding headache. Maybe later."

"Why don't I get someone to drive you over to the Grand? You can take some Advil and lie down while we take care of things here."

"I want to be here. I want to know if she has anything else of mine."

Chris raked a hand through her hair. She'd been doing it a lot lately. In this instance, it remained sticking up in the air. "Why don't you sit down somewhere and I'll see if Kate's got any Advil in that monster purse of hers?"

She got a quick laugh out of Taylor. Neither Taylor nor Chris were in the habit of carrying a purse, but Kate carried everything but the kitchen sink in hers everywhere she went. Taylor pulled out one of the dining room chairs. It looked like the safest place to sit. When Chris came back with Advil and a glass of water, Taylor was hunched over the table with her face in her hands. She straightened to take the Advil and Chris took a seat next to her.

"You should take a vacation. Take a week before you come back to work and go lie on a beach somewhere – de-stress."

The sound that escaped from Taylor's lungs was somewhere between a laugh and a huff. "Just fly off somewhere by myself and lie on a beach?"

"Sure, why not? You can afford it."

"When was the last time you laid on a beach?"

"I've never been anywhere outside of Ontario and Quebec; never flown on an airplane."

Taylor hadn't been outside of Ontario, up until she left on the book tour, so she wasn't surprised by it. "Maybe it's time you did then. God knows you could use some de-stressing after dealing with Sarah Johnson."

Chris still had a couple of weeks of vacation time that had to be used up by the end of the year or it was lost. It happened just about every year. She'd get to the end of December and still have a week or two she hadn't used. The only exception had been the couple of years she used up all of her time off working on her house. "Maybe. We'll think about it." She got up at the knock on the door and let the uniforms in.

They spent the next couple of hours searching through Lisa Harmon's apartment and came up with a pile of items that belonged to Taylor, including several dresses and eight more drawings that came from both Cail's apartment and Chris's house. Chris wandered into the bedroom where Taylor and a uniformed officer were still going through Lisa's closet. "I think we're just about done," Chris announced.

"When was the last time you wore that bracelet I gave you?" Taylor asked from her hands and knees with her head in the closet.

"I put it away when we got home from Gray's. I didn't want to lose it at work." She walked over to the closet and watched as Taylor pulled out a small box and lifted a gold handcuff bracelet out of it in a gloved hand. "Jesus."

"I'm not sure if it's the one I gave you or the one I had tucked in my suitcase to give Kate on her birthday." Taylor pushed the jewelry around the box with a finger then pulled out Cail's watch next. Just to be sure, she flipped it over then brushed her thumb over the inscription – 'I love you, TGS'. Pushing back to sit on her heels, she looked up at Chris. "Can you ask Cail when was the last time he wore the watch I gave him?"

"Last night," Cail answered from the doorway. "When I didn't have it on this morning, I thought maybe I lost it last night or I took it off and didn't remember." Anger was coursing through his veins again, but this time it wasn't Taylor he was angry with. He wasn't sure if he was angrier with Lisa or himself for believing and trusting her. Still, at the back of his mind, he was telling himself Lisa's addiction must be the reason behind her behaviour. The Lisa he knew would never do anything like this and she certainly wouldn't have let her apartment get into the condition it was in.

Taylor continued to poke through the jewelry in the box with her back to Cail. She didn't turn to look at him or respond to what he said. She wasn't sure what to say or what to feel. She was saved from the awkwardness that had descended upon them when a voice boomed from the other side of the apartment.

"What the hell are you doing in my apartment? Get he fuck out."

"Oh goody." Chris grinned and headed towards the ruckus. She made it out to the entryway just in time to see Lisa swing at Kate. Kate ducked under the right hook and took Lisa down in a graceful, sweeping move that had Chris beaming with pride. She grabbed the hand cuffs one of the uniforms offered and secured Lisa's wrists.

"Lisa Harmon," Kate began. "You're under arrest for possession of stolen goods. You have the right to retain and instruct counsel without delay. We will provide you with a toll-free telephone lawyer referral service, if you do not have your own lawyer. Anything you say can be used in court as evidence. Do you understand?"

"Fuck you."

"I'll take that as a yes. Would you like to speak to a lawyer?"

"Damn right, I would. You have no right to be in my apartment."

"Great. As soon as we get you booked into the jail, we'll get right on that." Kate yanked her up to her feet and turned her over to the uniformed officer, who searched her thoroughly.

"Check her purse, Kate," Chris advised before turning to the officer. "Get her processed through booking. I'll be down there to interview her in an hour or so."

"Oh dear." Kate smirked. "Been doing a little shopping, have you?" She pulled out a Ziploc bag containing dozens of smaller bags. She removed one of the smaller bags and inspected the crystal like substance inside. "Looks like crystal meth to me." She held the bag out for Chris's inspection.

"Looks like we're adding possession with intent, Lisa." Chris studied her with narrowed eyes. "Oh, and Kate forgot to add resisting arrest and assaulting an officer."

"For Christ's sake, Cail," Lisa pleaded. "You know me. That's not my stuff. I don't know how that got in my purse. Do something for Christ's sake."

Cail's eyes were hard. They didn't give away the sorrow he was feeling inside. "You need a lawyer. I'll meet you downtown."

Kate glared at him, but she held her tongue until the uniformed officer took Lisa out the door before letting loose. "Are you fucking crazy? What the hell are you doing?"

"She obviously needs help, Kate. She needs to go into a treatment program, not jail." With that he moved to the door and walked out.

Taylor stood in the bedroom doorway, not knowing what to think. She'd seen the toll crystal meth takes on enough people on the streets to see the signs in Lisa – the open sores, the weight loss compared to pictures of her around the apartment. "How could he not have seen that she's been using?"

"Maybe he didn't want to see it," Kate offered. "Maybe he didn't want to believe it."

Chris studied Taylor, but if she was upset at Cail offering to represent Lisa, she wasn't showing it. "Let's get the evidence bagged, tagged and transported to Headquarters."

* * *

The observation room was small and bland. Taylor leaned against the wall, staring through the two-way mirror as Cail and Lisa talked up a storm. Lisa's dirty blonde hair brushed over her shoulders as she shook her head, her wide brown eyes pleading for sympathy. She looked drawn and tired. Open sores dotted her hands, face and neck. She watched as Lisa broke out in tears and reached for Cail and she watched as he repelled from her and fended off her embrace.

"You okay?" Chris asked from the doorway. She just couldn't get a read off Taylor and knew Taylor had put up a shield. She also knew Taylor was going to respond to her question with a 'yeah, fine' and didn't know why she'd bothered to ask. "Damn it, Taylor. I wish you'd talk to me." That did it. She saw the shield drop just for a split second and caught the sadness and pain in Taylor's eyes. "You don't have to hold it all in. If you don't want to talk to me, talk to Gray … or Lane, but don't hold it all in."

With a nod towards the interview room, Taylor responded, "Let's get through this first." It wasn't the time or the place to spill her woes.

"Ready when you are, Sarge." Taylor heard Detective MaryAnn Blake's voice in the hallway and was surprised. She figured Chris was going to take Kate in with her to interview Lisa.

Before they got a chance to enter the interview room, Cail stepped out and addressed Chris. "She'll tell you everything you want to know in exchange for being placed in rehab. Drop all the charges and she'll go into treatment."

"I can't just put her in treatment, Cail. There are waiting lists at all of the treatment centres. It'll take at least six months to get her in. In the meantime, she's better off being locked up where she can't use."

"Damn it, Chris, help her. At the very least, run it by the Crown Attorney."

"Let's hear what she's got to say," Chris offered. "Then I'll call the Crown Attorneys' Office and see what I can do."

Kate joined Taylor in the observation room as Chris, Detective Blake, and Cail settled into the interview room with Lisa Harmon. They stood, side by side, looking through the glass. "You're not going to take him back, are you?"

Taylor's eyes moved from Lisa to Cail. Just looking at him had her stomach spinning. "What would you do?"

"Now, see? That puts me in a spot, doesn't it?" Kate frowned and crossed her arms in front of her. "I want to say I'd kick his sorry ass to the curb, but I don't want him to lose you. I don't know what the hell's gotten into him over the past few days, but he's just not himself. I keep wondering if the depth of his feelings for you is scaring him and he's unconsciously sabotaging your relationship. I just don't know how else to explain his behaviour."

It wasn't just the last few days, Taylor thought. He'd been hiding his relationship with Lisa from the beginning and he'd gotten angry with her before. It scared her to think that his aggression might escalate as time went on. "Well, maybe Lane can help."

"God, I hope so."

In the interview room, Chris busied herself writing in a file as Cail and Lisa sat watching her. Lisa gnawed at her fingernails as she waited. The only sounds were the whir of the heat seeping in through a vent, Cail's foot tapping on the floor, and the flipping of pages as Chris searched through the file. When she finally finished writing, Chris set the pen down and leaned back in her chair. "Let's start with the four drawings that were sold to a reporter named ..." she leaned forward again and flipped through the file folder. "Kyle Sledmore."

"Let's start with Troy Rappaport," Lisa countered as she continued to gnaw at her nails.

Chris pushed back in her chair so she was teetering on the two back legs. "Okay, let's start with Rappaport."

Everyone listened intently as Lisa relayed the story of how she met Kevin Laurey and Troy Rappaport at a party near the end of August. "I was just partying with them a couple of times a week at first, but I got hooked. I got hooked on ice and before long I was partying every night. I didn't know Troy was keeping a tab of the drugs I used. A few weeks ago, he tells me I owe him ten grand. How the hell am I supposed to come up with ten grand? What was I supposed to do?"

When no one answered her questions, Lisa continued. "I got the idea when I was at Cail's to meet up with Dave. I saw all those drawings and I knew someone would pay for them. Every time you turn on the news, Taylor Sinclair is on there. So, I figured someone would pay good money for them. I found Sledmore through his blog, online. It was so easy. Five grand, just like that," she snapped her fingers then went back to gnawing on them. "It bought me some time with Troy. He wanted to know where I got the money and I told him it was none of his business. But, then he dangled some ice in front of me ..." Lisa glanced up at Cail as if pleading for forgiveness. "I couldn't help it. I needed it." She turned back to Chris. "I gave him my keys to Cail's place."

"You had several items in your apartment that came from my house," Chris continued.

"I was with Troy a couple of nights ago when he broke in. I grabbed some of Taylor's stuff and then left him there. He wanted to wait for Taylor to get there."

"Was anyone else with you when you broke in?"

"Just me and Rebecca. We left in her car, but we stayed in the area to wait for Troy. He called us a while later and we picked him up. There were too many cops around, so we ended up dumping Rebecca's car and hopping on the subway. We crashed at my place that night, I think. Rebecca had to go home to her parents place, but Troy and I crashed at my place."

"How did Rappaport know Taylor was staying at my house?"

Lisa's eyes bounced between Cail and Chris. "Sorry. I'm sorry, Cail. I needed the ice."

"You told Rappaport Taylor was at Chris's? Goddamn it Lisa, what the fuck were you thinking?" Cail yelled.

"Counselor," Chris warned as she watched the horror seep into his eyes.

"I'm sorry. You told me where you were staying, so I took Troy and Rebecca there. I needed the fix. You don't understand what it's like."

"Do you have any idea what you did? You set Kate up. He would have raped her if it hadn't been for ..." Oh, God. If it hadn't been for Taylor. Disgusted with Lisa and furious with himself, he slammed his fist down on the table.

"Well, there you go, counselor. If you want someone to blame for Kate getting hurt, she's sitting right beside you." Chris glared at Cail.

"So what if I took some of her things," Lisa continued her plea to Cail. "It's not like Taylor can't afford it. She must be making a fortune with that book. She's a street person, Cail. You should be with me. She's just a street person. She doesn't deserve you."

Cail's fists clenched tight as pure, undiluted rage surged through his veins. The more Lisa said, the angrier he became. He hurt Taylor and blamed her for Kate being hurt when it had been his fault all along. "I can't do this. I can't represent you." His chair fell back as he shot up and stormed out of the room.

"Cail," Lisa called after him, her eyes wide.

"Where is Rappaport now?" Chris asked.

Lisa swiped her trembling hands over her face. "I dunno. The other night was the last time I saw him. He left the next morning and I haven't heard from him or Rebecca."

"Where did you get the crystal meth that was in your purse?"

Lisa's eyes darted around the room as she continued to gnaw at her fingernails. "Troy wasn't answering his phone. I needed a fix."

"Where did you get it, Lisa?"

"I knew where he kept his stash. I went there and no one was there. I really needed a fix, so I broke in and helped myself."

"Where?"

"He'll kill me. If he finds out, he'll kill me."

"You want to cut a deal?" Chris stared her down with a cool, hard glare. "You'll give up the address. Otherwise, you'll be in prison for too long to worry about what Troy Rappaport is going to do to you."

"He's got people ... everywhere. Everyone owes Rappaport. He'll just call in some debts and I'm toast no matter where I am."

"All right," Chris said with a nod to Detective Blake. They both gathered up their papers and stood. "No deal. I'll have someone take you back down to lock up."

Chris was almost out the door behind Blake when Lisa called out to her. "Okay, okay. Please. I'll tell you anything you want to know. I'll give you the address where he's keeping his stash. But, please, you have to help me. He'll kill me."

Chapter 28

Chris contacted Detective Pierson and gave him the information on Rappaport's stash house. In the observation room, she explained, "Pierson's crew will sit on the house and, hopefully, pick up Rappaport. In the meantime, we're done here. I want you to take it easy for a few hours before Ripkin shows up at my place."

"I'm fine," Taylor protested.

"That wasn't a suggestion, Sinclair. You're taking some down time."

Taylor sent a quick text message to Cail before they left Headquarters and checked her phone for messages all the way back to Chris's. There was no response from Cail. She ran a hot bath with Lavender oils to relax her and slipped in, closing her eyes with a sigh as the hot water eased the ache in her shoulders. She tried to empty her mind, focusing on the heat of the water and the aroma of the oils. It wasn't long before body and mind calmed and she eased into sleep.

"Tay?"

Taylor's heart jumped up to her throat at the sound of Cail's voice. She hadn't heard him come in. "There's a lock on the door for a reason," she gasped.

He didn't say a word. He stripped down and nudged her forward in the tub as he lowered himself down behind her, hooking his legs over hers. Taylor leaned back into him as he began to knead the tension out of her shoulders. His hands ran down her arms then hooked them, restraining them behind her and suddenly she was on the floor of a rundown apartment with Darryl Johnson restraining her.

Chris shot up from the sofa at the first gut wrenching scream. She pounded on the bathroom door and was about to kick it in when Kate used a coin to unlock the door. Taylor thrashed in the tub as Chris screamed her name. She grabbed onto Taylor's shoulders and tried to shake her out of the nightmare as she shouted her name.

Taylor sat up, arms flailing and sucking in air as if she'd been starved for oxygen. It took a moment for her to remember where she was and then a wave of embarrassment flooded through her as she pulled her legs up to cover herself. She dropped her head to her knees, refusing to let the tears take over again. She'd cried enough already today.

Chris was soaked, but she kept a hand on Taylor's trembling shoulder. "Jesus, Taylor. This has to stop. You can't keep going like this." With Taylor hunched over her legs, Chris got a good look at the bruising across the back of her shoulders right down to below her shoulder blades. It was like one big mottled bruise. She figured that's why Taylor was taking so many showers, to ease the pain and stiffness.

Taylor knew Chris was right. First thing in the morning, she'd call Lane's office and try to get in to see her. What was disturbing Taylor the most was that the nightmares were beginning with Cail. He didn't belong there. He didn't belong tangled up in the horrors of her past.

"Taylor, damn it. Talk to me."

Taylor's voice mimicked the trembling of her body. "Sorry. I'm sorry. I'll call Lane in the morning."

"Why don't I call her right now?"

"In the morning," Taylor repeated. "I'm fine now."

With a sigh of frustration, Chris stood and accepted a towel from the pile Kate held in her arms. "I brought a few extra to mop up the floor," Kate explained.

"I'll clean up. Just leave them." Taylor just wanted to be left on her own to swallow the humiliation and embarrassment once again.

Back out in the living room, Chris dropped herself onto the sofa and Kate sat next to her. "There must be something we can do to help. I feel so useless watching her suffer like that."

"She needs Cail," Chris said as she mopped her face and arms with the towel. "She doesn't have full blown nightmares when he's lying next to her."

"Wow," was all Kate could manage as she thought of the power of love. Her deep blue eyes glistened and her heart warmed as she realized the magnitude of the effects Cail had on Taylor.

"I need to get into some dry clothes," Chris began as she stood. "Would you call him?"

* * *

Cail found Taylor in the spare room dressed in a pair of yoga pants and a tank top as she brushed her hair out, her back to him as he peeked around the door. The first thing that struck him, that always struck him when he first saw her, was her breathtaking, heart-stopping beauty. His heart filled, until his gaze dropped to the dark mottled bruises spilling out from under her tank at her shoulders. His stomach churned to the point where he wasn't so sure if he was going to throw up. His chest tightened, nostrils flared in a flash of self-loathing. The choking, stuttered sound of the breath he drew in gave up his presence.

Taylor whipped around, her brush clutched to her chest, hair flying out as she turned.

"May I come in?"

"Yeah," Taylor nodded. Her eyes widened at the massive pile of flowers in his arm as he entered and closed the door behind him. She could smell their sweet fragrance all the way across the room and closed her eyes for a moment to breathe it in.

"I didn't know what flowers you like, so I got a few different ones. Maybe I got too many," he said, suddenly feeling like a bit of an idiot.

I bet he knows what kind of flowers Lisa likes, Taylor thought, then immediately chastised herself. "You're the only one who's ever bought me flowers, so I don't really know what I like. I like those ones with the bright colours," she said with a forced smile.

"Gerbera daisies. Yeah, the bold colours suit you. I should have known." They stood there staring at each other until Cail finally got up the nerve to speak. "I don't know how to apologize for the way I've treated you over the past few days. I don't think there are words to convey how sorry I am for being a complete asshat. I didn't mean to hurt you, Tay. I can't stand that I hurt you. I promised you I never would. I swear to God I've never laid my hands on a woman before. When I saw that video ... God ... I was shocked. I couldn't believe what I was seeing."

"I'm not going to say what happened was okay, because I can't be with a man who's abusive, physically or emotionally. I can't. But, I understand why you were so angry. If it had been me trying to get to Leila, I would have been enraged. So, I understand."

And that right there was one of the many things he loved about her. Her ability to empathize despite the abhorrent manner in which he had treated her floored him even though he knew he didn't deserve her empathy. "Are ..." he hesitated because he was afraid to ask, afraid to hear her answer. "Are you saying we're done?"

The look on his face was one of pure devastation and it nearly brought Taylor to her knees. "I don't want us to be," she whispered. "But, we have a lot to talk about, a lot of issues to work out."

A gust of air blew out of his lungs in relief. "You'll give me a chance to make things right?" Cail leaned over, dropped the flowers onto a chair, crossed the room in two long strides, and wrapped his arms around her. The warmth of her shuddering breath against his neck, the pounding of her heart against his, was as much of a relief as her words. "God, I miss you, Tay. I love you so much."

Chris tidied up the kitchen then made her way to the sofa to watch the news. She saw Kate standing in the hallway outside of the spare room. "What are you doing?" she whispered.

"I can't hear anything," Kate frowned as she whispered back.

With a devilish grin, Chris began to stalk Kate down the hallway. "They're making up. I think they might be a while." Kate was giggling like a teenager and Chris was trying not to laugh, but she kept snorting out a quick laugh before getting control of herself again. She caught up to Kate, silencing her giggles with her mouth. "God, you smell so good. How do you go through a sixteen hour day and still smell so good?"

Kate giggled.

As her mouth worked its way down Kate's neck, Chris's hands found their way under her bra. The sound Kate made in her throat before she started giggling again sent a thrill shooting straight to Chris's groin. She nipped her way across Kate's collarbone whispering, "I can't get enough of you. It's never enough."

Gasping, Kate combed her fingers into Chris's hair, holding her to her breast. "Don't stop. Just don't ever stop."

Straightening, Chris splayed her fingers over the sides of Kate's head and took her mouth with such heat that a shudder ran clear down Kate's body from shoulders to toes. "Bedroom." Chris began to move forward, forcing Kate to walk backwards down the hallway.

Hoping Chris was navigating them in the right direction, Kate pulled at Chris's shirt until she could get her hands underneath. Soft, soft skin over all of those rippling muscles. She loved the feel of her, could spend hours touching her.

Chris got them through the bedroom door and hooked her foot around it, slamming it closed with more force than she anticipated. Clothes flew in all directions as they made their way to the bed. And then they were lost. Completely lost in each other. It was always like this with Kate and it had never been like this with anyone one else. All consuming. Deliriously erotic. Powerful. Sensual. Love. This was love. This was what love could do. Tears welled in Chris's eyes and on a sob she took her lover over, soaring, soaring together on a wave of hedonistic bliss. "I love you," Chris cried. "God, I love you so much."

* * *

Taylor fell asleep with her head resting on Cail's shoulder, listening to the beat of his heart. Cail watched her sleep for nearly two hours before she began to tremble in his arms. He knew the moment the nightmare began. Her eyelids flickered as she trembled and let out a painful groan before her eyes flashed open. "Shhhh," he brushed his lips over her temple. "It's just a dream. I'm here. I've got you."

Taylor closed her eyes again, tightening her arms around him. His lips continued to brush back and forth over her temple until she felt calm and relaxed. "Sorry."

"For what?"

Taylor didn't answer. She wasn't quite sure why she was apologizing. For having a nightmare? For waking up shaking in his arms? When she didn't answer, Cail curled a finger under her chin and turned her face up so he could look into her eyes. There he could see the pain, the shame and humiliation, and he wanted to take it all away. "Are you dreaming about your baby?" He saw the flash of anger before she turned away.

"I don't want to upset you. I just want to help."

"I know." Taylor rolled onto her belly with her arms out in front of her and rested her cheek on the backs of her hands. "I'm not ready to talk about it."

"I want you to come home with me."

Taylor closed her eyes for a moment thinking 'here we go'. "I can't. I can't live there, Cail. Every time I walk into your room, I'll see Lisa and Dave in your bed. Or Lisa and you."

"We'll get a new place then. The super wants us to move out anyway. He said all the reporters hanging around are a nuisance to the other residents."

"I'm sure he's right. I've never had a place that's mine. I went from Gray's to the Academy to your place. I've never had a home that's mine."

"Are you saying you want to get a place of your own, without me?"

"No. I guess what I want is a place that's ours. I've never felt like your place is ours. I want something that's big enough to put in a

Unfinished Business

home gym and have room for Gray, Callaghan, and Gracie to stay when they're in the city."

"And you'll need an art room," Cail smiled.

"Art room slash office. I want to start writing again."

Cail lined himself up next to Taylor on his side and began brushing his fingers up and down her spine through the thin material of her tank. He grinned when she shivered in response. "What about a man cave?"

Taylor snorted. "What are you going to put in your man cave?"

"Big screen TV, comfy couches, pool table, bar, video games … there's so much to think about."

"We're going to need a really big place."

"It'll take us months to christen every room."

Taylor snorted again then locked her eyes on his. "I missed you." She laid a hand on his cheek, rubbing her thumb over the bristle of his beard. "I love you."

Cail's hand covered Taylor's. Closing his eyes, he sent up a quick prayer of thanks. "I love you, Angel." He leaned over, heading for her mouth, when she put her hand to his lips to stop him.

There were things that needed to be said, by both of them, but she wasn't sure how to say what she needed to say and ask what she needed to ask without making Cail angry. The last thing she wanted was to rouse his anger. "Cail?" she began and then she was at a loss as to what to say.

"Talk to me, Tay."

"We have a lot to talk about." Her stomach was full of butterflies as she summoned her nerve.

"I've been a complete asshat, Tay. I don't know what to say to make up for the idiot I've been, for how horribly I've treated you."

"Asshat?" Taylor pursed her lips, trying not to laugh.

Cail looked down into Taylor's eyes with laughter reflecting in his own. "If the hat fits ..." And they both let go and laughed together. He lowered to her side again and wrapped his arms around her. "Just say it. Whatever's on your mind, just say it."

She wished it was that easy. Still, she needed to get it out. She let out a quivering breath and then took Cail's advice and just blurted it out. "Were you going to Lisa for the things I haven't been able to give you?" Cail's arms released her and Taylor waited with her eyes squeezed closed for his reaction. But, it wasn't what she expected. His hands cupped her face and he tilted her head back until he was eye to

263

eye with her.

"Look at me, Tay." Cail waited for her eyes to open before he continued. "I was an idiot for being with Lisa last night. I was drunk and I was a complete fool. There isn't anything that I want or need that you don't give me. I love you. Only you. I don't want to be with anyone, but you."

Taylor was sickened that one of his excuses for what happened with Lisa the previous night was that he was drunk. Why would he drink so much that it affected his ability to make rational decisions? There was something that really bothered her about Cail turning to alcohol when he had a bad day. But, there were so many other issues they needed to hash out that she let it go and turned her focus back to Lisa Harmon. "You had oral sex with her. You didn't seem to have a problem with that, yet you put the brakes on when it came to intercourse."

"Jesus, Tay." Cail pushed away from Taylor, got up from the bed and turned away from her. "What the fuck gives you the right to use that ESP shit on me?"

This was the reaction she'd been expecting. She backed up to the middle of the bed and drew her legs in to her chest. "I already explained to you I wasn't trying to use it to see what you were up to. I'm worried, Cail. I'm worried that if I can't give you what you need, you'll just get it from someone else."

Turning back to her, Cail frowned when he saw her curled up tight. "God. I'm such an idiot." He crawled over the bed to get to her and wrapped her in his arms again. "I'm sorry I made you feel that way, Tay. I don't know how to reassure you that I don't want anyone else. I know I screwed up. I know I need to earn your trust in me, but you need to know I don't want anyone, but you. I made a stupid mistake, but it won't happen again. I don't want you to do anything that you're uncomfortable with. I don't want you to feel pressured into doing something you don't want to do because you're worried I'll go somewhere else. I won't, Angel. Never again."

"Let me ask you this then. If I hadn't seen you and Lisa together, would you have told me?"

"No."

Well, at least he was honest about that, Taylor thought. "Then how can I ever trust you? How do I know you haven't been seeing other women all along?"

"Ouch." Cail rubbed the heal of his hand between his pecs. "I suppose I deserve that." He let out a long, slow breath, telling himself to stay calm and then he cupped his hands on Taylor's cheeks and looked her straight in the eye with all of the sincerity he could muster. "I haven't been with anyone else since I first laid eyes on you in Tryst. I swear to God yesterday was my only fuck up. I don't know what to do or say to convince you, Angel. You have to believe me."

Taylor realized he could promise her he'd never cheat on her, he could promise he would never be violent with her again, but she couldn't be sure of either. Only time would heal the damage and answer the question of his fidelity. Maybe all of the questions she had about their relationship were best to be voiced in their sessions with Lane. "I want you to get tested before we're intimate again."

"W-what?" God, she didn't believe him at all, he realized. He'd completely destroyed her trust in him and it was something that he wanted desperately, maybe because he knew how difficult it was for her to trust. If only he could take back the last few days.

"She's been injecting drugs, sleeping with Dave, Kevin Laurey, and God knows who else. You had your mouth …" Yeah, she couldn't finish that one. "You don't know if she's clean."

Christ Jesus, he hadn't even thought about it. And suddenly it made complete sense why she stopped him from kissing her. "I'll get tested tomorrow," he said quietly.

Taylor nodded, feeling a tremendous sense of relief they'd gotten through that without Cail losing his temper, but they weren't finished yet. "I don't want there to be any limitations on our sex life. It's not that I don't want to do certain things with you, because I do. When we went through that sex book together, we basically just went by the illustrations. I've been reading the book and I've learned a lot about intimacy and pleasing each other. I want to explore all of those things with you. No more 'No-Go' list."

Cail's stared at her with his blue eyes bulging.

"There are reasons I haven't let you touch me." She'd been keeping her eyes locked on his, but dropped them now. "I'm not going to feel like the other women you've been with."

He felt like even more of an idiot. This whole time she'd been afraid for him to feel the scars from Sarah Johnson mutilating her. "Tay, I've felt your scars from the first time we made love."

"Maybe, some of them, but not all of them and you haven't *seen* them." She tried to gather the determination she felt when she realized why Sarah marked her, mutilated her.

"I don't understand how she could do what she did to an innocent child. I really don't get it."

Taylor dropped her head to her raised knees because she felt light-headed. She left it there because it would be easier to get the words out if she wasn't looking at Cail. "I didn't understand it until I went to see her the other day," she admitted. "All those things she wrote on Darryl's wall about marring my face and my eyes - I think she wanted to do those things to me, but she couldn't, for the same reason Darryl couldn't look me in the eyes. I look too much like Greg Johnson. So, she punished me for my mother's sins, for sleeping with her husband. She tried to make it so no man would want me."

"She didn't succeed, Angel." Cail ran his hand up and down her leg. "I want you. I don't give a damn about the scars. I love you with all of my heart and soul." When Taylor reached for him, he drew her onto his lap and held on for all he was worth.

"Thank you for that."

"I love you, Angel."

"Love you, too," Taylor murmured into his neck. "Why do you keep calling me Angel all of a sudden?"

With a quick laugh, Cail reached over to the nightstand to grab his phone. He found the photo he'd taken of Taylor at the library with rays of light from the skylights shining down on her and passed her the phone. "You look like an Angel," he whispered into her neck. "My Angel."

She hadn't even realized he'd taken a picture of her, but then she was beside herself worrying about their 'No-Go' list being reported in the media. Handing the phone back to Cail, she said, "Well, it's better than Bean anyway."

"You didn't like me calling you Bean?"

"No, I didn't. It's one of the names kids called me all through my school years. Stretch, Slim, Beanpole, whatever."

"Why didn't you tell me that? Now I feel like a real shit for calling you that all this time."

"How many times did I ask you not to call me that or tell you that my name is Taylor? When you didn't listen, I gave up."

"God, I really am an asshat."

They both laughed and Taylor turned her head to look up at him. "Yeah, you are."

Grinning at her, Cail said, "So, you really want to do away with the 'No-Go' list."

Taylor nodded, returned her head to his shoulder then Cail lowered his cheek to the top of her head. Reading the sex book had really opened her eyes to the fact that holding on to the limitations she'd placed on their love making was only cheating them both out of expanding their love and trust in each other. Apparently, there were a boatload of sensations that she'd yet to experience and she wanted to share those moments with Cail.

"But, one of the two things left on that list is me being behind you. It really freaks you out, Tay."

"Not always. I love it when you stand behind me, wrap your arms around me, and our hands join at my belly. I can lean back into you and feel your heart beating and your big, strong arms wrapped around me makes me feel so safe and cherished. I love when you hold me like that."

"Only when we're fully clothed and not thinking about making love. Any time I'm behind you in bed, you freak. Why? What is it that you think I'm going to do to you that freaks you out?"

"It's not anything that you're going to do that scares me." Taylor closed her eyes and blew out a breath. Communication was a key factor in making any relationship work and she knew she had to open up to Cail more if she expected him to be open with her and if she wanted their relationship to go forward. "I'm afraid of myself. I'm afraid that my dark side will come out." God help her if he asked what the hell she was talking about because she didn't think she could talk about it. As it was, she could feel the heat burning her face and ears.

Whenever he told Taylor that she was beautiful, she got angry and told him he was only looking at what was on the outside, that he didn't understand the dark places inside her. But, she never talked about the dark side of her and he'd never really seen anything in her he considered dark. "So you have some dark sexual desires, so what? You said you wanted to explore, so we'll explore."

Taylor shook her head and winced. The muscles in her back, shoulders, and neck were so tense that was getting a nagging headache. She kept trying to consciously relax her muscles only to find them tensed up again moments later. "No, you don't understand. It's not sexual. It's not something that I want to revisit." Since she came off the streets, she hadn't given in to that piece of her dark side. She was sure that since she was able to feel again after being numb for so many years she didn't need those dark desires anymore. She'd been so desperate to feel, especially after she lost her son, and Sarah Johnson gave her something to filled that void. If anyone knew she'd been willingly going to Sarah for the last thirteen or fourteen years and why, she'd be completely humiliated. If the side of her that craved pain and punishment surfaced again, she didn't know what she would do.

* * *

Cail made his way to the kitchen to make coffee for Taylor. He stopped half way across the living room. "What the hell?" Cardboard Taylor stood at the stove top wearing an apron.

"Ah-ha," Chris called out from the sofa. "They live. We thought we might have to come in there and rescue you."

Cail shook his head, and continued into the kitchen. "Mind if I grab a beer?"

"Help yourself. Where's Taylor? Did you wear her out?"

"She'll be out in a few minutes. She slept for a couple of hours." Cail was about to put some coffee on to brew, but there was a fresh pot sitting ready. Beside the coffee maker, Chris had set out a cream and sugar set and several mugs. Cail twisted the top off his beer then joined Kate and Chris in the living room. The two of them sat staring at him with big grins gracing their faces. "What?"

"Feel better?" Kate asked.

"I convinced her to take a nap and then we talked. I royally fucked up and it's going to take some time to repair the damage I've done."

"I hope things work out, Cail."

"Did you catch the news?" Cail asked, because he really didn't want to have this conversation in front of Chris.

"No," Chris answered. "But they're running the highlights non-stop – the last minute plea bargain, Taylor collapsing, the press conference, and a whole lot of speculation about what happened to the baby. It's like where's Waldo."

"That's not funny," Cail scowled. He glanced up at the flat screen in the corner of the living room. It was tuned into NNN, but the sound was muted. "Turn it off. She doesn't need to see that crap." When he turned around again, Taylor was leaning against the wall by the hallway, her hands filled with flowers.

"You think I don't know they're falling all over themselves trying to figure out what happened to my son?"

"Your son? Did he survive?" Chris asked with eyes wide open.

Taylor caught the flash of headlights through the living room window and nodded towards it. "Blades is here," she announced, then retreated to the kitchen to find something to put the flowers in and grab a cup of coffee. She saw cardboard Taylor wearing an apron and shook her head.

"Shit," Chris whispered under her breath as she got up to go to the door.

Kate turned to Cail. "Do you know?" she asked quietly. He only shook his head in response.

Chris opened the door to Blades. He was a ruggedly good looking man with deep brown eyes and shaggy brown hair. He was tall and rangy, a little under Taylor's six feet. Behind him stood a woman Chris pegged to be in her mid-fifties, dressed professionally in a dark suit, black leather coat and boots. She bore a striking resemblance to Blades, except her hair was blonde. Chris offered her hand to Blades. "Detective Sergeant Chris Cain."

"Blades," he returned then added, "Justin Ripkin. This is my mother, Dr. Evelyn Ripkin."

"Dr. Ripkin." Chris nodded and shook her hand. "Come on in." Kate took their coats while Chris went to the kitchen and brought out the tray of coffee, cream, and sugar.

Taylor was impressed. She hadn't realized Chris even had a serving tray. She followed Chris out of the kitchen and stopped dead in her tracks when she saw Blades' mother. "Dr. Ripkin."

Chapter 29

"Hello, Taylor. I'm sorry, I didn't mean to shock you. When Justin said he was coming to meet with you, I made him bring me along hoping you'd sign my copy of your book. It's good to see you."

"No, sorry. I … just … I guess I just wasn't expecting … sorry, that sounds rude." Taylor set her coffee down and moved towards Dr. Ripkin. Everyone stood staring as Taylor gave the doctor a warm hug. "It's good to see you, too."

Dr. Ripkin was startled at Taylor's show of affection. "You've gotten over your fear of being touched," she smiled warmly.

Taylor's cheeks flushed. She turned to Blades then, gave him a quick embrace, and pressed a chaste kiss to his cheek. "Blades."

"I hope you don't mind me bringing Mom," Blades whispered.

"Why don't we all take a seat in the living room," Chris offered. She raised her eyebrows at Taylor and got a glare in return. Oh, this should be good, she thought.

Before he sat, Blades stuck his hand in his jeans pocket and pulled out Leila's locket and Taylor's bracelet. "You're probably wondering how I got these." He placed them in Taylor's hand.

Taylor closed her fist around them. "You have no idea how much I appreciate getting them back. Thank you."

"My pleasure," Blades smiled at Taylor then turned to Chris. "You look like you're about to arrest me, Detective Sergeant, so I better explain."

Chris merely smiled. She remained seated on the arm of the sofa beside Kate, at the ready.

"I'm associated with Troy Rappaport, but it's not what you think. I've never hurt anyone, or threatened anyone, on Troy's behalf. He only believes I have."

"Uh-huh. And why's that?" Chris asked.

"What I'm about to tell you can't leave this room."

"Are you trying to say that you're on the job? You're working undercover?"

"No. We're self-employed, you might say," he answered with a quick glance at his mother. "Basically, parents at the end of their rope come to us to save their children from the streets. It's like performing an intervention. I find them then take them to my parents' detox and addictions treatment clinic."

"It's completely off the books," Dr. Ripkin added. "In order to do what we do, it's necessary to keep it undercover. The kids we treat don't know where they are. The location is kept secret because we're not always successful. If the dealers found out where we were … well, it would close us down."

"Wow," Kate commented. "That's seriously awesome."

Chris studied both Dr. Ripkin and Blades with narrowed eyes. There was a reason the Ripkin family dedicated themselves to rescuing kids from the streets and getting them off drugs or alcohol. "You lost a child to the streets," she said to Dr. Ripkin.

Ripkin's coffee cup jerked slightly. Chris only caught it because she was looking for it. When Ripkin's eyes met Chris's, they were slightly glazed. "Yes," she responded simply.

"Dr. and Mrs. Knightley retained our services to get Rebecca away from Troy," Blades continued. "Mrs. Knightley found Taylor's bracelet and locket in Rebecca's pocket when she came home on Monday night and she gave them to me. Rebecca has been at my parents' clinic since then."

Chris's narrowed eyes turned on Taylor. "You knew."

"I told you Blades would never lure a young girl to Rappaport. He saved my life. Blades and Dr. Ripkin saved my life. I promised never to reveal their secret."

"I'd already made one attempt to get Rebecca off the streets. She tried to set me up. I was never at that subway station," Blades explained.

Chris raked a hand through her hair. It was a crazy story, but she knew they were legit. "Where's Rappaport now?"

"He split. Nearly getting busted after he broke into your house on Monday night scared him. He's planning on laying low until the heat dies down and then he's going after Taylor, which is one of the reasons I wanted to meet with you. You're not safe, Taylor."

"Do you know where he went?" Taylor asked.

"If anyone knows, they're not saying."

"How long is he planning on lying low?" Cail asked. He wanted to know how much time they had.

Blades looked at Cail with disgust. After seeing the way he treated Taylor, he hoped she would have dumped him. "I don't know, but it won't be long and it's not just him you have to worry about. He's put the word out. He wants Taylor Sinclair alive and he's willing to pay. That puts all of you at risk, including Gray Rowan." Blades made eye contact with each of them to drive his point home. "He'll use any one of you to get to Taylor."

At that, Chris pulled her cell phone out of its case and dialed Callaghan's number. She stood and strolled across the room then paced back and forth as she waited for him to answer. Just when she thought it was going to go to voice mail, he picked up.

"It's Chris. Are you still at the Grand?"

Callaghan caught the concern in her voice. "Yeah, why? What's going on?"

"I'm going to send a couple of uniforms over. In the meantime, stay in your suite. Don't answer the door to anyone unless you know for certain who they are. Rappaport put word out that he'll pay for Taylor. That puts all of us at risk."

Chris heard Callaghan sigh in frustration. "No one's going to get to Gray. I'll guarantee that."

Her next call was to Cal Worthington. By the time she was off the phone, twenty-four hour protection was being organized for all of them.

Chris returned to her seat on the sofa then turned to Dr. Ripkin. "You treated Taylor at your clinic. That's why there are no medical records from Taylor's pregnancy."

"Chris," Taylor warned with a sharp tone and a threatening glare.

"As a doctor, you had an obligation to report Taylor's injuries to the police."

Taylor shot to her feet in anger. "Chris, back off."

"It's okay, Taylor," Ripkin soothed then turned back to Chris. "If I called the police, they would have finished what they started. Is that what you would've wanted?"

"You knew it was her case worker who had tried to kill her?"

"No. We knew she was scared to death for the life of her baby. She refused to let Justin call an ambulance or take her to a hospital, so he brought her to our clinic."

Taylor sunk back into her chair, trembling and nauseous. She buried her face in her hands as bits and pieces of her memories flashed through her mind. She would have fled if she thought her legs would hold her. Cail came over and sat on the arm of her chair, his arm wrapping around her shoulders.

It took one glance at Taylor for Chris to back off. She couldn't do this to her again. "I'm sorry, Taylor. I didn't mean to upset you."

With a tremorous voice, Taylor took a stand. "I'll tell you what I remember if you agree to stop picking my life apart trying to find charges to lay. It stops now, Chris. I can't take any more."

Chris went to Taylor, crouching in front of her with her hands on Taylor's knees. "I'll back off. I'm sorry. You don't need to tell me anything. If you tell me that the she-devil had anything to do with harming your child, I'll have to pursue it."

"It's not like that. I don't remember very much for the first few weeks after they beat me half to death."

"I could fill in the blanks for you, if you like," Dr. Ripkin offered. When Taylor nodded, Ripkin thought back to the first few weeks Taylor was in her care. "Most of your injuries were to your arms and legs – defensive wounds from protecting your child. But, you also had some head trauma. There were injuries to your lower back and your legs were paralyzed for the first few weeks. Once the swelling around the lumbar spine reduced, the paralysis faded. It was touch and go for the first couple of weeks. You gained consciousness now and then, but slipped back under after a few minutes. Every time you came around and saw that you were in a clinic, you became very agitated and pulled out your IV. Treating you was … difficult, to say the least. You refused any meds. It was only because you were unconscious for the most part of the first few weeks that I was able to get antibiotics into you. Most people would have begged for pain meds, but you absolutely refused. Add the haphephobia and it was certainly a challenge. We ended up moving you out of the clinic to a guest room in our home and you were much more settled there."

"Haphephobia?" Kate had no idea what that meant.

Dr. Ripkin offered Kate a friendly smile. "The fear of being touched," she explained. "We monitored the baby closely, but he was doing very well."

"Dr. Ripkin kept me on bed rest." Taylor remembered the rest. "A month before the baby was due, I went into labour." The room filled with silence as Taylor struggled to remain in control. She pressed the heel of her hand to her sternum to try to relieve the pressure she felt there. Then shaking her head, she wheezed, "I can't."

Dr. Ripkin took over again. "Taylor was just a child herself. Children just aren't built to bare children. It was a very difficult labour and Taylor wouldn't consent to a c-section. There were times I worried Taylor wouldn't survive it. I'm sure if it wasn't for the baby, she wouldn't have had the strength or the desire to survive." Ripkin stopped to pull some tissues out of her bag and wipe her tears. Very quietly, she said, "Taylor's son was still born."

"If she'd been in a hospital –" Chris began before she was cut off by Dr. Ripkin.

"No," she gently interrupted. "Because of Taylor's age and size, I brought in one of the top OB-GYNs in the country. "We did everything that could have been done."

"Satisfied?" Taylor mumbled through her hands.

Chris wasn't sure if she was trembling or if she was feeling Taylor shaking. She thought she felt guilty before for what she put Taylor through, but now she felt so much worse.

"There's more that I need to tell you," Blades announced after a few moments of awkward silence. "Rappaport didn't steal meth from DeCosta. Laurey and Spanner stole it from Rappaport. He's got a lab in a warehouse down by the docks. Rappaport and Laurey had been partners for years. They had a falling out about a month before Laurey and Spanner broke into the lab and made off with a couple of million dollars worth of meth. What the cops found in Spanner's trunk was only half the take. Laurey had the other half somewhere.

"Rappaport wasn't involved in the limo shooting either. I don't know who the second shooter was, but it wasn't Rappaport. He wouldn't have tried to kill Taylor. He's been obsessed with her for years. I figure that's maybe why Laurey tried to take her out."

Blades kept his eyes trained on Chris as he spoke. She knew he was telling the truth, yet she still didn't trust him completely. "Have you got proof of any of this?"

"I can give you the address of the lab." He rhymed off the address and then explained that access to the basement lab was via a key-padded door in the basement of the parking garage across the street from the warehouse. "I'm not sure where Laurey stashed his take, but he has a girlfriend. She might be able to lead you to it."

Chris took out her notebook and wrote down the address Blades gave her. "What's the girlfriend's name?"

"Lisa. Lisa Harmon. She lives over near Jane and Finch." Blades found himself amused at the wide eyes and looks being shot around the room. He particularly enjoyed watching Cail's face turn red. Obviously, Lisa Harmon was a name they were familiar with. "We should be going. Now that I've got your number, Taylor, I'll let you know if I hear anything."

Chris pulled one of her cards out of the side pocket of her pants and passed it to Blades. "I'd appreciate if you could keep me updated as well."

Taylor signed Dr. Ripkin's book then said her good-bye's at the door and retreated to her room. Chris watched her go then stepped out onto the porch, closing the door behind her. "You could have gotten her off the streets."

Dr. Ripkin stopped at the bottom of the steps with her back still to Chris. She turned slowly, resting a hand on the hand rail. The woman was relentless. She understood why Taylor wanted Chris to back off. "Other than terrifying screams and begging not to be taken to a hospital, Taylor didn't say one word for the first two months she was in my home. I have an excellent team of therapists and psychologists working at the clinic and not one of them was able to get through to her. In fact, the more time they spent with her, the further she withdrew. Every time I walked into her room, she'd scurry into the back corner of the bed, terrified.

"It was Justin who finally gained her trust. He spent an hour or two every day just talking to her. Just talking. She'd just sit there, pushed up against the headboard, staring at him as if she was waiting for him to strike. He called her 'Em' for her emerald eyes because we didn't know her name."

Blades stepped in beside his mother, looking up at Chris. "She'd been with us for ten weeks before she told me her first name. She never did give us her surname, even after the baby was born. She named him Leiland. No middle name, no last name; just Leiland."

"We gave him our last name," Dr. Ripkin continued. "We had a private service for him and buried him as Leiland Ripkin. The next morning, Taylor was gone. Of course, I had Justin look for her and when he found her, Taylor refused to accept our help, even when he explained to her we wanted her to stay in our home. She pleaded with him to leave her be."

"I kept an eye out for her. She went to summer school and got caught up on the school she missed. I didn't understand what kept her going until I read her book," he smiled. With a nod, Blades turned and started towards his car.

Dr. Ripkin lagged a moment. "You think that if we had taken Taylor to a hospital that the outcome would have been different for Leiland, but you're wrong. Leiland passed before Taylor went into labour. We didn't tell her because we needed her to be strong to deliver the baby. We didn't tell her he was gone until after his birth. She held him for about an hour before we had to take him from her. It was one of the hardest things I've ever done in my life."

Chris held her emotions in check by sheer determination.

"I don't think you realize the effect you and Gray Rowan have had on Taylor. I didn't believe she would ever overcome her haphephobia. You've managed to succeed where numerous psychologists failed. The progress she's made since I knew her is quite remarkable. Last month, the clinic received a very generous anonymous donation." She figured Detective Sergeant Cain was smart enough to figure out where the donation came from. "It will help a lot of kids." With one last smile, she turned and walked away.

"Dr. Ripkin?" Chris called out before she got into the car. When she turned back, Chris said, "If you ever need anything … if there's ever anything I can do to help …"

"Thank you. I'll keep that in mind."

Blades held the door while his mother settled into the passenger seat then strode back towards Chris. He stood at the bottom of the steps for a moment then turned as if he'd changed his mind and then turned back again and walked up the steps until he was face to face with Chris. "He intends to keep her. Rappaport. He intends to keep Taylor for his own pleasure." With that he bounded down the steps.

Chris stood out on the porch long after they drove away.

Kate popped her head out the door. "You're going to catch a cold standing out here. Come back inside and warm up."

Chris continued to stare off into the night. "Is Taylor okay?"

"Cail went in to check on her, but she told him she wants to be alone. He's giving her some space." Kate stepped out and closed the door again. She stood behind Chris and wrapped her arms around her, resting her chin on Chris's shoulder. "Are you okay?"

"Do you think she'll forgive me for digging into her past?"

"I don't think she holds it against you, Chris. I think it's more a question of whether you forgive yourself. It sounds to me like she just really needs to put it all behind her." Kate spotted the unmarked car down the street. "Surveillance is in place. We should really go inside."

"You worried about them seeing us together?"

A smile spread across Kate's face before she nipped at Chris's neck, just under her ear. "Now that my parents know and are okay with it, I don't care who sees us together. I've never felt so at ease with who I am. I'm happy, Chris. I love you and I'm so damn happy. I want to go inside because it scares me to think there are people out there who would use us to get to Taylor."

"We're not going to let them. They're not going to get to us or Taylor." Chris turned and reached for the door. She opened it and motioned for Kate to go in first. As Kate stepped towards the door, Chris grabbed her face in her hands and planted a soft, lingering kiss on her lips. "I love you, too," she whispered.

* * *

Taylor woke with a gasp then a low moan. Cail pulled her in close and whispered, "You're okay. I'm here."

Taking a moment to settle herself, Taylor snuggled into Cail's arms. "You stayed."

"I need to be with you," he replied sleepily. "If you can't stay at my place, I'll stay here with you." He nearly nodded off again when he had a thought. "You want me to stay, don't you?"

"Yes. I want you to stay." Taylor stayed bundled in his arms, letting the rhythm of his breathing wash away the remnants of the nightmare. It hadn't started off with Cail this time and Taylor hoped that he was out of her nightmares for good. She waited until she was calm again then slipped out of bed. Instead of a sketch pad, she picked up her laptop and went out to make coffee.

She was typing away, hours later, when Chris came down the hall. "You're up early," Taylor said quietly.

Chris dragged herself out of bed intentionally. She knew Taylor would be up and figured it was her best chance to talk to her alone. "You want a refill?" she asked as she put a fresh pot of coffee on.

"Yeah, sure." Taylor continued to type until Chris set a coffee mug in front of her and sat next to her on the sofa. She would have kept going, but she felt Chris sitting there staring at her. She saved her document and closed the laptop. "What?"

Chris took a sip of her coffee. "I want to apologize."

"Oh. Why?"

"For everything that I've put you through."

They sat there staring at each other for a moment while Taylor tried to figure out why Chris was apologizing. "You want to apologize for doing your job?"

"I should have backed off when I asked you about the baby at Gray's. I should have left it alone when you asked me to."

Taylor set the laptop down on the coffee table and picked up her coffee. She blew into the mug before taking a sip. "You wouldn't have found anything." She didn't know what else to say.

Chris couldn't imagine what it must have been like to give birth to a child at the tender age of thirteen, never mind giving birth to a still born. An image of a tiny white coffin kept popping into her head. She wished she kept her damn mouth shut instead of poking at Dr. Ripkin. "You cried yourself to sleep last night and that's on me."

It wasn't on her, Taylor thought. It was nothing to do with Chris. She hadn't been able to cry when they took Leiland from her. She hadn't been able to cry at his funeral. It felt good to finally shed those tears for her son. Maybe it even lifted a little of the sorrow from her heart. Taylor closed her eyes and tried to push the memories out of her head. "I'm not going to talk about it except to say you weren't responsible for those tears. Just leave it alone. Please."

"Sorry." With a smirk, Chris added, "Again." She got a quick laugh out of Taylor. "Can I ask you something?"

Taylor's eyes narrowed as she wondered where Chris was going this time. "Depends."

She couldn't blame Taylor for being leery, but she wasn't looking to investigate. She just wanted to know as a friend. "Why didn't you go to the youth hostels? You didn't have to be out there on the streets alone."

"When you go to one of those places, you have to sign in."

"And as a case worker with Child Services, Sarah Johnson could access the sign in sheets. Taylor, did you know it was her?"

There was a roar in her ears as the scene before her morphed into a small, sterile cubicle in an emergency room.

Sarah Johnson squeezed, her long, blood red nails digging into the back of Taylor's hand. When she tried to pull her hand out, Sarah's grip only tightened, digging those claw-like nails deeper into the flesh of Taylor's small, thin hand.

"Everything off, gown on with the opening to the back," the nurse explained, setting the small hospital gown on the exam table. Taylor could have recited it. They all said it the exact same way. At eleven, she knew the

routine very well. She knew what they did to little girls here.

Johnson closed the curtain and began pulling Taylor's shirt up. She knew it would only make matters worse, but Taylor tried to fight her off. One eye swollen shut, the other narrowed in anger, her bottom lip pushed out in defiance. "I can do it myself."

The claws dug into Taylor's arm, giving it a good tug. "Taylor Sinclair, you do what you're told or I'll take you over my knee and spank you into next week." It was an angry whisper, intentionally low enough that the hospital staff wouldn't hear and angry enough to make the little bitch obedient.

With tiny fists, she batted at Sarah's arms as Sarah tried to relieve her of her shirt. Sarah's arm cocked back just as the curtain flew open. Taylor froze, one big green eye wide with terror. Cop. The same cop, Detective Martine DuBois, showed up every time Johnson brought her here and asked her so many questions over and over again. But, Mrs. Johnson told her what cops do to little girls if they opened their mouths. She didn't want to go in the cage. She didn't want to be raped again, never again.

"Problem, Mrs. Johnson?" DuBois asked in her thick Québécois accent.

Johnson turned toward the sound of the metal rings sliding along the metal bar, her arm extending out behind her as if she hadn't been about to slam her palm across Taylor's bruised and battered face. "Detective DuBois, Taylor's acting up. I'm just trying to talk some sense into her."

"Uh-huh." DuBois eyed Johnson suspiciously. "Why don't you and I take a walk while Taylor changes into that gown?"

Chapter 30

"Taylor?"

The roar, like a vicious storm, passed through Taylor's ears again and she stared into Chris's big brown eyes. Concern. That's what she saw in those mesmerizing brown eyes. She had no way of knowing if she talked out loud or screamed during the flashback. It had been a very long time since she allowed a flashback to grip her so fiercely it stole her consciousness. "Huh?"

"Did you know it was her?"

"What was her?" Taylor watched as the concern in Chris's eyes deepened. She had to wrack her brain to remember what they'd been talking about before the flashback. "No ... or yes. I don't know. I think on some level, I knew, but I blocked it out ... or something. Her nails. She had those long, sharp finger nails." Taylor unconsciously rubbed the back of her hand. "And her voice when she was angry with me. You can't hide those under a mask."

Chris toyed with the idea of asking Taylor about the flashback it was obvious she just had and decided not to push it. "What about the Ripkins? You could have stayed with them."

Taylor took a long sip of coffee so she could feel the heat inside her, hoping it would warm her chilled bones. "It would have been a reminder. It's kind of like having the reporters throwing those questions at me all the time. It would have constantly been in my face."

And I'm just making it worse by drudging it all up, Chris thought. "You up to going back to work today?"

Her answer was immediate and definite. "Yes."

"I'm going to arrange a briefing with Pierson and Boone. Before that, we're going to sit down and you're going to tell me everything you know about Troy Rappaport and Kevin Laurey."

"Chris, the address Blades gave you for Rappaport's lab. That's the building we searched. I didn't know about the lab. I swear I didn't know about it."

"When did you start staying there?"

"When I left the Ripkins. It was a safe place, for the most part. I remember it coming up for sale and there was a lot of speculation that the buyers were going to tear the building down to build a strip mall or something. The for sale sign went down after that and I didn't hear anymore about it."

"Did Rappaport know you were staying there?"

"The first few months I was there, I was pretty messed up. The Ripkin's were going to adopt my baby, but they were going to allow me to take an active role in his life. When he was still born, I was screwed up for a while. I spent days just sitting on the roof, looking out over Lake Ontario. Rappaport found me there. I hadn't been eating. He knew something was up with me. He told me I was safe in that building. He started to offer his protection and I told him to piss off. The price for his protection was more than I was willing to pay.

"It was kind of weird, but he sat down next to me and said there were no strings attached with this offer. I could stay in that building and he'd ensure it was a safe place for me."

"So you took him up on the offer, with no strings attached?"

Taylor was just about to respond when she heard glass break followed by a *thwack* towards the back of the house. She automatically dropped to the floor, closely followed by Chris. Seconds later they heard the same sound again. Chris leaned over and turned the table lamp off, leaving the room in darkness, save for the stove light in the kitchen.

"Stay down," Chris whispered. "It's coming from the kitchen door." Damn it! There was a break glass alarm installed on that door. The alarm should be going off. "Do you have your phone on you?"

"It's in my coat pocket in the bedroom."

"Shit. I'm going to my room to get mine."

There was no way in hell Taylor was going to stay out there by herself. She crawled after Chris until they made it to the hallway and got to their feet. She followed Chris into the master bedroom and watched her grab her phone from the charger.

"Kate," Chris whispered as she put a hand on Kate's shoulder, giving her a little shake. "Wake up."

"Hmmmm? Too early," Kate murmured in the dark and rolled onto her side.

"Get up. Get dressed. Someone's trying to break into the house."

Kate bolted up, naked. "Jesus. Shit."

Taylor stepped back out into the hall to give Kate some privacy. Feeling a little braver now, she crossed the hall and opened the door to the spare room. "Cail."

"Yeah? You okay?" He sat up in bed.

"Someone's outside." Taylor figured he was still half asleep when he just sat there staring at her. "Someone's trying to break in."

Cail shot out of bed and quickly threw his pants on as Kate and Chris joined Taylor in the doorway. Chris had her phone to her ear.

"Who are you calling?" Cail asked.

"I'm waiting for dispatch to put me through to the unit watching the house."

"Have you got your weapon here?"

Chris raised her hand from her side, showing Cail the black Glock 27. On her phone, a male voice answered, "Reynolds."

"This is DS Cain. What's your twenty?"

"Ah … sorry, Detective Sergeant. We just went for a quick coffee run. We'll be back there in two minutes."

Chris's face flushed with anger. "Someone is trying to break into my house, Detective. You better haul ass." She ended the call with, "Fuck." Then she dialed 9-1-1.

"Now what do we do?" Taylor asked after Chris explained the situation to the 9-1-1 operator. The four of them stood in the pitch dark hallway.

Chris kept the line to 9-1-1 open. "We wait," she whispered. She hadn't heard any other noises. She kept expecting to hear the back door open and the alarm go off, but they were surrounded by complete silence.

Taylor leaned back against the wall and had an image flash through her mind that had her stomach lurching in response. "They're gone."

"We wait," Chris repeated. "I want the patrol units to clear the area before we move."

"They weren't trying to break in," Taylor announced. "They fired two shots through your back door."

They listened to the distant scream of police sirens until the ear piercing shrills were out in front of the house. It was another five minutes before the 9-1-1 operator told Chris they had an all clear. Chris darted straight for the kitchen and found exactly what she expected. Cardboard Taylor lay on the kitchen floor with two bullet holes in her chest. "Son of a bitch." She spun on her heal, hoping to stop Taylor from seeing it, but she was standing right behind her, staring down at the floor. "Christ. Cail, take Taylor into the living room and sit her ass down."

"I'm fine," Taylor insisted. "It's just a piece of cardboard … that probably just saved my life."

Kate went to the front door and let Detectives Reynolds and Martinelli in.

They barely made it in the door before Chris turned on them. "Do you want to explain to me why you abandoned your post, detectives?"

"We called in a relief. There was a squad here when we left on the coffee run," Martinelli explained in defense.

"Did you get the number of the squad?"

"Ah, no."

"How about the name of the officer driving it?"

Martinelli shook his head. "Sorry."

"Where was it parked?"

"Right in front of the house."

It was at that point that Chris knew he was full of shit. "What time did this mysterious squad arrive?"

"Must have been five fifteen, five twenty."

"Now see, that's interesting, because we were sitting in the front room and a car didn't pull up in front of the house. We would have seen the lights."

Detective Reynolds let out a long sigh. He knew Chris only had to check with dispatch and she'd know they were lying. "We didn't call for a relief, Detective Sergeant. We figured we'd only be gone for a few minutes."

"I appreciate your honesty, Reynolds. You're both on notice."

"Have you got a problem with me, Cain?" Martinelli fumed. His face turned red as his chest heaved and Taylor worried he might have a heart attack.

"I've got a problem with you abandoning your post and nearly costing us our lives. If you don't like being put on notice, take it up with your union rep." Chris stared him down until he turned and stormed back out the front door. "Asshole," Chris muttered under her breath. "Reynolds? Why did you leave at that particular time?"

"We both needed a pick me up."

"Martinelli didn't take a call shortly before you left?"

Reynolds put his hands on his hips and looked down at the floor. "Look, I don't want to get in any trouble. It was a long night and we were both starting to nod off."

"And procedure would be to call in for a relief or you could have had someone grab you a coffee. The timing of your little coffee run just seems a little too coincidental for me to believe it."

"I got a wife and kids. I can't afford any time off the job, Sarge."

"Come clean and I'll make sure you don't get any time off."

Reynolds didn't rat out fellow officers, but he was pissed at Martinelli for getting him involved in this mess. He didn't want the black mark on his file, nor did he want time off without pay for something he just happened to be stuck in the middle of. "Martinelli took a call shortly after oh five hundred. About ten minutes later, he started the car saying he wanted to go grab a quick coffee. I began to call in for a relief and he grabbed the mike from me. He said, 'Why bother when we'll only be gone a couple of minutes?' I just went along like an idiot."

"When I put in my report, I'll note your cooperation and request that no disciplinary action be taken against you. Thank you for your honesty, Detective."

When Reynolds was gone, Taylor pointed to Chris's fridge.

Chris turned to see the bullet holes in the fridge door. "Damn it." If it had just been a case of two holes being in her fridge, she could have just thrown some magnets over them. But, forensics were going to have to tear the damn thing apart to retrieve the slugs.

"I'll buy you a new one," Taylor offered.

A slow grin spread across Chris's face. "Mind if I shoot the oven, too?"

"Why bother?" Cail smirked. "You only need a beer cooler."

* * *

The view over Lake Ontario was spectacular. The penthouse suite featured the latest in technology and was decorated to the nines. Rappaport, surrounded by luxury and comfort, tuned the large flat screen to NNN. Breaking news of the shooting at Detective Sergeant Chris Cain's residence was front and centre. Seething, Rappaport picked up his cell phone.

There was no greeting, no need to announce who was calling. "Get a message to Kev. Any harm comes to Sinclair and Harmon will die a very slow and painful death." Clicking off, he hurled the phone across the room. Watching it smash into pieces against the stone façade of the fireplace did nothing to calm his rage. "Fucker. Goddamn son of a bitching mother fucker."

Chest heaving, he paced back and forth across the wall of windows looking out over the lake. "Call in some debts. That's what I need to do. Call in some fucking debts. And I know just the fucking cop for the job."

* * *

Lane sat poised in her usual seat in the comfortable sitting area in her office. Taylor took her chair across from Lane, pulling her knees to her chest and hugging her lower legs. It was a sure sign to Lane Taylor was upset, feeling vulnerable.

"I had a call from Evelyn Ripkin this morning," Lane began. "She was delighted at the progress you've made since she last saw you." While she waited for Taylor to respond, she studied her expression, her body language. Not just vulnerable and unsafe, she thought. There was fear there, in her eyes.

"Gray doesn't know. How can I tell her when she's pregnant and not freak her out?"

"Would you like me to talk to her, Taylor?"

Her ponytail bounced as she shook her head. "No. I think Chris will. I know that's taking the easy way out, avoiding the discomfort, but I don't think I can tell her. I don't think I can get it out and keep it together."

"You could wait to tell her when you're ready to talk about it."

"The rest know. I don't think it's fair to Gray and Callaghan to be kept in the dark when the rest know what happened to him."

"You never refer to your son by the name you gave him," Lane noted.

The conversation was going in a direction Taylor didn't want to follow. Not yet. She wasn't ready to go down that road quite yet. She pushed the image of her son in her arms out of her head and focused on the other things on her mind she needed to address. "Everyone I loved was taken from me - my mom, my sister, my son. It was too easy to give in to the temptation of staying with Gray. Now she and everyone I've come to love since she took me in are in danger because of me."

"You're afraid you're going to lose them all."

"It's pattern. It's what happens to people I care about."

"Bad things happen, Taylor. But, I believe that things happen for a reason. It took Gray coming into your life for you to be able to open your heart again. It took Gray for you to allow yourself to be loved again. I can't sit here and tell you you won't lose someone else you care about, but you can't live your life cutting yourself off from any emotional attachment to people because you're afraid you'll lose them."

"Sometimes I think I was better off when I did. Sometimes I wish I stayed on the streets where I was anonymous and alone. If I had, they wouldn't be in danger now. I should have gone back once Morse was back in custody."

"When you compare your life now to what it was when you were on the streets, don't you think that it's better, richer, for having the relationships you have now?"

"If anything happens to them, it's my fault. It's because they're associated with me. I couldn't forgive myself if they get hurt … or worse. Look what Rappaport did to Kate. That was my fault."

"No, Taylor. It's not your fault. It's Troy Rappaport's. It's his and his alone."

"On some level, I know that. I know I can't control what he does, but at the same time I can't help but feel responsible for the situation I've put them in."

"The situation Troy Rappaport put them in. Not you."

They were talking in circles now. Taylor felt like she wasn't going to get anywhere. She felt responsible, no matter how hard Lane tried to convince her she wasn't. She had a horrible feeling this whole thing with Rappaport was going to come down to how much she was willing to sacrifice for the well-being of those she loved. She left Lane's office without mentioning her nightmares, feeling just as frustrated as when she went in.

As soon as Taylor left, Lane was on the phone. Five minutes later, Chris appeared in her doorway.

"What's up?"

"Come in and close the door." Lane closed the file she'd been working on and gestured Chris to the sitting area as she took her usual seat. "I need you to keep an eye on Taylor."

"Why? What's up?"

"I can't tell you, Chris. But, I'm asking you to keep an eye on her. Make sure she's okay."

"You're worried about her."

"Yes, I am. And that's all I can tell you."

"Did she tell you about her son? Is it something to do with that?"

"No, it's not about Leiland." Lane stood and went to the window, looking out at the drizzly, miserable day. "You have a case from your first year with the Sex Crimes Unit. One that hasn't been solved."

"Jenny Devereaux. I keep her case file on my desk."

"Taylor was my Jenny Devereaux. I went to see her every day when she was at the Ripkin's. I was never able to get through to her."

"So when I asked you to see her, it was like you were getting a second chance."

"Yes, exactly. The woman who walked into my office that day had come leaps and bounds from the child I knew. Gray was responsible for that."

"Did Taylor know? Did she know it was you she was coming to see?"

Lane turned from the window and answered with a smile, "No. She got quite a shock when she walked in. Anyway," she waved a hand in the air. "This has nothing to do with why I'm concerned. Promise me you'll keep an eye on her. If you feel she needs me, call me. Day or night."

Chris got to her feet and stuck her hands in her pockets. "You're freaking me out, Lane. Do you think she's going to hurt herself?"

Lane closed the distance between them and placed her hands on Chris's face. "No, she won't hurt herself. She's got a lot on her mind, but she wouldn't hurt herself. Okay?"

"Okay." But, Chris still felt uneasy. She'd never seen Lane so fraught with worry.

* * *

Taylor sat at her desk in the Sex Crimes Unit. Chris wasn't in her office, so Taylor waited. All around her, cops were busy on their computers or on the phone. She watched as two detectives took a suspect into one of the interview rooms. On the other side of her computer monitor, Detective MaryAnn Blake busily tapped away at her keyboard.

She wished she had something to keep her busy so her thoughts didn't keep shifting to Cail in his disciplinary meeting. Pulling out her cell phone, she checked the time for the umpteenth time. How long could a disciplinary meeting take? Surely he must be done by now.

Sliding the phone back in her pocket, she decided she may as well try to look busy. She pulled her chair up to her keyboard and typed in

'Troy Evan Rappaport', bringing up his criminal records. Troy was twenty-eight years of age, five foot nine, one hundred and eighty pounds, brown and brown. He had a long list of tattoos on his arms, chest, and back and a long list of charges that included possession, possession with intent, assault, and assault with a deadly. Lots of charges, very little jail time. That was interesting. Kevin Laurey and Justin 'Blades' Ripkin were listed as known associates.

She ran Kevin Laurey next - twenty eight, five foot nine, one hundred and sixty pounds, brown and brown. Scar above right eye. Tattoos on his arms, right hand, and chest. He had a juvenile record which was sealed. Other than that he had a couple of possession charges and one trafficking charge which had earned him a couple of years in prison. Bet that pissed him off, especially when Rappaport keeps walking from his charges.

The sound of the coffee cup hitting her desk startled Taylor. She looked up to see Chris staring at her. Their eyes locked for a moment while Chris appeared to be studying her and then Chris slapped another cup down on Blake's desk before going in to her office. That was weird, Taylor thought. She peeled the lid back on the coffee and took a sip before turning back to her computer.

Taylor entered Justin Ripkin just for the hell of it. No criminal record. Next, she typed 'Chris Cain' and then sat looking at it. Maybe she should be entering Christine, or Christina. Odd, she thought. She didn't even know Chris's full name.

"Sinclair!"

Taylor nearly fell out of her seat at Chris's bark. "Yeah?" She looked up to see Chris walking away from her.

"You're supposed to follow her," Blake smirked.

"Oh." Taylor logged off of the computer and jogged to catch up. She followed Chris into a meeting room and Chris closed the door behind them. A long conference table took up most of the room, surrounded by black padded chairs. The large windows along the outer wall looked out over the back of the old Centre for Forensic Sciences and the Medical Examiner's Office. The front of the room sported a large white board and a projection screen.

"Okay." Chris slapped a file folder, writing pad, and her coffee down on the table and pulled out a chair. "Take a seat." Taylor obeyed and sat waiting while Chris arranged a second chair and rested her boots on it. Once she was comfortable, she set the writing pad on her lap and posed her pen. "Start from the beginning. When did you first become acquainted with Rappaport?"

"I've known him since I started school. He was a year ahead of me. It wasn't like I was friends with him or anything, but, when kids were picking on me, sometimes he'd step in and stand up for me. I think he was eleven or twelve when he started selling. It didn't take him long to figure out he could make more money if he recruited kids to sell for him. He started off with kids at school and then he began recruiting street kids. That's where he hooked up with Kev.

"He was successful because he treated it like a business and he didn't use the product."

"Did he ever try to recruit you?"

"He tried to recruit everyone. I wouldn't do it. He tried to convince me several times, but he pretty much left me alone."

"How did he try to convince you?"

"At first, he told me how much money I could make and what that money could buy me. When that didn't work, he'd tell me if I worked for him he could protect me."

"Protect you from what?"

Predators large and small, old and young, Taylor thought. When you lived on the streets there was constant danger. She answered the question simply. "The streets. I was thirteen the first time he said he would protect me if I was his girlfriend. He said he'd give me a nice place to live, give me anything I wanted, and all I had to do was be his."

"Did you ever get the sense he knew about Sarah and Darryl?"

Taylor blew out a long, slow breath. "He knew."

"Fucker." Chris tossed the pad of paper on the table and got up to pace. "Do you ever think what a fucked up world this is? Jesus." Knowing what the Johnsons were doing to Taylor, instead of helping her, Rappaport used it to try to lure her to him. Jamming her fisted hands in her pockets, Chris leaned next to the window and stared out. Getting angry wasn't helping Taylor, but damned if she could rein it in.

Taylor sat quietly for a moment, staring at a pile of white board markers. This isn't helping, she thought. We're focusing on the wrong thing. She picked up the markers and approached the white board at the front of the room. She drew two squares at the top of the board, writing Troy Rappaport in one and Kevin Laurey in the second. Drawing a line out from Laurey's box, she wrote Carlos Spanner. She tapped the marker against her lower lip for a moment and then added Lisa Harmon's name under Spanner's. From Spanner's name, she drew another line and then wrote Vincenzo DeCosta.

"If Blades is right, and I'm positive he is, then Laurey and Spanner stole the meth from Rappaport's lab. What would cause Rappaport and Laurey to have a falling out after running a successful business together for – what – seventeen, eighteen years?"

Chris turned from the window to see Taylor put the blue marker down and pick up the red one. With it, she circled Lisa Harmon's name. "A woman."

"A woman," Taylor said in agreement. "According to Harmon, she began partying with Rappaport and Laurey in August. She never said anything about being Laurey's girlfriend, yet Blades says she was. So maybe Laurey thinks she's his girl, but Lisa doesn't see it that way. She's too busy screwing Dave and whoever else. Maybe Laurey catches Rappaport bouncing on his girl and decided to take revenge by taking me out, who he knows Rappaport has a thing for." She tapped the marker against her lip again. "Could be, could be."

"Then Laurey gets busted and he points his finger at Rappaport for being his accomplice in the limo shooting and states he was Spanner's accomplice in ripping off the meth from DeCosta. Doesn't fit, does it? Why rip off DeCosta if you've got your own lab? If you're producing your own meth? Why piss off a mob boss when you can quietly continue your very lucrative business?

"Cops believe Laurey because they figure DeCosta's the only one with the kind of reach who could have someone snuffed when they're locked in a cell, alone. But, what did Harmon say? 'Everyone owes Rappaport.' He's got a lot more reach than the cops give him credit for." Taylor knew Rappaport had cops in his pocket. She'd seen him in the company of cops many times over the years and it never looked like they were shaking him down. It looked like he was doing business with them.

Taylor walked back and forth in front of the board, staring at it while she thought out loud. "So who was the second shooter in the limo incident? It wasn't Rappaport. He doesn't want me dead. Who does? Harmon? Would Lisa Harmon shoot up a limo thinking Cail and I were inside? She's pissed at Rappaport for telling her she owes him ten grand. Is that how she wanted to pay him back? Or … did Laurey dangle a bag of meth in front of her and say, 'just pull this trigger here and I'll give you the ice, sugar'. Maybe she thought it was just me in the limo."

Turning, Taylor caught a glimpse of Chris gawking at her.

"Oh, crap. Sorry." She set the markers down and stood facing Chris as if she was expecting a dressing down.

"No, keep going," Chris urged.

"It's just a bunch of speculation."

Chris picked up the markers and put them back in Taylor's hands, nodding to the board. "Put it in a timeline starting with Lisa Harmon hooking up with Laurey and Rappaport in August."

"It goes further back than that. In the spring, when I took Troy's car back, he'd been using. He was very strict about not using the product. He was proud of that. He claimed that's why he was so successful, but he'd been using. And Kev, too. Kev was spaced right out. It adds to it – their state of mind."

"Okay," Chris nodded towards the board again. "Write it down." And with a grin, she stood back and watched.

While Taylor wrote, Chris put in a call to Detective Pierson. "That address we got out of Lisa Harmon, did it pan out?"

"Bogus," Pierson replied. "A couple in their eighties live there. The hardest core drug we found on the premises was aspirin, but old Mrs. Carlson bakes a mean cookie."

"You got time to swing by for a briefing?"

"I'm in the field, but I could be back there in thirty minutes."

"Perfect." Her next call was to Detective Boone.

"You got something new on the limo shooting, Cain?"

"I've got a new angle, a new theory."

"Beats what I've got. I'll be there."

Chris moved to the board and began to read over Taylor's timeline. Taylor stood back, eyeing the names at the top, thinking, thinking. "Oh, God." Why hadn't she seen the connection? She took the black marker and circled Rappaport's name. "Did Rappaport hone in on Lisa Harmon ..." She drew a line from Rappaport to Harmon, then another line out from Harmon and wrote Caillen Worthington. "Because she's connected to Cail, who's connected to me?" She wrote in her own name then drew another line circling back to Rappaport. "Is that why Laurey and Rappaport had a falling out? Did Laurey find out he was just using Harmon?"

Before Chris could answer, Taylor drew an arrow from just above August in her timeline when Harmon hooked up with Rappaport and Laurey. She added in 'July 21st – media announces Caillen Worthington and Taylor Sinclair involved'.

"You remember the exact date?" Chris asked.

Why did that make her feel like an idiot, Taylor wondered. "It was the night of the Secret Garden Fundraiser."

"Oh, yeah, and someone's birthday." Chris laughed, giving Taylor a quick shoulder bump. Chris pointed at the board. "Okay, so we've got all of this speculation. Now, what do we do with it?"

Taylor stared up at the names across the top again. "We go back and re-interview Kevin Laurey and Lisa Harmon. See if we can get one of them to crack."

"That's my girl," Chris grinned. "But, first we have a briefing to get through."

Chapter 31

Cail walked into the briefing room behind his father and Kate. He knew the moment Taylor sensed him. She was sitting at the conference table, her back to him. Her head slowly turned on that long, lovely neck, completely exposed with her hair up in a French twist.

The first thing Taylor noticed was Cail's clean shaven face. Those adorable dimples that had been hidden in the few days' growth of beard were now clearly visible with Cail grinning like a fool. It was a moment before she registered he was in uniform and then her grin matched his.

He had to settle for a seat across the table from Taylor as she was flanked by Detective Blake and Detective Pierson.

Blake stretched her legs out and eased back in her chair with a long sigh. This briefing just got a hell of a lot more interesting. So what if the smouldering looks of love and lust Cail was shooting across the table were aimed at Sinclair. There was nothing wrong with a woman fantasizing that those looks were for her. God, the man was hot. How the hell did a street rat bitch end up with the prize of all prizes? Sinclair did nothing to earn a slot on the elite Sex Crimes Unit and she sure as hell didn't earn a spot partnering with Cain. Blake worked her ass off for three long years, jumping every time Cain barked out her name, doing all the grunt work, putting in the time. What did she get for it? Zip. At least having Sinclair on the team meant she had more opportunities to enjoy feasting her eyes on Cail's supreme good looks. The wide shoulders, narrow waist, bulging biceps, and an ass that made you just want to grab onto it and squeeze, made the Toronto Police uniform sexy as hell.

At the front of the room, Chris was about to begin the briefing when the door banged open and David Worthington entered with a smirk.

"Sorry. I'm running a bit late." He leaned over Kate, pressed a kiss to the top of her head and then dropped a set of keys in her hand before taking a seat next to Cail.

Chris waited until he settled then began the briefing by going over the information they had received from Blades and then flowed into the connections and timeline Taylor had written on the whiteboard. Taylor kept glancing across the table to analyze Cail's reaction to Lisa Harmon's possible involvement in the limo shooting and to the possibility Rappaport targeted Harmon because of her connection to him. Gone was the beaming smile, replaced by a clenched jaw.

Taylor's eyes were drawn to Dave who eyed her as if she was a piece of meat. She dropped her eyes, her stomach roiling. She couldn't stop her hands from trembling so she moved them under the table.

Beside Taylor, Detective Pierson brought up information on the address of the warehouse Blades gave Chris. When Chris finished, she asked Pierson for updates on the investigation into the meth confiscated from Carlos Spanner upon his arrest.

Pierson pushed his chair out and stood to give his update. "We've been through every inch of DeCosta's textile plant twice. We brought in heat sensing cameras and as far as we've been able to ascertain, there is no sub-basement. There is no meth lab in that place. We haven't been able to find any evidence tying DeCosta to the meth confiscated in the Spanner arrest or to Spanner's death. Which," he nodded towards Cain, "Would give your new theory some weight.

"I ran the address Blades gave to you and it's an old, supposedly abandoned warehouse down by the docks. The deed to the property is listed under the name Troy Evans, as is the parking garage across the street. That's an alias we weren't aware of. In fact, we don't have any information on Rappaport using an alias. The information we do have on him, puts him at a fairly low level dealer. Either he's been very good at covering his tracks all these years, or he's got connections covering them for him. My partner is hitting up the Crown Attorney for a search warrant on the warehouse as we speak. With any luck, we can secure that within the hour.

"This property is one of the locations Sinclair gave us on Sunday evening. You didn't find access to a basement level during that search?"

"I spent a lot of time in that building," Taylor put in. "I've never seen access to a basement and I've never seen people coming and going from there."

"There is a basement level," Pierson stated as he pulled up the buildings plans on his laptop. "If he's accessing it from this parking garage, it's brilliant. The building would look abandoned. No one would see anyone coming and going. Parking in the garage wouldn't raise any suspicion. It's brilliant."

"Could be where he's holing up," Chris said. "Will you keep me updated, Detective?"

"Will do." Pierson took his seat again and turned his attention back to his laptop.

Detective Boone stood and began his update without prompting. "Our investigation into the limo shooting has stalled, mainly due to the fact we haven't been able to locate Troy Rappaport and we had him pegged as the second shooter based on Kevin Laurey's statements. As you all know, two suspects fled from the scene of the limo shooting. Both were described as male, dressed in black – black coveralls, toques, gloves. Kevin Laurey was apprehended, but the second suspect got away clean. I've got one wit that swears the second suspect was female, but we disregarded that information as all of the other witnesses stated that they were both male, including Laurey." Boone stopped for a moment and his right hand came up to scratch the back of his head. "I have a hard time believing Laurey could put an AK-47 into Harmon's hands and she could operate the weapon with a fairly good degree of accuracy."

"Believe it," Dave responded. "Her father was a firearms specialist in the army. Lisa has had a fascination with guns since she was a kid. She still goes to the range every now and then."

Taylor wasn't surprised Dave would offer up that kind of information on a woman he's been sleeping with for years. She wondered if Dave hadn't said anything, would Cail have spoken up? She looked across at Cail again, trying to get a read on his reaction. She could see his anger simmering below the surface, but he seemed to be completely under control.

Boone knew it wasn't just about skill. "Firing weapons at the range is one thing, but would she have what it takes to commit murder, to fire a weapon at another human being?"

"She made it pretty clear she despised Taylor for taking Cail from her bed. I don't think she would have hesitated at the opportunity to take Taylor out. But," Dave continued. "She wouldn't have fired at that limo if she thought there was even a slim chance Cail was inside it."

Boone turned his attention back to Chris. "I think it's time we re-interviewed Mr. Laurey. I'd like to get your Lisa Harmon into interview as well."

"Harmon is still in lockup," Chris advised. "We'll need to get Laurey brought in from Palmerton."

"I'll take care of that," Boone stated.

Inspector Worthington rose then and moved to the front of the room. "What Detective Sergeant Cain failed to mention in her briefing," Worthington began.

"I was getting to it," Chris defended.

"Is that Troy Rappaport has a hard on for Constable Sinclair."

Taylor winced at his verbage. She glanced across the table at Cail then saw Dave poking his tongue in and out of the inside of his cheek. It was all she could do to suppress a gag.

"He wants her. Alive," the Inspector continued. "He wasn't involved in the limo shooting and he wasn't involved in the shooting that took place this morning at Detective Sergeant Cain's residence. As disturbing as the fact he wants Sinclair is, it's more so that someone out there wants her dead. Laurey tried for both Sinclair and my son, Caillen. Was he able to hire the job out from prison? Or is it someone else? I want the answers." He stood, an imposing figure of authority, and met the eyes of every cop sitting around the conference table. "I want the answers and I want the sons of bitches responsible locked up." Worthington gave the floor back to Chris, but remained standing.

"We start with the interviews. Detective Boone, I know you want Laurey and Harmon. Would you mind if I sat in?"

"It would be my pleasure, Detective Sergeant."

"Detective Pierson. You'll notify me of your progress with the warehouse?"

"Will do. I've got a team standing by. We're just waiting for the warrant."

Chris waited until Pierson and Boone left the room. "Anyone have anything to add? Any speculation, ideas?"

Watching Pierson run the warehouse address had given Taylor another thought. "We need to do a search of properties owned by Troy Evans," Taylor answered. "He's got his apartment downtown, but I'm betting he's got digs on the high end somewhere. His apartment is a front, isn't it? He wants us to believe he's a low level dealer. But, someone with the kind of money I imagine he has would want to live in luxury, wouldn't they?"

"Get to it then, Sinclair," Chris ordered. "See what you can find."

Taylor spared a quick glance at Cail as she rose, judging his anger level. She breathed a quick sigh of relief as he sent her a slow smile and a nod.

"Worthington," Chris addressed Kate as Taylor left the room. "Touch base with Palmerton Correctional. I want any and all communications to or from Kevin Laurey, including any visitors. Worthington," she nodded at Cail. "See if you can find any traffic cams near my residence. There couldn't have been a hell of a lot of traffic at oh five fifteen this morning. Let's see if we can find a vehicle connected to any of our players. Blake, have Lisa Harmon brought up to Homicide. Boone will give you the interview room. Worthington, David. You can review the traffic cam footage with Cail."

As everyone scurried, Chris was left with Inspector Worthington. Worthington put his hands in his pockets. "I didn't mean to offend you or undermine your authority, Chris. I wanted to make it clear my family is at stake here. I want the people responsible behind bars before any of you get hurt." Or worse, he thought.

"Understood, Inspector."

"I don't know how my wife put up with me being a cop all these years. Having all of my kids on the job ..." He shook his head, pursed his lips. "It's hard. Damn it, it's hard. You and Taylor are family, too. I want you as safe and protected as possible. Be smart. Don't take any chances."

"If it comes down to it, using Taylor as bait might be our only chance at Rappaport. I don't want it to come to that, so we'll do everything we can to get the bastard."

"I have complete faith in you. You know I do. I brought Kate, Dave, and Cail into the briefing because I know it will be impossible to keep them out of this one. You didn't even question it. You just put them to work."

"I wouldn't have been able to stay out of this one either."

"No." Cal offered her a weak smile. "No, I don't imagine you would have. Wrap it up, Detective Sergeant," he ordered as he made his way to the door. "Wrap it the fuck up."

On her way back to her office, Chris stopped at the desk Cail was using to go through footage from traffic cams. Chris propped her hip on the edge of the desk and addressed both Cail and Dave, who was sitting across from Cail. "Either of you going to be a problem with Lisa Harmon?"

There was no way Cail could wrap his mind around the idea that

Lisa shot at the limo, thinking he was in it. Then again, he wouldn't have pegged her for being hooked on ice or sleeping with his brother either. Was he that wrong in his perception of her? He could admit he didn't know what she was capable of at this point. If she had anything to do with trying to kill Tay, she deserved to pay for it. He looked Chris directly in the eyes. "No, it's not going to be an issue."

"Dave?"

"No issues here, boss."

"Okay." Chris was struck by how similar both Cail and Dave's eyes were to Kate's – the shape, the deep, deep blue, and the thick ebony lashes. Bedroom eyes. Every one of them had sexy as hell bedroom eyes. "If you want to hit the observation room once Harmon is brought over, you can get back to this later."

Turning to the desk across the aisle from Cail, Chris addressed Kate, "Anything?"

"Phone calls to his lawyer, Lisa Harmon, and his mother. He's had one visitor. Yesterday morning. Guy's name is Luca Jensen. I'm just running him now."

"I've got a plate that comes back to a Naema Raye Jensen, three blocks from your house at oh four fifty-five this morning," Cail announced.

"Fucking A," Chris grinned. "Run them both." Her next stop was Taylor's desk. "What ya got?"

"Nothing under Troy Evans, except the warehouse and the parking garage. I'm running variations of his name."

"Blake?"

"Harmon is en route to Homicide as we speak. Boone's going to tag me as soon as she arrives."

"All right. I'm heading over. You can all hit observation after Blake gets the tag."

As soon as Chris walked away, Blake asked, "Does Cail know that his brother is sexually harassing you?"

Taylor's eyes met Blake's over her computer monitor. "I don't know what you're talking about."

"I saw the way he was looking at you, Sinclair. And, I saw what it did to you."

Taylor looked across the room to where the Worthington's were working away in a tight group. Dave said something that had them all laughing.

Blake followed her eyes and then looked back at Taylor. "Look, I don't like you. I don't think you've earned the right to be here. But, no one deserves to be treated the way he's treating you, especially after all the shit you've been through."

"If I say anything, Dave's just going to deny it. It won't solve the problem." It would just make matters worse and probably drive another wedge between her and Cail. She thought he'd been protective of Lisa, but was sure he'd be doubly so of his brother.

"Dave gets off on honing in on his brother's women. You should do something about it before it becomes more than harassment."

Taylor didn't respond because Cail was walking towards them. He propped himself on Taylor's desk and brushed his fingers up her long neck, sending shivers of delight down her spine. "Working here," Taylor said in frustration, keeping her eyes on her monitor.

"You think Rappaport targeted Lisa because he knew she was connected to me. Got her hooked on ice and in debt to him so she would feed him information on us?"

Taylor's hands dropped to her lap and she swung her chair around so she was facing him. "I don't know. It's a possibility. Fits his profile."

"I know you don't want to talk about Lisa, but –"

"Not here," Taylor cut him off with a whisper. "Please, don't do this here."

The pain, the hurt, even the humiliation he'd caused her was so evident on her face, in her eyes. She was expecting him to do it again and Cail felt the hurt in that he'd caused this, too. He reached for her hand, knowing any show of affection in the middle of the unit embarrassed her. "Come with me for a minute." He made no move, simply waited for her to decide whether or not she'd go with him.

It was at that moment Kate slapped a photo they'd pulled from the traffic cameras, a close up of the windshield, down on Taylor's desk. It was grainy, but you could make out two individuals in the car, wearing all black including the balaclavas they had pulled down over their faces. It was the masks Taylor focused on; similar to the mask Sarah Johnson used to cover her identity. Taylor heard the roar in her ears as she flashed back to the first time the Johnsons pulled her off the street and threw her into a dark van. She hadn't seen Sarah initially. She was focused on Darryl. It wasn't until Sarah grabbed onto her ponytail and threw her across the van that she'd seen her, looked into the eyes hiding behind that mask. Devil's eyes, she thought – full of hate and anger and something sinister.

"Tay?" Cail gave her hand a squeeze.

Taylor felt Cail's hand and used it to draw herself out of the flashback, draw herself back to the present. She was still staring down at the photo. "Who are they?"

"Supposedly, this is Luca and Naema Jensen. When I couldn't get them on their house phone, I tried the next of kin. Naema's mother, Connie Spires, claims her daughter and son-in-law are enjoying the beaches of Aruba and have been for the past five days. Dave's just calling the hotel in Aruba. Apparently, they drove her car to the airport the night before their departure, parking it at the hotel's long-term parking facility. That hotel reports the car is in the lot at this time."

"Have they got video surveillance on the lot?"

Kate flashed Taylor a grin. "I've got a patrol unit heading over there to pick up the discs. Things are falling into place."

"Lisa Harmon certainly has," Blake announced as she hung up her desk phone. Boone's got her in Interview Room Four in Homicide. Let's head over."

"We'll meet you over there," Cail said. He kept his grip on Taylor's hand and waited until Blake and Kate were out of ear shot. "You're shaking, Tay."

"Am I?" She pulled out of Cail's grip and wrapped her hands tightly around her torso.

"Is this because of Lisa?"

"No."

"Luca and Naema Jensen are in fact enjoying the beaches of Aruba," Dave announced as he approached Taylor's desk. "Lucky sons of bitches."

"Interview Room Four over in Homicide. We'll be over in a few minutes." Cail nodded to his brother.

"Sure. Hey, can I borrow your cell phone, bro? Mine's dead and I need to confirm my dates for tonight."

Cail shook his head in disgust, but handed over his cell phone. Dave turned and walked away, whistling as he went.

Taylor kept her eyes down until Dave was gone.

"You were fine when I walked into the briefing room and now you're pale as a ghost and shaking. Talk to me, Angel. Tell me what happened. Did Blake say something to you?"

She glanced around at the other cops in the vicinity before Cail took her arm. "Come with me. We'll talk in Cain's office." Cail shut the door then took her in his arms. "Tell me."

Taylor wanted to tell him it was nothing, but she just couldn't shake the trembling. With a sigh, she nuzzled into his neck, the comfort of his arms around her settling her jangled nerves.

When she said nothing, Cail prodded. "Did you have a vision? Did you see Rappaport getting to you?"

"No. No. It's nothing like that. I just feel a little shaky."

"Something made you feel that way. Something triggered it in the briefing." Cail brushed his lips over Taylor's temple until he felt the trembling subside. Leaning back, he turned her face up to his and looked into her exotic eyes.

Those bright blue eyes boring into her were so intense. She wondered if he could see right into her soul. It was obvious he wasn't going to lay off until he had some sort of explanation, yet she felt like she couldn't tell him. He would believe his brother before he believed her and, really, he hadn't done anything but look at her wrong. "I just feel uncomfortable around certain people."

"This is more than uncomfortable, Tay. Who? Who set you off?"

Needing to escape the intensity of his glare, Taylor took a step back and wrapped her arms around herself again. It was going to piss him off, so she tried to prepare herself for his ire. "Dave. I feel uncomfortable around Dave."

She was right about his anger. She watched as his jaw clenched, eyes darkened, and his colour flushed. "Did he touch you? Did he say something to you?"

"No. Maybe it's just me."

Cail pulled her back into his arms, closed his eyes, and counted to ten in an effort to ebb his anger. He knew his brother's reputation with women was worse than his own. If Dave got his kicks out of sleeping with Lisa behind his back all these years, he'd probably get a kick out of trying it with Tay. It had taken him months to get close to Tay, to gain her trust, before she was even able to tolerate him holding her hand. There was no way in hell she'd fall prey to Dave. He didn't have to worry about that aspect of it. But, if Dave was making her uncomfortable enough to shake, there was something there. Even if it was just something she was sensing, there was something to it. Time to have another talk with his brother, he decided. "I won't let him hurt you, Tay. I won't let anyone hurt you again."

Not the reaction she was expecting. The tension in her eased again and she relaxed into his arms and as she did, Cail thought that she could feel safe in his arms was his miracle.

Taylor wanted to stay back and run aliases for Rappaport, but Cail convinced her to accompany him to the observation room. He wanted the opportunity to observe his brother in close proximity to her. Taylor stepped into the small, box-like room and stood next to Kate. Cail took up a position a few steps behind Taylor. He noticed she'd positioned herself so that Dave's view of her was blocked by Kate. Dave leaned against the wall and Blake stood at the back of the room.

Inside the interview room, Lisa Harmon sat alone. She looked ill, Cail thought as he watched her, pale and trembling as Taylor had just been. Albeit, for entirely different reasons. Twenty-four hours without a hit of meth was taking a toll on her.

"She's being monitored by medical staff," Chris announced from the doorway when she saw the concern on Cail's face. "They're helping her through the detox stage."

Cail just nodded, feeling guilty when Taylor turned to look at him. He was taken aback when he saw the sorrow in her eyes instead of an accusing glare. Everyone's attention focused on the small interview room as Boone and Chris entered. Boone read the salient information for the record then reminded Lisa of her rights.

"You lied to me," Chris started off. "I don't like liars, Lisa."

"I didn't," Lisa shook her head, eyes wide.

"You'll take the full hit on the possession and intent charges. The address you gave me for Rappaport's stash house was bogus. But, then, you didn't know where Rappaport's stash was. It was from Laurey's stash that you picked up the meth you had on you. You know where he stashed the meth he and Spanner stole from Rappaport and you helped yourself." The little colour left in Lisa's face drained. Chris watched her trying to think her way out, trying to figure out just how much she knew.

"Maybe I mixed up the address. I don't remember. I can't remember."

"Bullshit," Chris yelled and enjoyed watching Lisa's fear. "Do you think Laurey and Rappaport are going to back you up? They'll throw you to the wolves rather than take the rap. You're nothing to them. Nothing."

"No. Kev's not like that."

Chris leaned in. "I've got Laurey on his way from Palmerton. Once I sit down with him, he's going to give you up. You've got one chance here for a deal, Lisa. One chance. Then you go down for murder in the first for the murder of Jonathan Graham Williams."

Lisa jumped out of her chair, but her hands, cuffed to the D ring on the table, kept her from going anywhere. Her eyes were like saucers,. "What? Who? I don't even know who that is?"

"Jonathan Graham Williams is the limo driver you and Kevin Laurey killed." Chris tipped back in her chair and simply watched Lisa's reaction. Her eyes skittered all over the room as her legs gave out and she dropped back into her chair. Score one for Sinclair.

"No. This can't be happening. Rappaport was with Kev."

"Did you know Cail was supposedly in the limo with Sinclair, or didn't Kev give you that little detail?"

"No. No. I wasn't there." Tears filled her eyes.

"You said it yourself, Lisa. You'd do anything for your next hit."

"Not that. I wouldn't hurt Cail. I love him. Don't you understand? I love Cail. He was supposed to be at work. I checked his schedule. He should have been at work."

"So you didn't know Cail was in the limo. You thought you and Kev were taking out Sinclair."

"Kev wanted to get back at Troy. He knew killing Sinclair was what would hurt Troy the most."

"And, handy for you, killing Sinclair would open the door to you and Cail getting back together."

"I wasn't there. Rappaport –"

"No, Lisa. You just told us Kev wanted to get back at Rappaport. Rappaport has been obsessed with Sinclair for years. He wouldn't kill her. You were there with Kev. You and Kev."

"No."

"What caused Rappaport and Laurey to fall out, Lisa? They'd been partners for close to twenty years. Why'd they all of a sudden become enemies?"

"I don't know. I don't know." Lisa dropped her head to her hands on the table. "I need a hit. God, I need a hit."

A uniformed officer knocked on the interview room door and stuck his head in. He announced that Kevin Laurey had been brought in to Interview Two and then closed the door.

Cail had forgotten all about watching Dave. He turned his eyes to his brother as Chris told Lisa she was done.

"Time's up. Laurey's going to give you up and you'll do life for murder one."

"No, wait." Panicked, Lisa got to her feet and begged. "Please. I'll tell you everything I know."

"Gee, where have I heard that before?" Chris asked.

"I'll tell you the truth. Please. Give me a deal and I'll tell you everything."

It was at that point Chris and Boone heard a commotion coming from the observation room. They looked at each other then bolted from the room.

Chapter 32

"Son of a bitch." Cail rained punches down on his brother.

Dave got his feet back under him after taking a couple of hits to the face. He wrapped his arm around Cail's neck and took him to the ground. Taylor, Kate, and Blake tried to break them up as they wrestled and threw punches at each other. It took them plus Boone and Chris to pull them apart.

"You son of a bitch," Cail yelled as he tried to break free from Boone, Blake, and Taylor's grip. His face was red, the veins in his neck thick and pulsing. "You leave her the fuck alone. Do you understand? You leave her the fuck alone."

"Nothin' stopping a guy from looking, checking out the merchandise," Dave spurred with a smirk as his eyes roamed up and down Taylor.

Cail surged forward as his captors strained to hold him back.

"Take him to Boone's office," Chris ordered Kate as she shoved Dave towards the door. He made a kissing sound and winked at Taylor on his way out. Once he was out, Chris swung around to glare at Cail. "Your return to duty is conditional on you refraining from aggressive and violent behaviour. Want to explain to me why I shouldn't relieve you of duty and put you back on suspension?"

Cail huffed out breaths. Taylor could all but see the steam released with each one. He pulled his arms out of Boone's grasp. "The fucker's been eyeing up Tay, making her sick. Their eyes met in the glass and Dave … son of a bitch. He was waiting for her to make eye contact. He knew what that would do to her. He had to know what that would do to her."

As everyone's eyes turned to her, Taylor felt completely humiliated. Dave had already made her feel dirty, now the humiliation and shame sent her over the edge. With escape foremost in her mind, she charged out of the room. Cail started after her before Chris blocked the door. "Let her go. She's going to need some time."

"She's upset. I can settle her down," he pleaded.

"I think you need to calm yourself down first, Constable. We're in the middle of an investigation here, in case you didn't notice. Jesus, Cail. I should be suspending you."

"You can't blame the guy, Sarge," Blake put in. "Dave's been undressing Sinclair with his eyes and making rude gestures to her since the briefing."

"Why the hell didn't she say something?" Chris raked her hands through her hair, leaving it spiking up and messy. "Detective Boone, I apologize for the drama. Is it alright with you if we take fifteen here?"

"Yeah, sure. It will give Harmon a few more minutes to sweat it out. I'll do a coffee run and meet you back here." He gave Cail a couple of supporting slaps on the shoulder and headed out.

Chris nodded towards the door. "Go find her," she said to Cail. "And put some ice on that eye." To Blake, she asked, "What rude gesture did Dave just flash her?"

"It even made me feel sick, and that takes a hell of a lot." When Chris didn't settle for that as an answer, Blake rested two fingers against her lips and ran her tongue up and down between them. "Satisfied?"

"Jesus fucking Christ." Chris stormed towards Boone's office.

Kate had already applied an ice pack to Dave's jaw. He sat with his legs stretched out, comfortable in one of the chairs in front of Boone's desk. Chris kicked his legs before sitting on the desk, facing him.

Dave slowly sat up straight, a smirk still decorating his face. "What?"

"Wipe that damn smirk off your face before I charge you with sexual assault and you can kiss your fucking career goodbye." The smirk quickly disappeared to be replaced by an angry grimace as Inspector Worthington appeared in the office doorway.

"Detective Sergeant. I'll handle this if you don't mind."

"Sir." Chris lowered herself to the floor. The Inspector looked well pissed and so was she at the prospect of Dave getting away with his behaviour. The look of fear on Dave's face at hearing his father's voice did little to calm her anger. Chris, Blake, and Kate filed out of the office.

Before the Inspector shut the door, he told Chris to have Cail sent in.

"I'll get him," Kate announced as she marched off in the direction of the Sex Crimes Unit.

Chris dropped herself down into a chair at the first unoccupied desk she came to and scrubbed her hands over her face. "What a goddamn clusterfuck." When her phone began to vibrate, she didn't want to answer it. She looked at the screen, seeing Detective Pierson's number and answered. "Cain."

"We've got six under arrest and millions, goddamn millions, in methamphetamines. It's going to take us days to get an estimated value. He had to be supplying the whole fucking city, Cain, and the packaging matches the meth from Spanner's trunk and Harmon's purse." Cain listened as Pierson babbled on excitedly like a kid at Christmas. "The place looks completely abandoned from street level, but the basement contains the biggest meth lab I've ever seen."

"Anyone talking?"

"Not yet. They're on their way to our offices. I'm heading in to head up the interviews while Forensics continues processing the lab."

"Did you find any signs Rappaport has being staying on site there?"

"Nada. One of the guys we just busted said they hadn't seen him in a few days. Here's another interesting tidbit for you. We've got a black 2014 GMC Sierra pickup parked in the garage. No plates, but the VIN comes back to one Michael Allan O'Hara."

"Now we just need the body. Keep me posted." When she hung up, she looked up at Blake. "The dominoes are beginning to fall." Standing, she shoved her phone back into its holder. "I need to check on something. I'll be back in a few." She passed Cail and Kate on her way back to the Sex Crimes Unit and found Taylor working away at her desk. On her way past, she ordered, "My office," and continued on.

Taylor saved her work, logged off the computer, and then followed Chris.

"Take a seat," Chris ordered again as she closed the door.

Taylor sat, with her head bowed as she stared down at her hands in her lap. It didn't take an expert to read the body language. Chris had no idea what had Lane so concerned, but what had just gone down made matters much worse. Taylor seemed fine before the briefing, but she sure as hell wasn't fine now. "Do you need to go home?" She watched Taylor's face flush at her question.

"I want to work on trying to find Rappaport's place."

"You've seen something; sensed something. You know he has another place somewhere."

"I can see it, in detail. I just can't get a sense of where it is."

Chris lowered herself into the chair next to Taylor and laid her hand on Taylor's knee. "You know you can talk to me when something is bothering you or if someone is making you feel uncomfortable, right? You don't have to put up with people treating you like that. You don't have to keep it all bottled up inside."

"Says she who buries everything deep inside."

She got a quick laugh out of Chris. "Touché."

Taylor was about to ask Chris how she would have handled it, but she knew Chris would have called Dave out on the spot, in front of his family and his peers. At the sound of a long sigh from Chris, Taylor said, "I'm sorry."

Cupping a hand over Taylor's cheek, Chris turned her face up and waited for Taylor to make eye contact. Their eyes met for an instant before Taylor lowered hers again. "You've got nothing to be sorry for. Taylor, I want to help. I know you're dealing with a lot of shit and I just want to help." As Taylor's eyes pooled, Chris wrapped her arms around her and drew her in. She listened to Taylor's breath hitch before she broke down and cried. "There, that's better. Let it out."

It was bad enough she let the situation get to her at work without breaking down in freaking tears. God, she hated crying. She struggled to get herself back under control. Crying like a baby while in uniform was another level of humiliation. "Sorry," she blubbered.

"Stop saying that. You're pissing me off."

Taylor laughed through the tears and pulled out of Chris's embrace. "I hate crying and this isn't the time or the place for it. Don't you need to get back to work?"

"Not before I know that you're okay."

"I'm okay. Can I stay in here for a few more minutes?"

Chris let out another long sigh. She hated leaving Taylor alone like this. Leaning over, she pressed a kiss to Taylor's cheek and said, "Take all the time you need."

She was half way to the door when Taylor called out her name. Chris turned to find Taylor's eyes locked on hers.

"I never thought I would love anyone again the way I loved Leila. I never imagined having a best friend and a sister again, but that's how I feel about you. I love you, Chris. I'm glad we've had the opportunity to get to know each other on that level."

Tears pooled in Chris's eyes. She never imagined having a best friend and a sister either. Their life stories were completely different, yet on many levels they were the same. "I love you, too," Chris choked. But, damn it, she thought, why does it feel like you're saying goodbye?

Taylor sat in Chris's office attempting to use the meditation Quinn taught her to clear her mind. She'd hoped once the Johnson trial was put to rest everything would settle down and she could begin working with Chris with a clean slate, a fresh start. But, it seemed that before one monster had been dealt with, another stepped in to take its place. What was it about her that made her susceptible to predators like Johnson, Rappaport, and Dave Worthington? While she pondered that question, a light knock sounded on the door and Lane stepped in. One look at the concern on Lane's face and she was biting back her emotions again.

"Chris called you?"

Lane gave Taylor's face a good study before answering, "We're all worried about you, Taylor."

"I'm fine. Really. I just felt so exposed and humiliated."

A smile filled with pride lit up Lane's deep brown eyes. It wasn't the reaction Taylor had been expecting. "What?"

The smile remained on Lane's face as she took the seat next to Taylor. "You have a difficult time expressing your emotions, yet you just told me exactly how the situation with Dave made you feel without any prompting."

"I'm becoming all too familiar with those kinds of emotions." Taylor closed her eyes. "Most of the time I was on the streets, I didn't feel anything. Except maybe fear and anger," she added. "There were times I would have given anything just to be able to feel something - grief, sadness ... anything."

Lane thought Taylor may be on the verge of a breakthrough, so she remained silent and just listened.

"When Gray took me in it was like all of my emotions had been frozen inside me and they slowly began to thaw. It's overwhelming sometimes and I find myself wishing I didn't feel quite so much."

Not a breakthrough, Lane thought in frustration. A regression. "You're trying to convince yourself you were better off on the streets. You're not, Taylor. Please tell me you're not planning on walking away from all you've accomplished in the past seven months."

Dropping her face into her hands, Taylor shook her head from side to side. "No. I'm not planning to go back to the streets."

"Are you planning on walking away?"

"No," Taylor answered. But, she had a feeling she may be forced to.

* * *

Detective Boone and Chris went back in to interview Lisa Harmon with Blake and Kate in the observation room. Dave and Cail had still been closed up in Boone's office with their father.

As soon as they sat down, Lisa stated, "I was with Dave the day that limo got shot up."

Chris rubbed at the spot just between her eyebrows where the headache began to pound. "I thought we'd gotten past the bullshit stage, Lisa."

"I was. I was with Dave. You can ask him."

"Do I look stupid to you? Do I look fucking stupid?" Chris shouted as Lisa shrunk back in her chair. "We've got you on camera leaving Cail's building at eleven ten. The shooting took place at twelve fifty. Do you need a fucking calculator to do the math? You had plenty of time to meet up with Kev. You were there with him, shooting at that limo thinking Sinclair was inside it. I bet you shit your goddamn pants when you heard Cail had been with her."

Crying again, Lisa spoke with a quivering voice. "Kev was at my place when Dave dropped me off. He said if I helped him he would settle my debt with Rappaport. Then he got busted and I still owed the ten grand."

"How did you get away? How did you escape from the parking garage?" Boone asked in a calm voice.

"My ears were ringing from the guns and from the explosion. I couldn't hear anything but the ringing and then I realized it was sirens. They sounded so close. Kev jumped in the car. He took off before I could get in, so I ran to a stairwell and took off the black coveralls and stuff. I stuck them in my purse and just walked out. Cop cars were everywhere. One even stopped and asked if I had seen a man wearing all black. I told them I saw him running in the opposite direction and they took off. It was kind of funny. Then I saw Kev's car and I saw him get arrested."

"What did you do with the coveralls and the gun?" Boone asked.

"I don't remember."

"The meth you had on you when we arrested you," Chris began. "Where did you get it?"

"I don't remember."

"You got them from Kev's stash. Don't give me anymore bullshit, Lisa, or I throw you to the sharks and you don't get a deal."

For the life of her, Lisa couldn't figure out how this bitch seemed to know everything. She was fucked and without a deal she knew she'd spend a hell of a long time in prison. "Kev's got an apartment he rents under a friend's name so the cops don't find it." She gave Chris the address. "I was there with him a couple of times and I saw where he kept the meth. It's in one of the bedroom closets in a big black bag. I put the coveralls and the gun and stuff in that closet."

"Why didn't you just steal all of the meth, sell it, and then pay off Rappaport?" Boone asked out of curiosity.

"Kev would have killed me. I figured he wouldn't miss a few bags, but if I took more than that he would have freaked."

"He's going to be in prison for life. How would he have known?"

"He's getting out. Rappaport told me his lawyers would get him out."

"Yeah, right," Chris laughed.

Chris and Boone went straight from interviewing Lisa into Interview Two where Kevin Laurey sat waiting on them. Boone read off the particulars for the record and reminded Laurey of his rights. "We have you cold for the limo shooting and we've got the drugs you stole from Rappaport's lab. You're done, Laurey. You'll never see the outside of a prison again."

Laurey smirked up at Boone. "You brought me all the way here to tell me that."

"I brought you here to give you the opportunity to take Rappaport down," Boone answered.

"Nice of you. I enjoyed the ride and the fresh air. You can take me back now."

Chris leaned in and waited for Laurey's eyes to meet hers. "We've got Lisa on possession, intent, and murder one. Think about it, Kev. If Rappaport could get to Spanner in jail, he can get to Lisa and he can get to you." She watched the anger and fear wash over Kev's face.

The warning he received from Rappaport hours earlier rang through his head. He couldn't bear the thought of Rappaport torturing her, killing her. "You think you know, but you don't know shit. You don't know who Rappaport has in his pocket. You would shit yourself if you knew how many cops he has. Look around your fucking office. I bet you can't walk ten fucking steps without running into a cop Rappaport has a line on. You're fucking boss is probably in Rappaport's pocket."

"Is that why you brought DeCosta into the mix?" Boone asked. "Did you think he'd do Rappaport for you? I got news for you, Kev.

DeCosta will go after you. Rappaport's tucked away somewhere nice and warm, living the high life, and you're flapping in the wind, bro. DeCosta's gonna make sure you die slow. It ain't going to be quick and painless."

Laurey let out a slow laugh. "See, the way I see it, you figure Lisa and I are in danger, you gotta protect us. Put us in like segregation or something."

A wide grin spread across Boone's face as he leaned back in his chair. "I don't gotta do shit."

The expression on Laury's face turned cold as beads of sweat formed above his lip. Boone and Chris sat in silence, waiting him out. You could see him thinking, the wheels turning as he thought his situation through. "If I give you Rappaport's lab, you put me and Lisa in protective custody?"

"We've already got Rappaport's lab, Kev. Tell us something we don't know."

As Laurey sat thinking, Chris turned to Boone. "How do you think DeCosta will do it?"

"He'll probably use one of those bone crackers. They start with your fingers." He stuck out his pinky. "They start with the smallest bones and work their way up. I hear the thigh bone is the worst. Hurts like a son of a bitch, if they make it that long. I hear they beg for death long before they get to the legs."

"Huh. I figured he'd go for disembowelment."

"Jesus. I don't know where Rappaport is, okay? He's got a condo somewhere, but he never took anyone there, not even me. He wanted to keep it private. He used his apartment on Jane most of the time. I don't know where the fuck he is, okay?"

Boone and Chris just stared at him. He was white as a sheet now and sweating profusely. "I swear I don't know. I'll tell you everything if you give us protective custody or whatever, but I don't know where the fuck Rappaport is."

"What do you know about Mick O'Hara?" Boone asked.

"What's O'Hara got to do with anything? He's a runner. O'Hara and his chick, Rebecca, they run packages for Troy."

"Why would Rappaport want him dead?"

"I've been inside. I don't have anything to do with that shit."

"Answer the question, Kev," Chris ordered.

Kev narrowed his eyes while he thought. He couldn't believe the cops had Rappaport's lab. Rappaport was toast. If they knew as much as they seemed to, Rappaport was done. He needed to cut a deal for his own protection before it was too late. "Word is O'Hara was skimming off of his deliveries. He'd pick up a certain amount of meth or money, but not all of it made it to the drop off."

They walked out with a confession from Kevin Laurey that included putting out the hit on Taylor. Boone was going to pick up the two guys he hired. Pierson was working on tracking down and seizing all of Rappaport's assets and that left Chris with nothing but frustration. She wanted Rappaport.

Stepping into the observation room, she was surprised to see Dave and Cail leaning against the back wall with their father between them. They both looked like little boys standing in the naughty corner. Chris locked eyes with the Inspector.

"You want to use her as bait," he stated.

Cail jerked upright and was stopped dead in his tracks when his father simply raised his hand.

"I don't like the idea any more than you do, Cail," Chris began. "But, I don't know any other way to get to him. He's cozied up somewhere waiting for this to all blow over. Maybe he's working on changing his identity and he'll be in the wind. But, sooner or later, he'll come back for her. He's obsessed with her."

"You've done an incredible job today, Detective Sergeant. We're a lot further ahead than we were this morning."

"It was mostly Sinclair. She's got a hell of a mind for the job and she works very well with a visual. Once she got going it just all fell into place."

"Give it a rest for tonight," Cal ordered. "We'll reassess in the morning and go from there."

Chris nodded toward Cail. "Why don't you take off? You and Taylor have that thing."

"What thing?" Dave asked and was quickly shut down by a glare from his father.

Cail waited for a nod from his father before high tailing it out of there and heading for Taylor.

"We'll debrief in my office," Chris announced to everyone else.

* * *

Taylor stared at her face in the mirror wondering if it was what drew predators to her. She knew by the way most men and even some women reacted to her that she had what people thought of as a beautiful face. Chris told her once it was why the media was so enthralled with her and she supposed the media was a type of predator as well. Maybe instead of babbling about emotions, she should have asked Lane what she could do to prevent people from preying on her.

With a glance at the clock, she berated herself for her melancholy mood and gave herself one last check in the mirror before leaving her room.

Very slowly, Cail rose to his feet in Chris's living room as Taylor walked in from the hall. She took his breath away. Literally stole his breath. Her hair was up in an elegant twist. The shimmering bronze dress hugged her body down to the mid thigh, giving way to long, lithe legs covered in black silk and killer heels that matched her dress. When he got his breath back, Cail walked to her and brushed a finger tip over her unpierced ear lobe and down her unadorned neck. "You should be dripping in diamonds," he whispered. "Diamonds and emeralds. You look amazing. So beautiful."

"We should go," she whispered, uncomfortable with Cail's praise.

Cail handed her a sheet of paper and explained, "Here's the paperwork you requested."

Taylor scanned the paper and broke out laughing. "You were tested for STDs by a Dr. Ball Sack?" Chris and Kate doubled over laughing.

"Balzac." Cail looked offended.

"Is this a joke?" Taylor asked, still laughing.

"No. He's my family doctor and I've got a clean bill of health."

Grinning now, Taylor stepped into Cail's arms, sinking her lips into his. Cail tilted his head for a better angle, sealing their lips. It had been torture not being able to kiss her over the past twenty-four hours and he made up for it in one searing hot kiss that had Chris and Kate applauding.

Taylor was still grinning when they broke apart. "Thank you," she whispered then grabbed her long, black leather coat from where she'd left it slung over the back of a chair.

Chris rose from the sofa and addressed Cail as he helped Taylor into her coat. "You take damn good care of her." When Cail only grinned, she added, "I mean it."

Rolling her eyes, Taylor said, "Would you like us to text you every half hour to let you know we're okay, Mom?"

"Yeah, actually. I would."

Rolling her eyes again, Taylor started for the door and stopped dead in her tracks when she saw cardboard Taylor standing by the front door with two Band-Aids covering the bullet holes in her chest. She turned back to Chris. "We'll text. Maybe not every half hour, but we'll let you know we're okay." She stood at the door for a moment, her stomach churning with nerves. Bringing Gabriella and her family into her circle would put them in danger if Rappaport found out who Gabriella was to Taylor. The last thing she needed, or wanted, was more people caring about her and she caring about them. "Maybe we shouldn't go."

"We're going," Cail stated. "We're not going to let that scumbag stop us from living, Tay." With that, he took her arm and escorted her out to the SUV waiting at the curb.

They weren't gone ten minutes when a delivery truck backed into Chris's driveway. "Delivery for Chris Cain," the driver announced when Chris opened the door. He handed Chris an invoice stamped 'Paid in Full'.

"I didn't order anything," Chris said as she read over the invoice for a top of the line fridge, stove and dishwasher in stainless steel. "Jesus. Taylor."

Chapter 33

The closer they got to the restaurant, the faster Taylor's fingers tapped her thigh. Cail took her hand in his. "It's just dinner."

"What am I supposed to say to them?"

"I'm sure you'll think of something." Bringing her hand to his mouth, he brushed delicate kisses over her knuckles.

From there she placed her hand on his cheek and let her thumb brush over his dimple. "I never asked you how the disciplinary meeting went."

"Well enough. I'm back on the job."

"I noticed that. And the fact that you shaved."

"You like the clean shaven look better?"

"I kinda liked the bad boy look. But, I like you this way, too. I can see your dimples again."

Cail laughed before giving her a quick, soft kiss. "We're here."

"Crap."

They waited for the body guards to open the back door. With Taylor's hand still in Cail's, they crossed the sidewalk into the restaurant with the guards flanking them. Inside, Taylor saw Gabriella wave her hand from a table mid-way to the back. She let Cail lead her through the dining room. He took her coat before pulling her chair out for her. Gabriella made the introductions to her husband, Jackson, and her three children, Nate, Greg, and Arianna.

"We took the liberty of ordering champagne," Gabriella announced as Jackson filled Taylor and Cail's flutes.

"Thank you." Taylor smiled nervously. To Nate, she said, "I heard you own a construction company."

"Yeah, me and Greg."

"We're looking for a place. I'm thinking about an old warehouse or loft type of thing that we can renovate."

"How much space were you thinking?"

"I don't know. We want something big enough that we can put in a home gym and space to have our friends stay when they're in the city."

"And an office slash art room for Tay."

"And a mancave for Cail." Taylor and Cail shared a quick look that had Gabriella smiling.

"I take it you want something downtown. I know a place that's up for sale right now. It needs a lot of work, but you could probably talk the price down because of that. And, it will give you the opportunity to design the space to your specifications." Nate pulled up the real estate listing on his cell phone and passed it to Taylor.

Holding the phone so that both she and Cail could see it, Taylor flipped through the images. "What do you think?"

"I think Nate's right. It needs a lot of work." Cail took one look at the list price and nearly swallowed his tongue.

"Yeah, but he's also right about being able to design the space. We could make it perfect." Passing the phone back to Nate, she asked if he could send the link to her phone and gave him her cell number.

"You must be rolling in it since you published that book," Greg said, smirking when Taylor's face went red.

Taylor shrugged then laid a hand on Cail's thigh when she felt him tense.

"Greg," Gabriella admonished.

"I bet you're scared of your own shadow after the life you've led," Greg continued.

Embarrassment gave way to anger. "Actually, I find it's safer in the shadows. I've spent most of my life there."

Greg decided he liked Taylor Sinclair. "That's a shame. A gem like yourself should be admired in the light." Smiling now, he said, "Don't be offended, cousin. I don't seem to have any filters. What pops into my head, spills out of my mouth."

"Much to our horror," Gabriella added.

"Do you carry your police badge with you?" Arianna asked, hoping to remove the awkwardness lurking over the table.

"Yeah." Taylor opened her clutch purse and handed Arianna her badge.

"Do you carry your guns, too?" Arianna studied the badge intently.

"No," Cail answered before Taylor got the chance. "If we did, I would have shot your brother by now."

Laughter erupted around the table. "I can see why Taylor likes you so much." Arianna passed the badge back to Taylor. "If I had a gun, I would have shot him years ago."

Again, everyone laughed. Greg shot Arianna a faux pout.

"Your mom said you're in university. What are you studying?"

"Oh, you're not going to like this, Taylor. I'm majoring in broadcast journalism."

"At the rate we're going, Taylor's never going to want to see us again," Gabriella said. "Why don't we order so my kids can stuff their faces to keep them from talking?"

Taylor turned her attention to the menu. Seeing the multitude of choices always made her feel so overwhelmed. When you were used to picking through whatever seemed most edible in a garbage bin, being presented with a long list of choices was a shock to the system. She stared down at the menu, unable to decide.

Cail could feel the tension emanating from Taylor. He leaned over and whispered, "You like spaghetti Bolognese. Why don't you try that?" The look of gratitude in Taylor's eyes, had Cail grinning. He leaned over again and left a soft kiss at her temple.

How did he know what she'd been stressing over? Taylor wondered. Regardless, she was grateful he came to her rescue. How embarrassing would it have been to admit she wasn't capable of picking an entrée from the menu?

Despite the food, Gabriella's clan continued to talk. For a while, Taylor remained silent and just watched the dynamics of the family. They enjoyed each other, she discovered. Every now and then, one of Gabriella's kids would get a jab in to one of their siblings, but it just made the entire family laugh. Taylor was surprised to find she was really enjoying herself, as was Cail.

At the end of the main course, Taylor excused herself to use the restroom. She came out of the stall to find Cheryl Starr leaning against the wall. Taylor continued to the sink and began to wash her hands. "I guess it's too much of a coincidence that you just happen to find yourself eating in the same restaurant as me."

"Every reporter in the city has a Google alert on your name. I bet you barely made it in the door before patrons in the restaurant were posting on social media that you were here. I know the manager here, so he let me in the back. You're a hard one to pin down though, Taylor. You refuse to return my calls and you don't come out very often."

"Maybe because I get attacked by the media when I do. What do you want, Cheryl?" Taylor grabbed a couple of paper towels.

"I know you want to get the media off your back. I see what it's doing to you, Taylor. I think if you sat down with me and answered some of the questions everyone is asking, it would go a long way towards that."

"So, out of the goodness of your heart, you want me to sit down with you and give you the scoop of the year?"

"I'll let you lay down the ground rules. We could do it in the comfort of your home or at a place of your choosing. Just you, me, and the cameraman. Unless, of course, there were people you wanted to be there, like Caillen or Dr. McIntyre, for instance."

Taylor narrowed her eyes at the mention of Dr. McIntyre's name, wondering how the hell they found out all of this stuff.

"There wouldn't be any producers there to interfere or make demands. I know it looks like I'm just trying to get the scoop of the year, as you said, but, I really do care, Taylor. I don't want to hurt you."

Tossing the paper towels in the bin, Taylor started for the door.

"Think about it, Taylor," Cheryl said as she passed her a business card. "My private cell number is on the back."

Taylor took the card, staring down at it for a moment. "I'll think about it." She began to pull the door open then pushed it closed again, keeping her head down, her eyes staring blindly at the business card in her hand. "Have you ever been raped, Cheryl?" She knew the answer, but asked anyway.

"No, I haven't."

"I figure even if you've only been raped once, it weighs on you, haunts you for the rest of your life. I was doing okay when I was on the streets. I could put it away for periods of time. But, for the last six or seven months, everywhere I go it gets thrown in my face." Her head came up slowly until her glossy eyes met Starr's. "I can't escape it." With that, she yanked the door open and fled.

Starr went to the sink, bracing her hands on the counter. She dreamed of being a journalist since she was a kid. It had taken her years to climb the ranks and she took great pride in the fact that she'd gotten to where she was by hard work, intelligence, and sheer determination. But, for the first time in her life, being a journalist shamed her.

As Taylor made her way back to the table, she could see the sidewalk outside the windows at the front of the restaurant filled with people, some of them with TV cameras and microphones held out at the end of long poles – no *booms*, she remembered. The maître'd was bent over talking with Cail and the two body guards who'd been standing near the front entrance were now at her sides.

"I'm sorry," Taylor announced as she arrived at the table.

Cail got to his feet and pulled her chair out. "Sit," he ordered. "We're just about to order dessert."

"Cail?"

"We're going to finish our meal, enjoy our evening."

"There are mobs of them out there."

He could hear the panic in her voice and wanted nothing more than to brush his lips over her temple to calm her. Taking her hand, he whispered in her ear. "Don't let them take this from us. You were enjoying yourself. Let's continued to do that. We'll deal with what's out there when we're ready to leave."

Exasperated, she lowered herself into her seat and apologized again.

"This must be what's it's like to be a movie star," Greg stated. "You won't mind if I try to steal your limelight, would you? If I could get my face splashed across the news, I'd be a hit at the clubs. Think of how many chicks we could pick up, Nate."

"God, you're an idiot, Greg," Nate said.

"Yeah, but, you're thinking about it," Arianna said and the table broke out with laughter again.

"Let's get one thing straight," Jackson, who'd remained relatively quiet throughout the meal, began. "No one answers any questions about Taylor. You can play with them all you want, but you don't give them any information about your cousin."

"What cousin?" Greg grinned.

They ordered dessert, which Taylor passed on in favour of sipping another glass of champagne. She gathered up her nerve and asked Gabriella a question that had been haunting her since childhood. "You and Greg have the same olive complexion that I do. My mom and my sister were both quite pale. It bothered me that I was so much darker than them. I didn't know where it came from."

"Spain is where it comes from. My grandparents on my mother's side came to Canada from Madrid. My mother had the same gorgeous complexion, but my father was Irish and had very pale skin. Greg and I got the olive complexion and Darryl ended up with my father's ivory skin tone. He hated that. I think he always envied us for it. I don't think he ever realized he was a very good looking man, at least before the drugs. He was too busy envying what everyone else had that he didn't. And I've said too much."

"Speaking of Irish good looks," Arianna said. "You must have Irish blood, Cail."

"Irish and Scottish. My brother, sister, and I all got my mother's colouring. My father's has the dark hair, but hazel eyes."

"You've got a brother who looks very much like you?"

"I don't think you want to go there," Taylor warned Arianna.

"Who knows?" Cail said. "You saved me, Tay. Maybe Arianna could be the one to save Dave."

"Or maybe he's beyond that."

"We should all get together and go out to a club. Are you doing anything on Saturday night?"

"It's a bit of a crap shoot," Taylor tried to explain to Arianna. "Going out and taking the chance of the media finding out."

"So what? You've got body guards. All you have to do is push through the crowd and get in the car."

"Arianna," Gabriella said quietly. "I don't think it's just a matter of that."

"Well, I don't think you should let it stop you from going out and having some fun."

When they were preparing to leave, Taylor and Cail got set up with the body guards at the front of the restaurant as the Atwoods said their goodbyes. "You'd probably be best to wait until we drive away," Taylor advised. "Otherwise, they'll be all over you. It could be dangerous."

"Screw that," Greg grabbed his brother's arm and the two of them walked out the front door and got swallowed up in the mob.

"Deserve what they bloody well get," Jackson announced. "The rest of us will have a drink at the bar while things cool off."

"It was nice meeting all of you," Taylor said.

Gabriella gave her a warm hug and then one to Cail. "Thank you both for coming. We really enjoyed ourselves. Maybe next time you could come to the house so the media wouldn't find out. Do you still have my number, Taylor?"

"Yes, I have it. I'll give you a call."

Tears formed in Gabriella's eyes. Taylor giving her a call, making that connection on her own will was what Gabriella had been praying for. She gave them both another warm hug and then stood back to watch the frenzy as they made their way to the SUV waiting at the curb.

As soon as the doors opened, the shouts began and Gabriella felt her stomach knot as the first few questions were hurled out.

"What happened to your baby, Taylor? Did Sarah Johnson kill it?"

Taylor used the technique Chris had shown her to get through crowds. She placed her hand on the hip of the person in front of her and pushed. That person was easily swung out of the way and she repeated the procedure to the next. Questions about the baby and the sexual abuse she endured filled the air as she went. Obviously her plea to leave her alone had fallen on deaf ears. People were pushing and shoving, trying to get closer. There was a commotion to Taylor's left and one of the TV cameras, hard and heavy, connected with the side of Taylor's face, pushing her into Cail as stars circled in front of her eyes. She wavered, thought she might pass out, but she continued to push through with her hand clamped to the side of her face and Cail's arm around her waist. It seemed like it took ages before the car door swung open and she and Cail clambered inside. The dark, tinted windows helped to shield them. As soon as the body guards got in the front, they began to edge away from the curb while dozens of reporters and civilians surrounded the vehicle. Some of them banged on the windows and Taylor buried herself in Cail as she tried to block it all out. Cail waited until they cleared the crowds of pedestrians then asked the guards to ensure they weren't tailed.

* * *

Across the street, Troy Rappaport sat in his car, watching the SUV pull away. He got the heads up Sinclair was at Buca, but by the time he arrived, the place was surrounded by reporters. His breath caught when he spotted her coming out the restaurant's front doors. God, she cleaned up good. Not the same street rat she'd been about six months ago. No, she was elegant now, classy. She'd fit right in to the lifestyle he set up for himself. It was a sign she was meant to be with him. He watched as a domino effect of reporters and cameramen fell into each other and then that massive camera smashed into Sinclair's face. *Fucker!* The guy just damaged his property.

He figured following two cops and two body guards probably wasn't the smartest idea. They'd make him, for sure. Instead, he took out his cell phone and made a call. "I need to know where they're going now. Are they going back to Cain's?"

"How the hell should I know?"

"Don't give me any shit, asshole. You've got a lot on the line here."

"I don't know where they're going from Buca. They'll probably head home, to Cain's."

"You sure you got me the right codes for the alarm system?"

"I'm sure."

Rappaport didn't like the growing sound of frustration in the asshole's voice. "How sure? Where did you get them?"

"Look, they're the right codes. I got them from the alarm monitoring company."

"How'd you manage that?"

"How the hell do you think I managed it? I'm a cop for Christ's sake."

"And the cell number is right?"

"Dial it and check if you want to. It's Sinclair's number."

"Stay available," he ordered, then muttered, "Asshole," when he hung up. Maybe he'd fuck the guy over just for the hell of it, once he had Taylor in his possession. He sat there for a few minutes, going over the plan in his head one more time. Since he hadn't been out of the apartment for a few days, he decided he'd drop by the lab to make sure everything was running smoothly. Yeah, he had lots of time to check on the lab and then he'd get himself over to Cain's. Old habits die hard, so he knew Sinclair would wake up around two or three in the morning. He'd set his alarm for three and have her out of there before the rest of the house woke up.

* * *

Taylor slowly began to relax once they cleared the frenzy. She supposed she had a little too much champagne as she began to feel ill. Or maybe it was the crack to the face. She lowered her hand from her face then stared into her palm, surprised she didn't see any blood in it.

"How bad is it?" Cail tipped her head up. "Maybe you should get an x-ray." That usually sharp and angular cheek bone was now a puffy black mass and looked ugly enough to be broken. The swelling extended up to her eye which was half closed already.

"I just need an ice pack." No way in hell was she going to the hospital.

Cail wasn't going to push it. His lips brushed softly over her cheek. "Okay. Let's get you home then." He took out his cell and sent a text message to Chris to let her know they were on the way. A few minutes later he received a response from Kate.

Reading the text, he explained to Taylor, "Apparently, my dad freaked when he heard we were all still staying at Chris's after the incident this morning. Kate and Chris have gone to the Grand and are hanging out with Gray and Callaghan. They packed a bag for us and want us to stop by."

When Taylor's phone began ringing, she slid it out of her pocket and handed it to Cail as she remained with her head back and eyes closed.

"It's Gabriella," Cail announced as he answered.

Taylor listened as Cail gave her an account of what happened and assured her Taylor was okay. He told Gabriella he'd have Taylor give her a call tomorrow and let her know how she was doing.

A full house awaited them in Gray's suite. Cal, Rose, Chris, Kate, Gray, and Callaghan were all seated comfortably around the living room. Callaghan had the TV tuned into NNN with the sound muted, so they already knew Taylor had been injured. Gray rose to study the nasty bruise and swelling on the left side of Taylor's face. As Gray went to get an ice pack, Rose and Kate fussed over Taylor. Relieved of her coat, Taylor sank into one of the deep chairs just in time for Gray to administer the ice.

Having the Inspector there gave Taylor the opportunity to present the idea of using herself as bait to reel Rappaport in and put him behind bars. With the ice pack pressed to her face, Taylor steeled herself and jumped right in. "We need to lure Rappaport in. Until he's locked up, our lives are basically upside down. I don't know about everyone else, but I'm getting tired of constantly having a target on my back. Besides, if we set him up, we're in control. We set the time, the place, and the situation. Waiting around for him to make a move puts him control." All eyes focused on her. In Rose and Gray's she saw worry and fear, but everyone else's narrowed and cooled.

Cal studied Taylor with admiration. It took strength and courage to put herself in that situation, especially after what Taylor lived through. "Have you got a plan in mind, Sinclair?"

The ice pack was doing its job. Taylor's cheek was relatively numb, so she removed it and held it in her lap. "He knows I've been staying at Chris's. We could have Blades get word to him that I'll be there alone for a specific period of time."

"So you think it was a mistake for me to pull you out of there."

"Not a mistake, no. You were right about us being sitting ducks at Chris's, which makes it the perfect place to set me up as bait. He knows where it is, he's broken in before. He'll be confident he can nab me from there."

"You sure you're up for this?" Chris was planning to approach Taylor with the idea, but here she was offering herself up. That took grit and determination, not to mention complete trust in them to keep her safe.

"I'm up for it."

Yeah, Chris thought again, grit and determination.

"Tay?" Cail leaned forward and rubbed his hands over his face. Images of her limp in his arms after Darryl Johnson tried to kill her filled his head. "It's not worth the risk."

Taylor reached out and laid her hand on Cail's arm. "It's more of a risk to do nothing."

He couldn't argue with her. When he thought it through, he knew she was right. His hands dropped and he looked up at his father. "Okay, how do we play it?"

"The news is already running the video of that camera hitting me," Taylor said. "Blades can put out the word that I'll be staying home because of the injury while the three of you go into work tomorrow morning."

Chris's first instinct was she didn't like it. "I'd rather we stayed in the house instead of appearing to go out to work. I don't like the idea of leaving you there alone, even for a few minutes."

"He's not going to try to kill me. By the time you drive around the block, he could still be eyeing the house, making sure you don't come back." Taylor wanted them out of the house and out of harm's way.

"I'll put a surveillance van on the street tonight," Cal offered. "If we put too many people on the house in the morning, he'll spot them and spook. So, back up will be a couple of blocks out, but we'll have eyes on the house at all times."

They made the calls that needed to be made then discussed and debated the details until they had a solid plan everyone seemed comfortable with.

There was just one more thing that needed to be addressed. Taylor needed to try to ease some of the worry so evident in Gray's expression since Taylor brought up the idea of being used as bait. Her opportunity arose when Gray was alone in the small kitchenette washing mugs and glasses. She grabbed a tea towel and started drying. "It's better we do it this way than wait for him to come after me."

"I know." Gray turned her head and smiled at Taylor. "I guess I'd rather you found him using your gift."

"I've tried. I can see him in his apartment. Not the Jane Street one. This one's high end, expensive. I've run searches of luxury apartments, tried to figure out where he is from the view. There are so many new buildings in that area and I can't narrow it down. I'm not getting anything, except more and more frustrated." She put the mug she'd been drying away and picked up another one. "I can't keep living like this, Gray. Feeling like someone's out there hunting me. I can't sit around waiting for him to make his move like we did with Morse. I need it to end."

Gray took the mug and tea towel from Taylor and set them on the counter before wrapping her arms around her. "I'm still going to worry until I know he's in custody and you're safe."

"I'll call you the moment it's done."

"Chris told me about your visit from the Ripkins. I'm so sorry, Taylor. I'm so sorry for Leiland."

Raw emotions bubbled to the surface again. "I couldn't tell you. Not when you're expecting." Taylor squeezed her eyes shut then winced with the bruising around her eye. "I don't want you to worry for Gracie. That's not going to happen to her."

"I know. I've got your painting as proof." Gray kissed Taylor's good cheek and released her. With a smile, Taylor spread her hand over Gray's bump. She had a flash of Gracie in her mother's arms and could hear her laughter, feel that intense, unconditional love between mother and daughter. Gracie's little hands settled on her mother's cheeks as she giggled away, laughter lighting up her bright blue eyes and angelic face. Taylor's smile faded. "I wish I could show you what I see, what I hear and feel. She's so beautiful, so happy, so full of love."

On a whim, Taylor placed her hands on Gray's face, where she'd seen Gracie's. "Close your eyes," she whispered. "Picture her running towards you, laughing, her arms extended out to you. She's wearing pyjamas – little pink pants and a long sleeved top. You scoop her up in your arms, breathing in the scent of her, with a big smile on your face and your eyes sparkling with a mother's love. She places her hands on your face, like mine are, and you stare into each other's eyes. She plants a sloppy, wet kiss on your lips then nuzzles into your neck, still giggling."

Tears streamed down Gray's face onto Taylor's hands. "I can see her, smell her, hear her." She didn't know if what she was seeing and feeling was because of Taylor's words or if Taylor was putting what she had sensed in her mind. She could smell her daughter, just bathed with a hint of baby powder. She could feel a love stronger than any she'd ever known. She could hear her baby giggling and feel her nuzzling. So beautiful, so happy, so full of love.

Opening her eyes, Gray looked into the glistening emeralds before her. "Did you just give me your vision?"

Taylor's lip slowly curled up. "I don't know. Did I?" She'd been so focused on Gray, she hadn't noticed Callaghan stood behind her. His hand touched her shoulder and she jumped, startled.

"You're a gift, Sinclair. A gift that keeps on giving." He pulled his wallet out and took a small picture out of it, passing it to her. "We couldn't bring your painting with us, so both Gray and I carry this picture in our wallets."

Taylor smiled at the picture they'd taken of her painting of Gracie and them in their backyard in Balton. They'd zoomed in on Gracie so she filled the photo. "I can't wait until she's born. I can't wait to see the two of you with her in your arms."

"And we can't wait to see her in yours." Callaghan kissed Taylor's cheek. "So you better make damn sure you stay safe tomorrow."

"She will." Somehow Gray knew Taylor would be okay. She couldn't say why or how, but she knew Taylor would be there when Gracie came into the world. She just had to be.

As they were going out the door, Taylor turned back and embraced Gray. She whispered, "I love you."

It was the first time Gray had heard Taylor say those words. She had a terrible, sinking feeling in her gut. "I love you, too, Taylor. Why does it feel like you're saying goodbye?"

Chris stood in the hall with the same sinking feeling in her stomach wondering if this was why Lane was so worried. Was Taylor saying her goodbyes?

"I just want you to know how I feel about you and how grateful I am for everything you've done for me." When Taylor tried to step out of the embrace, Gray tightened her arms around her.

"Promise you'll call me tomorrow when he's in custody. Promise me."

"I promise. I'll call you tomorrow as soon as the handcuffs are on his wrists."

Gray took a step back but held onto Taylor's shoulders while their eyes met.

"I promise," Taylor repeated.

Chapter 34

When they got to their room, Cail turned on the TV and they watched the news, the top story detailing the shooting that morning. Then they showed the commotion outside of Buca and a heated debate on the media's obsession with Taylor followed. One reporter even went so far as to compare it to the media frenzy over Princess Diana.

The story of the raid on Rappaport's meth lab filled the screen next. Video of the warehouse ran behind the audio of the reporter's voice. Blue and red flashing lights played over the scene like strobe lights. The mobile forensics unit could be seen parked outside the parking garage with people in hazmat suits coming and going. Detective Pierson gave a short statement before they went on to other news.

"Bet that's going to piss Rappaport off," Cail said.

"Good," Taylor responded. She rose from her seat and made her way over to Cail as he turned the TV off. She inched the skirt of her dress up before straddling Cail's lap, running her hands up his rippled abs to his muscled chest then draped her arms over his shoulders.

Cail's ran his hands up Taylor's thighs and was shocked when he came to the lacy top of her stockings and then bare skin. His mouth dropped open, admiring the garter and thigh highs she was wearing. He'd never seen Taylor wear lingerie other than the multitude of colourful, lacy hip huggers she favoured from Victoria's Secret. The ones she was wearing tonight were black, to match the garter and thigh highs. "God, you look so sexy, Angel."

Taylor grinned in response.

"How's the face?" Cail's lips brushed over the bruise.

"I could ask you the same thing." Taylor shifted so she could brush her lips over the black eye Dave gave him before leaving a careful, chaste kiss there.

"What a pair we make."

"Ha." She'd been waiting until they were alone to talk to him about an apartment. She sensed his trepidation when they were looking at the pictures at dinner. "What did you really think about the place Nate showed us?"

"I think it needs a lot of work and it's a hell of a lot of money."

"We could go and take a look at it."

"If you want."

"Is it the money?"

"Is what the money?"

"Is that what's putting you off?"

"It's a lot of money, Tay."

"I could make enough of a down payment that we could easily afford it with our salaries and we can put in a low ball offer."

Cail's cheeks puffed out before he blew out a long, slow breath. "Why don't we go and have a look at it and then we can talk about it? Besides, don't you think we should look around and see what else is out there?"

"I've been looking online. The thing I really like about this place is that we can design it basically from scratch. We could get Nate to give us an estimate before we put in an offer."

Cail was leery of Nate showing Taylor a property that required major construction when the guy owned a construction company, but he didn't express that to Taylor. "It sounds like you've already made up your mind."

"No." Taylor rested her head on Cail's shoulder. "If we're going to do this, we have to do it together. It's just that I've never really had a home and we have the opportunity to make one exactly the way we want it."

The whole money thing was weirding him out. He had some money saved, but he also had a hefty student loan from law school. Maybe it was the way he grew up with his father bringing home the bacon and his mother being at home to raise the kids, but he always felt it was the man's responsibility to provide for his family. On the other hand, why should Taylor be denied the home of her dreams when she could afford it? Callaghan didn't seem to have any issues moving into Gray's mansion. "Call the realtor and make an appointment. We'll go and take a look. But, I want to know a ballpark of what our monthly costs are going to be once it's all said and done."

She managed a 'kay' before his firm lips melded with hers. They knew each other's bodies well now, knew just how to drive each other to delirium. Dragging her nails up his back sent his body into spasms. A soft touch across her belly and he watched her muscles pulsate. The pleasure was just as sweet whether you were on the giving end or receiving. But tonight, she was more than ready to take their love-making to a new level. She was ready to let go of her fears and focus on, not just pleasuring her man, but allowing herself to be pleasured in ways she'd never expected to open herself up to.

"I want you on the bed, naked," she whispered into Cail's ear. "Then I'm going to explore every inch of your body."

Cail shivered in response as he hurriedly unbuttoned his shirt and Taylor laughed at his eagerness. "I'm yours to command," he said and grinned from ear to ear.

Taylor peeled herself off his lap, took a step back and just enjoyed watching Cail's magnificent body being unwrapped, like a gift. She supposed it was. As soon as he stripped, he headed for the bed.

"Wait a minute." Taylor laughed again. "I think you better peel me out of this dress first."

There was no way to describe the way he walked back to her other than a prowl. She felt like prey ... in a good way. His hands brushed carefully over her face as he brought her lips to his and her arms folded around his neck. A slow slide of lips, a soft caress of tongues deepened until they were both in a haze of arousal. Cail's fingers found the top of her zipper and slowly began the journey down her back. His nails dragged lightly over her spine on the way back up and she arched into his touch, so sensitive and responsive she sent a thrill through him.

He broke away from her mouth to step back as he eased the dress over her shoulders and let it slide down, down, down. As it passed her hips, he gasped in delight. Letting the dress drop to the floor, he stood speechless before her. His eyes feasted up and down her lithe body, ending at the lacy tops of her thigh highs. "Keep them on," he growled.

Taylor's laugh turned into a moan when Cail's mouth met hers again. She backed him up towards the bed then broke away from the kiss to give him a shove. Cail dropped onto his back on the mattress with a laugh. He wasn't sure what had gotten into her tonight, but he liked it. Propping himself up on his elbows, he gloried in the sight of her as she raised her arms up, released the clip restraining her hair, and shook the long, silky strands, freeing it to cascade down her back. He'd never seen anything so sexy in his life.

The vision came out of nowhere. One moment her eyes were feasting on every peak and valley of Cail's heavily muscled body and the next she was seeing herself in the white room she'd seen in her dreams. Everything was white - the carpet, the walls, the furniture, the linens. It was completely devoid of colour. Somehow she knew this room was her prison; the price she would pay for the well-being of those she loved.

"Tay?" She looked like she had completely zoned out, then blinked a couple of times at the sound of his voice. He was about to ask if she was okay, but her lip curled up in a sexy smirk as she crawled up onto the bed with him. Her hands and mouth explored and caressed his body as if she was committing every inch of him to memory. Every slide of her palm, every caress of her fingers, every brush of her lips drove his desire higher and higher until he was half crazy with his need for her. When he couldn't stand it any longer, he reared up, reaching for her, but Taylor pushed him back down with a provocative grin.

"I'm not finished with you yet, I want to taste you. Tell me what you like. Tell me how to please you." With that she lowered her mouth to him.

Cail sucked in a sharp breath as Taylor's tongue circled around him. His head fell back, his back arching right off the bed. "Holy Mother of God."

Taylor purred at his reaction, the vibration causing a string of expletives to flow from his mouth. She realized she didn't need him to tell her what he liked. She was figuring it out pretty quickly using the knowledge she gained from the sex book and from his reactions. "Mmmm," she hummed around him, revelling in his groans of pleasure. Having the power to evoke such a reaction from Cail was a heady experience. The more he moaned and groaned, the more it turned her on until she was aching with desire.

"Okay, okay. Stop or I'm not going to last," Cail pleaded.

Taylor released him, only because she was desperate to take him inside her. She never would have dreamed she could enjoy taking a man in her mouth, that it could make her feel so powerful and feminine and ... sexy. God, yes. She felt incredible. She crawled back up Cail's body and positioned herself over him. One thrust was all it took to send her into a shuddering, convulsing state of utter bliss.

Cail's hands slid up her body and cupped her breasts. Rearing up, he closed his mouth over a tight, beaded nipple and the sound of her low, raspy voice screaming his name nearly took him over the edge. Taylor's fingers combed through his hair, holding him to her as she began to roll her hips. Arching back, her mouth dropped open as she tried to suck in oxygen.

Cail trailed his finger tips up and down Taylor's sensitive, sweat-sheened back making her arch back again. God, he loved the sight of her. She was such a lovely, sensual being and he ached to tell her just how beautiful she was. What a fool he'd been to risk losing her.

Cail held her to him and reversed their positions, propping himself up on his elbows so he could stare down into her intense green eyes. "I love you, Tay." The words didn't seem to be enough to convey what he felt in his heart.

"I love you." Taylor's fingers spread over his neck and ears, her thumbs caressing his face as Cail slowed to a tender pace, pouring his love into her through his brilliant blue eyes.

Her vision blurred, but she kept her eyes locked to Cail's. The way he was looking at her, the way he was making love to her filled her with such emotion and knowing this could be the last time was too much to bear. Her breath hitched as a fat tear spilled out of the corner of her eye.

"Tay?" The look in his eyes turned to pure concern.

Rubbing the tear away with her fingers, Taylor said, "It's nothing." She shook her head. "Sometimes you just make me feel so much, it's overwhelming."

Concern turned to love and adoration. Cail leaned in, nudged her nose with his then kissed her as slowly and sensually as he was making love to her until they rolled over the edge into orgasmic bliss together.

Cail nuzzled into her neck. She smelled so good. The light lavender mixed in with her shampoo and all he wanted to do was lay there and inhale her exquisite scent all night.

Taylor relished the few minutes after they made love where her mind was peaceful and her entire body was relaxed and sated. "So tired," she whispered lazily.

Cail rolled to his side, taking her with him so they were face to face with their legs entwined. "Go to sleep, then. I've got you."

His hands trailed up and down her spine making her shiver. "I wasn't done with you. There's so much more I want to explore."

Cail's eyes widened. She just kept surprising him tonight. "I think I better read this book." Laughing, he brushed a few strands of hair from Taylor's face then he pulled the duvet up over both of them. "Go to sleep my little nympho. We'll explore more next time." He wanted to ask her what she meant when she told him she was afraid of releasing her dark side. It wasn't until later he had remembered the marks criss-crossing her back that only appeared after he applied pressure and the blood was rushing back to the surface. Someone had whipped her, he was sure of it. And he wondered if she'd wanted it.

"Mmm, next time," she whispered, but she still had that sinking feeling there wasn't going to be a next time. She didn't want to go to sleep because she didn't know if they'd ever have the opportunity to lie in each other's arms, completely sated and relaxed like this again. So she kept her eyes open, enjoying the feel of his body against hers and the sparkle in his deep blue eyes.

"I could spend days just lying here looking at you," Cail whispered. He figured he was safe as he hadn't said she was beautiful, just that he enjoyed looking at her. She raised her eyebrows at him and he tried valiantly not to laugh, but lost the battle in the end. He supposed it was okay though because Taylor laughed with him. "Go to sleep, Nymph."

With eyes narrowed, Taylor asked, "You're not going to start calling me *that*, are you?"

"Maybe."

It was hard to be upset with him when he was grinning from ear to ear and his eyes were lit up like the fourth of July. "If I'm a nympho, it's all your fault."

"Now that's something I don't mind taking the blame for."

They both laughed and then Taylor decided if she was going to be called that, she might as well try to live up to the handle. She pushed Cail onto his back and dove on top of him.

Cail used her momentum to roll them both, until he was grinning down at her. "No more list?"

Taylor's breath caught. "No more list."

"Anything goes?"

Gone was his grin. He stared down at her with a look of serious lust and a delicious pang of arousal shot straight to her core. "Anything goes," she repeated in a raspy whisper. His hand skimmed down her side then his fingertips brushed lightly over the back of her knee and her body went taught in reaction. Her breaths came in quick, short pants in anticipation and a little bit of fear. She was pretty sure she knew the intended destination of that clever hand.

Cail lowered his mouth to her breast, distracting her while his fingers caressed their way up her inner thigh. Her fingers weaved into his hair, holding him to her as she arched up. Sucking her nipple hard just as his fingers met her slick heat had Taylor screaming out his name and arching nearly right off the bed. There was no more fear, no more worry. All was lost but intense pleasure. Shamelessly, she ground into his hand, wanting more, needing more.

He took her up quickly, then left her hanging on the precipice. "Oh, God. Cail. Please, don't stop." She was writhing beneath him, desperately reaching for that contact that would take her over the edge as his mouth began the journey down her six pack abs. "Oh, God," she rasped, realizing what was coming next. Her belly quivering, legs shaking, she didn't give her scars a thought. She was too entranced in the pleasure. Twice more he took her to the edge then reined her back in until she was pleading, begging for release.

When he finally took her over it was like been shot from a slingshot. Extreme, intense pleasure bordering on pain shot out in every direction as Cail moved up her body and thrust into her. Endless, mind-numbing convulsions tore through her until she didn't think she could take any more. Cail collapsed onto her, his face burrowed into her neck while their breaths heaved and their bodies continued to shudder. ·

"Holy shit," Cail wheezed. He grinned into Taylor's neck as his ears filled with her low, raspy laugh.

* * *

The Hawaii Five-oh ring tone sounded on Chris's phone at oh three eighteen. "Cain," she answered in a gravelly voice, still half asleep.

Kate kept her eyes closed, but listened to Chris's end of the conversation.

"When?" Chris sat up, fully awake now. "Is he in custody?"

Chris's sudden alertness had Kate opening her eyes, studying her as if she could figure out what was going on from Chris's expression.

"Shit." Chris ran her free hand through sleep tussled hair. "I'm on route with Constable Kate Worthington. ETA is approximately thirty minutes. Notify Inspector Worthington." Ending the call, she dropped the phone in her lap and rubbed her hands over her face. "Rappaport broke into my house. They lost him in a foot chase."

* * *

Taylor woke to the throbbing in her cheek instead of on the brink of a nightmare. Not wanting to wake Cail, she took a quick shower and got dressed so she could go down to the front desk to request an ice pack and some Advil. She was just about to walk out of the room when her cell phone began to vibrate. The call displayed a private name and number. She had enough time to register that sinking feeling again before she answered in a quiet voice.

"I've got people watching your boy around the clock, people he trusts. One phone call and he's a dead man or, if I don't call in at pre-arranged times, he's a dead man. Got it?"

Taylor recognized his voice instantly. She grabbed a pen and paper from the desk drawer and walked into the bathroom, shutting the door and turning on the fan to drown out the sound of her voice. "Leave Cail out of this, Troy."

"He will be left out of it as long as you follow instructions. Listen to me. I don't want to hurt you, Sinclair. What happened in the spring was fucked up. I don't want to take you like that, but I need you with me. I can give you things Caillen Worthington will never be able to give you. I can give you what you need."

Her legs shook so badly that Taylor lowered herself to sit on the edge of the tub. "The cops are closing in on you."

"Did you give them my lab?" Rappaport screamed into the phone.

"No. I didn't even know about your lab." Think, Taylor told herself. She couldn't afford to get him riled up and she needed to think her way out of this. "I swear I didn't know about the lab. I wouldn't have sold you out." The sound of his angry breaths was the only thing Taylor heard for the next few seconds. Taylor closed her eyes, trying to concentrate on background noise to see if she could get a bead on where Rappaport was.

"You've got thirty minutes to get to Union Station."

It wasn't enough time to figure her way out of this and ensure Cail's safety. "And then what?"

"Then you're going to be with me from now on. We'll be married as soon as I can arrange it."

"I need more time. I can meet you at seven."

His laugh sounded contrived. "So you can put a bunch of cops in play? I don't think so. You come now and you talk to no one."

"You're asking me to walk away from my life. I need more time. You know I won't do anything to jeopardize Cail's life. Give me until seven and then I'm yours." In the long silence that followed, Taylor focused on background noise again and thought she heard a car drive by, but she couldn't be sure. There was nothing to give her a clue to his location. Then she heard a scratching sound and Rappaport sucking in air. "You're using."

"That's none of your never mind."

"Yes, it is. If I'm going to be with you, you can't be using that stuff. That's why you lost control in the spring. I swear to God, Troy, if you try that crap on me again, I'll kill you."

"I told you I wouldn't hurt you like that again." He sounded like he was holding his breath as he talked then he let out a whooshing breath and Taylor could picture the blue smoke coming out of his mouth. "It was a mistake. I want you to want me, to come to me willingly."

Taylor closed her eyes, her nostrils flared as she sucked in air trying to quell the nausea. "That's never going to happen, Troy. I don't feel that way about you. You can't force someone to love you."

"I know what you need, Sinclair."

"You don't know anything about what I need. I need Cail. If you truly cared about me, you wouldn't be forcing me to marry you; you wouldn't be threatening to kill Cail to get me to come to you."

"You're better off with me. You'll see. Union Station at seven then, but I swear to God if you bring any cops or set me up, your boy will not only die, he'll die slowly and painfully."

Taylor didn't want to wake Cail, so she stood next to the bed and just watched him sleep for a few minutes. "I love you," she whispered and reached down to brush her fingers over his loose black curls.

Less than five minutes later, Taylor was getting into a cab at the front of the Grand. "Forty College Street. The faster you get me there, the bigger your tip." As the taxi pulled away from the curb, Taylor entered three hours and thirty minutes into the stop-watch app on her iPhone and the countdown began.

* * *

Chris stood with her arms crossed in front of her at the back door to her house watching Constable Luis Santana twirling the fine tendrils of his brush, spreading black fingerprint dust around the door knob and on the shiny new key that was left in the deadbolt lock. Kate shifted her weight from one foot to the other until she couldn't stand the pressure she felt for another second. "I need to speak with you privately," she whispered to Chris.

Chris raised an eyebrow at her then nodded her head and they walked towards the back of the yard. Kate had been acting nervous since they arrived and learned Rappaport used a key to gain entry into the back door and keyed in the correct code to deactivate the alarm system.

When they were out of earshot, Kate looked Chris in the eye with a pained expression on her face. "Yesterday, when we were in my Dad's office, Dave asked if he could borrow my car to run out to the drug store." Kate dropped her head in shame. "I gave him my keys."

"Come here," Chris whispered, drawing Kate into her arms. "It's not your fault. Do you hear me? We don't know that he copied the key. Rappaport had the code for the alarm system, too. Dave didn't have that, did he?"

"No, I haven't told anyone the code and Dave's never been here, so he wouldn't have seen us use it. But, I think he copied the key, Chris. Dave told me that his car was in the shop, but when we left Headquarters yesterday, I saw him get into his car in the garage."

"Shit. I don't want to have to tell your Dad it might have been Dave."

"I'll tell him. It was my fault, so I'll tell him."

"It wasn't your fault." Chris pulled back, looking Kate in the eyes. "It's not your fault. Don't blame yourself for something your brother might have done. Let's not get carried away until we know for sure." As she tried to comfort Kate, Chris a made mental note to check what stores cut keys in the vicinity of Headquarters and call the alarm company to inquire how someone would obtain her code.

* * *

Three hours and fifteen minutes. Taylor sat at her desk and waited for her computer to boot up. The first thing she did was type out her conversation with Rappaport along with the time the call was received and then printed it. Next on her list was identifying Rappaport's assassin. *People he trusts*, Rappaport had said. Had to be cops, but only one of them would have been tasked with killing Cail and it had to be someone Rappaport trusted.

She called up her Academy training, thinking about the steps to take when an investigation stalled. Go back to the beginning. But, where was the beginning? When she met Rappaport? When Rappaport started buying or blackmailing cops? Rappaport's beginning? She knew he'd been raised by his father, but she never heard him mention his mother.

She entered Troy Evan Rappaport into the system, pulling up his police and driving records. Father listed as Evan James Rappaport, nothing on his mother. Damn it. She scanned through Troy's entire history and came up empty. Next, she entered Evan James Rappaport into the system and discovered he'd been investigated in a Child Services complaint for neglect, but was never charged.

Switching to a Child Services database, she entered Evan James Rappaport again and two files were listed in the search results. The most recent was the neglect complaint when Troy was nine. The second file stated Troy was removed from the home at the age of two when a neighbour reported he was left in the care of his mother, Charlene Elena Rappaport, who was passed out drunk and high. She printed the Child Services file then entered Charlene into the system.

Charlene did a stint in jail for possession of a controlled substance following her arrest in the Child Services incident and when her divorce came through, she changed her name back to her maiden name. "Oh. My. God." Taylor recognized the surname and scrambled to print out Troy Rappaport's most recent mug shot and the driver's licence photo of a Toronto Police officer who shared Charlene's maiden name and set them side by side. Rappaport was short and stout and Charlene's second son was tall and thin, but if you compared the photos across the eyes, you could have been looking at the same person.

Two hours and forty minutes. The next problem was determining if Troy's half brother was in fact the assassin and Taylor had no idea how to do that in the limited time she had left. If she wasn't able to identify the assassin and prove it, she would have to turn herself over to Rappaport and convince Chris not to come after them until the threat to Cail was neutralized. She couldn't risk Cail's life, even if it meant her own.

For the next couple of hours, Taylor searched everywhere she could think of looking for a connection between the half-brothers including a physical search of the officer's desk and locker, all to no avail. She couldn't access his desktop computer because she just didn't have the e-skills to figure out his password. She couldn't even find evidence the two knew of each other's existence. Everywhere she turned she ran into a dead end.

Thirty-five minutes. She used most of the time remaining typing up a report for Chris that included her hunches and intuition. She was fairly certain Rappaport's condo was in the Cityplace Development based on what she'd seen in her vision, but that only narrowed it down to any number of buildings and she didn't have a name the condo was listed under. Still, if Chris had some officers show his photo around on the day shift, they might get lucky.

All of the documents she printed went into a new file folder. She stuck a post-it note on the front of the folder and wrote Chris's name then a note all but demanding they not look for her unless Rappaport's assassin was identified and in custody. She left the folder in the centre of Chris's desk then logged out of her computer. Fifteen minutes.

Her long strides carried her swiftly from College to Bay Street and then straight down Bay Street to Front Street, dodging cars when she came upon red lights. Slowing to a walk, the sliding glass doors welcomed her into the main entrance of Union Station with three minutes to spare.

* * *

Cail was used to waking up alone, but he expected Taylor to be in the room and she wasn't. He checked the bathroom before he found her note on the desk stating she needed some time to clear her head. What the hell that meant, he wasn't sure. Did she need a few hours, a few days? The more he thought about it, the more he questioned. He'd thought everything was back to normal with them after a night of making love and talking. Was last night a good-bye? Is that why she seemed to be memorizing every inch of him? The more he questioned, the more he worried.

Chapter 35

Chris's first stop once she arrived at Headquarters was Lane's office. "You were worried she'd cut and run."

"I was."

Frustrated, because she knew Lane wasn't going to divulge much, Chris dropped into a chair facing the desk and sighed loudly.

"Let's not get ahead of ourselves. We don't know if she's gone, Chris. Cail's note said she needed some time. Let's give her some."

Chris shook her head. "She said her good-byes."

It was Lane who let out a loud sigh this time. She sunk back into her chair and asked, "Any idea where she might go?"

If she did, she'd be out there searching for her, Chris thought. The only place she could think of was the warehouse and she was sure Taylor would steer clear of it for that very reason. She shook her head with another sigh. "Cail's out looking for her, but I don't think he has any idea where she might go." When Lane only frowned again, Chris became even more frustrated. "I don't get it. Why would she skip out after all of the progress she's made?" She managed a surprised look from Lane this time.

"Think about it, Chris. She lost everyone she loved beginning with her mother. Then Leila and Leiland. She's worried that she'll lose all of you because she cares about you. She feels responsible for putting all of you in danger and believes the only way she can protect you is to walk away."

When they finally did find Taylor, Chris was going to kill her. "Maybe she's not as smart as I thought," she fumed. "Does she really think we'd just let her walk?"

Lane didn't get the opportunity to answer. Cail appeared in the doorway looking distraught. "Come in Caillen. Give us an update."

Cail lowered himself into the chair, taking time to get his emotions under control before he could begin. "She got in a cab at the Grand at oh three thirty. I contacted the cab company and she was dropped off here at Headquarters. She was seen at her desk on and off until about oh six forty-five. CCTV shows her leaving through the front doors at about that time. Where she went from there I have no idea."

* * *

Chris leaned in the doorway of the observation room waiting for Inspector Worthington. She turned when she heard someone approaching and nearly ran into Detective Pierson.

"Just wanted to let you know, Mick O'Hara's body was pulled out of Lake Ontario this morning. He was less than five hundred meters from the warehouse. Rebecca Knightley is in the wind. No one has seen her since Monday night."

Chris knew Rebecca had been picked up by Blades and was now a guest at the Ripkin's clinic. How much she could reveal to Pierson, she wasn't sure, so she kept her mouth shut. "Thanks for the update. I appreciate it."

"We're still sorting through the mountain of evidence confiscated from the meth lab."

"If you find anything that will give us a clue as to Rappaport's whereabouts, will you let me know?"

"You'll be the first," Pierson said as he headed out.

Chris stepped into the observation room again and watched through the glass as Constable David Worthington sat with his head resting on his forearms on the table.

When Inspector Worthington joined her, he took a minute to check on his son through the glass. "Is he fucking sleeping?"

"I believe so, sir."

"Time for a wakeup call." He was first through the door to the interview room, but said nothing. Taking his seat, he let Chris take the lead.

Chris read off the attendees and case number and then read Dave his rights. He stared at her in shock for a moment, his eyes still heavy from sleep. "What the hell is this about?"

Opening her file folder, Chris laid a photo in front of him. "At oh nine hundred hours yesterday, you met with the Alarm Monitoring Station Supervisor at Burn Security to obtain the alarm codes for my home alarm system." The image in front of him was a still from the security cameras showing him entering Burn Security. "At eleven ten, you borrowed a set of keys from Constable Kate Worthington. At eleven twenty," she placed another video surveillance photo in front of him. "You entered Luke's Hardware, one block from this location, and had a key for my home cut from Constable Kate Worthington's key ring. You then gave both the alarm code and the key to Troy Rappaport."

"This is bullshit," Dave began before his father slammed his fist into the table and stood, glaring down at him.

"Look at the evidence in front of you. What the fuck were you thinking? You put your own family in danger."

"You're overreacting," Dave began before being cut off again.

"Bullshit. You knew Rappaport was after Taylor. You knew. And you gave him the alarm codes and key to allow him into a residence your own family lives in."

"Dad?" Dave looked at his father as if he was shocked at the accusation.

"What does Rappaport have on you?"

"Nothing. Dad? Please?" Dave's voice actually broke on the *please*. Chris wanted to reach across the table and bitch slap him.

"Do you owe him money? Are you doing drugs, Dave?"

"No."

Cal took out his phone and dialed Kate's cell and put her on speaker. She was searching Dave's apartment. "What have you got?"

Kate's voice came back dripping with sorrow. "He's got meth, coke, and crack. I'm not sure of the amounts, but it's more than personal use, Dad. It's much more than personal use."

Cal closed his eyes for a moment and breathed out a long, steaming breath. "Bring it in." He hung up and turned back to his son. "How long have you been selling?"

"What? Dad? I'm not selling." Again he looked stunned.

"You just heard what Katie found in your apartment." He turned to Chris. "I want him piss tested before you take him to booking." He got up and was heading for the door when Dave called out.

"Dad, wait." When Cal turned back, Dave looked at Chris. "I need a few minutes with my Dad."

Chris turned to Cal and got a nod before she stood and left the room. Cal sat across from his son again, still fuming.

Dave looked his father in the eye, the look on his face more serious than Cal had ever seen him. "I've been working with Internal Affairs for the past eighteen months trying to identify all of the dirty cops

Rappaport has under his thumb. The drugs that are at my apartment are part of that investigation. We've identified eighteen cops Rappaport has control of, but there's still more we've yet to identify. Rappaport has a meeting scheduled on Sunday with a high ranking Toronto cop and a contact from Palmerton. That contact at Palmerton was how he was able to kill Spanner. We're days away from identifying two very important people in our investigation. I had to give Rappaport what he asked me for."

Cal's anger was by no means diminished by Dave's confession. "I want to know who gave you the order to give Rappaport access to your own fucking family."

"If I hadn't given him what he asked me for it would have fucked up an eighteen month investigation when we're days away from our goal."

Rappaport broke into Cain's just after oh three hundred and Taylor left the Grand at approximately oh three thirty and was now missing. It was too much of a coincidence. "What else did you give him?"

"Just the key, the alarm code, and Taylor's cell phone number."

"Who gave the order?"

"Dad?"

"Who gave the fucking order?" Cal yelled.

Dave swiped his hands roughly over his face then quietly answered, "Chief Clarke."

Chris stood in the hall when Inspector Worthington stormed out of the interview room. "Cut him loose," he ordered.

"No fucking way." It was the first time Chris disrespected her commanding officer.

Cal spun around, glaring at Chris. "Cut him the fuck loose, Detective Sergeant. That's an order. I'll be with the Chief." He turned and stormed off.

* * *

Toronto's top cop, Chief Madison Clarke, sat at her desk with two men in suits sitting across from her when Inspector Cal Worthington burst through the doors with his raging hazel eyes focused on her. "Gentlemen, if you'll excuse me, I need to deal with this."

"Of course." Both men scurried quickly out of the office, steering wide of the Inspector.

"Explain to me why a fucking investigation took precedence over my family's lives."

"Why do you think I told you to make sure they weren't staying at

Cain's place until Rappaport was in custody? The last I heard, you moved them all to the Grand."

"Goddamn it, Maddy. Taylor's fucking missing."

* * *

Chris walked into her office as the phone began to ring. She just wanted fifteen quiet minutes where she could sit down and run everything through her head. "Cain," she answered, the aggravation clear in her tone.

"Your presence is required in the Chief's office, Detective Sergeant."

Shit. What now? "On my way." Chris hung up and caught a glimpse of the file folder sitting in the middle of her desk on her way to the door. Whatever it was, it was going to have to wait. "I'll be in the Chief's office," she told Detective Blake on her way by her desk.

She arrived at the Chief's outer office to find Boone and Pierson sitting waiting. "What's up?" Chris asked. Both Boone and Pierson shrugged their shoulders. Chris was about to take the empty seat next to Pierson when the Chief's office door opened and her aide, Constable Brandon Moody, waved them inside.

Chris knew it had to do with the Rappaport investigations based on Pierson and Boone also being in attendance. She walked into the Chief's office behind the other two detectives to find Chief Clarke sitting at a conference table with Inspector Worthington, Constable David Worthington, and two detectives - one male of East Indian decent and one Caucasian female with short brown hair and stylish glasses who she recognized from Internal Affairs.

"Please, join us." Chief Clarke motioned to the empty seats around the conference table. She waited until the new arrivals were seated and her aide had retaken his seat at her left. "I realize this is unconventional, but I'm going to ask you to cease your efforts in locating Troy Evan Rappaport until Sunday evening. Internal Affairs is at a critical point in an investigation involving Rappaport and we need him to believe he is free and clear until their investigation comes to a conclusion."

Chris glanced at Pierson and Boone to try to gauge their reaction. It was Boone who spoke first. "Chief, with all due respect, leaving him out there is dangerous. We believe he is responsible for at least two recent deaths, Carlos Spanner and Michael O'Hara."

"Once Internal Affairs completes their investigation, evidence pertaining to the death of Carlos Spanner will be released to you, Detective Boone. Perhaps I should rephrase my earlier statement. I'm not asking you to wait until Sunday evening, I'm ordering you to."

Chris's eyes narrowed at the Chief, her frustration level from dealing with Dave earlier increased. She looked down the table at Dave and found herself questioning why he was sitting in on this meeting. Cal had stormed up here after their private conversation and suddenly they were being told to back off of Rappaport. What had Dave said to get off the hook for supplying Rappaport access to her home and having a shitload of drugs at his apartment? Was he involved in the IA investigation, working undercover? Had to be.

Damn it, but she needed that fifteen minutes to think and pull it all together. Timeline, she thought. Rappaport breaks into her house at oh three hundred and gets away after a short foot chase. She gets the call at oh three eighteen. Then what? "Oh, fuck." Sinclair flees the hotel at oh three thirty and spends three hours at HQ before disappearing into thin air. What was she doing for three hours? The file folder on her desk. Damn it, she wasn't saying her goodbyes because she was walking away. She was saying her goodbyes because she had a vision about Rappaport getting her.

"Is there something you would like to share with us, Detective Sergeant?" Clarke asked in a derisive tone.

"No, ma'am. May I be excused?"

"Hang on a minute, Chris." Cal spoke in a relatively calm manner, but his ire was unmistakable as he turned to the Chief. "You're asking that Rappaport be hands off for another forty-eight hours because Internal Affairs has been unable to determine the identity of a high ranking officer under Rappaport's control. Am I correct?"

Chris's gaze bounced between the Inspector and the Chief. "Are you saying Internal Affairs is investigating dirty cops?"

The female IA detective joined the conversation. "Before this goes any further, let me just say that anything you hear in this room, stays in this room. You don't discuss the details of our investigation with anyone. Am I clear?"

Before anyone could answer, Clarke said, "Let me make this a bit easier. Detective Boone, do you have any issues with holding off on arresting Rappaport until Sunday evening?"

"No, ma'am," he answered.

"Detective Pierson?"

"No, ma'am."

"Very well. You are dismissed with my gratitude for your cooperation."

The room fell silent as they waited for Pierson and Boone to leave. Once they departed, the female IA detective responded to the Cal's question. "We believe we have identified everyone Rappaport has under his control with the exception of a high ranking officer and someone high up at Palmerton Penitentiary. All of the suspected officers are under surveillance."

Chris glared at her. "You *believe* you have identified all of them? Excuse me if that doesn't sound very reassuring, Detective."

"That's enough." Clarke narrowed her eyes at Chris. "I won't have you questioning an intricate investigation you know nothing about. Detectives Bollard and Singh are not here to justify their work to you. The issue here is whether you can wait forty-eight hours before arresting Troy Rappaport."

"Can I ask what's going down on Sunday evening?" Chris was putting it together as she spoke. "Whatever it is, you *believe* it will identify the ranking officer and Palmerton official."

Singh made eye contact with the Chief before he spoke. "Rappaport is preparing to flee. We intercepted a transmission stating he's set up a meeting with the two individuals we've yet to identify in order to finalize cash payments for their services. The meeting is scheduled for eighteen hundred hours on Sunday. Rappaport is booked on a flight out of Pearson at twenty-two hundred hours under an alias."

"Oh, I guarantee that they will be long gone by eighteen hundred on Sunday," Chris snarled.

"If you've got information in connection with Internal Affairs' investigation, you need to put it on the table." Clarke glared at Chris again. "Now, Detective Sergeant."

Fuckin' eh, Chris thought, her face burning with anger as she pushed up to her feet. "One of my officers is missing and very likely in Rappaport's custody. I'm not waiting around -"

"There is no proof Sinclair is with Rappaport," Clarke cut Chris off. "I will not allow you to undermine an eighteen month long investigation on assumption."

"Give me five minutes to go to my office and I'll bring you your proof on a silver fuckin' platter."

"Chris," Cal warned.

Glaring at Cal, Chris fired back, "We're dealing with the life or death of one of our own here."

As Chris yelled, the door to the office swung open and Kate rushed in with tears streaming down her face followed closely by Detective

Blake. Kate put the brakes on when she saw everyone sitting around the conference table. "I'm s-sorry for interrupting, but no one was answering their phones." She walked to Chris and handed her a file folder. "This was on your desk." She turned to the Chief with her hand covering her mouth. "It's urgent. It couldn't wait. I'm sorry."

Constable Moody leaned over and whispered something to the Chief then quickly and quietly left the room.

Cal stood and took a step towards his daughter. When she saw him, Kate sobbed and launched herself at him. "Dad. She gave herself up to Rappaport to save Cail's life."

Chris was still on her feet as she scanned the file. She looked up, searching for Moody and realized he'd left. "Fuck." Her fingers dug a path through her short hair. "It's not a high ranking officer you're looking for. It's an officer who works with the *highest* ranking officer. Where the hell did Moody go?"

"What are you talking about?" The Chief asked as she rose to her feet.

"Brandon Moody is Rappaport's half-brother." She tossed the file folder towards Chief Clarke and it slid across the table. "And here's your fucking proof Rappaport has Sinclair."

* * *

It was the screaming, burning pain in her shoulders that drew Taylor out of a deep state of unconsciousness. She slowly became aware of her arms stretched out in front of her and then the bindings squeezing her wrists as she tried to pull her arms in to relieve the pain. Panic surged through every fibre of her being as she twisted and pulled at the restraints. Breathe, she told herself, knowing that panicking wasn't going to help her.

She was on her knees, bent over a soft platform. A mattress? Her arms stretched out above her head. She tried to move her legs, but it was like they were strapped to the floor. She couldn't move. There was no way to ease the burning in her shoulders and lower back. Barely keeping the sense of panic at bay, she opened her eyes and saw nothing but a white blur in front of her. Her eyes fluttered as she struggled to focus. Raising her head slowly, she tried to focus on what was binding her wrists and saw the thick brown leather straps wrapped tightly around each wrist with metal chains linking them to the white posts of the headboard.

She began twisting and pulling on the restraints again, desperate to free herself, until her wrists were so raw that they began to bleed. Dropping her head, Taylor tried to calm herself down and think. It was then she realized she was naked and then a new sense of panic threatened to take over her sanity. What had he done while she was out?

Taylor couldn't see below her waist where she was folded over the end of the bed, but she soon realized that she was still wearing the jeans she had put on that morning. Was it that morning? She had no idea how long she'd been unconscious and strapped to the bed. It was only her upper body that had been stripped, but why?

Peering under her arm, she began to study the room. Everything was white, from the carpet and walls, to the armoire on the far side of the room. This was the prison she saw in her vision the previous night and in some of her dreams over the past few days.

She dropped her head again, letting her anger build and then she used her rage in a new fight against the leather straps binding her. A great roar of frustration filled the room when she failed to even loosen the restraints.

When she lifted her head again she noticed the brown curling pattern in the centre of the bed. At first she didn't comprehend what she was seeing. It was a moment before she could focus properly and then the realization hit her like a fist to the sternum. A bull whip, so carefully arranged in a spiral in the centre of the white duvet it almost looked like a work of art.

Did Rappaport know her so well that he knew what the deepest, darkest parts of her craved? As she stared at the stupid thing, that need suddenly burned inside of her like a raging inferno.

"No."

She didn't have that need anymore. She didn't need it. Because Gray Rowan had given her a gift so much more precious than a roof over her head; more precious than the hope and confidence that she could make something of herself; more precious than the means to fulfill her promise to Leila. Gray had given her the ability to feel again - from the stab of fear she felt when she first saw the report of Ralph Morse's escape and knew he was going after Rowan, to the unexplainable connection she felt with Gray.

So she didn't need the crack of the whip and the burning pain slicing across her back in a desperate attempt to feel something, anything.

Did she?

Taylor couldn't take her eyes off the coiled length of leather, nor could she extinguish the burning need to feel it connecting with her skin. She could almost feel the burn blazing across her back and then the burn receded and a warmth spread through every cell of her body. Did Rappaport leave the whip there to screw with her mind? Because, holy hell, it was working.

Hours passed, days. It seemed like it anyway with no relief from the burning in her shoulders and lower back. Her knees joined the party and if she didn't get some relief soon she was sure she'd go stark, raving mad.

As she stared at the whip, a form began to materialize above it. At first she thought she was hallucinating - who knows what was in that needle Rappaport stuck her with as soon as they entered his apartment - then she remembered the only times Leila appeared like this was when she needed to go somewhere else in her mind; when she needed to focus on something other than what was happening to her body.

"No," Taylor sobbed. "I can't go through it again. I can't."

"Look at me, Tay." Leila's voice was as ethereal as her form as it hovered over the bed.

As Taylor lifted her head, the heavy door to her left swung open. Her eyes shot to the door, only it wasn't Rappaport who crossed the threshold, it was Brandon Moody, dressed in his uniform. Something boiled in Taylor's blood, rushing through her and giving her a surge of strength. It was something more than rage, something more than hatred and disgust that she couldn't even identify. Warm blood trickled down her arms as she yanked ferociously at the restraints again.

Moody sauntered across the room, coming up behind Taylor. "Well, well, well. What do we have here?"

"Touch me and I promise I will kill you with my bare hands," Taylor growled. Her jaw was clamped so hard her teeth hurt.

Moody's laughter echoed around the room. "Like you're in a position to do that."

"It may not be today. It may not be tomorrow. But, at some point I will wrap my hands around your throat and squeeze the life out of you."

The slow, controlled growl that Taylor spoke in actually had Moody paling and that just pissed him off. He'd be damned if he let some chick intimidate him. He picked up the bull whip from the centre of the bed and walked behind Taylor. "You into this shit, Sinclair?" He gave the whip a couple of test strikes in the open air. On his third try, the whip snapped as he drew it back and a surge of power shot through him. "Yeah, I can see how this could be appealing."

Panic, rage, fear, and desperation had Taylor putting everything she had into freeing her arms. She was trying to use her body to pull the chains from the posts while twisting her wrists. Adrenaline coursed through her system so she didn't even feel the pain.

She heard the crack a moment before the pain seared across her back. It was nothing like the strikes Johnson had given her. It wasn't a burning pain she felt. It was like he'd ripped the flesh right off her back. The feeling of warmth spreading through her didn't stand a chance before the next strike was upon her. She screamed out in bloody murder.

At the next strike, Rappaport roared before charging across the room and tackling Moody.

With a brawl going on behind her, Taylor blinked open her eyes and saw Leila's image fading. She whispered, "Don't go. Don't leave me again. Please. Leila, please."

"I'm always with you, Tay. Always," Leila responded as she faded away to nothing.

Taylor felt something shift inside her. She was left with that simmering rage and a determination to never be a victim again, to never be weak and helpless again. Something Lane told her repeatedly came to mind and finally made sense. She was the only one who had control over her emotions. She could choose to be embarrassed and ashamed of all of the crap she lived through; she could choose to let the media's constant harassment affect her; or she could choose to hold her head high and not give a damn about what anyone thought of her.

Like Chris once told her, her past didn't define her. She'd been listening to this kind of advice from Gray, Chris, and Lane for months, but only now did it seem to click. She could choose to be weak, innocent Taylor or she could be strong, resilient Taylor who didn't take crap from anyone.

"Like you give a shit what happens to her when you've got her tied up like that?" Moody shouted at Rappaport. They'd stopped throwing punches and were hurling words now.

"She's mine. You keep your fucking hands off her."

"Whatever, man. We need to talk. Shit's gettin' real. I want my money and I want it now."

"There is no money, asshole. All of my accounts are frozen. I can't fucking touch it."

Unfinished Business

Taylor tried not to think about the blood pouring down her arms and back. "Release my hands," she ordered in a raspy, low voice.

Rappaport stood behind Taylor, staring at the gashes across her back and didn't know what the hell to do. He didn't know first aid and he couldn't very well take her to a doctor. "I'm sorry, Sinclair."

Taylor was surprised at how shaky his voice sounded, like he truly was upset at her injuries.

He paced back and forth then scrubbed his hands over his face. "That shouldn't have happened. Fuck. I don't know what to do."

"Release my friggin' hands," Taylor screamed.

With trembling hands, Rappaport undid the buckles on the wrist restraints and freed Taylor's hands. He felt sick when he saw she basically rubbed the skin right off her wrists. "I'm sorry. Jesus, I'm sorry." He left her to figure out the restraints on her legs herself.

Moody paced back and forth. He couldn't believe they'd gotten to this point and the money wasn't there. He risked everything and he'd be damned if he would go down without a fight. "They don't have your Legend ID. You've got money tucked away under that alias."

"The money's gone," Rappaport yelled again. "You didn't do your fucking job and the money's gone, you asshole."

Moody pulled the Glock from its holster as he rushed up behind Rappaport. He grabbed a fist full of his hair and shoved the Glock to his temple. "You've got money in your safe. Let's go." He pushed Rappaport towards the door, made him key in the code and shoved him out the door in front of him.

With her arms free, Taylor leaned back on her heels and studied the ropes tying her legs down to the legs of the bed. She was shaking uncontrollably, probably in shock, she thought, and the sight of her own blood was making her feel faint. It took her several minutes, but she finally got herself free. Now that she knew Moody was taking money from Rappaport, she was confident he was the one Rappaport had ordered to kill Cail. She needed to find a way to let Chris know where to find her and fast. There was no telling what Rappaport and Moody would do now that they knew everything was crumbling around them. She didn't know if it would work, but she did some deep breathing to calm herself and then reached out to Quinn.

351

Chapter 36

Chris was kicking herself. If she hadn't been so wrapped up in Dave's shit, she would have figured out this mess with Taylor and found the folder hours ago. She sent half a dozen officers over to Cityplace with photos of Troy Rappaport while she searched Moody's apartment with Detective Blake and Kate. She'd issued a BOLO for Brandon Moody and his vehicle and, thank God, had the Chief's blessing to take down Rappaport as soon as they tracked him down.

They decided to leave Cail out of the loop. He was on patrol with his partner, Tara MacNeil, which was a much better use of his time than freaking out about Taylor. When they did find her, Chris didn't want Cail there just in case she was in bad shape or worse. Tara had been updated on the threat to Cail, and Cal arranged for a security detail to keep an eye on him. Both Cal and Chris believed Moody would be the guy Rappaport trusted to take Cail out and they believed he'd be too busy worrying about saving his own ass to bother with Cail.

The search of Moody's apartment didn't give them an address for Rappaport. Chris had his computer, bank statements, passport, and ten grand in cash taken into evidence and put a unit on the street to watch for Moody returning. If he was planning on fleeing the country, he would have to go back to his apartment for his passport and cash. She'd taken his bank statements because they showed regular deposits of large amounts of money that had to be payments from Rappaport. She'd use the statements to apply for a warrant to freeze his accounts. They had no proof Moody was who Rappaport had charged with killing Cail. Chris wanted Moody's cell phone. She was sure there would be damning evidence on his cell if he didn't erase it before they got to him.

Frustrated, they returned to Headquarters and Chris made contact with each of the officers she'd sent out with Rappaport's photo. So far, they hadn't found anyone who recognized Rappaport, so she increased the search area.

"Fuck." Chris dragged her hands through her hair for the hundredth time and pulled. "We need a freaking miracle right now."

Just as she said those words, Quinn Paylen knocked on the door jamb of her office. Chris, Kate, and Blake all looked up at her at the same time. "Hey," Chris began. "What can I do for you?"

Quinn gave Chris a weak smile, but her smoky grey eyes only showed concern. "I believe I have your freaking miracle." She handed Chris a piece of paper with an address written on it. "She's hurt. She needs medical attention."

"Where'd you get this?" Chris asked.

"Taylor, of course."

"She called you?"

"Do you believe in her gift, Detective Sergeant?"

Chris nodded. "Yeah, I do."

"That address showed up in my head and I saw Taylor. I think I felt what she was feeling. She's in pain and I think she's in shock. I tried to get more information. I tried communicating with her several times on the way here, but I'm not getting anything."

Chris picked up the phone, called Inspector Worthington, and requested a tactical unit. Within twenty minutes she had a full Emergency Task Force team plus Kate, Dave, and Detective Blake in a meeting room. Taylor had been right about Cityplace. The address Quinn gave them was smack dab in the middle of it. Chris let the tactical team leader dictate the plan of entry. Once they got the all clear, she'd go in with Kate, Dave, and Blake.

"I'm coming with you." Lane stood at the door dressed in jeans and a warm coat with her medical bag at her side. "She may need me."

Vibrating with rage at the thought of what might have been done to Taylor, Chris answered, "If he raped her, Rappaport's going to need medical attention in the form of a fucking autopsy. Let's roll."

* * *

"You fuckin' idiot." Rappaport raged, as Moody shoved him into his bedroom closet, facing the floor to ceiling safe.

"I'm not the idiot here. You're screwed, Troy. It's time to bail."

"They took my lab, my accounts are frozen. What the fuck, dude? You're supposed to be on top of this shit."

"It's out of my control. Internal Affairs is rounding up all of the cops you've been paying off. It's only a matter of time before they make the connection between us. There's nothing I can do anymore, Troy. I want my money and I'm out. Open the fucking safe."

"You want your money?" Rappaport's voice came out high pitched and hysterical. "For what? Your job was to keep the heat off of me. Do your fuckin' job."

"It's out of my hands. There's four different departments investigating you. You want to blame someone? Blame your fuck buddy, Kev. His shit put you front and centre. And this shit with Sinclair, man, you're up a creek. Dump the bitch and let's get the hell out of here."

"Even if my accounts weren't frozen, do you really think I'd give you a dime after what you just did to my woman?"

Moody's head spun. All the shit he'd done for Troy and just when he's about to get the big payoff the money is gone. This couldn't be happening. There had to be money in that monstrosity of a safe. He spoke slowly, articulating every syllable. "You have money in your safe. I. Want. My. Money."

"So do I, asshole. But thanks to you the money I've spent my entire life earning is gone. Fucking poof." He held his fingertips together then flared them out as he yelled *poof*. "Gone. You want your money? Go get it from your fucking boss." Rappaport's laugh started off slow and pathetic and quickly turned into hysterical. "I just made the Toronto fucking Police richer than hell."

Moody stood there steaming, staring at the mess his brother had become in the last six months. He'd lost about thirty pounds and looked like he hadn't slept in weeks. The worst part though, was Troy had fried his fucking mind. Moody aimed his Glock at the floor and fired.

Rappaport nearly jumped right out of his skin. "Holy fuck, man. Be careful with that thing." The barrel was still burning hot when Moody pressed it to Rappaport's temple again.

"Next one's going in your head. Open the fucking safe."

With trembling fingers, Rappaport turned the dial on the safe, first to the right, then left, then right again. As soon as he pushed down on the handle and the safe door cracked open, Moody smashed the gun into the side of Rappaport's head and he went down like a sack of potatoes.

When he came to, head throbbing, Rappaport looked up at the open safe door and started laughing. There hadn't been a dime inside. It was filled with meth and it didn't look like Moody had bothered to take any of it. He wouldn't know where to liquidate it. Still laughing, Rappaport reached over and pulled up a section of the carpet. The safe hidden below it contained about a million in cash.

He stumbled out to the bedroom and picked up a pipe and a lighter from the dresser. Holding the flame to the end of the pipe, he inhaled deeply. What the hell, he thought, and dropped a few more crystals into the pipe.

In his office, he sat at the computer. He couldn't be sure what Moody would do, so he had to do something with the money he had in accounts under his Legend alias. It was the only money he had left other than the cash in his closet floor safe. Before he got down to business, he turned on the TV and turned it to the channel that displayed the building's security cameras.

* * *

Standing in front of the panel listing the names of all of the residents in the building, Chris found the code for the building superintendent and dialed the number on the intercom. When a staticy male voice answered, she said, "Detective Sergeant Chris Cain, Toronto Police. I need to speak with you regarding one of your residents."

"I'll be right down."

It only took a few minutes for the super to arrive in the lobby, but it felt like a lifetime. Chris paced back and forth like a caged animal and then pounced on him as soon as he arrived. She held a picture of Rappaport in front of his face. "Recognize him?"

"Hmmm." The fiftyish man in jeans and a blue button down shirt squinted at the photo. "Yeah, he lives in the building, but I'm not sure what unit."

"I need the name of the occupant of this apartment." She showed him the slip of paper Quinn had given her.

The super took the slip of paper and held on to the side of his glasses as he read the address. Scratching his balding head, he said, "Ah, I'll have to go back to my apartment and get the listing."

"You do that. In the meantime, we will be entering that unit. Call me at this number when you've got it." She gave him her business card and headed to where the tactical team had both elevators waiting.

"Yes, of course." He stood back and watched Lane, Chris, and the rest of the officers split up between the two elevators. "I guess I'll take the stairs," he muttered to himself and shuffled off.

They emerged from the elevator on the top floor in silence. The tactical team leader communicated with his team using hand signals. There were only six units on this floor and the one they wanted was in the southwest corner of the building. The tactical team took up positions on either side of the door with a battering ram at the ready. They wanted to go in fast, not giving Rappaport the opportunity to use Taylor as a shield or as a hostage.

They rammed the door and six officers stormed the apartment yelling, "Police." Seconds later the yelling became frantic. "Put down the gun. Lower your weapon."

It felt like another lifetime before the team leader came out and addressed Chris. "We've got a hostage situation. He's holding a gun to Sinclair's head and I'm pretty sure that he's higher than a kite. He was waiting for us. He knew we were coming. We're going to need paramedics on standby."

"Fuck," Chris muttered. She entered the apartment and headed straight for the living room. Rappaport stood with his arm around Taylor's neck and a flashy silver pistol pressed to her temple. The five tactical officers all had their weapons trained on Rappaport.

The only injuries that Chris could see on Taylor were her wrists, but she was trembling like crazy wearing jeans and a white silk negligee. Her hands gripped Rappaport's arm around her neck, her eyes closed.

"Back off. I swear to God I'll pump her head full of lead if you don't get the fuck out of here," Rappaport screamed.

Taylor desperately tryed not to think about the blood dripping down her back. Her right hand was only inches from the gun, she was just waiting for the right moment to grab onto the barrel and twist it out of Rappaport's hand.

Chris stepped forward, holding her hands out to the side and spoke softly. "Let's not get all fired up here, Troy. You know this isn't going to end well. Let Taylor go and set the gun down."

"I'll tell you how this is going to end. We're going to walk out of here and you're all going to stay the fuck out of the way. Move out of the way or I shoot her."

"And then what?" Chris asked. "Taylor will be dead and one of these tactical officers will put a bullet in your head before she hits the ground. Is that what you want?" Chris took another step closer to Rappaport.

"Easy DS," one of the tactical officers whispered. "He's high on meth."

She could see that he was pissed by his red face and his flaring nostrils. The meth would make him aggressive and unpredictable. "Is this the way you treat someone you care about?"

"I didn't hurt her," he said through gritted teeth. ""I passed out. I only meant to take a short nap. When I woke up, Brandon was in there with her. Brandon hurt her."

"Really? Who lured her here and left her alone?" It made her sick that he was trying to dump the blame on his brother.

His face was even redder now, his neck corded and strained, and he hissed out breaths through his clamped jaw. "Fuck you." Spittle flew from his mouth as he spoke.

"Do you care about her, Troy?"

The emotion her question brought to his face surprised her. His hazel eyes glistened and in them she saw guilt, remorse, and love. She thought his was a sick, twisted form of love, but he did care for Taylor. Rappaport nodded in answer to Chris's question.

"She's hurt and she's in shock." Chris took another step forward.

Rappaport just stood there shaking, in rage or in fear, Chris wasn't sure, but she thought he was about to give up. She started to take another step towards him and he freaked.

"Back the fuck off. Everyone get the fuck out." Spittle flew as he screamed and a couple of the tactical officers began to yell over him.

"Drop the gun. Drop your weapon."

With everyone yelling and screaming, Taylor took the opportunity to make a grab for the gun. Just as her hand wrapped around the barrel and began to push forward, it went off. Taylor dropped to the floor, her fist still gripping the weapon. White hot pain blinded her. Her left hand came up to cover her eyes and became slick with the blood. Everyone was still screaming, but Taylor was oblivious to it.

The tactical officers tackled Rappaport and he fought them like a son of a bitch, but they quickly cuffed him.

Chris dove straight to Taylor as the Team Leader headed to the door to let Lane in. The back of the white negligee was soaked with blood. Chris placed her hand on Taylor's upper arms, pushing her up so she could get a good look at her face. "Taylor, it's Chris," she soothed. "I've got you. Lane's going to look at your injuries. Okay?"

"Is Cail okay?" Taylor asked, her voice steady and strong despite her trembling body. "Is he safe now?"

Lane spoke in a soothing tone as she kneeled next to Taylor. "Cail's fine. Can you show me your face?" She'd already studied Taylor's back and wrists. She could see the powder burns around Taylor's right eye and the blood flowing from her nose and left eye. She was more concerned about treating her for shock at the moment.

"Did he hurt you in any other way, Taylor?"

It didn't take a rocket scientist to figure out Lane was asking her in a very gentle manner if she'd been raped. "No. Moody hit me a few times with the whip then Rappaport came in and fought with him."

"Rappaport is in custody. All of the cops Rappaport was bribing or blackmailing are being rounded up as we speak."

"What about Moody? If he's still out there, Cail's not safe." There was an edge of panic in her voice now. If Moody got to Cail, she'd gone through all of this for nothing. "You weren't supposed to come for me until the threat to Cail was neutralized."

"We won't let Moody get to Cail. There's a BOLO out for him. He'll be in custody soon enough. What's more important right now is that we get you to emerg to be treated for shock and your injuries."

"I know," Taylor answered. She knew she was going to have to go to the hospital and that was nearly as terrifying as being strapped to that stupid bed. But, she couldn't focus on that until she knew Cail was safe.

"Will you let me give you something for the pain?"

Taylor shook her head once. "Nah, I'm good." It was her eyes that hurt the most. It felt like someone was jabbing ice picks into them. If it got much worse, she might just give in and take the pain meds.

"The paramedics are going to come in, but I'll treat you if you don't want them to touch you." When Taylor nodded, she asked again if Taylor would let her take a look at her face.

Taylor carefully peeled her hand away from her eyes. Lane pursed her lips as she studied the damage. Taylor's left eye just went to the top of her list of concerns.

Lane opened up her medical bag just as a male and a female paramedic guiding a gurney came into the room. Lane stood and introduced herself. "I'm Dr. Lane McIntyre. Taylor is haphephobic, so if you don't mind, I'll treat her."

"Sure, doc," the male paramedic answered. "Just let us know what we can do to assist."

Lane took Taylor's vitals then the medics prepared bandages and an I.V. line as Lane worked on Taylor. She refused to allow Lane to bandage her wrists, but calmly submitted to everything else.

As Lane worked on her, Taylor gave Chris a play by play of the events from the time she arrived at Union Station until the ETF officers arrived. Chris wasn't sure how she was holding it all together, but Taylor seemed to be no worse off from her ordeal and Chris was as relieved as hell Taylor hadn't been raped. As it was, she felt responsible for Taylor's injuries.

"Are you sure Cail's safe?" Taylor asked Chris.

Chris crouched down in front of Taylor. "You should have trusted us to protect him. Coming here ..." She didn't want to berate Taylor for her actions, but she was so frustrated Taylor put her life on the line instead of trusting them to ensure Cail's safety.

"I couldn't risk Cail's life. How do we know someone he trusts isn't still out there waiting for a call from Rappaport that isn't going to come?"

Chris explained IA's investigation into the cops under Rappaport's control, but she knew Taylor was still uneasy about Cail's safety. She did her best to reassure her, but until Moody was in custody, they would all be on edge.

"Can you see if you can find something warmer for Taylor to wear?" Lane asked Chris.

She returned moments later with a thick hoody from Rappaport's closet and helped Taylor into it, being careful of her wrists and the IV line.

Lane and Chris helped Taylor to her feet and led her to the gurney. The paramedics wrapped blankets around her. It was when they buckled the strap around her legs and tightened it that Taylor's composure began to fray. She couldn't handle being tied down.

"I can give you a sedative," Lane offered. She'd been surprised how well Taylor was coping, but it could be a different story once they got to the hospital.

Taylor shook her head. "No drugs."

"Let's see how you do, shall we?"

As Lane went off with Taylor, Chris stepped into the master bedroom where Detective Blake had begun a methodical search. "Could you take over here if I head to the hospital?"

"Yeah, no problem, Sarge. There's a huge safe in the closet, wide open and full of meth. We found another one on the floor under the carpet. Rappaport won't cough up the combination, so I called in a safe cracker."

"I've got a couple of patrol officers picking up Rappaport. They're going to get him processed through booking then I think Pierson and Boone are going to interview him. I'll either come back in tonight or I'll interview him in the morning. Pierson and Boone are both sending a couple of detectives over, so you'll have some help. I'm going to steal Kate and take her with me."

Blake gave Chris a look with a raised eyebrow and a smirk. "Something going on between you and Kate?"

"Why?"

"Oh, I don't know. You two seem to be inseparable lately. Either something's going on or she's your new shadow."

Chris rolled her eyes. "We've pretty much been living together since we started seeing each other in July."

"Whaaat?" Blake grinned. "Detective Sergeant bump 'em and dump 'em, bed 'em and shed 'em, fuck 'em and chuck 'em, is in a committed relationship?"

"Jesus. How many names to people have for me?"

"Oh, there's plenty more. Boff 'em and doff 'em, kiss 'em and diss 'em, mash 'em and trash 'em." Behind Chris, Kate popped her head out from the closet and grinned. Blake suddenly felt like an idiot.

"Okay. Shit, shut up already." Chris stuffed her hands in her pockets, thinking people had way too much time on their hands. "I think Kate's ... you know?"

"No." Blake was enjoying Chris's sudden discomfort. It was totally out of character for her commanding officer. She glanced at Kate, who held a finger to her lips and winked. "Kate's what?"

"Pfff." Jesus, how did she get into this conversation anyway? Staring down at her feet, she kicked at the carpet. "She's it. The one that I want to spend the rest of my life with."

Blake's mouth dropped open. She didn't think she'd ever hear Chris Cain say something like that. Once she recovered from the shock, a grin spread across her face. "You're a lucky woman, Kate."

"I know," Kate beamed. Chris whipped around and her face went bright red. Blake nearly fell to the floor she was laughing so hard.

"Hey, you," Chris began. "Come out of the closet."

Both Kate and Blake laughed as Chris took a step forward, grabbed Kate's face and planted a deep, sensual kiss on her lips. When she stepped out of the kiss, she pointed to the door. "Hospital, now. And call Cail. Tell him to meet us there, but break it to him gently." On her way through the doorway, Chris turned back to Blake and winked with a big ass grin lighting up her face.

"Well, holy shit. She's absolutely, head over heels in love." Blake went back to work, shaking her head and smiling.

* * *

Cail ended his call from Kate and stuck his phone back in his pocket. The injuries she described had him thinking about the marks he'd seen criss-crossing Taylor's back and wondering if Rappaport had been the one who put them there. Instead of heading to the hospital, he went straight to Rappaport's condo. He walked through the open space of the living room, dining room, and kitchen area to the hallway looking for Dave. He found him in a room Rappaport had set up as his office and came to a dead stop, staring at the wall covered in pictures of Taylor from when she was very young to very recently. There were even photos from her book signing a couple of days ago and from the day of Sarah's trial.

"Holy shit," Tara said from just behind Cail.

Dave turned from searching through the desk at the sound of Tara's voice. "Hey, bro. What the hell are you doing here, man?" He tried to take Cail's arm and lead him out of the room, but Cail pulled out of his grasp and continued to study the wall.

There was a black and white photo of Taylor walking down the street. She couldn't have been more than ten or eleven and directly behind her was Darryl Johnson looking like he was about to pounce on her. Rappaport, the son of a bitch, had known and let it happen. Another photo showed Taylor at about the same age, squatting with her arms wrapped around her lower legs in a cardboard box in an alley during a snow storm. She was wearing jeans that were too short on her long, thin legs, a sweatshirt, and running shoes.

The more photos he looked at, the more it hit home just how hard Taylor's life had been. He read about it in her book, talked to her about some of it, but looking at the pictures made it so much more real.

"Cail, come on. You really shouldn't be in here, bro." Dave took his arm and gently tried to steer him out of the room. When he started to resist, Tara took his other arm.

He let them lead him out to the hall and just stood there for a moment with all of the images running through his head. What he hadn't seen, and had been looking for, were images of Rappaport using a whip on Taylor or of her back with welts all over it.

"Why don't you let Tara take you to the hospital?" Dave asked. "You really shouldn't be here."

"I want to see the room he locked in and then I'll go."

ave put his hands on his hips, shaking his head. Then he pointed across the hall. "Make it quick."

The first thing Cail noticed when he stepped into the overly bright room was the smell of blood. Everything was blindingly white except for the brown leather whip laying on the floor like a snake and the bright red blood decorating the bed and the floor at the base of it. The leather wrist cuffs, stained with blood, were still attached by chains to the posts on the headboard and white ropes were barely visibly against the white carpet the end of the bed.

He hadn't gotten any further than the doorway, but he'd seen enough. It was either get the hell out of there or he was going to deposit his lunch all over the pristine white carpet.

Chapter 37

As soon as the sliding glass doors to the emergency department slid open, Taylor was hit with that distinct, sterile smell of hospital. Between that, the shock, pain, and being strapped down, Taylor was on the brink of completely losing it. By the time they transferred her onto the bed in an exam room she was hyperventilating.

The first nurse who tried to touch her nearly got taken out by a right hook. The only thing that saved her was that Taylor couldn't see what she was swinging at.

"Back off," Taylor screamed. It seemed like everyone was crowding in on her and she just needed a few minutes to get it together.

Lane cleared the room, spoke soothingly to Taylor. "I'm going to give you a sedative to get you through this without injuring yourself or anyone else."

"No," Taylor wheezed.

Lane sighed in exasperation. "Taylor, if you're going to be treated properly you need to be relaxed. If you continued to be aggressive, they'll want you strapped down."

The thought of sleeping through this ordeal sounded a hell of a lot better than trying to deal with people touching her and doing whatever they needed to do. Besides, she didn't know how much more of this pain she could take. The gashes she could deal with, but her left eye hurt like a bitch. "Okay, do it."

Lane injected a sedative into her IV line and within seconds, Taylor's entire body began to relax and she felt like she was floating away.

The next thing she knew she was caught somewhere between sleep and consciousness, but just couldn't seem to break through the fog. It was like being underwater, floating to the surface only to find it had frozen over and she couldn't break through that last barrier. She was aware of the sharp, piercing pain in her eye and voices somewhere nearby, but she couldn't make them out. Then she felt herself being pulled back down into the depths of unconsciousness.

The next time she tried to surface, she was moving. She could feel the cool air brushing over her and shivered. Her arm felt so heavy and awkward when she tried to lift her hand to her eyes.

"She's coming around."

That sounded like Lane's voice. Someone gently lifted her hand and put it back at her side and she felt herself slipping away again.

When she finally managed to break through that barrier to full consciousness she found she couldn't open her eyes. She was on her back, propped up in a semi-sitting position. She felt groggy, probably from the sedative they'd given her. Varying degrees of pain consumed her entire body. The gashes and her wrists stung, her shoulders and lower back ached, her knees ached, and she still had that stabbing pain in her left eye and a burning pain in her right. She raised her hand to her eyes and found they both were bandaged. A surge of panic sent a horrible, sinking feeling into her belly.

She sucked in a deep breath through flaring nostrils and realized the sterile smell of the hospital was absent. It didn't smell like Chris's place or Gray's suite at the Grand. Another deep breath in and she caught the masculine, spicy scent that was Caillen Worthington. She reached out and found his hand, entwining her fingers with his and blew out a slow breath as a sense of calm filled her.

"You're awake."

The edge in his voice was unmistakable and the sense of calm quickly evaporated. "You're angry."

"I think we need to talk about your history with bull whips and Rappaport's involvement in it."

For a moment she forgot about the pain in her eyes because she had that roiling feeling in her gut like you get when you're on an elevator that suddenly drops too fast. "I don't know what you're talking about."

"I've seen the marks on your back, Taylor. The ones that look like you've been whipped repeatedly. The whole time we've been sleeping together, you've been lying to me."

With every sentence, Cail's voice grew louder and louder and Taylor had no idea what to say to calm him down. She let go of his hand and pulled herself up to a sitting position. "How have I been lying to you? I don't understand."

She heard him let out a rush of air, like he couldn't believe what she was saying.

"I've always tried to be careful with you, not knowing what might set you off, and the whole time you've been into pain. Should I have been taking my belt to you all this time? Is that your idea of foreplay? Jesus, Taylor, you're probably more suited to Dave than you are to me."

Okay, that hurt. She was shaking and wasn't sure if it was from physical pain or the emotional pain he just threw at her. "It wasn't like that. It wasn't sexual."

"Bullshit," Cail screamed. The bed dipped as Cail pushed off of it to his feet and continued yelling at her. "Are you going to sit there and tell me you didn't get off on it? Bullshit."

She'd always thought of the euphoric warmth that spread through her body after the initial burn of Sarah's whip blazing across her back as a kind of high. Could it have been arousal that she'd been feeling? She hadn't known what arousal felt like back then, but the more she thought about it now, the more she thought he could be right. Her stomach roiled, nausea seeped in. "If you'd stop yelling at me for half a second, I could explain."

"That's just it. You should have explained it to me a long time ago. All this time I've had no idea who you are, what you are."

"Caillen."

Well, at least she had an idea of where they were now. The sound of Rose's voice had Taylor flushing with embarrassment. How much had Cail's parents heard?

"I need to get ready for work."

Taylor listened to Cail's retreating steps then heard a door slam. Someone walked into the room and sat on the bed next to her. A warm hand covered Taylor's trembling, cold one.

"How's the pain?" Lane asked.

"Not so good," Taylor answered. Then she asked the question that had sent that surge of panic through her when she woke up. "Am I blind?"

Lane made a sound of disgust. "Didn't Cail explain anything to you when you woke up?"

"He had something else on his mind." Taylor wasn't sure if Rose was still nearby. Since Cail didn't want to hear her explanation, she wanted to talk to Lane about it. She felt the need to talk to someone about it.

"You're not blind, Taylor." Lane patted Taylor's hand in comfort. "Dr. Hawthorne is the ophthalmologist who examined your eyes. She covered both of your eyes to try to limit the movement until your left eye has a chance to heal. You've got a torn cornea. The right eye sustained some minor powder burns when the gun discharged. Dr. Hawthorne repaired your left eye lid and Dr. Rhampoor, who is one of the top plastic surgeons in the city, sutured the rest of your wounds. You were in surgery for a couple of hours and when you came out of recovery, we snuck you out of the hospital under the noses of the media. I didn't want you in there any longer than necessary. We kept you sedated and brought you here to Cal and Rose's hoping the media don't figure out where you are. Dr. Hawthorne is going to stop by this morning and check on your eyes. She wants to examine them daily for a few days. And Chris will be by sometime this morning to take your statement.

"Here," Lane put two tablets in Taylor's hand then put a glass of water in her other hand. "Those are Tylenol Threes for the pain."

Taylor swallowed the pills without argument. Lane fluffed her pillows and explained they wanted her to rest in a semi-sitting position to keep any pressure from her eye. Just as she got settled, she heard footsteps coming down the hall and felt the tension in the air as Cail came in and grabbed his wallet and phone from the night stand.

"Are you going to let me explain?" Taylor asked.

"I've got to get to work." Cail's response was short and sharp.

She reminded herself she wouldn't be a victim ever again. "If you walk away from me right now, don't plan on coming back."

Cail stopped dead in his tracks and turned back to Taylor. "Excuse me?"

"I'm not going to put up with you verbally assaulting me every time you get your panties in a knot. Either we deal with this now, or we're done." She supposed she had her answer when she heard him walk out of the room. She breathed out in exasperation and settled back into the pillows.

"Want to talk about it?" Lane asked.

"Yes." Taylor could almost feel the surprise in Lane at her willingness to discuss the issue between her and Cail. She was pretty sure the whole house heard every word Cail yelled at her. She took a deep breath and then just poured her heart out. "This goes way back to when I started living on the streets. It was like I lost the ability to feel.

Or maybe I shut off all of my emotions after the first time Tremblant raped me. I'm not sure, but I just remember feeling hollow, empty. It was worse after I lost my son. I loved him a little more every day he was inside me and when I lost him I was empty again. I didn't feel grief or sadness and I desperately wanted to feel something, anything."

Taylor took another deep, stuttering breath before continuing. "The first time Darryl got me after that, he took me to this underground parking garage. There was a door leading into a mechanical room. He took me in there, took my shirt, and tied my hands around a thick pipe above my head. Then he left me there." Not being able to see was making it easier to say what she needed to say. She could almost make herself believe she was alone. "I don't know how long I was there before Sarah came in. I wasn't afraid. I didn't feel anything. It was like I just didn't care what happened to me at that point.

"She wanted to know what happened to my baby. You know, I can look back at it now, knowing what I know today, and I can almost make some sense out of it. She freaked out when she realized I was pregnant. She totally lost it. But, I think after she cooled down and realized what she'd done she regretted it. She hated my mother so much because my mom was able to give Greg Johnson the one thing Sarah desperately wanted and couldn't give him. A child. After she beat the crap out of me, I think she realized she just screwed up her chance at having a baby, my baby.

"When I wouldn't tell her what happened to the baby, she let loose with her whip. That first strike was pure agony. It was like fire blazing across my back. But, when the burning faded, this warmth ... I don't know how to describe it. It was a wonderful warmth that spread through every cell of my body and I can remember thinking, *Oh my God, I can feel this. Finally, I can feel something and it's absolutely euphoric.* I couldn't get enough of it. I craved it. But, it wasn't just how it made me feel. I wanted to be punished for losing my baby. Does that make any sense?"

Taylor didn't wait for an answer. "I ended up making a deal with Sarah so that we both got what we wanted. She wanted to punish me and I wanted to be punished. Win, win," Taylor laughed, although she didn't think it was the least bit funny.

"Troy Rappaport knew she was whipping you," Lane said quietly.

"He must have followed me at some point," Taylor shrugged. "In all the times she whipped me, she never once broke the skin. She knew

367

what she was doing and could place every strike with pinpoint accuracy.

"When Gray took me in, my emotions came flooding back. I didn't need that anymore because I could feel again.

"Then I came to in that room at Rappaport's and he had my wrists in leather cuffs, chained to the posts on the headboard and my knees tied to the legs of the bed. I was pulled tight, my shoulders and my lower back were killing me. And that whip was curled up perfectly in the middle of the bed. He left me in there like that for ages. I don't know how much time past, but it felt like days. I don't know if he planned on using it or if he was just messing with my head. I stared at the stupid thing and I started to crave it. I wanted to feel it lash across my back and I wanted to feel that euphoric warmth."

She took another shaky breath and braced herself for more humiliation. "This morning, Cail said that I get off on it. I never thought of it as sexual. I didn't know what arousal felt like before him. I suppose he is right in a way because I did get off on it, but it wasn't sexual. It was a relief."

Taylor reached out trying to find the glass of water on the night stand, then took a long drink when Lane placed it in her hand. "When Cail gets angry at me like that, he says things that hurt. I guess that's one of the downsides of emotions. They're not all good ones." A half laugh, half sob rushed out of her lungs. At that moment, she hated herself for crying, for being weak when she told herself she wasn't going to be weak anymore.

"Are you satisfied with your sex life with Cail?"

"Yes," Taylor answered, her throat raw with emotion.

"Do you need pain in order to climax?"

Horrified at the question, Taylor's answer flew out in a rush of air, "No."

"Then I don't think you have to worry about the rush you got from Sarah's whip being sexual. It was a desperate attempt by a traumatized young girl to feel again or, more likely, to forget for a short time. Most children of abuse turn to some sort of coping mechanism to deal with the abuse. For many, it's drugs or alcohol. For others it's promiscuous sex. For you it was pain."

That made sense to Taylor. She used the feeling she got from being whipped as an escape, a release. She craved it, needed it. "Pain was my drug."

"Exactly."

"So, I'm an addict?"

"Do you think you're an addict?"

The things Cail made her feel were so much more powerful than what she'd gotten out of being whipped. If she put the two together, and if it was sexual as Cail had said, then she probably would be addicted. What heights would he have been able to take her to by adding an element of pain to their lovemaking? Her mind took her on an erotic journey as she thought about the possibilities.

"Taylor?"

Taylor was sure her face just turned flaming red. Thank God Lane couldn't hear her thoughts. Cail had been right. She did get off on it, but not in a sexual way. She craved it because it did something very similar to what their love making did - it made her forget. "I think, maybe, on some level, I might be."

"Hmmm." Lane smiled. "That answer was as clear as mud."

"When I was experiencing the pain of that whip, I forgot about everything else. It was the only time in my life I've been able to let go of the memories." Until recently, at least. "Until Cail and I made love." A thought struck her so hard she nearly crumbled. Was she using sex with Cail as a replacement for Sarah's whip?

"The pain and making love with Cail both give you a release from your emotional pain?"

Taylor nodded. "Is that bad?"

"Why do you think it's bad?"

"Using sex as an escape?"

"Taylor, do you sleep with Cail for the escape or because you love him?"

"I don't sleep with him specifically for the escape, but it's a nice benefit."

"Do you love him?"

She nodded again and whispered, "Yes. I never would have been able to sleep with him if I didn't."

"Do you still crave the pain?"

When she really thought about it, she realized she didn't. It was a need when she'd been desperate, but it wasn't something she wanted to bring with her from the past into her new life. "No. I don't."

"Do you still feel the need to be punished?"

Taylor had to think about that one for a moment. She hadn't even thought about punishment since she came off the streets. Maybe because she was being punished enough by the damn media. "No, I don't think so."

"What about your relationship with Cail?"

"I just gave him a choice and he chose to walk away. I've been treated like crap my whole life. I'm not going to take it anymore. Not even from Cail."

Lane cared for both Taylor and Cail, so it was hard to see them breaking up when she wanted so much for them to work things out. But she had to be proud of Taylor for taking a stand and refusing to be treated the way Cail treated her when he was angry. She patted Taylor's hand again in support. "Why don't I go down and get us some breakfast? What would you like?"

"Just a coffee, please. I'm not really hungry."

"Okay." Lane gave her hand a pat. When she stepped out into the hallway, she nearly walked straight into Cail leaning against the wall just outside the door with tears streaming down his face and his head hung low. Lane's mouth dropped open in shock at seeing him standing there eavesdropping. Then she pursed her lips, giving him a disapproving look, and walked around him to the stairs.

Taylor listened to Lane's retreating steps and heard her come to a stop then continue on again. It was only moments later she heard the floor boards creaking as someone made their way quietly to the stairs. Someone had been listening outside the door and it had to have been Cail. She couldn't imagine Rose eavesdropping on them like that. If he was in such a hurry to get to work, why did he stand there listening instead of letting her explain?

Male and female voices drifted up from downstairs, along with the sound of dishes clattering and the smell of bacon, but Taylor couldn't make out what the voices were saying. She threw the covers off, sat up and dangled her legs over the side of the bed. She was wearing one of those awful gowns from the hospital. Pushing to her feet, she pulled the gap at the back closed and held it with one hand as she felt her way around the room with the other. She found a window and stood in front of it, tilting her face up to feel the sunlight, even if she couldn't see it. Despite the warmth from the sun, the window felt cold and she knew it would be a brisk day.

She knew she was facing the road as she could hear the street traffic. Odd how all of her senses seemed to be heightened with her lack of vision. A car door closed in the driveway below and she knew it was Cail. She waited for the sound of the car starting, but it was a while before it came. Had he seen her standing in the window? Had he been watching her?

Maybe it was for the best she let him go now. She knew from the start Cail wanted a family much like his own and at some point he would leave her because she couldn't give it to him. She figured they'd have more time than this though and she had wanted to take as much time with him as she could, because she knew deep in her heart she would never feel for another man what she felt for Cail.

At one point, she thought they might have that same special connection Gray and Callaghan shared. But, she'd never seen Callaghan and Gray get angry at each other or say hurtful things to each other. The same went for Chris and Kate. Although they'd had that rough patch a few days ago, they were always laughing and joking around and they looked at each other the same way Gray and Callaghan did, like they adored everything about each other.

Was it her? Was she so messed up no one could love her with the intensity that Callaghan loved Gray?

She stood at the window until Lane came back in with a coffee for her. Sitting on the edge of the bed, sipping her coffee, she asked, "Do you think I could go back to Chris's today?" She didn't want to stay at the Worthingtons' with the way things were between her and Cail.

"Chris and Kate will be working and I don't want you home alone, at least until you have one eye uncovered."

Taylor wished she could go to work to keep busy. She felt like she was locked inside herself, locked in darkness. She couldn't write or draw or even go for a run. "Gray's suite at the Grand then?"

"Rose is quite happy to have you here, Taylor. She loves to dote on her kids and she considers you part of the family now."

"I don't want to seem ungrateful, but I'd feel more comfortable with Gray." Staying here left her open to Cail coming in anytime he wanted and she really didn't want to face his anger again. She needed time to get used to the idea of being alone again. Time to heal from her physical and emotional wounds, she supposed.

Lane patted her thigh. "I understand. I'm sure Gray will be stopping by to see you. You can ask her then."

* * *

Chris arrived just as Dr. Hawthorne was packing up. "I brought you some clothes and your toothbrush and stuff," she said as she set a duffle bag on the floor then crossed the room to look over Dr. Hawthorne's shoulder.

The thought of brushing her teeth and getting into her own clothes made Taylor sigh. "Thanks, Chris."

"I'm leaving my card on your nightstand," Dr. Hawthorne explained. "I'll plan on seeing you at the Grand in the morning, but if that changes, you can get someone to call my office."

"Thank you, Dr. Hawthorne. I appreciate you making the house calls."

"My pleasure," she said as she patted Taylor's leg. "I'll see you tomorrow then."

As soon as she heard Hawthorne's steps retreating down the hall, Taylor swung her legs out of the bed. "I'm dying for a pee and I don't know where the bathroom is."

Chris laughed. "I'll guide you there, but I draw the line at helping you pee."

"Can you grab my stuff?"

Chris led her down the hall to the bathroom and left her with her bag. Doing everything by feel wasn't easy. After relieving herself, Taylor managed to wash her hands and brush her teeth. It took her a few minutes to find a wash cloth then she gave herself a quick sponge bath. She brushed her hair out and re-secured her pony tail. Doing her hair by feel was easy.

Dressing proved to be the biggest challenge. She hoped her underwear and tank top were on right side out and not backwards. Jeans were easy enough and then she put on a button down shirt, hoping the buttons lined up. She opened the bathroom door and Chris waited there to guide her back to the bedroom although Taylor thought she probably could have found her way back.

"Has Moody been arrested yet?" Taylor asked, anxious for an update.

"No, not yet. But, don't worry about Cail. We've got him covered. Did I hear Hawthorne say you'd be at the Grand?"

"If it's alright with Gray. I'd just be more comfortable there." She didn't know whether to tell Chris about her and Cail or not. There were other things she wanted to talk about instead. "Have you talked to Rappaport?"

"Pierson and Boone got him in to interview last night, but he lawyered up. Then his lawyers dropped him like a hot potato when they heard all of his assets had been seized as proceeds of crime. Looks like he's going to have to settle for a public defender."

"So is he willing to talk since his lawyers dropped him?"

"Not exactly." Taylor heard Chris sigh. "He's willing to talk, but only to you."

"Okay. Take me ito Headquarters and then you, Pierson and Boone can fill me in on what you want me to ask him."

Chris shook her head, amazed that Taylor was so willing and eager. "You sure you're up for that?"

"Yeah, why wouldn't I be? It beats the hell out of sitting around here doing nothing." It beat the hell out of sitting around here stuck in her own head. Anything she could do to get her mind off Cail was a blessing.

Taylor talked to Gray and got the okay to stay with her for a couple of days. She thanked Rose, feeling guilty for bailing on her, and then Chris took her to Headquarters.

Chapter 38

Chris took Taylor into Headquarters through the parking garage and whisked her up to her office. The only people who saw her were the few detectives who were in the Sex Crimes Unit. The fewer people who saw her, she figured, the less embarrassing for Taylor.

Once she got Taylor settled with a coffee, she made phone calls to Pierson and Boone to arrange for a meeting. Then she called Detectives Bollard and Singh and invited them so they could get their two cents worth in. She took Taylor's official statement and then led her into a conference room. While they were waiting for the detectives to arrive, Chris filled Taylor in on Internal Affairs' investigation. Eighteen Toronto Police Officers had been arrested, Moody was still on the loose, and they hadn't identified Rappaport's contact at the Palmerton Penitentiary.

"Moody's mother lives in Pickering. Have they checked her place?"

"I don't know," Chris answered. "But, here's Detective Bollard. You can ask her."

"Ask me what?" Bollard pulled up a chair across from Taylor and Chris made the introduction.

"Have you checked Moody's mother's place in Pickering?" Taylor repeated her question.

"Yeah. She says she doesn't know where her son is. She's lying her ass off, but we've got her house under surveillance." Bollard opened her briefcase and pulled out a clear evidence bag containing a leather journal. "Constable Dave Worthington found this in Rappaport's office." She placed the journal on the table and patted it with her hand. "Our entire case is solved with this one piece of evidence. In it, Rappaport has recorded every officer he paid off or blackmailed including amounts, dates and grounds for blackmail. We also have payments recorded to Kyle Sutherland. He's the warden at Palmerton. Or, he was until last night," she grinned.

"So, you don't need Taylor to question Rappaport on your behalf?"

"Nah, we're good." Bollard returned the journal to her briefcase and closed it. Standing, she said, "It was good to meet you, Sinclair. I hope you're feeling better soon."

"Thanks. Nice to meet you, too." Taylor offered a weak smile.

Detective Boone was the next to arrive with Pierson right on his heels. They took seats across from Taylor and Boone placed several file folders on the table in front of him.

"Why don't I start?" Detective Pierson began. "Our case against Rappaport is solid. The packaging on the meth confiscated from his condo, listed under the alias Ivan Michael Legend, matches the packaging from his lab. We also have a journal listing all of his distributors that was found in his office at the Legend condo."

Chris snorted. "Egotistical bastard, isn't he?"

"What?" Pierson asked, looking at Chris in confusion.

"I.M. Legend?"

"He'll be a legend alright," Pierson laughed. "In prison."

"So I guess it comes down to me," Boone said. He opened the first folder in front of him. "Mick O'Hara. We've got him driving Mick's vehicle on the night he went missing and the vehicle was later found parked in the garage across from Rappaport's lab. But, we don't have anything concrete. I need to get a confession out of him."

Opening the next folder, Boone continued, "Carlos Spanner. I interviewed Kyle Sutherland last night and I have his confession that Rappaport paid him fifty thousand dollars to arrange for Spanner's death. He transferred ten thousand dollars into the account of one Desmond Arroya, currently a resident of Palmerton Pen for assault with a deadly and a long list of narcotics and trafficking charges, after the deed was done, for a tidy profit of forty thousand dollars.

"Sutherland has also accepted money for putting the fear of God into Kevin Laurey. He stated Rappaport had his lawyers working on getting Laurey out, so he could finish him off himself. No love lost between those two, apparently."

"What was the cause of death in the O'Hara case?" Taylor asked.

"He had the shit beat out of him before they slit his throat. He was tossed into Lake Ontario post mortem. There was water in his lungs, but drowning wasn't the cause of death. We think he had his head held under water, probably as a form of torture, before they cut his throat.

The properties of the water found in his lungs identified it as city water, tap water. Forensics are running tests to match blood found in an office at the meth lab. They cleaned up pretty good with bleach, but there was a lot of splatter from when he was beaten, so we've got blood samples. We should have confirmation today if that was in fact the kill site."

"So, basically all you need from me is to get a confession out of Rappaport for O'Hara?"

"That's right. We've got Kevin Laurey's statement that O'Hara was skimming from his deliveries. We need Rappaport to tell you who beat O'Hara and cut his throat. If it wasn't Rappaport, he had someone do it for him."

"Okay." Taylor gave a slight nod of her head. "Is there anything else?"

"I've got a few questions, but why don't we arrange for Rappaport to be brought over first," Chris said. "If you don't mind, I'd like him brought to one of my interview rooms, so Taylor doesn't have to navigate all over Headquarters."

"I'll make the arrangements," Boone said as he gathered up his files.

When they were alone again, Chris went over the questions she wanted put to Rappaport.

* * *

Rappaport was passed out with his head resting on his arms in the interview room. A nurse from the jail sat in the seat next to him. Chris led Taylor in and waited until she was seated before taking the seat next to her. "Rappaport," Chris yelled. When he didn't move she reached across the table and slapped him on the shoulder a couple of times.

"He crashed," the nurse explained. "He's coming down from the meth." She shook his shoulder, calling his name and he finally stirred.

"Sit up, Rappaport. You wanted to talk to Taylor, so talk. Or we're leaving and you can go back to your cell and rot."

Rappaport pushed himself up then leaned back in his chair with heavily lidded eyes. "Oh, shit. I'm sorry, Sinclair. I never meant for you to get hurt."

"Holding a gun to someone's head usually results in someone getting hurt," Taylor responded coldly.

"Ah, God." Rappaport scrubbed his face with his cuffed hands. "Honest to God, I didn't want you hurt."

"I suppose you didn't want Mick O'Hara to get hurt either."

"Who?"

"We've got you on video driving his truck with his girlfriend on the night he disappeared. His truck was found in the parking garage that you own across from your warehouse and his body was found in the lake within five hundred metres of your warehouse. We know why you killed him. He was skimming from his deliveries." Taylor waited for a response, but there was only silence and the whir of heat blowing out of a vent near the floor. "Okay," Taylor said as she got to her feet. "I guess we're done here."

Chris stood and pushed her chair in so she could lead Taylor out of the small room.

"Wait. Wait," Rappaport called out.

Taylor stopped, but didn't turn around to face him. "I thought you wanted to talk, but if you've got nothing to say I'm not going to waste my time here."

"I didn't kill O'Hara. I don't do murder. I'm a dealer, not a killer," Rappaport grinned and laughed.

"You were there. You ordered his death."

"Nope."

"Let's go," Taylor said to Chris. "I don't have time to sit here listening to his lies." They made it all the way to the door this time. Chris opened it and was guiding Taylor through it when Rappaport called out again. "Okay, okay. I'll talk."

"You're going to be in prison for the rest of your life whether you talk or not. There's enough evidence against you to put you away for good. If you think I'm going to sit here and listen to your lies so you can gawk at me, you're wrong." Taylor took another step into the hallway and the door began to close behind her and Chris.

"I said I'll talk," Rappaport yelled. "I'll tell you anything you want to know."

Chris pushed the door open again. They came back in and took their seats. The silence that filled the room for the next few minutes was almost deafening. Taylor felt like getting up again and walking out for good. "You were going to tell me who you ordered to kill O'Hara."

Rappaport slumped back into his chair again and blew out a long, slow breath with a, "Pffffff."

"You can either start talking or I'm going to get up again and walk out that door, only this time I'm going to keep going."

"Brandon," Rappaport said in defeat. "Brandon did all of my wet work."

"Brandon who?"

"You know who. You met him yesterday, didn't you?"

"Brandon who?" Taylor repeated with an icy tone.

"Oh, for fuck sakes. Brandon Moody. Constable Brandon Moody. He's my brother, my half-brother. He's supposed to keep the cops off my back, give me a heads up if the cops are lookin' at me for anything, and he does all my wet work. He likes that sort of thing, likes hurting people until they beg him to end their lives. That's his drug of choice, his high."

Chris slid a pad of paper across the table and slapped a pen on top of it. "Start writing the names of everyone Moody killed for you."

"Like I can remember their names?" A mocking laugh spilled out of him before Chris's frigid glare shut him up. "I got them written down in a book in the desk in my office. A leather bound book with the names of my contacts and shit. You'll see I didn't kill anyone. That's all on Brandon."

So, it was written in either the book Bollard had or the one Pierson had. Either way, Rappaport would get slapped with a shitload of conspiracy to commit murder charges and Moody would get hit with multiple murders. Chris could picture Boone doing his happy dance in the observation room. She didn't bother to let Rappaport know he'd get just as much jail time as Moody for the killings. He'd find out soon enough.

"What happened between you and Kev?" Taylor asked. "You were running a very successful organization until the two of you started using and warring with each other."

"Fuckin' Kev, man. Ruined everything. Over a stupid fuckin' chick if you can believe it. He got stupid over that bitch Lisa and when he found out I was using her, he went ape shit crazy. Like she was good for anything but a quick fuck. She wasn't even that good. Funny as hell though. Shoot some meth into that chick's veins and her clothes flew off. She'd fuck anything that moved, male or female, two, three at a time. I've seen your boy's brother do her six ways to Sunday. Funny as hell."

"Lovely," Taylor said under her breath. That really wasn't a picture she wanted in her head. "So, you used Lisa to get information on Cail and I."

"Lisa. Dave. It wasn't like I had to twist their arms. You'd be surprised at the shit your boy told both of them. There isn't a hell of a lot I don't know about you and your boy, Sinclair." Rappaport pulled himself upright with effort and leaned over the table, lowering his voice. "You never told him how you like to dance under Sarah's whip, did you?"

Taylor could feel the heat spread up from her neck to her face and ears, but she didn't give Rappaport the satisfaction of responding to his question.

"See, I could have given you that, Sinclair. I could have given you that and anything you could possibly want."

"No, you couldn't," Taylor said quietly. "Because the only thing I wanted was Cail."

* * *

Taylor spent the next couple of days going stir crazy in Gray's suite until Gray downloaded some audio books for her to listen to. Gabriella came by to visit every morning and brought home cooked meals so she and Gray just needed to warm them up in the microwave. Cail's parents, Lane, Chris, and Kate came by a few times. Chris brought her more clothes and took her laundry home with her. On the third day, Dr. Hawthorne finally removed the bandages from Taylor's right eye. Her vision was a little foggy and she had no depth perception, but it beat the hell out of being blind.

As soon as Dr. Hawthorne left, Gabriella drove Taylor and Gray to meet up with a real estate agent at the place Gabriella's son, Nate, recommended. Andrew Gemini met them in front of the house. He matched Taylor in height and had an adorable baby face that made him look like he was fresh out of high school. To his credit, he didn't even flinch at the bruising and the gash on the bridge of Taylor's nose.

Andrew unlocked the front door, opened it and then stood back to let Taylor enter. She put one foot over the threshold and froze as a vicious vision overwhelmed her. Blood spattered across the walls, the ceiling. Screams of terror filled her ears and she quickly stepped back out, her breaths coming in short, rapid bursts. "Something bad happened here. Something really bad. A mother and her children. Slaughtered. So much blood."

"Okay," Andrew took Taylor's arm and gently led her back down the stairs. "Let's just cross this one off the list." He jogged back up the steps and secured the door, thinking he'd never bring another client to this place.

He joined the three ladies on the sidewalk again. "I've got a new listing about a block from here that just came on the market this morning. The owner has been transferred to London, England and he needs to sell the place quickly. It has just had a complete renovation done and it's similar to this place with the loft style, exposed brick and beautifully refinished plank floor boards. I think it would really suit you and it has a gated entrance from the back alley. You just have to push your remote and the gate will open. You can drive in, close the gate behind you and you don't have to worry about reporters or anyone hounding you."

"It sounds perfect," Taylor responded.

They walked the block and a bit to the second location, giving Taylor the opportunity to check out the neighbourhood. There was a grocery store on the corner and a Tim Horton's just down the street. The outside of the house was refinished in a medium grey stucco with black shutters on the oversized windows. From the outside, it looked fantastic.

Taylor stepped over the threshold and was pleasantly surprised by the warm, cozy feeling that enveloped her. This place had a much better feel to it. A short stair case took them onto the main floor where the wide floor boards had been stained dark and finished with a glowing coat of varnish. A floating stair case beside the exposed red brick wall lead up to the top floor. To the right, the main floor was a massive open space with the kitchen towards the back. Granite counters, stainless steel appliances, and a breakfast bar complete with four stools matching the dark wood of the floors impressed Taylor. At the front of the house, French doors opened to a room that would be perfect for an art room and office. Taylor couldn't wait to see the rest.

Andrew took them downstairs first. There was enough space here for a home gym and a rec room. A heavy door opened to the two car garage. Not only could she drive in the gate, she could drive right into the garage and if there were any media people hanging around, they wouldn't even get a picture of her.

Taylor was nearly jumping up and down in excitement when she saw there were essentially two master bedrooms with en suites and plenty of space for a sitting area. They each had gas fireplaces and the en suites had modern soaker tubs, glassed in shower,s and granite topped vanities. Two smaller bedrooms shared a bathroom. Taylor swirled around, grinning from ear to ear. "It's perfect. Gray, you and Callaghan could stay here when you're in the city and Gracie could have one of the spare bedrooms. Oh, my God. I want this house. What do I need to do, Andrew?"

With a laugh, Andrew showed Taylor the listing and explained the process. They went downstairs to the kitchen and Andrew drew up the offer right there and then. Once Taylor signed all of the papers, she took another look through the place. In one of the master bedrooms, she stood at the oversized window looking out across the street. The ledge was about a foot deep with a marble sill. She could sit right in the window and watch the world go by on the street below. She loved watching people on the street and it was something she didn't get a chance to do very often anymore.

Directly across the street was an empty three story building with oversized windows similar to the one she was standing at. The windows on the first floor had been boarded up. As she stared at the building, she could almost see it as a hostel for street kids. One day, she thought to herself.

"Well?" Gray asked from behind her.

Taylor continued to stare out the window. "I love it." Turning to Gray, she asked, "Do you love it? Can you see yourself staying here?"

Gray laughed at Taylor's exuberance. "Yes, I can see us staying here, but you don't have to do that for us, Taylor."

Grinning, Taylor crossed the room and hugged Gray. "I don't have to, but I want to. Andrew said they want a quick closing. We could be in here by Christmas and you could stay here when you're waiting for Gracie to pop."

"God, I hope it's as easy as a pop," Gray laughed.

"I wouldn't describe it as a pop," Gabriella said from the doorway. "But, it's definitely worth it." She took a couple of steps into the room. "The house is amazing, Taylor. When you're offer is accepted, we'll have to celebrate."

"I'm going to be a basket case until we hear. I hope it doesn't take too long."

"By the sounds of it, if they're as anxious to sell as Andrew says, you should hear back quickly," Gabriella advised. "I'm thrilled for you, Taylor." Gabriella was taken aback when Taylor pulled her in for a hug. A huge knot of emotions rose up from her chest and caught on a sob in her throat.

"Oh, no, no, no." Taylor took a step back and placed her hands on Gabriella's shoulders. "There is no crying allowed in my house."

Gabriella laughed through her tears. "I'm just so happy. Happy for you and happy you're accepting me into your life. I just wanted you to accept me and let me try to make up for all the years we've lost."

Taylor wrapped her arms around Gabriella again. "We'll make up for it, Aunt Gabriella."

Taylor calling her Aunt had Gabriella crying even harder.

They had lunch at the Grand. Just as they were finishing their coffee, Taylor's phone began to ring. Pulling it out of her pocket, she saw Andrew's number on the screen and was so nervous she was afraid to answer. When she pushed talk, her hands were shaking. "Hey, Andrew. I've got you on speaker. Gray and Gabriella are with me."

"Hi ladies."

"Hi, Andrew," Gray and Gabriella said in stereo.

"Taylor, would you like the good news or the bad news first?"

Oh, crap. Wincing, Taylor answered, "Start with the bad."

"Aaah." There was a long silence and Taylor nearly burst from holding her breath. "There is no bad news. Your offer was accepted with the closing date in the middle of December."

Taylor's mouth dropped open. "Oh, my God. Really? Are you serious?"

Every head in the restaurant turned to stare at them as all three ladies began screaming.

Laughing, Andrew replied, "Completely serious. Congratulations Taylor."

Chapter 39

Taylor spent the next week at Gray's place in Balton. Every time they watched the news, there were stories about Cail making his rounds of Toronto's pubs and clubs. He was filmed leaving Delaney's several nights running with a gorgeous red head who had been identified as Ireland Delaney. It hurt to see him with someone else already and she felt sick at how drunk he appeared. It looked like the red head was holding him up.

When she returned to Toronto for her appointment with Dr. Hawthorne, she was anxious to get the dressing off of her left eye and return to work.

The next two weeks were going to be crazy busy. She and Gray had done a lot of shopping online while she was recovering in Balton, but she still had a lot of stuff to buy for her house. She didn't know what she would have done without Gray helping her to make a list of everything she would need. She sat in the waiting room at Hawthorne's office trying to organize an action plan in her head to get everything done. It wasn't that she didn't like shopping, but it overwhelmed her with the amount of choices there were. Grocery stores were the worst. Cail had done all of their grocery shopping because she would walk in, see all of the choices, and begin to panic. She figured if she made a list of exactly what she needed from each store before she went, it might be a bit easier. Chris hated shopping, but Kate seemed to enjoy it. Maybe she could get Kate to come with her and help her out.

She left Dr. Hawthorne's office wearing an eye patch. With the patch off, her vision was blurry so she had an appointment the next morning to get her eyes tested for glasses. The scar across the bridge of her nose and especially her left eye lid was nasty, but Hawthorne had told her to massage Bio Oil into the scars and it would help to reduce the scarring. She recommended Taylor massage it into the scars on her back twice daily as well, but she didn't know how she was going to manage that.

Her next stop was Headquarters to talk to Chris about returning to work. She knew she would be stuck on desk duty for a bit, but that was better than sitting at home. She had just made it to the door of Chris's office when her phone began to ring. She didn't recognize the caller's number, but answered anyway. "Hello?"

"I've got your boyfriend, Sinclair."

Taylor recognized Brandon Moody's voice and put the phone on speaker as she stepped into Chris's office. "He's not my boyfriend."

"You've got money from that book you wrote. I want five hundred thousand if you want to see Cail alive again."

Chris was out of her seat as if she hit an eject button and reading the incoming phone number from Taylor's phone. Then she busily tapped away on her own phone, texting Brice McLean in the eDivision.

"I don't have that kind of money, Brandon. I just bought a house." The phone was shaking in Taylor's hand. All she could think of was Rappaport saying how much Brandon like to hurt people.

Chris wrote frantically on a pad of paper and then held it up for Taylor to read. *Keep him talking. Brice is trying to trace the call.*

"You can get the money," Brandon yelled. "If you don't have it, that writer friend of yours does."

"I want to talk to Cail. I want to know he's okay, that you haven't hurt him."

There was a long silence before Moody spoke again. "You've got an hour to get the money. You'll get proof Cail is okay before I call you back. One hour." The line went dead.

Taylor looked up at Chris. "We need to verify he has Cail. Can you call Kate and see if she can track him down?"

Instead of freaking Kate out while she was working, Chris called upstairs to Inspector Worthington. She filled him in and then left him to try to locate his son. Then she called Brice. "Anything?"

"I didn't get a trace, but I've got his service provider on the line. We're trying to see if we can get a GPS location on his phone."

"Keep me posted."

Taylor was still shaking, that horrible sense of dread knotting in the pit of her stomach. She knew the colour had drained from her face. She could feel it. If she used her money to get Cail back, she'd lose her house. She didn't think the bank would give her a mortgage for that kind of money based on her police salary. When she weighed having a house against Cail's life, his health, there was no hesitation. "I need to go to the bank."

"I think you need to sit down for a minute. You're not looking so great, Taylor." Chris moved around her desk, intending to get Taylor to sit down.

Before Chris could reach her, Taylor was out the door saying, "There's no time. We've only got an hour."

Chris grabbed a jacket and took off after her. "We'll take my car," she said as she caught up to Taylor.

The Inspector called Chris back while they were driving to Taylor's bank. Cail had the day off and had been playing hockey with a group of friends. After the game, they were supposed to meet up at a nearby pub. Cail hadn't made it to the pub. He had a squad car en route to the rink to see if Cail's car was still there.

"Can you use your psychic ability?" Chris asked.

"I don't think so," Taylor answered. "I'm too anxious. I don't think I could concentrate enough."

Chris pulled into a spot at the curb just down the street from Taylor's bank. Taylor was out of the car and running before Chris could get her seatbelt off. When she caught up to her, Taylor was speaking with a stern looking teller in her fifties. Her name tag identified her as Carol.

"The funds for your house have been transferred into a trust account by your lawyer. You don't have five hundred thousand dollars available."

Taylor looked at the available balance on her account. "Two hundred and fifty thousand then." Moody would take what he could get, wouldn't he? Would he even know the difference?

Carol pursed her lips and glared at Taylor. "I can't just give you two hundred and fifty thousand dollars in cash. We'd have to special order that high of an amount."

"Get the manager out here," Taylor ordered.

Carol's nostrils flared as she lifted her head to stare down her nose at Taylor, as if she was completely offended by the request.

Chris slapped her badge on the counter. "Get the manager, Carol. Now."

Carol stomped off and within minutes Taylor and Chris were being escorted into the manager's office. Once Taylor explained the situation, she got the same answer from the manager that they couldn't disburse that amount of cash on short notice. Ten minutes later, they were on their way back to Headquarters armed with a certified cheque and Taylor was nearly hyperventilating. They went straight to Inspector Worthington's office. Cal took one look at Taylor and called Lane. He got her admin assistant and requested that she send Lane to his office immediately.

"Cail's car is still parked at the arena," Cal informed them, grim faced. "I've got a couple of patrol units searching the building, but it's not looking good."

"Surveillance cameras on the arena's lot?"

Cal just shook his head in answer to Chris's question.

"How long ago was he supposed to have been leaving the arena?" Taylor asked. God, her chest was so tight she could barely talk.

"They came off the ice at fifteen hundred hours. He showered and changed and was the first one to leave the dressing room about twenty minutes later. He told one of the guys that he had something to take care of and he'd meet them at the pub."

Taylor received the call from Moody just before seventeen hundred hours. Moody had Cail for over an hour and a half before he called her. He could have used that time to take Cail away from the city or he could have used it to hurt Cail. She couldn't see Moody taking him far. He had to know she would demand to see him before she gave Moody a cent. Where would he take Cail, she wondered. She was so wrapped up in trying to figure Moody out that she was surprised when Chris took her arm.

"Sit your ass down, Taylor. You look like shit and you need to slow your breathing down before you pass out." Chris led her to a chair and Taylor dropped into it then dropped her head into her hands.

"Breathe." Chris bent down in front of Taylor, coaching her to slow down her breathing. When Lane arrived, Taylor was beginning to get some colour back.

"God, this is all my fault. If he hurt Cail ..." She couldn't finish the thought, never mind the sentence.

Cal went to her, laying his hand gently on her shoulder. "This isn't your fault, Taylor. I need you to stay calm and get through this. We'll get Cail back, but you need to be strong."

She couldn't understand why Cal wasn't pissed as hell at her until he said that. He needed her to get his son back safely. He was holding it together until he got his son back and she would do the same. She sat back up in the chair, nodding her head. "I'm good. I'll get through it."

Lane carefully took Taylor's wrist, scabbed and healing from her injuries. It was a moment before Taylor realized she was taking her pulse. "I'm good," she repeated, but let Lane finish. As Cal was filling Lane in, Taylor's phone whistled, signalling an incoming text message. The first thing Taylor noticed was that it was from the same number Moody called her from. Opening it, she found a picture of Cail strapped to a chair. He was slumped over and she could see bruising and swelling on the side of his face. Bearing down, she studied the background. "It looks like he's got him in some kind of mechanical room." She looked up and met Cal's eyes. "Are we sure he's not still in the arena?"

She barely got the question out when Chris's phone began to ring. "Cain," she answered. "Okay, got it. Thanks, Brice." Chris ended the call and announced, "Moody's cell phone is hitting off of a tower at Bay and College. He's in the fucking building. What mechanical rooms do we have in the basement?"

Within minutes, Cal had an ETF team on standby and the maintenance supervisor, Lars Magnussen, in his office with floor plans of all of the mechanical rooms in the building. Taylor showed Lars the picture Moody had sent. "Yeah, yeah. That's a riser room on the garage level. I'm not sure which one, they all look pretty much the same." He spread the floor plan of the garage level over Cal's desk and pointed out nine fire sprinkler system riser rooms.

"He's going to call any minute now," Taylor announced nervously.

"We could send enough men in to check every riser room simultaneously," Chris suggested.

The shrill ringing of Taylor's cell phone had everyone freezing and turning to her. "I'm putting it on speaker," she announced before answering the call. "You hurt him. I can't tell from the picture you sent if he's alive or dead."

"Shut up." Moody yelled then let out a frustrated roar. "Just shut up. You didn't look like you were carrying five hundred thousand dollars when you left the bank."

"They don't have that amount of cash sitting around. It takes time to order it in. The best I could do was a certified cheque."

"No. No, no, no." Moody sounded like a spoiled five year old having a temper tantrum.

"If you want cash it's going to take a few days."

Everyone in the room was focused on Taylor or her phone, except for Chris who was furiously typing into her phone.

A few grunts and groans came through Taylor's cell and everyone waited for what seemed like eons. When he finally spoke it was fast and short. "I'll call you back." The line went dead.

"He's on the edge," Lane announced. "It's very likely he's about to break."

"What does that mean?" Taylor asked. "Is he about to go ballistic or what?"

"Brice, tell me you got him." Chris paced back and forth with her phone at her ear. "That's okay. We've got the level." She hit end and announced, "North-east corner of the building."

"Five," Lars called out. "Riser room five."

"How often are you in those rooms?" Chris asked Lars.

"Once a month to inspect the risers, unless we have to shut one down to replace sprinkler heads or work on the system. The last time we were in that particular room was probably in the first two or three days of the month."

Chris leaned over Cal's desk, studying the floor plan. "What's this box next to riser room five?"

"That's the Chief's private elevator."

"So Moody would know this area of the garage very well. He'd come and go through this elevator with the Chief. What do you bet the bastard has been hiding in this room for the past ten days? Right under our fucking noses."

"Lane?" Taylor was still waiting for an answer to her question. She was scared to death Moody was going to take his anger out on Cail.

Lane pursed her lips, a stern look on her face, but she gently laid her hand on Taylor's and gave it a reassuring squeeze. "He's unstable, unpredictable. He could become very aggressive and act out or he could shut down and not be able to function. I would say he's having a difficult time making decisions because he didn't know what to do when you gave him the ultimatum about the cash."

Cal was on the phone giving the Chief of Police an update and requesting to send some of the tactical officers down to the garage in her private elevator. He got the go ahead and hung up. "Cain, you're with the tactical team in the Chief's elevator. Everyone else hangs here."

Taylor shot to her feet. "I need to go with Chris."

With a scowl, Cal held his hand up in front of Taylor. "Touch my hand," he ordered.

Taylor flinched back when Cal's hand came up then reached out, but was a good six inches away from his hand. Damn, she was sure his hand was right in front of her. She dropped her hand to her side in frustration.

"I'm not sending you into a volatile situation when you've got no depth perception. I want everyone to come out of this unharmed."

The tightening in her chest was threatening to steal her breath again. She couldn't sit here waiting to hear if Cail was okay or not. She reached up and pulled her eye patch off. "Problem solved." Her vision was blurry, but she'd be damned if she told anyone that. She knew everyone was staring at the ugly scar on her half closed eyelid and she didn't give a damn. She needed to be in that elevator. She needed to get to Cail and make sure he was okay.

"You haven't been cleared for full duty," Lane said softly, but firmly.

Taylor inhaled sharply. She felt like she'd just been punched in the gut.

Cal made eye contact with Chris and gave a slight nod towards the door, giving Chris the order to move out. She didn't waste another second. She darted out of the office while Taylor stood fuming, blocked in by Cal and Lane.

Glaring at Cal, Taylor spat, "How can you just stand there doing nothing when your son is down there in God knows what condition?"

"Is that what you think I'm doing, Sinclair? I've sent in a team of highly trained members of the Toronto Police Service. Men and women who deal with this kind of thing on a regular basis. Are you telling me you don't have faith in them? That you don't trust Chris?"

Taylor had worked herself up to hyperventilating again and now she disgraced herself by making it sound like she didn't trust the officers under Cal's command or his judgement as a ranking officer. "I apologize. I just need to know that he's okay." She sank back down into the chair, and lowered her head into her hands,. Lane's warm hand found her wrist, taking her pulse, making Taylor feel like a complete idiot for telling Cal she would remain strong and then breaking down again.

"You've gone above and beyond in protecting Cail in the last couple of weeks. The way he's been acting, I'm surprised you bothered going to the bank, surprised you would put up five hundred thousand dollars to ensure his safety."

Taylor lifted her head, perplexed at Cal's comments and all she could think of to say was, "I could only get two hundred and fifty thousand."

Cal and Lane made eye contact, both of them trying to stifle their laughter. Taylor was completely oblivious to it, too wrapped up in her own misery and fighting for control. She jumped when her phone began to ring again. Before she could answer, Cal said, "Try to keep him occupied while the tactical unit gets into position."

Taylor hit talk. "I want to talk to Cail. I need to know he's okay."

"You're not in a position to make demands. Just shut up and listen to me. There's a key in your desk drawer. Take it to the main level of Union Station and find locker number two thirty six. Put the cheque in the locker. Once I've cashed the cheque, I will let you know where you can pick up your boyfriend."

"I'm not handing over the cheque until I see Cail. I'll trade you the cheque for Cail or no deal."

"I make the demands," he screamed like a spoiled child again. "Not you. Not you. I'm running this show."

"I see Cail before I give you the cheque or you can go and screw yourself. He's not even my boyfriend anymore. Don't you watch the news? Haven't you seen him running around with that red head all week? Why don't you call her and ask for five hundred thousand dollars?" Taylor hit end and then immediately regretted her outburst. "Oh, God. I'm so sorry."

* * *

Chris drew a diagram of the riser room in relation to the elevator for the tactical team. When they were ready, they gathered in front of the elevator. Chief Clarke pressed the button and the elevator doors opened. When she took a step inside, Chris laid her hand on Clarke's arm. "Where do you think you're going?"

"The elevator requires a key card and security code to operate," Clarke informed her.

"Do you mean to tell me that Moody could have been using this elevator over the past week and a half?"

"Absolutely not. I had his card deactivated and the security code changed as soon as I read over the file Sinclair put together." With a slight smirk, she added, "I'm the Chief of Police. Give me a little credit for being security conscious."

"Ah, shit. Foot, meet mouth."

With a laugh, Clarke inserted her card and then entered the security code before stepping out and holding the doors for the tactical team to enter. "God speed," she said just as the doors were closing then winked at Chris.

"One of these days, I'm going to learn when to keep my mouth shut." Laughter filled the elevator, but by the time the doors opened to the garage level, no one was so much as smiling.

* * *

Cail regained consciousness slowly. It was like a fog slowly dissipating around him. The last thing he remembered was feeling a sharp pinch at his neck as he loaded his hockey bag into the trunk of his car. He kept completely still, remaining slumped over. He could hear someone moving around behind him and muttering something, like he was talking to himself. Opening his eyes, he blinked several times until he could focus. There was duct tape wrapped around his torso and he could feel it securing his wrists behind his back and his ankles to the legs of the chair he was sitting in.

Glancing around, he could see that he was in some kind of mechanical room. He couldn't see the guy behind him, but he risked pushing up with his feet slightly to see if he was able to move the chair. He would bide his time and wait for an opportunity to take the guy out by throwing himself, chair and all, into him and hope for the best.

"You're not in a position to make demands. Just shut up and listen to me. There's a key in your desk drawer. Take it to the main level of Union Station and find locker number two thirty six. Put the cheque in the locker. Once I've cashed the cheque, I will let you know where you can pick up your boyfriend."

Oh, holy mother of God, Cail thought. That's Moody and he has to be talking to Tay.

"I make the demands. Not you. Not you. I'm running this show."

Out of the corner of his eye, Cail could see Moody jumping up and down stomping his feet. "Bitch. Bitch, bitch, mother fucking bitch." Two long strides put Moody right beside Cail and something cold and hard pressed to the back of his neck. "I'll show that fucking bitch. I'll put a fucking bullet in your head."

Cail clamped his jaw tight, determined not to make a noise as Moody shoved the barrel of the gun into the back of his head several times. A loud bang echoed through the room and Cail thought the gun had gone off. Another bang sounded and the door exploded open. Cail pushed off of his feet with all of his strength and sent himself and his chair into Moody's side. They both crashed to the floor as complete chaos ensued. Cail heard the bone in his left forearm snap before he registered the blinding pain shooting up his arm and down to his fingertips. He could hear people yelling even over his own screams of agony.

"Drop the gun. Drop the gun."

One of the officers stepped on the gun that was still gripped in Moody's hand as he lay sprawled out on the floor. In seconds, he was cuffed and being pulled to his feet.

"Let's get an ambulance in here."

"Chris," Cail croaked, recognizing her voice. The edges of his vision were fading to black. He shook his head, refusing to give in to the darkness. There was no way in hell he was going to faint in front of a bunch of tactical officers. "My arm. Oh, fuck, my arm snapped."

The moment word came through that Moody was in custody, Taylor bolted from Cal's office. Ignoring the elevator, she slammed the stairwell door open and began her descent taking two or three stairs at a time. How she made it to the bottom without falling, she had no idea. She burst into the garage and took off at a sprint to the far side where she could see an ambulance parked and several of the tactical officers standing about.

She came to a skidding halt as Cail emerged from the riser room, his left arm secured in a splint, the right side of his face battered and bruised. He looked a mess with his hair in disarray and a couple of days' worth of growth shadowing his face.

It wasn't her place to run into his arms anymore and it was all she could do to stay in place when Cail's beautiful blue eyes found her. The corner of his mouth slowly raised and then bloomed into a gorgeous, heart stopping smile. He walked towards her, his good arm extended and then he just wrapped himself around her. Taylor's arms found their way around his neck. "I thought ..." Her breath hitched.

"I'm okay now that you're here. I missed you so much, Angel."

ABOUT THE AUTHOR

Wendy Hewlett is a British born Canadian author who began writing in earnest in 2011 with *Saving Grace*, the first book in the Taylor Sinclair Series. She enjoys writing strong female protagonists in the mystery/crime fiction genre.

She has enjoyed many exciting jobs including working on cruise ships in the Caribbean, Security & Fire Supervisor at General Motors Canada, and Clinical Associate (Addictions Counselor) at a private Addiction Treatment Centre.

She has one son who she credits as being her finest achievement.

She dreams of spending a year exploring and writing in her birthplace, Scotland, as well as England and Ireland.

Look for *Saving Grace*, *Unfinished Business*, and *Runed* at your favourite online bookstores.

Book 4 in the Taylor Sinclair Series is due out later in 2019. Wendy also plans to publish several unrelated novels in 2019.

Visit the author's website at: wendyhewlett.com and sign up for her Monthly Newsletter to stay up to date on news, new releases, giveaways, and more.

Follow Wendy on:

Reviews are the bread and butter of an Indie Author's career. Please take a moment to write a quick review on Amazon, Goodreads, or your favourite online book retailer. It is greatly appreciated and allows Wendy to continue writing and publishing page-turning novels with wonderful, strong female protagonists.

34547435R00219

Made in the USA
Lexington, KY
25 March 2019